I0760328

The Serpent's Keep Trilogy

---

the complete series

DAVID R. BESHEARS

Greybeard Publishing

THE SERPENT'S KEEP TRILOGY

The Serpent's Keep Trilogy
the complete series
Omnibus Edition

ISBN 978-1-947231-51-1 *(omnibus hardcover edition)*

Greybeard Publishing
P.O. Box 480
McCleary, WA 98557-0480

Serpent's Keep

ISBN 978-1-947231-31-3 *(hardcover edition)*

Serpent's Keep Two – the Six Temples

ISBN 978-1-947231-32-0 *(hardcover edition)*

Serpent's Keep 3 – the Outland

ISBN 978-1-947231-33-7 *(hardcover edition)*

CONTENTS

| 1 |

Serpent's Keep

Chapter One

Jacob Quigley reached down and picked up the travel bag. Ahead of him was a wooden double gate set into a rough stone wall ten feet high that enclosed the entire village. One side of the gate stood open and a guard watched the new arrival with casual interest. He saw a young man, probably in his early twenties, definitely from the outside.

Jake looked back behind him at the old, 40s era bus that was slowly disappearing down the dusty, narrow road winding its way through a landscape of grassy fields, twisted scrub oak and yellow and brown brush. The sound of the engine faded away, leaving behind an ominous silence.

As he neared the gate, he started to say something to the guard, but before he could open his mouth the man stepped calmly to one side and made way. Once through, Jake started down the main thoroughfare of Serpent's Keep.

The village lay comfortably in the Outland, isolated from the rest of the world and unaffected by external events. Its narrow cobblestone streets were quiet pedestrian thoroughfares where it was normal for citizens to stop and converse with one another, both of recent goings-on in the village and of adventures from long ago, in lands distant and mysterious. That is not to say that all of the citizens of Serpent's Keep could be trusted, neither in word nor deed, but all in all, the small village was a pleasant place in which to live. It was peaceful, filled with interesting characters, dark secrets, enduring mysteries, and the inevitable skeleton in the closet; a small community safely enclosed within its protective walls, hidden away warm and snug, deep in the Outland, and long ago forgotten by the real world.

Quigley Mansion sat alone, midway along one of the narrow side roads in the village. The estate took up most of the north side of the lane, surrounded on all sides by a high fence, making it accessible only through the tall, narrow front gate.

Jake looked in through the wrought-iron bars, dropping his travel bag at his feet. The house looked too small to be called a mansion, but he knew from his summer visits years before that it was one of the larger houses in the village. Still, just a child back then, to Jake it had been just a big old house, and the grounds had been just a big yard.

Across the street was the village plaza, a park of sorts that took up the entire south side of the road. Much of the plaza was surrounded by its own high wall. Directly across from the Quigley Estate was the north entrance to the plaza, an opening in the fence some forty feet wide. Through this opening, Jake could see several children playing in a large, grassy area. The plaza held a number of massive oak trees, some shrubs, a few benches and an occasional table. There were expanses of lawn, expanses of flagstone, and meandering cobblestone pathways.

Jake watched the children for a few moments before turning his attention again to the Quigley Estate gate. He reached into his jacket pocket and pulled out a large, ornate key. He inserted it into the lock, turned it, and pushed down on the latch handle. Picking up his bag, he pushed the gate open. It swung closed behind him as he started up the walk toward the house.

A large, dragon-shaped doorknocker hung in the center of the front door. Lifting and dropping it several times, it didn't sound nearly as impressive as it looked. Still, after a minute's wait, which gave Jake time to survey the grounds from the porch, the door opened and a tall, thin, graying gentleman stood looking down at him.

Mr. Griffin hadn't changed much over the years. Jake had last seen the man through the eyes of a twelve year old. He had been old then, and he was the same old now.

"Mr. Griffin?" Jake mumbled. Mr. Griffin twitched an eyebrow, but other than that, there was no movement. Jake cleared his throat. "Mr. Griffin, it's me... Jake. Jacob... Jacob Quigley."

"Good afternoon, sir." Despite his age, Mr. Griffin looked and sounded as alive, as fit, and as able as always.

Jake fumbled in his jacket pockets. He pulled out the gate key, continued searching, finally reached into the side pocket of his travel bag. He pulled out a folded and battered envelope. He held up the key and letter together. "I got the letter. I came as soon as I could."

Mr. Griffin took a step back into the foyer and made way for Jake. "You have been expected, Mr. Quigley," he said, without emotion. Mr. Griffin had always referred to him as *Master Jacob* when he was a child. He noted the change to *Mr. Quigley*. He wasn't sure what the change in status meant, but sensed that he had somehow lost something.

"Thanks," said Jake, stepping into the house. Once in the main hall, he set his bag down and took in the place. "Hasn't changed much, has it?"

"What would you have us change, Mr. Quigley?" The man's attitude hadn't changed, either. The patronizing, self-righteous—

"I don't know... new rug?" It was his turn now to raise an eyebrow. "A chair?"

Mr. Griffin was able to smirk without actually smirking. "I shall look into it," he said.

Jake let the matter drop. *The old fart...* Yet, in spite of the man's sanctimonious condescension, Jake liked him. His air of assurance and stability had always been a source of calm for Jake during his summer visits to Serpent's Keep. He was the essence of quiet strength, no matter what turmoil may be surrounding him. He was security.

Mr. Griffin was the house administrator for the Quigley Estate; as such, he was much more than just the butler. He had been with Uncle Tobias for as long as anyone could remember... at least fifty years. Jake couldn't imagine the one without the other.

Jake stood silent, Mr. Griffin patiently waiting behind him. He sensed an emptiness in the mansion. It looked the same, but it didn't feel the same.

There were two doors along the left wall of the main hall. One he remembered led to a sitting room, the other to Mr. Griffin's apartment. Straight ahead were the stairs to the second floor. To the left of the stairs there was a short hall and a door under the stairs that opened to a narrow stairwell that lead down to the basement. At the far end of the right wall was a wide arch that opened into the dining room.

It all seemed very still. The house too seemed to be patiently waiting on Jake.

"I was real sorry to hear about Tobias," he said at last.

"Your uncle shall be greatly missed, Mr. Quigley."

"Stop calling me that."

"Sir?" The question came from some place on Snob Hill.

"*Mr. Quigley.* Stop it." Jake stuffed his hands into his pockets. "Call me Jake."

Mr. Griffin's face visibly retracted. "I don't think so."

Jake's face slowly morphed into a slight grin, "All right. Jacob, then."

Mr. Griffin paused all activity, as if his entire being was sorting through a difficult problem. Once the mental processing was complete, he nodded imperceptibly. "Very well."

Jake noticed a young woman standing in the archway to the dining room. She might have been there for some time. Jake wasn't sure. She was still, unmoving.

"Who's that?" he asked. The woman was small and unassuming, probably eighteen or nineteen years old.

"That is Meara. She assists Mrs. Hodges on a part-time basis."

"Cleaning and like that?"

"She assists with the cleaning."

Jake nodded. Good ol' Mrs. Hodges. The housekeeper and cook for the estate. She had to be getting on in years.

"I guess Mrs. Hodges can use a hand around the place."

"Maintaining the estate is a considerable task, sir. If you require a meeting to review the Quigley concerns, I shall arrange it."

"Yeah," Jake grumbled. "Later."

"I shall arrange a time convenient to us both."

"Yeah," Jake said again. He watched as Meara moved back into the shadows.

"Meara," Mr. Griffin raised a hand in her direction. "Come here, girl."

Meara stiffened abruptly, then stepped cautiously into the main hall. Mr. Griffin waved impatiently at her. She took the last several steps quickly and stopped short.

"Sir?" she stood before Mr. Griffin.

"Meara, this is Mr. Quigley... the master of the estate." Mr. Griffin's statement held finality. It was now Meara's responsibility to respond. Meara turned to Jake.

"Mr. Quigley. Welcome, sir."

Jake glanced very briefly in Mr. Griffin's direction. With only a subtle change in Mr. Griffin's facial expression, he had made it quite clear that Jake was not to allow Meara to become familiar with "the Master of the Estate". There was to be no "call me Jake".

"Thank you, Meara," said Jake, and left it at that.

"You may return to your duties," said Mr. Griffin.

"Thank you, sir." Meara gave a slight curtsy, backed away, turned and left, disappearing back into the dining room and probably on into the kitchen.

"Shy, isn't she?" Jake asked, once she was gone.

"Meara is unaccustomed to strangers... Jacob." Mr. Griffin made the word 'Jacob' sound very much like 'Mr. Quigley'. "Your uncle hired her and asked that I find a position for her."

"You disapprove?"

"She would not have been my choice, were I looking to hire someone to assist Mrs. Hodges."

"Yet you kept her on, after..."

"Her work has proven satisfactory."

Jake was pretty sure that Mr. Griffin had felt then and felt now that it was his responsibility alone to manage the house and the staff. He was also pretty sure that Uncle Tobias had stayed out of Mr. Griffin's way, for the most part. He wondered what would have caused him to bring home a stray.

"So, does she live here?"

"I am the only member of the staff living on the estate." Mr. Griffin stated flatly, paused a moment, then took a step away from Jake and started toward the stairs. He gave only the slightest indication that Jake should follow.

Jake picked up his bag and followed.

Mr. Griffin spoke over his shoulder as they climbed the stairs to the second floor and started down the hall. "Mrs. Hodges prepared your uncle's meals at 8:00, 12:30, and at 6:00 in the evening."

"Yeah, well... I like 7:00, noon, and 5:00."

Mr. Griffin took the statement in stride. "I am certain that Mrs. Hodges can adapt." He opened a heavy door and held it open. Jake stepped through and walked into the room, tossed his bag on the bed.

"Where is Mrs. H?" Jake remembered a kindly woman, always fussing about, and frequently flustered by Jake's summer visits.

"She has gone to the marketplace. Purchasing vegetables, I believe."

"Tell her no cabbage." Jake mumbled, looking around the room. It was the room that he had stayed in as a child. "And no peas. I hate peas."

Mr. Griffin raised his level of snobbishness just a bit. "Perhaps you should prepare a list of your likes and dislikes."

"Maybe I'll do that."

Mr. Griffin stepped back into the hall and took hold of the doorknob.

"I'll leave it to you, then." He closed the door, leaving Jake alone in his room.

"Sure a lot smaller than the last time I was here..."

Chapter Two

Jake stepped out of his room and into the upstairs hallway. He glanced once at the staircase leading down to the first floor, but decided to wander around first, do a little exploring. He hadn't been in here in years, and now was as good a time as any to get reacquainted.

The master bedroom wasn't much larger than his old room, and the furniture wasn't all that different. There was a large bed, a desk, a dresser, and a few chairs. The only real difference was the private door that led to the one and only upstairs bathroom, which had its main door opening onto the hall.

Jake sat on the bed and looked carefully around the room; some nice paintings, a set of heavy drapes over the window, dark-paneled walls; an oval rug on the floor. The bed was firm but comfortable. The room was clean and comfortable.

He found nothing in the desk drawers but a few odds and ends, and the dresser had been emptied. Jake wondered what Mr. Griffin had done with Tobias' clothes.

He went back out into the hallway. The upstairs hall was in the shape of a large L. His old bedroom was at one end, with the upstairs bathroom and then the master bedroom along the north wall. At the other end was the library. Across from the master bedroom were the stairs leading down to the first floor. On either side of the staircase was a door.

Jake chose the door on the right. It led out to an open deck, enclosed on three sides and open to the west. He had spent many hours playing there as a child. Just as many hours were spent staring out across the village toward the Outland beyond the west wall.

People in the village spoke of how dangerous the Outland was, when they spoke of it at all. It was a strange land of dark forests and darker lakes, great cliffs and menacingly shadowy valleys and canyon-like ravines.

And yet there were hints of civilization in the Outland. There was a large farm to the north that supplied foodstuffs to the village. A day's hard march to west was a temple where a group of monks lived. And people spoke of a highway out there somewhere that seemed to start from nowhere and led nowhere.

And there was the narrow, single-lane, winding road that connected the outside world to the village. It wasn't visible from the deck, coming as it did from the south. It cut through the Outland like a thin, twisted wound, and was the only visible sign of the outside. Traveling this road, there was little to be seen on either side and there were no exits. The seldom-scheduled bus would bring the infrequent traveler from the outside world to the front gate of the village, and quickly retreat back to the real world. Jake had made that journey each year growing up, and to a small boy it had simply been part of the mystique of his uncle's home. Only now did he consider just how peculiar this place was, and now he would try to become a part of it. He turned away from his view of the west and went back inside.

The village was an island in the Outland, and the estate was an island in the village. The Quigley Mansion was old; perhaps as old as the village. It was well cared for, well kept, but its age showed. The furniture, the floors and carpet, the wood trim, the tapestries and paintings and drapes, all looked clean and cared for... and old. The very air had the smell of antiquity.

The mansion fit in well with the rest of Serpent's Keep. This was a world of no cars and of cobblestone thoroughfares, where everyone knew it was the twenty-first century but no one lived in the twenty-first century; where you could find oil lamps and electric light bulbs in the same room.

Jake walked past the head of the stairs and went on to the bend in the hall. There was only one door in this section of the hallway, located at the very end. It opened into the upstairs library.

Jake remembered his uncle Tobias spending quite a bit of time there, but had only been in the room a few times himself. It was high-ceilinged, with shelved walls and a cherry-wood desk and leather chair. Two high-back chairs sat in one corner beneath a single pole lamp. It wasn't a very large room, and all available space was filled with books. Jake read titles as he walked slowly past the shelves: 'Flora and Fauna of the Ancient Rainforest', 'Creatures of the Deep', 'Ancient Religions', 'The Science of Labyrinths', 'Spelunking', 'Desert Ecosystems', 'Survival in Extreme Environments', 'Holography', 'Cryptography and Pictographs', 'The Art of Symbolism', 'Beyond the Fourth Dimension'.

Uncle Tobias had very diverse interests.

"Mr. Quigley?"

Jake turned sharply, startled from his thoughts. Meara was standing near the door.

"Geez, Meara."

"I'm sorry, sir."

"No..., no it's all right. You just startled me." Jake waved a hand at the room around them. "Just doing a little exploring."

"Yes, sir."

"What is it, Meara?"

"Mrs. Hodges is back from the marketplace. She's quite eager to see you."

Mr. Griffin appeared suddenly behind Meara.

"That'll be all, Meara."

Meara turned quickly about, stepped past Mr. Griffin as he moved aside.

Mr. Griffin stepped fully in to the library. He gave the room a quick, cursory examination.

"Master Jacob... I thought perhaps now might be a good time to meet with Mrs. Hodges."

"That so?"

"You might want to discuss your meal schedule with her." Mr. Griffin raised a brow. "Perhaps you could present your list of likes and dislikes.

"Yeah, well..." *What's up with Mr. Griffin?* "Never got around to writing it."

Mr. Griffin stood in stoic silence. Jake grew increasingly uncomfortable and finally stepped away from the wall of books and started toward the door.

"Yes," said Jake. "Do let us attend to Mrs. Hodges." He stepped past Mr. Griffin and left the library.

Mr. Griffin examined the library more studiously, backed out and closed the door.

The kitchen was open and airy, and everything was overlarge. The cabinets reached all the way up to the high ceiling. The counters reached deep, and there was a large island of a countertop in the center of the room. The refrigerator and stove complimented each other, each being quite large and heavy duty.

The kitchen was very functional, and harkened to decades past.

Mrs. Hodges was putting away the last of the groceries. A two-wheeled, wire handcart stood next to the back door.

She turned when she heard Jake and Mr. Griffin enter the room.

"Master Jacob!" she beamed.

"Hey, Mrs. H," said Jacob, smiling broadly. She had grown older, but she was definitely Mrs. Hodges.

"The place hasn't been the same without your visits."

"Is that bad or good?" They hugged, and Jake felt that she was genuinely glad to see him.

"A lot quieter, that's for certain."

Jake heard Mr. Griffin emit a slight *harrumph* from his position by the door. He ignored him.

"I'll try to keep the rough-housing down to a minimum."

"Oh, don't you dare."

"That's very kind of you."

"Not at all. The house is in need of a young man's voice." There was melancholy in Mrs. Hodges' smile.

Mr. Griffin, still standing near the door, took the quiet moment to speak up. "Mrs. Hodges. Young Mr. Quigley has some concerns regarding food selections and meal times."

"No cabbage," Mrs. Hodges said with a mock scowl.

"And no peas," Jake added.

"I have not forgotten," she said. She went to a bin set into the far wall and pulled out half a dozen potatoes. There was work to be done, company in her kitchen or no.

Mr. Griffin gave another almost silent *harrumph.* "And he wishes the meal times adjusted."

Mrs. Hodges set the potatoes in the sink, turned on the water, and began scrubbing them. "Meals in this house are served at 8:00, 12:30 and 6:00," she said flatly.

"Why?" asked Jake, just as flatly.

"Because that's when the meals will be ready."

"But what if I want them at 7:00, 12:00 and 5:00?"

"Why?"

"Because that's when *I'll* be ready." Jake watched as Mrs. Hodges continued to scrub the potatoes clean. He could feel Mr. Griffin watching them both, no doubt relying on Mrs. Hodges to knock Jake down a peg or two. He must have been frustrated at the love-fest going on just a few moments earlier.

"7:00 is too early," said Mrs. Hodges at last.

"Lots of people eat breakfast a lot earlier than that."

"Your body's not ready for food at 7:00," she said firmly. "But 12:00 and 5:00 will do."

Jake turned away and started out of the kitchen. He nodded a silent good-bye to Mr. Griffin and spoke over his shoulder to Mrs. Hodges. "Love you, Mrs. H."

"I love you too, sweetie."

§

His old bed was comfortable enough, but with all that had happened throughout the day, Jake hadn't been able to sleep. He had lain staring up at the ceiling, listening to the faint sounds the old house made late at night. The ancient roof timbers creaked against a strong wind blowing in across the sleeping village from the Outland to the north, the large handmade nails that held the walls together shifted about and complained noisily; a loose shutter in a downstairs window fought against its latch. Shadows came and went, sliding from wall to ceiling and down again as the half moon outside moved in and out amongst dark clouds and moonlight shone in through the large window.

So Jake found himself standing out on the open deck in the early hours before dawn, looking out over the village. The sky was still dark and filled with stars.

Gas lamps were evenly spaced along the main thoroughfare and several cross-streets, but most of the illumination came from the bright, full moon.

The village was very quiet in the early morning. The sun hadn't been up long, and the streets were mostly empty. Jake walked down the center of the main thoroughfare, a wide cobblestone avenue lined with single-story, well-worn stone buildings set side by side, with heavy wooden doors and small, square windows. There were a few people out and about, and each one looked curiously at Jake as he passed. He had been a child when he had last walked these streets, and would be a stranger now to most who saw him.

He didn't go straight to the sheriff's office, but instead decided to wander about some first. He found the bank, the general store, the café; at the far end of the main thoroughfare was the wide entrance to the market place.

He reached the sheriff's office, but it was closed. According to the sign, Sheriff Smith wouldn't be in for another hour. Jake supposed that if there was an emergency, most would know where the sheriff lived.

He stood on the step and looked up and down the road. A woman was pulling a small, two-wheeled cart into the market plaza. The booths inside would be opening up soon. Produce, clothing, household supplies, hunting equipment, and just about anything else a person would want, was available in the marketplace.

Jake decided to have breakfast at the café. He could guess what Mrs. Hodges would have to say when he got back to the estate, after she had made and then cleared away breakfast, but he wasn't ready to head back without seeing the sheriff, and he might be able to pick up some information at the café. Besides, if he was going to be living here, he would need to get to know the folks.

The inside of the little restaurant was quiet, and Jake could tell that it hadn't been open for more than a few minutes. Looking about from just inside the door, he saw that all the heavy wooden tables were empty. A woman was moving efficiently from one to the next, setting out salt & pepper shaker sets and napkin holders. She slowed imperceptibly as he came in, glancing at him warily out of the corner of her eye. She looked to be about Jake's age.

He walked over to the nearest table and sat down. The waitress finished setting out the table sets and moved behind the counter. She looked once at a man who appeared at the kitchen 'food up' counter as she reached for the coffee decanter and a cup. The man nodded silently at the waitress and gazed unblinking at Jake.

"You're new here," said the waitress as she reached the table. Not a question; a point of observation.

"I've been gone a while." Jake watched as the waitress poured a cup of coffee and set it on the table in front of him.

"Yeah?" she asked cautiously.

"Jake. Jake Quigley."

The waitress looked somewhat taken aback. She looked quickly at the man watching from the kitchen, then back at Jake. "You're—"

"Tobias is my uncle."

She smiled faintly. "Yeah. Yeah, I remember you. It *has* been a while. You used to come visiting summers. You were just a kid."

"I grew up," Jake said calmly. He took a sip from his coffee. It was hot and very strong.

"I used to see you around," said the waitress. "I'm Sparta Vesper."

"Of course," said Jake. He remembered the name. How could he not remember that name? He didn't remember the face. "You've changed some."

"I grew up," she said, then nodded in the direction of the kitchen. "That's Wallace. He didn't. What can he do for you?"

"Scrambled eggs?"

"Coming up," said Sparta, starting back to the counter.

"Call me Jake," he said, calling after her.

"Call me Sparta," she called over her shoulder.

Jake sat back with his coffee and took another look around the café. It was definitely something out of the past—the distant past—which fit in well with the rest of Serpent's Keep. It was a bizarre mix of different periods from the past, with only the occasional glimpse of the present.

A dusty ray of sun shone through the one window, creating a bright square of light on the reddish-brown wooden floor. The surface was incredibly smooth from decades of cleaning, sweeping, scrubbing, polishing, and tens of thousands of footsteps.

Jake's breakfast came after a few minutes, and he ate quietly, thinking on what little he had already seen this morning, and how much more there must yet be to discover. First up, though, was to talk with the sheriff and find out what had happened to his uncle.

He had finished his eggs and was on a third cup of coffee when the door opened and a man came ambling in. The man was startled by Jake's presence, and faltered slightly as he entered, but managed to gently close the door behind him. He stared at Jake as he did so, then crossed the room and sat at the table set against the far wall. Sparta followed after him with a cup in one hand and the pot of coffee in the other.

The man mumbled at her as she filled his cup. He turned his head slightly at her response, giving Jake another few seconds look before focusing on his coffee. Sparta grinned at Jake as she turned away from the man's table.

"Regular for Mr. Dante," she called out to Wallace.

"Dante regular, coming up," he called back.

Mr. Dante sipped from his cup and carefully set it down on the table in front of him. He turned it slightly, so that the handle was just so, then looked up at Jake.

"So, you are Tobias Quigley's nephew, then."

"That's me," said Jake. "Jacob Quigley."

"Ah," the man nodded. "I am Cosmo Dante, Mr. Quigley. I run the bank here in Serpent's Keep."

"Nice to meet you, Mr. Dante."

"You should drop by the bank, at your convenience. I will personally assist you with the transition of the estate." Mr. Dante adjusts the position of his cup. "You will need to be able to draw on the account, allow or deny others access, and so forth."

"Others?"

"Griffin and Hodges," said Mr. Dante. "Griffin currently has free access, and the Hodges woman can charge to the account."

"I see."

Dante lifted his cup to his mouth and took a sip, slowly set it down again, adjusted its position on the table. "Mr. Quigley was trusting of those whom he deemed had earned that trust. An honorable man. I believe a good man."

"I thank you for your kind words, Mr. Dante."

"Few in the village would have any but kind words in regards to Tobias Quigley." Mr. Dante turned at the sight of Sparta coming from around the counter, his breakfast in hand. He smiled broadly, spoke as he carefully watched Sparta approach. "Excellent food, excellent service, eh, Mr. Quigley?"

Jake raised his cup in answer.

§

Al Smith had been the sheriff of Serpent's Keep for almost twenty years. He was well respected, and was probably the most trusted person in the village. He had a smile and a considerate word for everyone each and every time he saw them.

Jake came up on Sheriff Smith as the big man opened the front door to his office.

"Good morning," said the Sheriff, seeing Jake approach. "You must be Mr. Quigley, recently arrived from the real world."

"That would be me." Jake held out his hand and the sheriff took it. The man had a solid handshake without overdoing it.

"Nephew of our own Tobias Quigley," the sheriff said approvingly. "Come on in."

Jake followed Sheriff Smith into the office. It was a small room with a desk, a filing cabinet and a couple of chairs. Jake assumed the second door in the room led to the back room where there would be cells, maybe a bathroom and a storage closet.

"Have a seat, Mr. Quigley." The sheriff walked around the desk and sat down.

"Call me Jake."

"Okay, Jake." The sheriff leaned back and the old chair squealed loudly. He smiled and pointed in Jake's direction. "I remember you. It's been a while."

"A long while."

"Don't know that I would have recognized you, but I got word of your arrival." He sat up and put his elbows on his desk. The chair squealed again, but the sheriff apparently didn't notice. "What can I do for you?"

"I was wondering about my uncle's disappearance."

"What about it?"

"I'd like to know what happened... What were the circumstances? And how did a disappearance become a death certificate so quickly?"

"Well, as for what happened," Sheriff Smith wrinkled his brow, "your uncle was on another of his Outland excursions, last known position somewhere near the Temple. We know that he stopped there. And that's it. He was never seen again. As for the circumstances, he had been on this particular trip for only three days when last seen; he had left the village with two weeks' worth of food, and he had been gone for just over three weeks when Mr. Griffin notified me of Tobias Quigley's failure to return."

"Had this ever happened before?"

"Tobias being reported missing? No. Griffin did inform me that Tobias would sometimes return later than planned, but not so late as to cause any serious concern."

"Do many people go missing in the Outland?"

"Enough to keep the village population stable," he said dully.

"Oh."

"Yes, sir." The sheriff stood and walked to a small, square table set in the far corner of the room. There was a fairly new coffee maker on the table. He put in a fresh filter, pulled the lid off a can of ground coffee and scooped in three heaping spoonfuls. Jake watched in silence. The sheriff picked up the decanter and went to the second door. When he opened it, Jake could see a row of bars running down one side. Sheriff Smith disappeared around the door, returned half a minute later with the decanter filled with water. He spoke as he poured the water into the back of the coffee maker.

"I found no sign of your uncle. Not a clue. I had no idea where he had gone, or where he had been headed. The only bit of luck I had was in coming across three monks from the Temple. They were on the main west trail, heading this way. They told me that your uncle had spent the night at the temple several weeks earlier, and had left the next day."

"I thought they didn't let strangers stay at the temple."

"They don't. Tobias Quigley wasn't a stranger."

"I mean anyone other than the monks."

"Tobias Quigley held more than a few special privileges in the Outland. A few here in the village, for that matter." Sheriff Smith returned to his chair and plopped down heavily. The chair gave out another painful screech. "Anyway, that's where the trail started and that's where it ended. There's been nothing since. If anybody had come across anything out there, they'd have brought it to me. Assuming they survived the encounter."

"Then what do you think might have happened to him?"

The sheriff looked at Jake for several long seconds. Jake assumed that he was trying to think of a friendly way to tell this uppity outsider from the real world that he had just spent ten minutes telling him that he didn't know what happened to Tobias Quigley, so why the hell are you asking me what happened to Tobias Quigley?

"There are a thousand ways to die in the Outland, Mr. Quigley. Nine hundred of them are going to leave no sign. Your uncle was probably the greatest Outland explorer that ever lived. So let's say, for the sake of this discussion, that he's not likely to succumb to most of those nine hundred...say eighty percent of 'em. He's going to see those coming, or at least he's going to know what to do. That still leaves... what? Almost two hundred of that nine hundred?"

Jake let out a surrendering groan. "Hundred and eighty."

Sheriff Smith gave Jake a consoling look. "I'm sorry, young man. I really am. Tobias Quigley was a friend, and an important and well-liked member of this community. If anything, absolutely anything, comes up, I'll be on it; in a big way. You can count on it."

Jake nodded slowly and stood up. The sheriff stood and held his hand out across the desk. Jake took it. "Thank you, Sheriff."

"Anytime, Jake."

Jake was all the way to the door. "Sheriff..."

"Yeah," the sheriff said, sitting back in his chair.

"You never told me how a death certificate was issued so quickly."

The sheriff smiled openly. "This isn't the outside, Mr. Quigley. We have our own way of doing things. The death certificate was issued because the circumstances surrounding your uncle's disappearance warranted a death certificate."

Jake stood at the door, hand on the knob. He thought about the finality of that statement. If his uncle wasn't dead, then he would have come back. Since he didn't come back...

"Thanks again," he said.

The sheriff watched as Jake left the office.

Chapter Three

Jake came into the kitchen just as Mrs. Hodges was coming in from the pantry. The smell of breakfast still hung in the air.

"Sorry about missing breakfast, Mrs. H."

"Quite all right, Master Jacob." It didn't sound quite all right.

"I had some business to take care of," said Jake, hoping to sound *masterly*. He didn't pull it off very well.

"As I said—"

"Quite all right... yeah." Jake leaned his hip against the island counter. He watched as she went about putting things in order. He knew that she would soon be leaving the kitchen and starting in on the upstairs cleaning. "Mrs. H., what do you know about Meara?"

"Don't you be getting involved with the little Missy, Master Jacob."

"No, no, nothing like that," Jake said quickly. "What do you know of her family?"

Mrs. Hodges kept at her work, but she looked to be ordering her thoughts. "Her mama runs a booth in the market, trinkets and such. Her daddy disappeared in the Outland a couple of years ago."

"What did he do?"

"Hunter."

"Did he do any scouting?"

"Couldn't say. He certainly knew the Outland well enough."

Jake nodded slowly. "Did my uncle ever hire him?"

"Possible I suppose, but Master Tobias knew the Outland as well as anyone in Serpent's Keep. I don't know that he'd need a hunter or a scout."

"Mmm," Jake nodded. "A couple of years ago? Is that when Meara came to work here?"

"I reckon the Master brought her in to help out the child's family. Putting in a few hours a day here helps set the girl's head right, and the few dollars she makes supplements what her mama brings in."

Jake nodded again.

With her morning work in the kitchen finished, Mrs. Hodges turned and faced Jake. "I'll have to be getting upstairs, Master Jacob. Will that be all?"

Jake returned Mrs. Hodges stare, frowned slightly. "Thank you, Mrs. H."

Mrs. Hodges started out of the kitchen.

"Sir," she said crisply.

"Sorry again about missing breakfast," he called after. Once she had gone, he pushed himself away from the counter and walked slowly over to the small kitchen table. A bowl of fruit sat in the middle of the table. He pulled the small bowl near him and grinned. Mixed in amongst the apples and pears was a pomegranate. She knew how much he loved pomegranates.

Jake was sitting in one of the high-back chairs in the library. The pole lamp beside him shone yellow light, putting Jake within a faint glow. The library, and the house in which in resided, had an air about it of the heavy quiet of a warm afternoon.

Jake stared off into the distance. He looked over at the door, closed now. He looked over at the book resting on the desk. He glanced over at the wall of books that he had been looking at when Meara and Mr. Griffin had drawn him away the last time he had been in the library.

He stood slowly then, walked over the desk and looked down at the book. As before, the title read "The Science of Labyrinths".

He rested a hand on the book, looked again at the wall of books to his right.

Jake stepped to the shelves and glanced again at some of the titles: "Flora and Fauna of the Ancient Rainforest", "Creatures of the Deep", "Ancient Religions", "Spelunking", "Desert Ecosystems", "Survival in Extreme Environments", "Holography", "Cryptography and Pictographs", "The Art of Symbolism", "Beyond the Fourth Dimension."

He pulled out a book. The title was "The Theory of the Parallel Universe." Casually flipping through the pages, he found references to trans-universe relationships, physics diversity theory and parallel universe interfacing. The volume, he noted, had opened at a passage discussing the intermediate plane thought to exist between all parallel universes.

Jake closed the book and put it back on the shelf, noting its location. He thought he might be looking at that one again someday.

He saw a large book with the title "Creatures in Myth", the lettering plain and the words faded. The volume itself wasn't much different than any other, less conspicuous even than the last. Still, something told Jake that this one was special. Looking at it sitting there on the shelf, it just...felt... different, though he couldn't say why. Maybe Uncle Tobias had said something about it years ago and the title had burrowed its way into the back of his mind.

He reached up and pulled at the book. Its position on the shelf was awkward and the book didn't want to come free. He realized then that it was stuck on something.

Not stuck...attached to something.

He heard a catch release. The sound had come from behind the shelves. Looking to his left and right, Jake didn't see anything. He took hold of one of the shelves with both hands and pulled.

Nothing.

He sidestepped to one side, to the next section of shelves, and pulled again. This time, he felt movement. Grasping one edge with his left hand, he pulled again and the shelf section opened out, hinged on the right side, the width of a narrow door.

Oh, boy..., thought Jake. *Just great... haunted house stuff. Uncle Tobias, you crazy old sneak...*

Jake had been quite serious about his search, but he hadn't really expected to find anything as exciting as a secret room. At most, some secret papers; maybe a stash of some ill-gotten riches. He had been looking for skeletons in the closet that Mr. Griffin seemed to have wanted to keep hidden.

It appeared now that Jake may have gotten far more than he had asked for.

Tobias Quigley had been the sort of uncle that any kid would have admired. Mysterious, secretive, always off and about on one adventure or another, none of which he was able to provide specific details about, yet from which he had drawn many a wild tale. When he had spoken to young Jake, the man's eyes had sparkled and his smile had been broad and genuine. He laughed and shouted and waved his arms over his head and spoke of grand quests and dangerous lands.

And then he would hide away for days on end, buried in books and charts and old parchment bearing old smells.

Jake had loved his Uncle Tobias more than anyone else on Earth. And Tobias Quigley had left Jake Quigley everything.

Everything...

Jake peered into the darkness behind the shelves. He could tell there was a cavernous space beyond, but nothing more. Taking one last look at the library behind him, Jake stepped through the bookshelf opening. He felt along the wall to his right, and then to his left. He found a switch and flipped it up. Three recessed ceiling lights lit up the room.

It was more of a hall than a room, about twelve feet wide and twenty feet long. Six statues stood on short pedestals, three along each side wall, set about five feet apart. They reached nearly as high as the very high ceiling.

Dragons...

Serpents...

Each was a unique species of dragon. One was winged. One was snakelike and clearly lived in the water. One was heavyset, well-muscled, and looked ready to breathe fire and destruction. One reminded Jake of an overly large desert lizard. One looked thin and agile, with delicate hands and fingers. One looked cerebral and protective.

On the face of each pedestal was an image of a geometric shape; oddly shaped polygons set in raised relief.

Jake walked cautiously down the center of the hall of statues and through an arched opening at the far end. He found another light switch on the wall just inside.

This room, running to Jake's left, wasn't much larger than the hallway that he had just come through, about twelve feet across and running less than twenty feet to his left, with the ceiling set at a much more familiar height of less than eight feet. The main difference between this room and the last, however, was that this room appeared to be very functional.

There was a large, heavy desk near the far end, facing the left wall. The only chair in the room was a large, leather chair behind the desk. A large, hand-drawn map hung on the wall behind the chair.

Jake approached the desk. The top was clear. The bottom left drawer was empty. There was a small, thin, leather-bound book in the top left drawer. He sat down and set the book on the desk in front of him. He opened it.

It looked to be a notebook of some sort, but only the first few pages had anything written on them. The first had a diagram containing a set of six geometric figures pulled together into a single, six-sided form. The individual polygons looked like those that he had seen on the serpent pedestals in the Hall of Statues.

The second page contained two short paragraphs:

It has been known for centuries that this time would come... the gathering together of the artifacts and restoration of the path. Each step is a dangerous one, but none so feared as that final footfall when the way is opened and I must step through to the other side.

The preparations are almost complete. It is difficult to awaken after having been asleep for so long... I dread what is to come.

The third page contained a darker passage:

The Rhetani must be prevented from recovering the artifact and opening the way. I am dismayed that this action, which I have anticipated for so long, for which I planned and yet hoped would never come, has arrived. More troublesome still are recent events that must be dealt with, and I grow increasingly concerned that the gathering and the restoration may fall to my nephew. Such was not to have been his fate, but I can find no other solution.

Jake closed the book and leaned back in the chair. He felt numb. This sounded major, in a very major way. What had his uncle gotten himself into?

What was going on?

He spun slowly around in the chair.

The statues, and the artifacts spoken of in the notebook, these were clearly related in some way. The geometric shapes...

The gathering of the artifacts...

Such was not to have been his fate...

That didn't sound good.

Jake sensed the presence of someone else in the room. Looking up, he saw Mr. Griffin standing just inside the room, one foot still in the Hall of Statues.

"Hey, Griff," he said calmly.

"Good evening, Master Jacob."

"Been expecting you."

"Sir?"

"You seemed anxious when you found me in the library before."

"Not at all, sir." Mr. Griffin walked toward Jake. Jake frowned and turned the chair so that he was again facing the desk.

"Whatever."

Mr. Griffin stepped nearer. He indicated the room, at the notebook in particular.

"Are you sure that you should be doing this?"

"Why try and hide all this, Griff?"

Mr. Griffin looked again at the notebook, glanced then around the room. He said nothing at first, finally stiffened his resolve. "Master Quigley was very secretive regarding his activities. Even with me. I accepted that there was a part of his life that I was not to be a part of."

Jake leaned back. "Yeah... and?"

"And... I do not know your uncle's wishes."

Jake straightened, startled. He smiled then, almost laughed.

"Poor ole' Griff." Jake looked long and thoughtfully at Mr. Griffin, closed his eyes a moment, then opened them and sat up straight, spoke as if quoting: "I bequeath to my nephew, Jacob Quigley, all that I own, all that I dream, and all that I am, in the hope that my life's quest will become his quest."

"Master Quigley's last will and testament."

"In its entirely. Exactly one sentence."

"Yes."

"I think he meant more than the furniture. Don't you?"

"I believe so."

"He quite clearly meant more than material wealth. And when he spoke of 'life's quest', I think he meant more than some spiritual or philosophical state of being. I think that it was something quite tangible."

Mr. Griffin appeared to think that one over. "I would suppose so, Master Jacob."

"Come on, Mr. Griffin. You were with my uncle since before the invention of fire. You may not have known exactly what he was up to, but you knew it was something heavy. And you knew about this room; and about that hall of statues, which I am for damn sure certain has some significance. And have a look at Tobias' choice of reading material: labyrinths, spelunking, holography, cryptography, extreme environments, parallel universes..."

"As I have said... Master Quigley chose not to include me in that part of his life."

"Yeah, yeah," Jake waved impatiently. "Get over it. You knew that this was going on. And I know that you are one smart old fart. Are you trying to tell me that when you read his will, you didn't make the connection between that reference to 'life's quest' and all of this?"

"I did make the connection," Mr. Griffin said flatly.

Jake leaned forward, spoke softly now. "Uncle Tobias has turned over to me some lifelong mission of his. He didn't make it obvious to an outside observer, but to you and to me, he made it clear."

It took a moment, but Mr. Griffin finally nodded in agreement. "Have you discovered what this... *quest*... might be?"

"Not exactly." Jake absently tapped a finger on the top of the desk. "On that, Tobias was extraordinarily cryptic." Jake glanced up at Mr. Griffin, "Quite the man of mystery... he never told you anything about it? Nothing at all?"

"No." Mr. Griffin paused and looked about them. "He never so much as spoke of this room. I never entered it, until now."

Jake grew thoughtful again. He placed a palm on the leather notebook. "Secret places, hidden accesses, mysterious journeys. It has something to do with gathering artifacts."

"Sir?"

Jake looked tired. "Nothing."

"Yes sir." Mr. Griffin managed to show some concern. "Why don't you come downstairs, Master Quigley. Hot tea would do you good."

Jake gave a tired grin. "You go on, Griff... I think I'm just going to sit here a while."

Mr. Griffin finally nodded and stepped back. "Very well, sir."

The command center was nearly dark. The overhead light had been turned off. The desk lamp was on, though, and it gave the top of the desk a dull shimmer, spread its glow across Jake.

His head rested on his folded arms. He had fallen asleep.

Something woke him...

He slowly lifted his head. He looked the top of the desk, then at the wall beyond.

He looked curiously then at the base of the wall. There was a very thin sliver of light where the wall met the floor. Pushing himself back from the desk, he stood and walked around the desk, never losing sight of the light.

Approaching the wall, he laid his palm against it, pushed at it, tapped at it. He gave the wall a light slap.

The wall had been designed in sections, flat panels separated by raised vertical strips. Jake began pulling and pushing at the strips, then pushed at the panel above the light.

Nothing...

He lifted his hand up to a horizontal strip a foot above his head. He pulled. He pushed.

Jake heard the clicking sound of a catch release.

He lowered his hand and used the flat palms of both hands to push.

The section panel opened.

The room beyond was barely six feet wide, twelve feet long. A tiny window was set in the far wall, allowing the colorful rays of the early morning sun to stream in.

A high counter ran down the left wall. A scattering of supplies were on the counter and on shelves set above the counter. There was a small backpack, a utility belt, canteen, an assortment of knives, a compass, several flashlights, batteries, handheld mining lamps, first aid supplies, wooden matches.

Jake looked closely at a box filled with small, sealed pouches. These turned out to be an assortment of dried fruit, trail mix, and jerky.

Hanging on a hook beside the door was a ring of keys. Lifting them from the hook, Jake was surprised at how heavy they were. In the morning light, he could see they were very ornate, but couldn't really make out the designs. He took them back to the desk and looked at them under the light of the desk lamp.

Six keys; stamped onto the face of each key was a geometric shape.

The polygons were the same as those he had seen in the notebook... and those on the face of the pedestals...

Jake looked in the direction of the Hall of Statues.

"Oh, dear uncle..." he whispered. *Secret places, secret rooms. Mysterious quests... what the heck are you all about?*

Jake absently weighed the keys in his hand, wandered in the direction of the archway. The hall was dark. Running a palm against the wall to one side of the archway, he found the companion to the switch on the far side of the room. Flipping the switch, the overhead light came on.

The six statues, three on either side of the room, towered over the aisle running down the center of the room.

Three dragons on the left, three dragons on the right.

Jake looked at the keys in his hand. He started down the center of the hallway. He looked at the geometric images set into the faces of each pedestal. As he passed each statue, he looked up at the face of each dragon. The winged dragon, the water serpent, each of the others in turn...

He stopped in front of the husky beast of fire and destruction. He found the key with the same geometric pattern as the one on the pedestal, looked up into the face of the monster looming over him.

"What do you have for me, old boy?"

The creature stood silent, mocking. Looking closely at the polygon shape itself, Jake could see no place to insert the key.

"Won't talk, eh?" Jake studied then, inch by inch, every feature, looking for the keyhole where this key belonged. He knew that he was on the right track, but the intricate design work hid the keyhole, and whatever lay beyond, very well.

He studied the statue all the way to the base, and then studied the base. Finding nothing, he moved around to the side of the statue and began again. Moving then on to the back, he sensed that here was where he would find the home for the key. He studied the top of the pedestal first, the surface of which was made up of large whorls of carved stone.

And there it was. He knew that it was what he was looking for, even though to all appearances it was little more than a shadow. He inserted the key. It slid in cleanly. He turned the key and some hidden apparatus within gave out a solid, satisfying click.

One small section of the top of the base released and popped up just a little. The section was one foot square, with the key set in the center. Jake lifted up the lid and peered down inside.

In the small compartment was a leather scroll, rolled and bound loosely with a leather strap. He reached in and lifted it out. It was very smooth and very soft. With the scroll in hand, Jake lowered the lid and removed the key. He hurried back to the desk where he would have room to examine the scroll under the lamp.

Chapter Four

Jake walked slowly around the desk, eyes never leaving the scroll that now lay flat on the desktop. The words were clear and easy enough to read, but it seemed shrouded with inner meaning.

> *Seek a northerly path and find now the pylon within the stone. The one will point the way to where footfalls echo down empty streets and windows be but dark and lifeless eyes.*

Northerly path. Well, that he got. He could do that. The north gate out of Serpent's Keep opened to a northerly path. That would get him going. As for the rest of it...

Pylon. Wasn't that some sort of support post? A tower?

Within the stone? Was he supposed to find a stone with a post sticking out of it? That didn't make any sense at all. That had to be wrong.

The one will point the way... That could mean anything. The one what? Would somebody be there to guide him? Would there literally be a "1" on this stone?

As for *empty streets* and *lifeless windows,* that sounded like an abandoned town. But Jake couldn't remember ever hearing of an abandoned town to the north; or in any direction, for that matter. It seemed, though, that if he found and traveled a certain path in the north, and found this stone with a pylon, that it would lead him to this... place. And once he got to this place, he would do... what?

Jake circled around the desk once more and sat down. He pulled the scroll around and read it again. He held his head in his hands. Slowly then, a thought crept into his mind.

Gateway... Couldn't a pylon be a gateway?

A gateway within a stone. That didn't make any more sense than a post in a stone. But perhaps, when taken with everything else... Jake stood up, grabbed up the scroll and went to wake Mr. Griffin. Jake needed a sounding board to bounce ideas off of.

Mr. Griffin, standing precisely in his full-length dressing gown and wiping sleepily at his eyes, stared down at the scroll laid out over the counter in the kitchen.

Jake was leaning over the counter, staring down at the scroll.

"I think that somewhere to the north I'm going to find a very special stone. A specific path will lead me to it."

"Yes sir."

"Hidden on or in this stone is the secret to a gateway. I think that's what this reference to a pylon means."

Jake watched Mr. Griffin nod silently.

"So," Jake continued, "If I can find this gateway, and go through it, I'll find a town or a village. It will probably be abandoned.

Jake looked uncertainly at Mr. Griffin, as if expecting the old man to break into hysterical laughter. Mr. Griffin, however, held his silence.

"I know..." Jake said defensively, "find a stone with a gate, somehow magically walk through this mystical stone... all pretty weird."

"Not at all, sir."

"Really?" Jake was surprised. "Sounds pretty weird to me."

"I believe you have surmised correctly," said Mr. Griffin. "But I have never heard of such a place."

"Yeah."

"Many questions remain."

"A few," Jake grumbled. "If I can find this stone, how exactly do I then find the secret that will lead me to this gate? It must be well camouflaged. Simple logic tells me that it wouldn't be out in the open for just anyone to find."

"The one will point the way," quoted Mr. Griffin.

"Yeah. So it says. I need to find out what that means."

"You may not be able to resolve that question without actually examining the stone."

"But will I recognize the stone without knowing what 'the one' reference means?"

"I cannot say."

Jake appeared to scrutinize the scroll, but was in fact looking far beyond. "If I find the stone, if I find the gateway, if I find the town... what then? What am I supposed to do when I get there?"

"I do not believe you have has yet discovered anything left behind by Master Quigley that would definitively answer that question."

Jake stared at Mr. Griffin in frustration. "Whatever it is that I'm supposed to do... why hasn't Uncle Tobias already done it? What was he doing when he disappeared?"

"The answer to that may very well have an impact on the task at hand."

"Doing *whatever it is I'm supposed to do* may require that I first accomplish whatever it was my uncle was attempting at the time that he vanished."

"He was last seen at the temple."

"So I should go there first..."

"They do not openly welcome strangers, Master Jacob."

"Maybe not, but you're right. That's where I need to go. And they're going to talk to me."

Now that Jake had a plan, or at least the beginnings of one, he was both excited and a bit anxious. Mr. Griffin had asked to go with him, but Jake had said no. As tempting as the offer was, he felt that Mr. Griffin would be more valuable at the mansion. He was certain there were more answers to be found in the secret rooms, in the pages of the books that filled the library shelves, in places as yet undiscovered.

So Jake spent the following day preparing for his journey. He filled the small backpack with some of the provisions and gear from the supply room, along with some extra clothes. He put the compass and some matches into a side pocket, and put the canteen and knife onto the utility belt. He wasn't ready to live on jerky and trail mix alone, so he asked Mrs. Hodges to make up a couple of lunches and some hardboiled eggs. His plan was to only be gone a few days. He knew the trip out to the temple wasn't that far, and he would most likely want to come back to Serpent's Keep before going out again in search of this abandoned town alluded to in the dragon scroll.

Back in the Command Center, he studied the large, handmade map of the Outland that was mounted on the wall. As he had noted before, it was a bit light on details. There were the known landmarks: the river, the Great Cliff. The Farm to the north was represented, and of course the Temple to the west. The major trails were displayed, and a handful of the lesser.

Jake thought it best to keep the original map safe at the mansion. He found paper and pen in the desk drawer and set about to make a smaller version of the map. Once he was finished, he stuffed the copy into the side pocket of the backpack and went downstairs to see if dinner was ready. He would be leaving first thing in the morning.

Meara was waiting for him at the foot of the stairs, dressed in night clothes.

"Master Jacob," Meara nodded nervously.

"Is everything all right?" Jake reached the last step and stopped.

"Yes, sir," Meara started quickly, and then paused.

"You sure?"

"Master Jacob... You should not be going into the Outland alone. Begging your pardon, sir."

"I can find my way, Meara." Jake stepped around Meara and started across the room. "I'll be fine."

She started after him. "Let me guide you, sir."

That stopped Jake short. He turned and looked carefully at the girl, trying to decide whether or not she was joking. She was not.

"You know the Outland?"

"Very well."

"Your father?"

"I went with him many times," she gave a sharp nod. "He was a hunter and a guide."

"So I understand," said Jake. "Did he ever serve as guide for my uncle?"

"Master Tobias needed no guide."

"So I've been told, but—"

"He did sometimes seek my father's counsel."

"Did they ever go into the Outland together? Not as master and guide, but as collaborators?"

"Yes."

"When your father disappeared?"

"Yes." Meara stood silent, offering no more. Jake chose to ask no more, at least not for the moment. He suspected that it was all tied together somehow; Meara's father, Uncle Tobias, the temple, the quest, the statues and what they represented; whatever Tobias was after when he disappeared.

Meara was young, certainly not yet twenty, but there was little doubt that she had more experience in the Outland than Jake. Perhaps she could keep him alive long enough for him to reach the temple and ask his questions.

"To the temple and back," he said. "No more."

"Yes, sir," she said excitedly.

"Your job is to keep me from making a fool of myself out there. Keep me out of trouble and keep me from getting lost."

"I can do that."

"Yeah, well, that may not be as easy as it sounds." Jake leaned close. "No heroics, Meara. I mean it. You're not my bodyguard."

"Yes, sir. No, sir."

Jake turned away again and started in the direction of the dining room. "We leave before first light. Get your gear together. I'll bring mine down later and you can look it over, make sure I haven't forgotten anything."

Meara was already turning about and rushing toward the back of the house. Jake had a sneaking suspicion that she was already packed.

Mr. Griffin watched Jake and Meara from the front door. He was quite distressed and had let Jake know of his concern all through the prior evening and again in the morning. The very thought of taking Meara along on the trip, no matter that it was only to the temple and back, was quite ill conceived. If Jake felt it absolutely necessary, then he should allow Mr. Griffin to accompany them.

Jake would have liked the additional company. But more than the fact that there were tasks at the mansion that needed doing, Jake, for right or for wrong, was concerned about Mr. Griffin's age. Griff had been an old man for as long as Jake had known him. He was probably the oldest man Jake had ever known. He seemed in good shape and was to all appearances a healthy man. But he was still an *old man,* and Jake had no way of knowing what to expect out there.

Jake said none of this to Mr. Griffin. He felt guilty enough just having such thoughts; he could never voice them aloud. He just told him that he needed Griff at the mansion, and that was that.

Jake could feel Mr. Griffin's cold eyes watching him now as he stepped through the estate's front gate, Meara following after. He looked up then, gate held half open. "Three days, Mr. Griffin," he called up to the dark figure on the porch. "After four, notify the sheriff. You have the route we'll take."

"Very well, sir."

Jake closed the gate and followed after Meara, who was already half a dozen paces down the walk.

"Good luck, Master Jacob," said Mr. Griffin, though by now Jake and Meara were already out of sight.

The morning air was damp and slate-gray. There was a slight breeze blowing down the main thoroughfare, cold and sharp against the face. Jake was glad when they turned onto a narrow side road and out of the wind.

The sun wouldn't be up for another half hour, and they saw no one until they reached the West Gate. All citizens of Serpent's Keep had to do their time standing watch at the gates, and the poor soul at the West Gate this morning thought at first that his relief had finally arrived.

"Where you been?" he asked. "You're late."

"Not really, no," said Jake. He and Meara stopped two strides from the heavy wooden gate. The young man on watch remained in the three-walled four-by-four shed that served as the watch post.

"Hey, Frankie," said Meara.

"Meara?"

"We're heading out."

Frankie stared blankly at her, not quite sure if he had actually heard her speak.

"So we'll be needing you to open the gate," said Jake.

"You're going out?'

"That's the plan," said Jake.

"Yeah... okay." Frankie moved in between Jake and the gate, reached down and lifted the heavy timber that served to lock the gate. All the while he gave Jake a careful study, not quite sure what to make of this stranger heading into the Outland with Meara.

It took all his strength to half-carry, half-drag the timber to one side and out of the way. That done, he stepped back in front of the gate and pushed down on the large, strong latch and leaned back, pulling at the heavy door with all that he had.

Jake stepped quietly through the opening as soon as there was room. Meara followed after, calling back over her shoulder, "Thank you, Frankie."

The main west trail out of Serpent's Keep was eight feet wide and cut straight into a thick forest of scrub alder and tangles of underbrush, with an occasional lone evergreen standing stark and solitary. A fog hung overhead, hiding the treetops, occasionally drifting down to the forest floor and floating smokily across the trail.

They traveled in silence for several minutes, with the only sounds disturbing the predawn quiet being the rustling of fallen leaves stirring in the breeze and the scurrying of small animals.

They reached a fork in the trail where both directions appeared to be well traveled, both narrowing only slightly from the path they were on.

As Meara watched Jake pull out the map he had made, she pointed first to the left fork, "We need to go left," she said.

Jake nodded as he studied the map. He found the fork on the map, the path that each route took. As he folded the map and put it away, he glanced up at the glowing fog. Somewhere beyond that fog, the sun had risen.

"We should reach the temple by late afternoon," said Meara.

"Is the trail like this all the way?" he asked. Up to now, the trail had been clear and open.

"It narrows just up ahead, but the route between the Keep and the temple is the most used in the Outland, other than the farm road."

From his research, Jake knew the farm road was the route running between the village and the farm to the north.

They started forward again, Jake leading the way down the left fork. It narrowed beyond the first bend, closing in on either side until it was only four to five feet wide. The vegetation began to change as well, becoming darker and thicker; much more evergreen, and more heavy moss, more moisture hanging in the air, more dew hanging on the leaves of the underbrush.

A thousand yards further and there was another split in the trail. Meara told him to continue left. He went left without pause. Over the next few hours they came up on several more side trails, and at each one his guide pointed the way without much thought. She definitely knew her way around this part of the Outland.

They stopped at a wide spot in the trail about midday, the sun high overhead and doing its best to burn through the last of the low clouds, and set about to have lunch.

The clearing looked like it was frequently used for midday breaks; a fallen tree that lay across the back of the clearing offered a place to sit, and appeared to have been worn by years of such use. A small circle of stones in the center of the clearing held the ashes of dozens of past cooking fires.

Jake studied the perimeter of the clearing as he climbed up onto the fallen tree and set his pack beside him. He could see numerous trails leading away from the clearing and into the woods. Each small path was lost quickly in the shadows of the forest.

"Some folks try to hunt out there," said Meara, who was studying Jake rather than their surroundings. "Most don't."

"The hunting's not good?"

"It is better to bring your supplies with you."

"Dangerous?"

"Can be," she said. "When you go out there to take care of business, don't go far and don't stay gone long."

"Got it," said Jake. He took a strip of dried meat and a chunk of cheese from his pack and used his knife to cut a piece from each. Meara did the same and they ate quietly for a few moments. "Your father taught you well," Jake said finally.

"He knew his way around, sir."

"He spent a lot of time out here?"

"He liked the Outland."

"And he passed that fondness along to you?"

"Not so much," said Meara. "I respect the Outland, but that's not the same thing."

Jake wondered if the reason that Meara didn't like the Outland was because she felt that it was responsible for her father's death. He wanted to ask, wanted to know if it might be related to Tobias, about whether or not it was Tobias' sense of duty and responsibility and guilt about her father's death that had led to her position in the household.

But in the end, he couldn't.

"Do you know if my uncle felt the same way about the Outland as your father?"

"I don't think so," said Meara. "He knew the Outland better than anyone, but I don't think it was so much that he liked it out here. I think he needed to be out here."

That's quite an assumption, thought Jake.

"He used to spend a lot time out here, but only in the last couple of years did it become... something more."

The temple was a sprawling structure, the original building lost and misshapen from numerous additions globbed onto it over the years. Three tall, narrow, cylindrical spires rose above the treetops. The thick walls were made of wood and stone and concrete and mortar. The main door, set into the center of a protruding forward wing, was made of dark, heavy wood and black metal straps.

Meara climbed the two steps and stopped, staring at the door. After a moment's pause, she lifted and dropped the large knocker set in the center of the door. It gave a solid, resounding thud. She lifted and dropped it a second time, then turned and looked down at Jake. "Let's see what we get," she said.

Jake nodded solemnly and the two of them waited. After a full two minutes, they heard the sound of a wooden cross bar being lifted, and the door smoothly glided open. A tall man in a heavy robe and hood stepped forward and stopped. Jake saw that the monk took in the surroundings before finally turning his attention to Meara.

"Yes?" he asked simply.

"Hello, John," said Meara.

She knows him, thought Jake.

"Meara," said John.

"Don't give me your monk posturing."

"What do you seek, Meara?"

"We seek to get inside."

"You know the tenets of the temple."

"And you know that I wouldn't be here if it wasn't important."

"That doesn't really matter."

"You let my uncle stay here," Jake blurted out. He kept to the foot of the steps. The monk looked down at him, then quickly back to Meara.

"What do you seek, Meara?" John asked again, choosing to ignore the stranger's outburst. Without further information, there was as yet no purpose in initiating a second conversation with Meara's companion.

"We seek knowledge," Meara droned.

"As do we all."

"Airs again."

"I need to find out what you know about Tobias Quigley," said Jake.

Meara saw a flash of interest pass across the monk's face. "Master Quigley was his uncle," she said.

John the monk turned his full attention to Jake for the first time, studying his features and his stance. "Tobias Quigley was a good man," he said. "His absence will be deeply felt."

"Can you help us?" Jake climbed the first step. He watched as John stiffened and then calmly took a step back into the doorway. He thought for a moment that the monk was going to close the door on them.

"I can promise you nothing," said John. He backed fully into the front hall and made way for Meara and Jake.

The front hall had a high ceiling, a floor of wide, wooden planks, and walls of square stone on which several torches flickered red and orange flame.

A low open archway opposite the front door was the only other access to the room. John closed the door behind them and led them through this and down a narrow, dimly lit passage. They passed several open doors, beyond which Jake occasionally saw a monk sitting at a table or working over a desk.

They followed John around several turns and down several side passages before coming finally into a library. The book-lined walls rose twenty feet on all sides, with several tall, very narrow windows set into the far wall. Gas lamps were placed in the center of each of four large tables. Two more lamps hung from the high, beamed ceiling.

John walked to the first table and signaled for them to be seated. "I shall return," he said, stepping away from the table just as Jake was sitting. The monk left by the door through which they had come, closing it behind him.

Jake stood and walked toward the nearest wall.

"They know you around here," Jake stated.

"All my life, sir."

Old leather-bound books lined the shelves. Jake walked along the wall to where the shelves were replaced with diamond-shaped cubbyholes. Sitting in these cubbyholes were dozens of leather tubes, each two to three inches in diameter. Sliding one out, and then several others, he found they ranged in length from about eighteen inches to as long as two feet or so. Painstakingly written on the side of each was a title, most of which he couldn't understand, as they were written in a language he wasn't familiar with.

He turned from the scrolls and was moving back toward the table just as the door opened and John returned. Another man, shorter and much older, was following him. At the sight of this second man, Meara hurriedly stood and bowed her head.

"Master Peter," she said.

Peter waved his hand for her to sit. "Always a pleasure to see you, my dear," he said pleasantly. He turned his sharp gaze to Jake. "I am told that you are nephew to Brother Tobias."

Meara spoke up quickly, not yet daring to sit, "This is Master Jacob Quigley, recently arrived in Serpent's Keep."

"Call me Jake," said Jake. He held out his hand. Peter looked at it curiously, as if completely perplexed as to what to do with it. He smiled finally and took Jake's hand. His grip was sure and strong.

"Brother Jacob," said Peter, as if correcting Jake.

"Okay," said Jake. "Should I call you Brother Peter?"

"That would be fine." He waved again for them to sit, then nodded curtly to John. The younger monk walked over to the wall of cubby-holes and searched through one section until he found the canister that he wanted. He returned to Peter and handed it to him.

Peter opened the tube and pulled out an old scroll, set it on the table in front of Jake and Meara. "I think you should look at this," he said, unrolling it. "It was the reason for Brother Tobias' last visit."

"He was looking at this?" asked Jake.

"And not for the first time," Peter nodded.

Jake hovered over the aging scroll. "You do know that I have no idea what it says..."

"It is an ancient script," said Peter. "Rarely used and unknown to most."

"But not unknown to you," said Jake matter-of-factly, looking at John, then at Peter. "...or to my uncle."

"That is correct," said Peter, resting a silencing hand on John's arm. He laughed lightly. "Your uncle called the script Old Scratch. He said that he much preferred the *entertaining vulgarity* of today's tongue."

Jake mumbled as he stared dazedly down at the scroll. "That certainly sounds like Tobias." He leaned back in his chair. "Why show me a scroll that you know I can't read?"

Peter held up a hand, raising a finger as if to indicate that Jake had struck upon the point.

Meara spoke up. "What does the scroll say, Master?"

"There are several ways to interpret the script, and so the exact meaning is dependent on that interpretation."

"Naturally," grumbled Jake. "How did Tobias interpret it?"

"He did not fully confide in me, Brother Jacob."

"But you do have an idea."

"I can extrapolate, make assumptions... based on his queries of me."

"And?"

Peter gave a long sigh, smiled distantly and leaned forward over the scroll.

"And the reason I wished to show it to you." he said, indicating the first section of text. "This passage refers to gates. And there is an inference to other existences. The *other existence* reference is rather ambiguous, but I interpret the phrase as *place not of here.*" Peter paused and then pointed to the next section. "It then speaks of the necessity to protect all existence, and later the hiding or disguising of '*the ways*'."

"Does it say anything about how these ways are disguised, or how to recognize them?" Jake asked.

"I am sorry, no. And that didn't seem to be a concern of Brother Tobias."

Jake furrowed his brow. Peter took this as a sign to continue.

"Here it refers to an object, an artifact, used to make clear the way. This particular phrasing of '*the way*' is different than the others. The wording is slightly different, and the interpretation places a different level of importance on it." Peter looked up from the text. "Your uncle showed a repeated interest in this passage."

"Any idea why?"

Peter gave an apologetic expression. He then slid a finger down to another section of the writing.

"A later passage," he pointed to another section of text, "speaks of defense of all existence, and the *segmenting* of the artifact."

Now that is *interesting...*

"The final passage refers to the closing of the path to those who would bring about destruction." Peter straightened, eyes darting from the scroll to Jake and back again.

Meara whistled softly. "I don't know if your interpretation makes it any clearer than the original script."

"Some of it does," said Jake. It confirmed, in Jake's mind, his own interpretation of pylons as gateways. And then there was the segmenting of the artifact.

"I am glad," said Peter.

"What can you tell me of this artifact?"

"Only that it was of supreme importance in an earlier time," said Peter. He studied John the monk, then Meara, trying to decide how much to allow them to hear. He finally turned back to Jake. "There is another scroll, older perhaps than this one. It speaks of a Guardian. This Guardian is closely tied to the Artifact, and the scroll states that it was the Guardian who was responsible for the partitioning of the Artifact into individual segments."

"So if we could find out more of this Guardian—"

"But he must have died thousands of years ago," said Meara.

"The scroll states that the bond between Guardian and Artifact was eternal," said Peter. "And I believe it likely that Brother Tobias was somehow bound to both."

The guest cell to which Jake was shown was just large enough to hold a bunk, a small table and a chair. There was a narrow window set high in one wall. An oil lamp on the table emitted a dim, warm glow, creating soft shadows that danced across the stone walls.

Jake sat down on the bed, turned and lay back, stared up at the heavy-beamed ceiling. He tried to relax. He was exhausted, but there was too much going on in his head for him to sleep. He feared that sleep would be a long time coming, and they had a very early start in the morning.

Once they had finished up in the library, Peter had shown Jake and Meara to the dining hall, where they were given a plain but filling meal. None of the other monks spoke to them, but the two strangers were under constant, if discreet, observation. After dinner, they were allowed to clean up before retiring to their cells.

They were to remain in their rooms until morning bell, one hour before dawn. After the morning meal, they would be leaving the temple.

Chapter Five

Jake and Meara reached the west gate of the village two hours before sunset. They had stopped several times along way, and had taken a few side trips down paths that had looked interesting, despite Meara's restrained objections. Jake wanted to get a better feel for the lay of the land. He knew that he would soon be spending some time out here.

The gate looked larger and darker from the outside. There was a large, metal ring hanging on the wall beside it. Meara reached up and gave it a long pull; Jake heard the peal of a heavy bell beyond the door.

"Who is it?" asked someone from the other side of the gate.

"Master Jacob Quigley," said Meara.

Jake heard the wooden bar lock slide over and a few moments later the door opened.

"Welcome back, folks," said the young man on guard. He was not the same person that had let them out the day before. Their exit had no doubt been logged in somewhere, and their return had been anticipated.

Jake stopped at the intersection of the side road and the main street of the village. It was quiet, with only a few people out and about. He would have thought it would have been busier this time of day. He turned to his guide and companion. "Why don't you head on home, Meara?" he suggested, his voice as quiet as the village around them. "We can discuss the trip in the morning."

"Of course, sir," said Meara.

"And thanks. I appreciate all your help."

"Glad to, sir."

Was she more formal now that they were back in Serpent's Keep? He started to say something, but thought better of it. "Tomorrow, then," he said, and started across the street.

The street to Quigley Mansion was empty and still, though he could hear people in the plaza on his right, mostly the laughter of children some distance away. He had his key in hand when he reached the gate, and was quickly through and starting up the front walk when Mr. Griffin opened the front door.

"You waiting for me all this time?"

Griffin raised one brow, but otherwise was still as stone. "Simply good timing, Master Jacob."

Jake climbed the steps and started through the front door. He looked tired.

"Not worried about me?" he asked. He sounded as tired as he looked.

"Was your trip successful, sir?" Griffin asked, following him into the house.

"Made it back. That's something."

"Quite so, sir. An unexpected, but most welcome outcome."

Jake started doggedly up the stairs. He spoke without looking back at Mr. Griffin.

"Think I'll clean up." He needed to rest.

That evening after dinner, Jake returned upstairs and went out onto the deck that looked out to the west. It was just after sunset and the sky was splashed in orange and red and purple, sending colorful streaks of light across the treetops of the Outland. He sat in the large wooden lounge chair and watched as the colors shifted and stretched with the sinking of the sun. At one point a streak of light struck at what must have been one of the spires of the temple, some thirty miles away, creating an intense star of light in the heart of the Outland.

As dusk slowly crept up on the village, flickers of light shone as street lamps were lit and as light poured out through the small, square windows of the homes and shops throughout Serpent's Keep. Sounds seemed to carry further in the oncoming dusk, though they were strangely muffled, as if the oncoming night was throwing a heavy blanket over the land.

Jake let his mind wander in the calming backdrop of the village settling in for the evening. His thoughts were conflicted, however, and he found himself torn between what sometimes felt like two very different objectives. The first was to find his uncle, whether alive or dead; the second was to identify and pursue the task that his uncle had started and apparently expected his nephew to carry on and complete.

He knew where he wanted to focus all of his attention, but also felt an obligation to the quest that he had been given.

Was there a way to pursue both?

That had been easy enough to do up to this point. Seeking clues for the first was the same as seeking clues for the second. Now, however, he was afraid that was going to change.

Or was it? If he set out on the first stage of the quest, would he be following the path that his uncle had taken before him? Would he therefore, sooner or later, overtake his uncle, or at least find another clue as to his whereabouts and his fate?

What else was there to do?

He was still missing so much. He didn't know what he should be searching for or where to look for it.

Jake heard the sound of someone coming out onto the deck. There were only so many possibilities as to who it might be, and only one whom it was likely to be.

"Hey, Griff," he said, without turning.

"Master Jacob." Mr. Griffin stepped up beside him. He cast his gaze in the direction that Jake was looking. After so many decades, the old man knew every twist and turn and shadow of the village. Of the Outland beyond the wall, however, he knew almost nothing. It mattered little to him, though, beyond the interest that his former employer had held for it. "Mrs. Hodges asked that I see about you."

Jake didn't respond. After several moments, Mr. Griffin continued, still not looking at the young man. "Apparently, you didn't have much of an appetite." Mr. Griffin made every effort not to display any shared concern.

Again Jake said nothing. This time, Mr. Griffin patiently waited. For almost a minute, the two of them looked out at the scene laid before them.

"My uncle had an interest in parallel universes," Jake said at last. It was a casual comment, not intended to draw a response. "Alternate universes." A shrug. "The books in the library."

Mr. Griffin looked calmly to Jake, then again turned his attention to the village.

Jake continued. "Take that, and tie it to the reference in his notebook... the one where he said that '*a way would be opened*', and that he would have to step through to the other side."

Jake grew quiet again. After a few moments, Mr. Griffin looked side glance at him. He considered speaking, considered saying something, *anything*, but chose to remain silent. Eventually, Jake went on.

"I think Tobias found a way to travel between these... *alternate...* universes." Jake turned to look directly at Mr. Griffin. "There is a scroll at the temple that refers to *gates* and *other existences.*"

Mr. Griffin felt it was now appropriate to chime in with a thought of his own. "Our own serpent's scroll; its reference to the pylon in the stone."

"Yes." Jake nodded. "Have you noticed that each of the six dragons looks like it comes from a completely different environment? Six worlds, each residing in an alternate universe." Jake looked back out at the village, at the Outland beyond. The colors of the sunset were growing darker. "Numerous occurrences of the six polygons, and in the notebook... the joining together of these into a single geometric shape."

"The Artifact," said Mr. Griffin.

"The scroll at the Temple speaks of the segmenting of the Artifact."

"The individual polygons."

"Each polygon can be found on a serpent's pedestal in the Hall of Statues. Each serpent, and therefore each polygon, represents another world."

"And the gathering together…" Mr. Griffin said flatly.

"I have to go to each of these other worlds and find the artifact segments. I have to bring them back and somehow restore the Artifact to a single piece."

"Sir." Mr. Griffin spoke coolly. "For what purpose?"

"To open the way."

"Master Jacob… it sounds as though the way was closed so as to prevent something dreadful from happening."

"I know." Jake's tone grew self-questioning. "The notebook. *'The Rhetani must be prevented from recovering the artifact and opening the way'*. And the scroll in the temple spoke of hiding the way, closing the path against those who would cause destruction."

"And yet now you speak of opening the way."

Jake shook his head tiredly. "Tobias clearly wants me to restore the Artifact. I have no doubt of that."

"Tread carefully, Master Jacob." Mr. Griffin wasn't quite as certain.

Jake stuffed his hands into his pockets. He was beginning to feel the chill of the oncoming darkness, both real and metaphorical.

"I have to go north. I need to find this stone. I need to find the pylon, the *gateway*, that will lead me to this other world."

Chapter Six

Jake watched the odd little man cross the street and approach him. He had left the mansion to gather some supplies for his next trip out and was about half way to the marketplace.

"You're Quigley," the man stated. He took a final step and blocked Jake's path.

"Yeah," Jake said warily.

The man nodded and eyed Jake. "You went out to the temple."

"That something I should have checked on with you first?"

The man chuckled at that. "Not at all, not at all."

"Glad to hear it. Thought maybe I had violated some rule."

The man lost his smile. "I's curious, though. Wha'd you go there for? Why take the girl? It's dangerous out there."

"So, I *am* supposed to check in, then? Clear my reasons with you?"

"Just curious."

"And I'm busy."

"Not trying to stir up trouble," the man raised a hand defensively. "It's... it's dangerous out there."

"So you said."

"I's lost friends out there."

"Sorry to hear that," Jake made to go. The man managed to move without really appearing to move, continuing to block Jake's path. "I really do have to go," he told the man.

"I's almost killed out there."

"Good to see you made it back in one piece."

The man tapped his temple. "Not exactly one piece," he said softly.

"Well, alive then." Jake tried to step around the man again, but was blocked yet again. "If you don't mind," he said.

"There's bandits out there," the man said, more urgently now. "They'll take your stuff, and your life."

"Apparently, it's not all that safe here in the village."

"Worse yet, there's creatures. Creatures ya' won't find nowhere else."

Jake was pretty sure this guy was nuts, but that didn't mean he hadn't seen something out there. Still, he was afraid of encouraging him. "So I understand," he finally said.

"Creepy-crawly things, and wolves with brains; and flyin' things."

"Flying things?" he asked, despite his own good judgment.

"Why do ya—"

"On your way, Mason," came a voice from behind Jake. A moment later, Sheriff Smith stepped up beside him. "Don't you be bothering Mister Quigley."

"I twarn't botherin' nobody," Mason said defensively. "He oughtn't be takin' the youngin' into the Outland."

"That's not for you to decide," said the Sheriff.

"Still 'tain't right," he mumbled.

"Meara has spent half her life in the Outland, and you know it," said Sheriff Smith. "Now move on, before I drag you in for being a nuisance."

Mason started to say something, but the Sheriff's sharp look decided him against it. He turned aside and walked quickly into the street and away. Sheriff Smith watched the retreating figure until he was certain the man wasn't going to turn back and renew his harassment of the newcomer. He turned then to Jake.

"Mister Quigley. I see you've returned safely from your trip to the Temple."

"I imagine you knew I was back three minutes after I came through the West Gate."

"Not quite that fast," said the sheriff, scratching at the back of his neck, "But most likely before you reached home."

Jake pretty much assumed that was the way of things. There was little doubt the sheriff knew all the goings on, at least within the high, stone walls of the village.

"Listen," said Jake. "About Meara..."

"An excellent choice for a guide, Mister Quigley. Pay no attention to Mason."

"She insisted—and she seemed to know what she was talking about."

"She is her father's daughter."

"I made it absolutely clear she was not to put herself in harm's way."

Sheriff Smith held up a silencing hand. "Son, I consider myself a pretty good judge of character, and I don't believe you would knowingly put Meara Gyles in danger. And Meara is about as smart as they come when it comes to the Outland."

"Well, I—"

"I would say only this..." Sheriff Smith's tone grew just a tad ominous. "Her father had more Outland smarts than she did. He's gone. Your uncle Tobias had more Outland smarts than Meara and her father and everyone else in this village put together; and he's gone." He pointed in the direction that Mason had gone. "Whatever he told you about the dangers of the Outland, you can take that and double it."

"I'll do that," said Jake.

Sheriff Smith stepped away and started across the street. "Have a pleasant morning, Mister Quigley."

The marketplace was a large open square, a grassy plaza lined on all sides with three-walled booths that offered everything from clothes to vegetables to kitchenware to gardening tools. As a child, Jake had found it an interesting world within a world. Now, as he walked the rows of booths and looked in at the wares, he was certain that many of the faces that looked back at him were the very same faces from those years long past.

He stopped at a booth lined with pots and pans and ironware.

"Hello, Mrs. Numidia," he said. Mrs. Numidia hadn't changed at all. She looked exactly as she had years earlier, when Jake would run around the grassy plaza, taking in all the sights and sounds and people. He probably remembered her most because Mrs. Numidia was the wife of the blacksmith. A blacksmith was something special to a twelve year old boy.

"'morning to ya, Master Jake," she continued about her work, organizing her wares in preparation of the day, but her tone of voice was pleasant. "Thought I wouldn't recognize ya, eh?"

Jake smiled. "You heard I was in the village, and how many other strangers do you see?"

"Oh, I know ya anywhere, boy," she said, then quickly put on her sad face. "Sorry to hear 'bout Master Quigley."

"Me, too."

"So, what brings you to the market? Anything I can offer? I give ya' the welcome back special, I will." Her returning smile was genuine and yet just a little unsettling.

"Nothing just yet, Mrs. Numidia, but I'll keep that in mind." Jake started forward, on towards the next booth.

"Nice to have ya' back, just the same, Master Jake."

Jake passed by several more booths, stopping then at a booth selling a variety of leather clothing. After a bit of good-natured haggling, he bought a pair of hiking boots and two pairs of pants. His feet were still sore from his last trip out, and he could use footwear designed for the travels that he had in mind.

Jake stood at the bench in the supply room off the Command Center. He had brought back gear and supplies from the marketplace, some of which he had stowed away, some he had packed for his trip. To the gear he had packed, he added additional equipment from the supply room, most of which he had taken with him on his short jaunt to the temple. He was putting in more rations and there were the heavy-duty clothes he had purchased. He had found that his city clothes weren't going to hold up very well in the Outland, and he had no idea what to expect if he actually found a way through the gateway.

Mr. Griffin appeared in the doorway. He showed mild interest in the items on the counter, but remained silent.

Jake continued putting his supplies together. "Ya' know, I asked the guy selling knives where I could find something with a little more... you know... *oomph*... and he clammed up tight. I mean he turned to stone; just stood there."

"Such things are not available in the market," said Mr. Griffin.

"You don't say?" Jake said sarcastically.

"His response was to be expected, sir. The market in which such items are to be found is not publicly acknowledged."

"Items?"

"Implements of battle. Defensive and offensive."

Jake closed his pack and lifted it off the counter. "And you know where to acquire such... *items?*"

"I may have heard rumors, sir."

Jake slipped one arm through the shoulder strap. He walked out of the supply room and into the command center. "Why don't you see what you can find out? Maybe we'll do some shopping when I get back."

Jake reached the Hall of Statues and stopped. Before him hovered the six dragons, towering over him, threatening and mysterious. "I've a feeling I'm going to need some help from this unspoken of dark underbelly of Serpent's Keep."

"Yes, sir."

They made it as far as the bottom of the stairs before Meara confronted them. She looked as prepared to go as Jake.

"Not this time, Meara," said Jake.

"You must let me come with you."

"No," he said.

"You're going to need me, sir. More so than before."

"That's enough, girl," said Mr. Griffin. He was much more stern than Jake. Nonetheless, Meara wasn't quite ready to give up.

"Master Jacob, to go out there alone is just foolish."

"No more," said Mr. Griffin.

This time, Meara did give up. She bowed her head in silent acknowledgement and shuffled away. Jake watched her leave, then started toward the front door.

Chapter Seven

Jake walked north down the center of the village's main thoroughfare. Dawn was still an hour away, and the street lamps burned low, sending a golden glow across the thick fog that hung above the street and lay across the tops of the buildings on either side. Shadows crept out of the doorways and down the side streets. Jake saw no one until he reached the North Gate.

It was much the same as the West Gate; a heavy wooden door set into the city perimeter wall, a thick beam holding it closed against the Outland beyond. The woman on watch stepped out of the small guard station.

"Good morning, sir," she said. She didn't appear surprised to see him.

"Good morning," said Jake. He stopped and nodded at the gate. "I'd like to go out, please."

"You bet." The woman braced herself and slid the beam aside. She lifted the latch and pulled at the heavy door. Once opened, she stood to one side and made way for Jake.

"Good luck to you, Mister Quigley," she said as he passed her.

Beyond the gate, Jake stopped to take in the scene. Ahead was darkness, the forest pushing in towards the village perimeter wall. Behind him, the door creaked on its iron hinges as the guard pushed it closed. After a few moments, he shifted the pack on his back, adjusted the utility belt around his waist, and started forward.

It wasn't totally dark. Jake could see the trail winding its way through the Outland's north woods, a path of brown dirt with scruffy patches of grass and weed, with trees and brush creeping in from either side, reaching in from black shadows that moved and shape-shifted as he strode forward.

The darkness grew steadily grayer as the early morning approached dawn. By the time he reached the first fork in the trail, Jake could read the hand-drawn map that he pulled out of the side pocket of his backpack.

He had expected this fork, had been anticipating it and had begun to worry that he had somehow missed it. He looked to the map for verification and to remind himself of what to expect next. Satisfied that he was indeed where he thought he was, he refolded the map and continued ahead.

He knew that the left fork would continue north and in the direction of the farm that supplied much of the food for the village. The right fork, the path that he believed he had to take, struck out northeast into land largely unknown and only sparsely mapped.

The trail narrowed almost immediately, and the brightening sky was frequently hidden from view by high branches reaching across from one side of the path to the other. There were sounds in the woods; animals scurrying across the loamy forest floor and in the branches of the brush and the trees. Jake occasionally heard the movement of larger animals, but never saw them. Several times, he heard what sounded like animals fighting. Once he heard what he could only imagine to be the cries of an animal dying unpleasantly.

He stopped every couple of hours to rest, drink from his canteen, and snack on jerky or cheese. He studied the map, marked what he believed to be his path and his current location. Three times he came up on a fork in the trail when there was no indication of it on the map. Each time, after making note, he chose the path that kept him going in a northeasterly direction; always deeper into the unknown.

By early evening he was far from any mapped trail, and was marking the map with what he believed to be the path he was taking. At one point the trail withered away and ended, and he had to turn back and take another route. He wondered if his uncle had traveled these trails, and if he had, why he hadn't included them on the map.

§

Jake came into a small clearing and decided to stop for the night. It was a few hours until dark, and this would give him time to set up a decent camp, gather wood and make a fire, and cook a hot meal.

Taking heed of what Meara had said, his first trip off the path and into the woods was short and brief. Once personal business had been taken care of, he set about to gather the wood for the fire. He found that he was able to get all that he needed while staying within twenty feet or so of the clearing. Walking just beyond the perimeter of the clearing, within tossing distance, he quickly picked up and threw into the clearing all the wood that he would need.

Finally, with a small fire going, Jake settled in for the evening. He set a small pot of water on the fire and started it heating. As it warmed, he took a chunk of smoked meat, a potato and several raw vegetables from his supplies and cut them into pieces, letting them drop into the water. With the soup going, he sat back and took out his map. It would be some time before dinner was ready, and he thought he might as well put the time to use.

He felt warm and relaxed, his mind was calm and the campsite was peaceful in the glow of the firelight. The sun had set but the sky hadn't yet turned dark.

Jake stiffened suddenly at the sound of an animal sound that came from the shadows behind him. It was a low, guttural noise, as if coming from deep down in a large animal's barrel chest.

Without standing or turning, he reached down and pulled his knife free from its sheath. The throaty noise continued, and he could also hear the rustling of dried leaves and branches—whatever it was, it was coming towards him. He looked from side to side, carefully watching the perimeter of the clearing. He saw nothing; no other movement. He heard nothing but the sounds coming from behind him.

Jake jumped to his feet and turned sharply about, his knife held out in front of him.

A shift in the shadows just beyond the edge of the clearing; a movement between trees, behind a large bush. The guttural sound stopped. There was only the sound of snapping twigs, the rustling of dead leaves and pine needles.

A very large wolf stepped out of woods and into the clearing. Jake took a step back and crouched slightly, readying the knife.

Large wolf... lots of sharp teeth...

City boy... little knife... primary use: cutting up carrots...

"Oh, boy..." Jake mumbled, backed up another step. The wolf moved forward a step.

Jake had never seen a wolf close up before, but even so he thought this one looked somehow... different. It was bigger than he had seen on television, and broader, bulkier. It had a large head and its face was almost flat but for the snout, with its mouth full of teeth.

It paced smoothly to one side, always watching Jake. Jake kept the knife pointed at the animal.

Jake froze suddenly. Something was wrong; he could feel it.

He saw a shadow out of the corner of his eye. Turning his head slightly to the left, he saw that another wolf had come into the clearing—out of the woods that he had been certain were empty.

Turning his head slightly to the right then, he saw another wolf, just inside the clearing, watching him.

Jake turned back to the main wolf, the leader. He saw something in the face, in the eyes. The animal seemed to be saying something...

gotcha...

Jake gave an involuntary shiver. He knew the wolf hadn't actually spoken, but he knew that's what the animal was saying.

There was the hint of a grin on the wolf's face. The eyes sparkled.

Another sound then... from behind him.

Oh, man...

"Back off," came a woman's voice.

Meara?

"I don't think I can do that," said Jake. He did not look back, dared not take his eyes off the wolf.

"Not you, sir," said Meara. Then, to the animals that were preparing to move in on Jake, "You don't want to do this."

The lead wolf appeared as though he was rethinking the situation, looking past Jake at Meara standing somewhere behind him. The two wolves on either side looked to the lead wolf for guidance.

The wolf lost the hint of the grin, now wore a scowl. It looked directly at Jake again. The piercing eyes and dark expression seemed to say *we will finish this later.* It turned about sharply and leapt out of the clearing. His two companions turned about and disappeared into the shadows.

"What the heck was that about?" asked Jake. He turned around and faced Meara. "And what are you doing here?" He sheathed his knife.

"I'm sorry, sir," said Meara.

"That's it?"

"I couldn't let you come out alone."

"You couldn't *let me*? Isn't there some rule in Serpent's Keep about the staff having to do what the Master of the House says?"

"Yes sir." Meara lowered her gaze. "I suppose so."

"And what do you think Mr. Griffin is going to say when he finds out?"

"I couldn't say, sir."

"He'll probably ground us both." Jake looked back in the direction the lead wolf had taken away from the clearing. He looked again at Meara. "How'd you do that?"

"We have an understanding."

"An understanding..."

"Yes sir."

"You and the wolves. You have an understanding."

"Yes sir."

"How does that work, exactly?"

"They agree to leave me alone; I agree not to kill them."

"Pardon?"

Meara shrugged halfheartedly, embarrassed. She moved nearer the fire. "My father had a confrontation with them a long time ago. Since then, they know better."

"Some trick," said Jake. Sooner or later he was going to have to get a little more from her than that. He moved up beside Meara and sat beside the fire. Meara sat to one side.

"My father had no choice," she said. "So now..."

"Yeah. They know better."

Meara shrugged again. Jake would to let it go for now. He picked up several sticks from the pile beside him, absently fed the fire.

"They're smart... aren't they?" *Wolves with brains...*

"Yes."

"I mean, *really* smart."

"Yes."

Jake slowly nodded, looked out beyond the clearing. Seeing this, Meara looked into the woods, studied the shadows, listened to the sounds.

"I don't think they'll be back tonight," she said.

Jake decided to accept that. He looked questioningly at Meara. "And so now what am I supposed to do with you?"

"Sir?"

"Did you at least let someone know that you were coming out here?" he asked.

"My mother."

Jake nodded silently.

"And there's the gate records," she said.

"Great," Jake grumbled. "The sheriff knows by now. One more headache I have to deal with."

"Sheriff Smith looks beyond mere appearances, Master Jacob."

"I didn't mean—"

"I don't see the problem, sir."

"I'm responsible. If something was to happen, I couldn't forgive myself. And I don't think the folks back at the village would forgive me, either. I wouldn't blame them."

"How important is this quest?" she asked suddenly.

"Very."

"Serious enough that you are willing to risk your life," she stated flatly.

"But not yours."

"It's worth your life, but not the life of someone else?"

"That's not—"

"Will something bad happen if you fail?"

Jake doesn't answer. His expression said it all.

"So." Meara raised a brow. "Don't you think you should give yourself the best chance of succeeding?"

This is just great, he thought. "You're standing the late watch," he said at last.

Over the next several days, Jake and Meara mapped a large section of the northeastern Outland, carefully documenting each fork in the trail, recording the locations of major features, hazards and obstacles. They didn't see the wolf pack again, though Jake was certain that he heard them several times as they traveled, and once on the second night as they camped. Meara was certain it was something else, but could not or would not say what that something else might be.

It wasn't until midday of their first day together that Meara asked what they were looking for. Jake didn't have the slightest idea. He could only hope that he would recognize it when he saw it. He told Meara to keep her eyes open for anything just a little bit different, just a little bit out of place; anything that made her go '*hmmm*'.

She seemed amused by this.

On the fourth evening they set up camp on a wide ledge overlooking a large ravine. It was hundreds of yards across, a thousand yards deep, and ran east to west as far as he could see. The sides of the ravine were steep and the floor was hidden beneath a canopy of dark trees and darker undergrowth.

Meara called it the Great Ravine.

Jake couldn't understand why a natural feature as significant as this wouldn't be on the map. Meara said that it was spoken of now and then, but no one she knew had ever seen it or knew where it was. Not her father, not anyone. Jake asked how that could be, and Meara simply shrugged, saying that it was really out of the way and there wasn't much to bring a body out this far.

"What do they say about it?" asked Jake.

"They say that it is a gash in the skin of the world; a wound that has never healed."

"Well, if they talk about it, then somebody has seen it, and if somebody's seen it, then why isn't something this big on a map?"

"Not everybody puts things on paper, sir."

Jake studied their surroundings. Wouldn't Tobias have documented it? And since he hadn't, did that mean that his uncle hadn't been here?

Maybe Tobias had intentionally left the ravine off the map. If so, why?

"Let's keep a sharp eye out," said Jake. "Just in case tourists around here get eaten."

The clearing was wide, allowing them to make camp well away from the trees and away from the edge of the ravine. They gathered firewood from the perimeter of the clearing, stepping warily into the shadows and returning quickly into the fading daylight. They took out three large bushes that lined the eastern edge of the clearing, opening up the perimeter there and making it more difficult for anything that might want to creep up on them in the night to do so without being seen.

They had a campfire going by dusk. Jake unpacked food supplies and together he and Meara heated up rations of meat and potatoes.

As they settled in around the fire and ate their dinner, Jake began to notice a change in the noises around them. The world was growing... quiet. The sounds of nature that he had become accustomed to over the previous days and no longer heard on a conscious level now slowly faded away.

Their absence had drawn his attention.

Putting another bite of potato into his mouth, he glanced over at Meara.

She had noticed it, too.

The world around them had gone silent.

Jake set down his plate and slowly rose to his feet. He studied the woods that encircled the clearing, but saw nothing, heard nothing. Looking up at the sky, he saw only one small wisp of cloud in the dusk of a darkening sky.

He looked again at Meara, now standing. She was looking in the direction of the ravine.

Oh, man... thought Jake. He sucked in a long, cool breath and slowly let it out. Not letting himself think anymore on it, he walked cautiously toward the edge. As he drew nearer, he began stretching forward, leaning forward, as if this somehow made it all safer. He could hear Meara beside him, saw her then out of the corner of his eye.

He stopped at the very edge of the ravine. Far below, the world was dark, with varying shades of black and gray, the treetops poking up from the darkest shadows.

And there was movement.

"Do you see that?" asked Jake, very quietly, very calmly.

"Yes sir," whispered Meara.

Shadows skimmed above the treetops. Large, black silhouettes, gliding silently, creating darker shadows that danced in the trees below them. At first, Jake saw only three of them, but as he watched, he saw another and another, until finally there was at least half a dozen.

From their position on the ledge high above, it was impossible to judge their size, and because of the distance and the shadowy darkness, it was impossible to discern what they were.

There's creepy-crawly things, and wolves with brains, and flyin' things...

"I don't think those are bats," said Jake.

"No, sir. Those ain't bats."

"So, what are they, then?"

"I couldn't say, sir."

Not out loud, anyway, he thought.

"Yeah," he said aloud. "Me neither."

Jake and Meara stood at the edge of the ravine until it was too dark to see, then returned to their fire and fed the dying embers until the flames were a foot and half high. They took turns on watch, as they had previous nights, but neither got much sleep. From what they could tell, the *flyin' things* never left the ravine... but something had scared nature into silence when the sun went down.

By morning, the world had returned to normal. They could hear the sounds of birds and small animals in the trees and brush beyond the perimeter of the clearing. Low clouds had come in before dawn, and the sky hung low and gray above them. Looking down into the ravine, the trees and floor were hidden from view beneath a thick blanket of fog. Jake saw nothing in the mist.

They decided to follow the ravine east. This would take them ever farther into uncharted territory and further away from Serpent's Keep, whereas west would have taken them in the direction of the farm, though probably far north of it.

They were able to follow the edge of the ravine for most of the morning before the terrain finally forced them to move into the woods. Travel was difficult until, an hour after midday, they found an animal trail that wound through the thick undergrowth and eventually brought them again to the ravine's southern edge.

The fog had cleared away and they were able to see the thick forest that covered the floor of the ravine. It was much shallower here, only a third as deep as further up-ravine. Continuing east, the trail they followed moved steadily downhill, the ravine grew steadily shallower, the floor seeming to rise up to meet them. By late afternoon, Jake and Meara were at the mouth of the ravine.

Jake watched Meara cross a wide clearing and stop at the dark brush that crowded the mouth.

"Here," she said. She had found a narrow path into the ravine.

"Here, Meara," said Jake. He stood at a large stone standing in the center of the clearing. Other than a few scraggily weeds, there was nothing else in the clearing. "Have you ever seen anything like this?" The rock was five feet high, irregularly shaped, four feet wide at its widest. There were numerous flat surfaces. He cautiously laid hand on stone. It was cool to the touch.

"I believe that's granite, sir," said Meara.

"Yes it is," said Jake. "But that's not what I mean." He had seen exposed rock in weathered, eroded hillsides, and in the side of the ravine they had followed. But this was different. A lone rock, on level ground, the only object in the center of a clearing.

As if it had been put there.

Meara returned to his side. "Is this it? What you're lookin' for?"

"I think so... maybe."

"What do we do?"

"I don't know." Jake pulled his hand back and rubbed it on his shirt.

Somehow, I have to make this thing give up its secret.

Chapter Eight

Jake had no idea what to do. He had hoped that once he found the stone, he would then find some further clue. As yet, however, he had nothing.

Camp was established. Meara sat off to one side, having made herself comfortable where she could sit and watch Jake, while at the same time watch the dark, heavily wooded mouth of the ravine. Jake would sit and stare at the stone, stand and circle the stone, stare up at the sky high above the stone, and occasionally walked to the mouth of the ravine that opened to the clearing in which the stone rested.

Find now the pylon within the stone...

The one will point the way...

Some one or some thing...

Jake studied the variations in the surface of the stone, looking for images of a one, or one of something, but found nothing. He tried shining light on the stone from various angles, looking for shadows that could be interpreted as a one, but again found nothing.

With the setting of the sun came a whole new set of images, shadows created by the flickering flames of the campfire. Meara kept the fire burning big and bright, pushing back the darkness that crept in from all sides, the shadows that reached out from mouth of the ravine.

Jake appeared to ignore it all, focusing all his attention, all his frustrations, on the stone standing complacently in their midst, waiting in silence for someone to speak the correct incantation, press the right button, twist the right knob, dance the right dance...

He grew increasingly concerned that there was something left behind at the estate that he needed—something still hidden away or locked away, some final key that would open the stone.

He slept little. Meara looked on most of the night; she watched Jake, and she watched the shadows. She watched the mouth of the ravine. Strange sounds and strange smells came from in there. Animal sounds that were something other than animal sounds. Sounds of live things moving, flying, creepily and stealthily walking. Sounds from the throat that did not come from the throat of any animal that Meara had ever seen or ever heard; thoughtful, studious sighs…

Animal smells that Meara had never smelled before; musty, musky, peculiarly leathery and yet not leather…

Meara knew that *they* knew were out there, watching as she watched, waiting as she waited. *Observing...*

They never came out of the dark of the ravine. They chose not to… perhaps they knew what Master Jacob was trying to do and they wanted him to succeed.

Morning gray came slowly to the clearing. Another hour passed; sunlight crept across the clearing and up across the stone. It brought no revelation, revealed no secrets…

Jake held his hands out in frustration. "What do you want?" he demanded.

The stone was silent.

Jake saw the shadow of his hand move across the stone. Not for the first time, he was drawn to the different shapes and shadows on the rough surface. But there was nothing there. There was nothing there…

The answer is here...

Jake turned away from the stone and looked at Meara. He didn't know what to do. Meara shrugged a shoulder and shook her head. She stood then, slowly, looking behind Jake, looking in the direction of the mouth of the ravine.

Behind him... at the dark, menacing, shadowy mouth of the ravine. He felt a cold, terrifying chill. Behind him. Behind him... It took everything he had to turn around and face whatever it was that awaited him.

It was a serpent... a dragon... *something...*

It stood just inside the clearing, watching Jake, studying Jake. Without moving its head, it turned an eye to Meara, then returned its attention to Jake.

It stood twice as high as a human. Its hide was scaly, colored in multiple shades of green and brown. It had powerful hind legs, slightly smaller front legs that looked as though they could be used as arms and hands. Massive leathery folds were bundled up on its back. Wings?

Is this the shadow they had seen when looking down into the ravine?

A flying dragon?

It took a step then, startling Jake, who took a stumbling step backward. The creature paused a moment, then took a second step, and then glided smoothly to the stone. It climbed atop the stone and settled itself in as though it was some gigantic, massive bird making itself comfortable on its perch.

It turned its horned head and stared down at Jake with one gleaming yellow eye.

"Tobias..." it said. The sound came from somewhere deep inside the creature, pushing up through its throat and pushing out harsh and low.

Did the dragon think that he was Tobias, or was he asking for his uncle?

What do you say to a dragon?

"I'm Jake," he finally stammered.

"Tobias," the dragon stated again. It raised its head up and took in the entire clearing, stopping its visual sweep only briefly on Meara. She stood fast; did not run, but did not move any nearer.

"I'm sorry," said Jake. "Tobias isn't here."

The dragon turned its head sharply and stared down at Jake. "Where... Tobias?"

"I don't know."

The dragon leaned forward and studied Jake closely. Its breath was hot, pressing down and taking the air away. It sniffed noisily, drew a breath in through its long, hollow nostrils, suddenly raised its head up and back. It eyed Jake curiously. "Blood," it said.

*Geez, it wants to eat me...*Jake thought in a panic.

Meara took a step forward. "Yes," she said. ""Master Jacob is blood. Tobias and Master Jacob."

The dragon glanced at the small human at the far end of the clearing, then looked down again at Jake. "Tobias' blood," it stated firmly.

Jake stammered. "My uncle. Tobias... my uncle."

"Tobias," it said again, this time with some affection.

What does this creature have to do with my uncle? What does it want of my uncle?

Meara slowly approached, finally standing directly beside Jake. The dragon continued to watch them, shifting position slightly in order to make itself more comfortable. The stone that it sat upon looked to have been worn down from years, perhaps centuries, of serving as the dragon's perch.

The one will point the way...

Is this the one?

Meara whispered, "The one—"

"—will point the way..." Jake finished.

"The *one* is a dragon?"

The dragon was calm, breathing easily. It seemed somehow comforted by Jake's scent—Tobias' blood...

"Its claws," Meara whispered, nodding her head in the direction of the stone perch. Jake saw again how the stone had been worn down from years of service as the creature's roost. The three claws of each foot fit snugly into deep grooves in the rock.

Jake realized then what Meara was suggesting.

The one will point the way...

Jake looked carefully at each deadly claw.

Not the dragon... the claw.

One of the claws pointed to a blemish in the great stone; a dark recess no larger than the width of Jake's thumb, no deeper than the knuckle.

Jake stepped forward, afraid to look up and see what the serpent's reaction might be. He sensed nothing from the creature and continued toward the stone. He reached a hand out and without taking time to consider what might happen, pushed his thumb into the dark blemish, the dragon's claw not half an inch away.

The area around the stone grew warm, as if the rock was heated from a noonday sun. The clearing was bathed in a suffuse light, centered at the stone.

The great stone began to fade in the wash of bright light, the colors disappearing first, and then the shape itself; the dragon all the while maintaining its perch, unperturbed, now sitting atop a soupy cloud of bright whites and grays. Seconds passed, and the cloud began to coalesce, until finally a primitive stone archway, seven feet high and seven feet wide, stood where the great rock had once stood. A clear shimmer swirled within the opening. High atop the ancient gate sat the dragon.

"Enter the gateway, Blood of Tobias," it said.

Jake looked quickly over his shoulder at Meara. "You wait here," he said.

"No sir," she said sharply. "I'm coming with you."

"No you're not. I mean it. If I don't come back, I need you here. If I don't come back, you go for Griff." Jake didn't wait for her to respond. He turned back to the gateway, glanced briefly up at the dragon, then stepped determinedly into the arch.

Chapter Nine

A tiny point of bright light appeared in the center of his vision. At the very instant it appeared, it rushed at him, growing rapidly in size, until half a heartbeat later it was on him, over him, all around him, turning his world into white nothing. Another half heartbeat and the white turned dull gray.

Jake felt an odd sense of falling forward, though nothing in his surroundings, if it could be called surroundings, gave any indication of movement. He involuntarily held his hands out in front of him, and was taken aback when he realized that he had no hands, no arms, no body. He had the peculiar sensation of sucking in a panicked breath though he had no mouth, no chest, no lungs, and there was no air.

Two virtual heartbeats later, Jake saw another tiny point of bright light appear in the center of his virtual vision. As before, it rushed at him, pressed against him, pushed at him and over him. This gray in-between place turned white. Immediately after, there was a sudden explosion of color and Jake stumbled forward into a different world.

The sky overhead was clear blue, brushed with only a few wispy clouds floating high overhead. The sun looked liked the sun back home, felt warm on the face, felt comforting and reassuring. He could breathe the air, though it smelled a little different. It had a faint metallic taste.

Directly ahead was the main street of a small town—strangely still and quiet. He turned and looked behind him. A stone archway like the one he had just stepped through stood stoic and silent in the middle of an open field. As he watched, it shimmered and faded, the colors of the stone began to coalesce.

In place of the rustic archway stood a four-sided stone pylon, slate gray and smooth as glass.

Jake's gateway home was gone.

That... could be a problem, he thought, but then noticed a small design recessed in the center of one face of the pylon. Looking closely, he saw that it was the same polygon design as he had seen on the key for this gate; the same as one of the shapes used in the design of the complete artifact image.

He was pretty sure then that if he found the artifact piece, it would fit.

He turned about again, a bit more reassured, and started forward toward the town. He had no choice now. He had to find the artifact in order to get home.

Coming into the town, he saw that many of the buildings were boarded up, giving no indication of what may lay within. There was no movement but for a single curtain drawn out of an upper-floor window, left open and unboarded, fluttering in the light breeze.

There was a sharp bend in the main street where the road jogged right, and just around the corner Jake saw one lone automobile parked on the street. It was a four-door sedan, but not of any make or model that Jake had ever seen. It was boxy and nondescript, so dusty that he couldn't see in through the windows. The tires were low and the car now rested on the rims.

The entire town appeared empty... abandoned.

Directly ahead was a restaurant, fronted by two large windows with faded curtains drawn; not very inviting. To the left, the main street turned again and continued on for a good distance. Jake decided to walk around a bit and get the lay of the land before going into any of the buildings. He crossed the street and followed the road left, striding down the center of the thoroughfare.

Not far ahead was a side street. He could see a general store midway on the left. He made a mental note; there might be some supplies there. Continuing down main street, he passed more cross streets, a newspaper office, and a small hospital (more of a clinic, really). The road continued to wind around and he passed the city hall, and then a church.

Finally, the main street turned sharply and sharply again, and abruptly ended in a cul-de-sac. Turning about slowly in the center of the dead end, Jake found himself looking at an old wooden house. Small, narrow, single-storey, it appeared out of place in a commercial setting, however small-town this community might be.

Gotta' start someplace, he thought, and walked toward the home. He knocked on the front door and waited. When no one answered, he opened the unlocked door and entered the living room. There was a couch, a chair, and a couple of end tables. Dull light shone in through the window. A picture hanging above the couch depicted a dilapidated barn in a wilderness setting, with tall trees shadowing a swayback roof.

In the dining room was a wooden table with six chairs. Dust had collected on the smooth tabletop.

The appliances in the kitchen were fifty or sixty years out of date. The refrigerator, stove, toaster, all looked right out of the mid-twentieth century. Even the overhead light globe and small chrome-trim breakfast table looked late-fifties era. Jake reached over and opened the refrigerator—and found it empty. In the cupboards he found one can of carrots. He noticed the words on the label were in English.

Jake hated carrots, and put the can back on the shelf.

Leaving the kitchen, he turned into the narrow hall. There were four doors: two on the left, two on the right. The first one on the right was the bathroom. As with the kitchen, everything looked like it came out of an old nineteen fifties movie. The tub had claw feet and a shower curtain hung from a metal ring frame. The toilet tank was set high on the wall, with a long pull chain. Jake gave it a yank and was a bit surprised to find that it worked.

The other doors in the hall led to the bedrooms. Two had full-size beds, one had a twin. All had old-style furniture. The closets still contained clothes, different in style to anything Jake had seen before, but not too bizarre.

There was a small writing table beneath a curtained window in one of the bedrooms. In the drawer, beside a pad of paper and pencils, Jake found an old revolver. There were three bullets in the spindle. He decided to take this with him, and put it into his pack.

Across the street from the house was a small schoolhouse. Just as with the house, the front door was unlocked. Jake stepped into the main foyer and looked around. A bulletin board on the wall displayed several notices behind a glass face. One stated that all five classes were going to dismiss early on Friday so that the teachers could conference.

The notice was dated *May 12, 1959.*

Was time different here than it was back home?

Or... had the town been abandoned for half a century?

He reread the notice. *Five classes?*

To the right, just beyond the bulletin board, was the door to the front office. Just beyond this and straight ahead, the foyer opened to the main hall. Glancing into the hall and looking left, he saw a number of doors, each inset with fogged glass windows.

Jake turned back and went into the front office, deciding to check this out first. There were several desks behind a counter to right, and on the left an open door led to the principal's office. On the principal's desk was a daily desk calendar with Tuesday, May 12 sitting on top.

Did something happen on May 13?

He gave the room one last look before going back into the front office and on into the front foyer, then into the main hall. The linoleum floor had once been smooth and shiny but now was dull with a thin layer of dust. If he looked carefully enough, Jake could see the occasional tiny footprint of rodents.

Whatever had happened, at least something had survived.

The first door that Jake came to had a large black "1" stenciled in the center of the glass panel. Going into the classroom, he stood beside the teacher's desk and looked down the four rows of small student desks. Clearly this was a very early grade, probably first or second. The alphabet, displayed in a row high along one wall, reinforced his assumption.

He was heartened to see all the familiar letters represented. With this and the other evidence he had found, it appeared to Jake that this world was very close to his own. If that were true, then any encounters he may have should be that much easier to deal with.

He walked down the center aisle to the back of the class. He had the eerie sensation that twenty ghostly young faces were looking up at him. The silence was like a loud ringing in his ears.

Running the length of the back wall was a waist-high set of shelves divided into twenty box-like compartments, each labeled with a student name. He noticed something odd in the spelling. There were a lot of w's and y's where there shouldn't be: Dwnn, Dowglys, Lwanne, Shywn.

Staring at the names, he recalled reading somewhere that there was an old dialect that used w and y as vowels. Welsh? He couldn't remember, but that sounded right, though these weren't Welsh names or spellings; he wondered, though, if there might be a Welsh influence. Was this alternate world somehow tied to Wales? That would be bizarre. Maybe this was a Welsh town in this alternate world.

What kind of a weird connection would that be?

He left the first classroom and stepped back into the hall. There was a water fountain directly across from him, and he went over to it and pushed down on the plunger. After a few seconds, water began gurgling out. He let it run for a full thirty seconds before bending over and taking a cautious sip.

He quickly decided to let it run a bit longer.

After another minute or so, he tried again. Not quite so bad this time; he assumed the lines had finally cleared and he was getting water from the source. He pulled his canteen free and opened it, took a deep swig, and then filled it from the fountain. This done, he continued his search of the classrooms.

The second class was much the same as the first, maybe a grade or two higher. He opened a few desks, looked in the teacher's desk, but nothing really caught his attention.

He found a slingshot in the teacher's desk of the third class, mixed in with other odds and ends that must have been confiscated from the students throughout the school year. A *wrist-rocket* if he remembered right, and he knew that it could do some serious harm to an enemy. It might come in handy if he ran out of bullets for the pistol.

The last two classrooms had full-size desks, but from the books and wall displays, Jake figured this school didn't go beyond sixth grade. Stepping into the student closet at the back of the last classroom in the hall, he found a closed umbrella leaning in the corner. It was tall, with a wooden handle and a metal tip. Jake picked it up on a whim and used it as a walking stick, stepped smartly out of the class and down the hall, tapping the tip on the linoleum.

Once again outside, he walked out into the cul-de-sac and began backtracking the way he had come. Reaching City Hall, he climbed the two steps and went inside.

On the wall behind the counter was a large sign that read: *Welcome to Rwndyll.*

"Rwndyll," said Jake. He tried several pronunciations, finally deciding to go with giving the 'w' a 'u' sound, right or wrong. He stepped around the counter and went into the back rooms. He found the office for the mayor, a conference room and a supply room. The supply room looked as though it had been ransacked; the shelves were bare but for a few empty boxes and some paper strewn about. He poked and pushed the litter about with the closed umbrella, then went back out to the main lobby. He had just gone into one of the side rooms off the lobby when he heard the front door open and the sound of footsteps.

Jake quickly pushed himself up against wall between the lobby and the office at the first sound, carefully pulled the pistol out of the side-pocket of his pack. The sound of muffled voices trailed away to the back rooms.

"He's here, I tell ya'," came as a harsh whisper. "I saw him."

Jake slid along the wall toward the door.

"And he had gear," said the same man.

"I saw it, too," said another. "New gear."

That doesn't sound hopeful, thought Jake. *I don't think I want to meet these guys.*

He peered through the open doorway. When he saw no one, he stepped out into the lobby and started hurriedly toward the front door.

"There he be," said someone, and then Jake heard the shuffling and scrambling of a dozen feet coming. He didn't turn to look behind him, but flung open the door and leapt over the steps of City Hall and down onto the street. He cut left and the left again, realizing too late that he was heading toward a dead end. Up ahead the road 'T'd. If he went left, he would be entering the cul-de-sac with the school. He would be trapped. Instead he cut right and was quickly confronted with a high stone wall. The road ended.

He noticed then a storm drain in the center of the road. The lid was a heavy metal lattice that allowed rain runoff to empty into it. Jake thought quickly, trying not to panic. He could hear loud voices and heavy footsteps. They were getting closer.

He knelt down and laced his fingers into the lattice and pulled.

It was stuck.

He thought of using the umbrella as a pry bar, but immediately dismissed that idea. It wasn't strong enough. He stood over the drain, one foot on either side. Reaching down, he pulled again, this time straight up. The lid lifted free and Jake hurriedly walked it forward and set it down. Without looking to see what he was getting into, he quickly scrambled down into the drain, reached out and pulled the lid over after him. He started down the narrow ladder, looking up only when he heard the thumping of rushing footsteps and loud, peculiarly jovial voices. Several faces were peering down at him through the grate.

"Hellooo there, rat."

Jake didn't respond. He continued down the ladder. Another half dozen rungs and he reached the bottom.

"Ya' not gonna' like it down there," the man taunted, to which the others laughed heartily. "You come on back up now, and you'z can walk away from this, pretty'z ya' please."

Okay... definitely not Welsh...

What little light that reached down from above showed Jake that the only direction open was south. He had to lower his head to step into the drain and moved forward in a crouch; he was immediately wrapped in darkness. He could hear the gang of marauders taunting him from above. *"Hey, come on back... hey, at least leave us the gear, dude..."*

Jake swung his pack around so that he could reach into it. Rummaging around, he found the hand lantern and pulled it out. It had a manual crank charger. He gave the handle six or seven good turns and flipped the large switch. The yellowish light didn't reach out too far, but it was enough to keep his panic at bay. He pulled the umbrella free of the pack's side strap and shifted his pack back into position. Holding the closed umbrella defensively out in front of him, he started forward again.

He hadn't gone more than a few yards when he came up on a junction; one line came in from the left, and the line he had been following continued straight ahead. He decided to continue forward.

The sounds of those on the street above slowly faded, and Jake finally found himself all alone. The world was only as large as the reach of the light from his lantern; not much more than five feet high (the height of the tunnel), and reaching not much more than six feet ahead. Each step he took pushed this tiny universe forward the same distance that it collapsed into darkness behind him. The only sounds were the echoing scrapings of his feet on the concrete floor, his own heavy breathing, and an eerie, hushed, wind-like white noise coming from the darkness ahead.

After a few minutes, Jake began to notice a very subtle change in these sounds. His footsteps, his breathing, even the white noise, all began taking on a deeper, more hollow timbre. Hardly noticeable at first, but with each step the shift in resonance become more distinct, more real.

And then Jake took a step and knew without a doubt that he had entered a chamber. The low ceiling overhead lifted away and he was able to stand up straight. The wall on his left continued ahead into the darkness, but the right wall was gone, was replaced with the deep black, a void that stretched away to some unseen ominous threat.

There was no telling how large the chamber might be.

There's something in here...

Jake was absolutely positive that he wasn't alone. He tried to quiet his breathing, to push away the white noise. The only sound left was the beating of his heart.

No—wait—there was something else...

Breathing...

How many? More than one... More than five...

There's something in here...

Jake took half a step back, uncertain as to what he should do. The beating of his heart grew louder, the pounding in his chest more powerful.

This must be what the marauders were talking about. *"Ya' not gonna' like it down there"*, they had said.

Well, I am definitely not liking it, he thought. *I am really, really not liking it.*

He continued to listen, studying the sounds, trying to sense changes, increasing threats.

Breathing... definitely breathing.

Should he go back? But did he want these things, whatever they were, coming up behind him in the tunnel?

Maybe he should face them here, whatever they were.

Jake cautiously inched back into the chamber. He held the lantern up with one hand, the closed umbrella with the other. He took another step, moved the lantern slowly from left to right, looking for some sign, looking for anything that wasn't floor. He kept close to the left wall, feeling some security at the presence of that solid slab of concrete close beside him.

Claws on floor...

Jake stopped. A very, very cold chill washed through him. He turned and pressed his back against the wall, jabbed the tip of the umbrella at the dark. He held the lantern up high. Nothing, nothing; there was nothing.

Claws on floor...

He could hear something moving out there in the dark. He waited, umbrella moving slowly left to right, right to left.

Shadows then, just outside the range of the lantern; dark grays in the black, shifting smoothly, gliding just beyond the light.

Flickers of bright white, shimmering sparkles, *reflections of the eyes...*

And then something stepped into the light.

It was just about knee-high, and looked like a gigantic rat.

No. Not a rat. A tiny dragon, but not a dragon.

What the...

Kind of a cross between a dragon and a rat...

A dragon rat? A rat dragon?

Jake felt a little woozy. He watched the thing squat down in the center of the circle of light provided by the lantern. It looked intently at Jake, pushed its two front legs out in front of it, each foot brandishing three dragon-like claws. Its skin had a brownish-green, serpent-like look to it. The nose had heavy nostrils, and two horns swept back from its head.

Dragon, and yet it had a very distinctive rat-look about it.

A second rat dragon came up beside the first, slowly squatted down beside its companion, never taking its shimmering eyes off Jake. A moment later a third came up on the other side of the first and sat back on its haunches. As it stared at Jake, it casually scratched its belly with one long, curved claw.

The shifting shadows behind them meant there were more out there.

"Hey," Jake said nervously. The first rat dragon cocked its head sideways, but otherwise there was no response. The one sitting up raised its scratching claw and studied it, as if it expected to find something, and then rested its paw on its round belly.

Jake took a slow, easy step to his left, attempting to continue his progress south. The three watched him, but made no overt moves. Encouraged then, Jake took another step and then another.

And bumped into the corner of the chamber.

If there was another way out of the chamber, it was on the other side of the room, through these three creatures and however many more waited in the dark.

"This is a dead end, isn't it?" Jake asked rhetorically. *This chamber has one way in and one way out.*

The middle rat dragon cocked its head again. The scratching rat dragon reached around behind with its scratching claw; Jake didn't want to think about where the claw was going or what it was scratching.

Jake started moving back the way he had come, keeping his back pressed firmly against the wall and his closed umbrella between himself and the creatures. He was within a few slide-steps of the exit out of the chamber when he saw a quickly shifting shadow move into his path. He stopped and warily moved the lantern to his right. He took another cautious step, and the circle of light pushed up and over a fourth rat dragon that was sitting up tall and staring him down.

Jake glanced back at the others. The one in the center had a curl to its lip and a sparkle in its eyes that gave Jake the unsettling impression that it was amused by the situation.

"Now, I just want to get out of here," said Jake, his voice quivering slightly. "No trouble, now."

The rat dragons didn't look as though they were inclined to step aside. Jake continued pointing his umbrella from one to the other. It didn't look particularly frightening or dangerous.

Jake had a thought. "Quigley," he said sharply. "My name is Quigley." He nodded jerkily. "Tobias was my uncle. Tobias. Uncle. Uh... blood! Him and me. Me and Tobias Quigley."

He really did half expect these ugly little creatures to move aside at the mention of the name. They, however, did not appear to be the least bit impressed.

Jake suddenly, and quite accidentally, pressed the button on the shaft of the umbrella and it quickly opened with a loud *whump*. The three rat dragons jumped backwards into the dark. The fourth creature, stationed at the exit to the chamber, scurried backwards into the tunnel. Jake, seeing his one and only opportunity, turned and ran towards the startled dragon, pushing the opened umbrella at it as he went. After a few steps he found himself falling, stumbling, jostling over the rat dragon. He, the rat dragon, the umbrella, the lantern, all enmeshed in a scrambling, flailing jumble. Jake frantically pushed himself forward, wanting only to get past the creature and escape down the tunnel. The rat dragon, for its part, was desperately thrashing about defensively, not sure what had happened or what was going on.

After several seconds of blind struggling, Jake found himself on his hands and knees with only concrete beneath him. He stumbled hurriedly to his feet and ran. He didn't know if the rat dragon, if any of the rat dragons, were following, and wasn't about to slow down to find out. The sphere of light created by his lantern bounced into and out of existence as his whirling arms sent the lantern behind him with each swinging stroke.

He almost missed the junction that he had passed earlier. Sliding to a stop, he quickly turned into the side tunnel and continued running. It wasn't until he had gone a hundred yards or so that he slowed down enough that he could take the time to listen out for anything that might be following him. Slowing his step, slowing his breathing, he tried to stretch his hearing out behind him, tried to pick up the sounds of claws on concrete.

For the moment, it seemed, he was alone.

He passed another junction, another line going south, decided to continue east just a bit further. Another few minutes, and the line that he was traveling turned sharply south. He was now paralleling the line that he had passed before.

Smaller drain lines, set into the walls about chest high, emptied into the tunnels every 30 or 40 yards. Jake could feel cool air coming in through these lines from the streets above, and was thankful for it.

Without it, the air in the tunnels would quickly grow stagnate and stifling. As it was, he was feeling very claustrophobic, especially knowing there were things down here, in the dark, perhaps just beyond the range of his lantern.

The tunnel Jake was following made another sharp turn, this one back to the west. At the next junction, he took the south route. He wondered if he would be able to find his way out, should he have to return the way he came. With that in mind, he stopped long enough to map out in his mind the path he had taken, returning to the junction that, left would take him to the rat dragon nest, right would take him to the ladder leading up to the street.

He went on then, choosing routes that kept him going south whenever possible, choosing east if he felt he had traveled a considerable distance west, and west if he felt he had traveled too far to the east.

He estimated that he had traversed most of the distance back through under the town, and was now somewhere near the southern city limits, when he came into another chamber. By the deep echoes of his footsteps, Jake was pretty certain this room was larger than the last chamber he had been in.

"Oh, man..." he whispered. The sound of his hushed voice rolled away from him and rolled back, making him shiver. He listened, anticipating that creepy sound of dragon claws scraping across the floor, holding the lantern out as far he could reach. There was only darkness and the sound of his own breathing.

He stepped cautiously into the chamber, following the wall but always looking into the black void in the center of the room. After a few steps, he stopped.

Is something there?

There seemed to be a dark mass just beyond the sphere of light created by his lantern. He leaned forward, towards the center of the room. The mass took a more distinct form, but was still beyond the range of the lantern.

Straight lines, straight edges; not a creature.

Jake stepped away from the wall and slide-stepped into the center of the room.

It was a staircase of some kind. A concrete staircase set into the center of the chamber. He held the lantern up high and looked upward, up to where the stairs led. He could see nothing.

Taking a nervous breath, Jake held his umbrella out in front of him, pointing it up the staircase. Only then did he notice that the thin metal framework of the umbrella was bent and broken, the cloth canopy ripped to shreds, and the staff bent at a 30 degree angle. It had taken quite a beating back during his tumble with the rat dragon.

He tried to close the umbrella and shape it into some semblance of a stabbing weapon, and took the first step up the stairs. He was climbing into darkness.

After seven steps the open staircase transformed into an enclosed stairwell. Continuing upward, he knew that by now he had to be above ground and must be inside one of the buildings that he had passed when he first walked through the streets of town. Another dozen steps and he was standing on a small landing, enclosed on either side by concrete walls. Straight ahead was a large, heavy wooden door.

Jake tucked the umbrella under his arm and pushed down on the latch. Pushing the door open an inch, daylight streamed in. Peaking through the narrow opening, he saw blue sky above and beyond, and a wooden railing two steps beyond the door.

He turned off the flashlight and tucked it into an outside pocket of his backpack. He found the pistol, and with weapon in one hand, the umbrella in the other, he pushed the door fully open and stepped outside.

He found himself on a raised walkway, four feet across, with a wall behind him and a waist-high deck rail in front of him. From here he could see most of the town laid out in front of him. He could see the streets that he had taken traveling north, and he thought he recognized which rooftop belonged to city hall, and which belonged to the school.

Stepping to the rail, he looked down on an enclosed courtyard. It was a twenty-foot drop to dirt and weeds and stone. Looking off to his left, he saw a steep, narrow staircase leading from the walkway down to the ground. In the center of the courtyard, twenty yards or more from the staircase, stood a stone pedestal. Sitting atop the pedestal was a small box.

Jake slowly walked along the catwalk, towards the staircase, continuing to study the pedestal. As he reached the top of the stairs, he noticed a large, open archway set into the opposite wall. The wall was a good sixteen feet high, and the opening reached almost to the top. Jake could see eight or ten feet into the room beyond the archway; nothing moved.

There's probably something really, really bad in there.

He glanced again at the pedestal, at the box sitting on the pedestal.

That's it, he thought. *What else would it be?* Where *else would it be?*

Jake started down the narrow, rickety staircase, watching the opening in the wall on the other side of the courtyard. Reaching the bottom of the stairs, he started cautiously toward the pedestal. The enclosed area had a strange smell. *Fire and brimstone,* Jake mumbled to himself.

He was halfway to the pedestal when he heard the sound: the loud *whump* of large, beating, leathery wings. He looked up into the sky and saw a dragon pass overhead, swing around and come to rest on the top of the wall. It was a massive creature, with a large, broad chest and horned head. It gripped the lip of the wall with huge, deadly-looking claws.

It looked down at the puny human standing in the middle of its yard. After several seconds, during which it sized up the situation, it spread its wings, pushed off the wall and dropped down to the ground a dozen yards from Jake. It folded its wings, shifted its feet and turned its head slightly to better study the intruder.

Jake, the *intruder,* took one step back and waited. The dragon shook its head jerkily from side to side and took two dragon-sized steps forward. Jake stumbled backward and almost fell.

"No fear," said the dragon. "Blood."

Jake could barely speak. "Quigley. Yes."

"Blood," the dragon repeated. "Not me to fear here. Not *Rhetani* fear here."

Jake nodded, regained his footing and tried to stand straight.

The dragon cocked its head. It sniffed the air. "Tobias?" it asked. "Blood."

"Blood," Jake placed a hand on his chest. "Blood. Tobias. Uncle. Tobias, my blood."

"Blood," the dragon stated flatly.

"Yes," said Jake.

The dragon took another step forward. "*Hu*-man to fear here."

"Yes," said Jake. The dragon had to be talking about the marauders. "The bad humans."

The dragon snorted, as if thinking about the marauders left an unpleasant taste. "Bad," the dragon repeated back.

"And those little ones," said Jake. "Like you."

The dragon looked at him curiously, clearly trying to understand the human's words. It suddenly rolled its head back and let out a deep, bellowing howl. Jake fell backward, terrified, dropping to the ground and scrambling. The dragon continued howling, and Jake tried to aim the pistol and continue scooting away from the giant beast all at the same time. It took him a handful of seconds to realize that the dragon was laughing.

When the dragon finally looked down again at Jake, it tried to reassure the foolish human. "Chenling," it said. "Chenling. No fear chenling."

"Chenling," said Jake, as if he understood what the word meant and that knowing this would somehow make everything all right.

The dragon clearly saw through this and grew very thoughtful. After a few moments, it gave a slight snort. "Pets," it said.

"Pets?" Jake blurted.

The dragon gave him a studied look, trying to understand what the human's peculiar response might mean. Had it used the wrong word? No. It remembered quite clearly. Tobias Quigley had called them *pets.*

They were pets. It leaned closer to the human of Tobias' blood. "Pets," it stated again.

Okay, thought Jake.

"No fear," said the dragon.

"I won't."

The dragon straightened up, leaned back and again grew thoughtful. "*Hu*-mans-bad hurt chenling."

"They're a nasty bunch, all right."

The dragon turned its head slowly to look over at the box on the pedestal. It let out a long, slow breath. The air in the courtyard grew warm and there was a strong, metallic smell; the same smell that Jake had noticed when he had first entered this Other World. The dragon looked sad. "Time take box?" it asked. Its voice was low and coarse.

"I think so," said Jake. *What did the dragon know about this?* He decided not to ask. The blood of Tobias Quigley should already know what it was all about.

"Take box," said the dragon. It turned then and walked in the direction of the archway. "Fear *hu*-mans-bad."

"I'll be careful," said Jake. He watched as the great dragon disappeared into its lair. Once he was alone again in the courtyard, he put away his pistol and walked over to the pedestal. The box was made of a dark wood and the lid lifted easily. The artifact piece was inside. It had the look of a small stone tablet, but was made of some metal or plastic unknown to Jake. It was smooth on front and back, cool to the touch. It was light, but he could tell that it was made to last. It was shaped like the image that he had seen on the pylon, and on the pedestal of the serpent statue in which he had found the scroll, and on the key that he had used to open the compartment. It was one piece of the full artifact that he had seen drawn in his uncle's notebook.

Jake pulled his backpack around and put the artifact inside.

Time to go home...

He looked around the courtyard. The only way out was back the way he had come. He went to the stairs and climbed them up to the catwalk. After walking up and down the walkway and deciding there was no safe way down, he returned to the door that would take him back into the storm drains. Before going in, though, he turned and looked back across the rooftops of the abandoned city. He found once again the likely location where he had first entered the drains. It was a long way back, and if he didn't find another way up, that's where he was going to have to go. He wondered if the band of marauders was still lurking nearby. Probably not; they no doubt figured the rat dragons had gotten him.

Assuming he made it all the way back, and assuming the marauders were gone, he would then have to travel the streets all the way back this way again.

Oh, man...

He opened the door and stepped back into the darkness.

Backtracking through the drains was easier than he thought, but it still took time. Along the way, he found several ladders leading up to grated drain lids, but discovered that none of them could be opened. He supposed this was intentional. One way in, one way out, with the only other access to the surface being the dragon's courtyard.

He made a few wrong turns, circled back around on his path a few times, backtracked several times, but eventually reached the original storm drain access that had brought him down. He climbed the ladder and listened for any activity on the street. When he heard none, Jake carefully lifted the lid and climbed back up onto the street.

The sky was already starting to gray, and if this world was anything like his world, that meant the sun was going down. Dusk was coming. He didn't want to get stuck here overnight. Besides, if he was gone too long, he knew that Meara would either try to come in after him or hurry back to Serpent's Keep for help. Either way, she would be putting her life in danger. Jake had to get back to the clearing.

If he had more time, he would have liked to go into the small hospital. He had to suppose the place had been ransacked more than once over the years, but he may have been able to find a few supplies that had somehow been missed by others. He resisted the urge and continued cautiously but rapidly through the streets of the abandoned city.

He had just passed the newspaper office when he heard voices coming from down one of the side streets. Quickly stepping back, Jake slipped into the front lobby of the small-town newspaper.

The main room had the front pages of editions from years past framed and set behind glass on the walls. Jake noticed that these too were in a dialect of English, if not his English. He glanced out the small front window for signs of danger before going behind the counter.

There were a few things tossed about, indicating that vandals had been through the place, but they hadn't really done too much damage. There were papers scattered about, cans tipped over; an old phone sat undisturbed on a desk. He couldn't help but pick it up and listen: no dial tone.

He found an old style printing press in the center of one of the back rooms. Beside it sat racks of type. Interesting, but he really had to get moving. He was about to step out of the room when he noticed there was paper still in the press.

Were they printing the latest edition when whatever happened, happened?

Jake leaned in over the page and read the article headings of what looked to be the front page.

The main headline stated "Mayoral Debate Tonight".

Nothing ominous there...

Other headings were just as ordinary. There was an article about city elections, a small blurb about conserving water, and one of their sports teams was doing very well this year.

The date of the unfinished edition was Wednesday, May 13, 1959.

The principal's calendar at the school: May 12, 1959.

What happened on the thirteenth?

Jake went back out to the front of the office and glanced out the window. The street appeared empty. He opened the door a few inches and listened. It was quiet. Before stepping outside, though, Jake decided to arm himself. He pulled out the pistol and made sure one of the three bullets was next in the spindle.

He wasn't taking any chances. He had the artifact piece, the way out of town was a few minutes away, and the gateway was a few minutes beyond that. He wasn't going to let a gang of thugs keep him from getting home. Not just for himself; this quest that Tobias Quigley had set him on was important.

He had to get home.

Jake had made it another couple of blocks when he again heard the sounds of men bantering amongst themselves, joking and laughing. This time, the voices came from behind him, and Jake quickly turned down the next side street and ran into the general store. He hurried past the one checkout counter and down an aisle of empty shelves. Reaching the back of the store, he turned and knelt on one knee, facing the front door of the store, pistol held ready.

Seconds passed. He could hear the voices growing louder as the group came nearer. From their tones, it didn't sound as though they suspected he was nearby. They were simply passing by.

When it was quiet again outside, Jake stood and returned to the front of the store. A bulletin board on the right wall had several notices pinned to it. There was a call to attend the Mayoral Debate for Tuesday evening.

Someone was giving away their beloved parakeet, including cage.

A stack of newspapers was on the wooden check out counter beside the old cash register. They were dated Tuesday, May 12th, 1959.

Jake didn't take the time to look through the rest of the general store. He didn't think there'd be much left, and he was within reach of the town's southern boundary. He slipped quietly out the door, turned right and hurried back to the main street. Within minutes, he was out of the city.

The pylon containing the gateway was still there, waiting to reveal its secret to one with the knowledge. Jake was certain he had that knowledge. He took the artifact from his pack and placed it into position in the pylon. It fit perfectly.

Nothing happened.

Jake removed the artifact and stepped back. *What am I missing?*

"I really need for you to open up," he said, growing concerned now.

Nothing.

Jake raised a hand to lay it on the pylon. He thought maybe it would recognize who he was. But instead of feeling the smooth, cool surface, his hand disappeared into the pylon. Startled, Jake quickly pulled back. He rubbed his fingers together and made sure that everything had come back intact. He smiled, then.

Some sort of *hologram* was hiding the stone archway—his gateway home.

A hologram that looks just like the original pylon... He knew that it had been a solid form earlier. He had laid a hand on it when it had changed from the stone archway to the pylon.

And it had been solid just a minute ago when he had placed the artifact into it.

So the artifact had opened the gate, as he had thought it would... it just didn't look any different.

Jake felt a sudden rush of anxiety—He had opened it... It was open... *right now* it was open. How long would it *stay* open?

He hurriedly tucked the artifact into his pack, raised his hands out in front of him and stepped into the pylon.

As before, he found himself in the in-between place. This time, he knew what to expect, and he watched for it. He saw the white speck of light appear, rush at him, and turn the world into white for a brief moment; he watched existence shift to dull gray. Again he had the sense of falling forward. Again he saw another tiny point of bright light appear far in the distance, though distance was not the right word, and watched as it hurtled across the gray plane towards him, push at him, press against him, and then rush over him.

Again there was an explosion of color and Jake stumbled into the clearing at the mouth of the ravine in the Outland.

There was Meara, waiting for him.

No... She wasn't waiting for him.

The wolves were in the clearing, and Jake had arrived in the midst of some sort of confrontation. The wolves looked startled, surprised at Jake's sudden appearance. Meara took the opportunity to strike at the nearest wolf. She swung a five-foot staff as if taking the ball out of the ballpark. Jake heard bone break and watched the large animal lift off the ground, its limp body flung to the edge of the clearing.

"What's going on?" Jake asked stupidly.

"Welcome back, sir. Good to see you."

The remaining three wolves shifted position to better defend against this new situation. They were very careful to maintain a safe distance from Meara's weapon, and were still trying to evaluate the threat that Jake might pose.

Jake regained composure and quickly swung his pack around and dropped it to the ground, pulling the pistol free from the side pocket. Seeing this, the nearest wolf leapt at him, somehow knowing it was now-or-never. Jake stumbled back, fired once and missed. As he fell to the ground, he fired again, striking the wolf in the neck. Injured but still alive, the wolf was on him, clawing at Jake's belly, swinging its massive head up to his throat. Jake shoved the pistol up to the animal's head and fired again.

The last bullet...

This time the wolf went lifeless, its body lying heavy on top of him. Jake struggled to push it off. As he did, he saw that Meara had moved nearer to him and turned to defend him against the two remaining wolves.

One of them looked an awful lot like the pack leader they had faced days earlier.

Meara thrust the staff toward the lead wolf, keeping it and its companion at bay. The two stayed just beyond the reach of the weapon, continually watching for an opportunity, studying and reevaluating, knowing that sooner or later Meara would make a mistake.

Jake rolled up onto his side and attempted to sit up. He froze then, suddenly, hearing the sound of snapping brush and breaking tree branches.

Something was coming out of the mouth of the ravine.

Oh, great...

The dragon pushed its way between two trees and came roaring into the clearing. With two quick strides it was on the wolves. The lead wolf jumped aside, but the other wasn't fast enough. The dragon dropped its clawed foot down on the animal and held it. The wolf struggled to free itself, digging frantically with its front paws, but it wasn't going anywhere. Ignoring its efforts, the dragon turned its attention to the other wolf.

The leader of the wolves had moved to the far edge of the clearing, where it stopped and now watched and waited. It clearly wanted to get back into the fight, to win whatever prize it had come for, and was displeased at this turn of events.

It knew that it had lost, and didn't like it one bit.

It gave its companion a final glance and looked up into the eyes of the dragon that held it prisoner. Knowing that it could do nothing to save the other wolf, it growled angrily at Meara and Jake, then turned and disappeared into the surrounding woods.

The dragon turned and looked down at Jake, gave him a studied, knowing gaze. Jake nodded, as if to say *yes, I have it...*The dragon then curled its claws around the wolf, gripping it so that the helpless animal couldn't move. The dragon opened out one great wing, stretching it its full length, then stretched out the other wing. It gave two heavy beats of these massive wings, pushed off with its powerful rear legs, and leapt into the sky. It circled high overhead and turned into the darkness of the ravine, carrying the wolf with it.

"Master Jacob!" Meara ran to Jake and dropped to her knees. She grasped his arm and held him up.

"I'm okay," said Jake.

"No, sir," said Meara. She saw that his shirt was torn at his left side, and the fabric was blood-soaked. "I don't think you're okay at all."

She carefully pulled the shirt away from the wound and studied the injury with a trained eye. She gave a *hmmph* sound and stood up, hurried over to her gear and returned with a small cloth bag. Using a damp cloth, she cleaned the wound, then took out a small tin and pulled off the lid.

"What's that?" asked Jake.

Meara sprinkled green powder onto a cloth bandage and carefully applied it to the wound. "A mix of this and that; something my father always kept on hand." She began wrapping the bandage ties around Jake's torso.

"Some sort of family secret?"

"Not really," Meara sat back on her heels and studied her work. "You just have to know where to shop."

"So I keep hearing. I'll have to bring you along come next shopping day."

Meara smiled, but she still had a look of concern on her face.

Jake looked at the dead wolves scattered about the clearing. "I thought you had an agreement."

"As did I. Something's got 'em stirred up."

Jake started to stand, then thought better of it. Sharp burning pain streaked out from his injury in all directions.

"I think we'll be safe enough here," Meara urged. She nodded in the direction of the ravine. "He'll watch over us."

"Maybe you're right," Jake nodded. "It'll be dark soon. May not be all that safe out there at night."

"We can get an early start in the morning," Meara agreed.

"Exactly," said Jake. "A good night's sleep under the watchful eye of our friend would do us both good."

Chapter Ten

The artifact lay in the center of the desktop. Jake sat in the chair, elbows on the desk, chin in his hands, staring at it. He heard Mr. Griffin come into the Command Center, but tried to ignore him. The man had been glowering at him ever since he had returned from the Abandoned City.

Mr. Griffin stepped from the Hall of Statues and strode smoothly across the room. He stood stiffly beside the desk.

"Master Quigley," he said, quite formally.

"Hmmm," said Jake, continuing to stare at the object on the desk.

"You should be resting."

"I am resting," Jake said absently. He finally lifted his head from his hands and pointed at the artifact. "One of these things for each one of those statues."

"Yes, sir. Please, sir."

"I wonder what the other worlds are like."

"You should return to bed," Mr. Griffin stated firmly. "You must give yourself time to recover from your injuries."

"I'm fine."

"I do not believe so, sir." Mr. Griffin put on his most stern look. Jake had returned from the Outland three days earlier, a difficult journey by Meara's accounting, and Mr. Griffin had been trying, without much success, to keep the young man in his room and at rest.

Jake nodded inattentively. He leaned back in the chair, still studying the artifact. "I'll be better prepared the next time," he said, almost to himself.

Mr. Griffin allowed himself a few more moments of proper consternation, then relaxed his severe expression and let his gaze move to the artifact on the desk. While he hadn't been in the least surprised that the rash Master Quigley had returned to the village injured and near death, he had been quite astonished to find that that the young man had returned with artifact in hand.

"You did very well, sir," he said.

"Thank you, Mr. Griffin." He let out a heavy sigh. "Does May 12 or 13 mean anything to you? Nineteen fifty-nine?"

Mr. Griffin thought a moment, shook his head. "Should it, sir?"

"That's when whatever happened to that town, happened."

"But, does their calendar follow ours?"

"I don't know. But there are so many things similar between that world and ours. What if it's our world in a parallel universe? What if most things are the same, and there's just a few things different?"

"Dragons, sir?" Mr. Griffin said doubtfully.

"Ah, but there's a dragon in our world, Mr. Griffin. Probably a bunch of 'em, in that ravine."

"Perhaps they originated in that Other World."

"Or yet another," said Jake, pointing a finger at the elderly gentleman. "We're talking not just dragons, but *talking* dragons. Now, what if there's a planet somewhere where dragon-like creatures have evolved to intelligence? What if Uncle Tobias found this planet? And what if he made friends with them?"

"From what you have said of your encounters with the creatures, they do consider Master Quigley an ally."

"Brothers in Arms against these *Rhetani* that we keep hearing about." Jake looked again at the artifact resting on the desk. "A dragon watching the gateway. Another watching over this artifact."

"You may encounter others."

Jake leaned forward and picked up the artifact. "Those dragons looked like the one in the hall over there. The very statue that held the scroll."

"Coincidence is unlikely," said Mr. Griffin.

"Exactly my thought," said Jake. "So let us pursue our hypothesis, dear sir. Let us see what we find in dragon Number Two."

"Sir?"

Jake stood up. "Let's do it." He took the artifact piece into the supply room and returned with the set of keys. He removed the one he had already used and tossed the set to Mr. Griffin.

"Pick a key, Mr. Griffin. Any key."

"I'm not sure that—"

"Just pick one."

Mr. Griffin cautiously studied the keys, an anxious look on his face. He finally held one key delicately between two fingers.

"An excellent choice," said Jake. He grabbed at the key ring, keeping the selected key separate from the others. "Let's see just what that choice be." He led the way to the Hall of Statues. Turning into the hall, he looked at the polygon shape on the key and slowly walked past each statue. He stopped finally at the lizard-like creature. He warily eyed the monster.

"Aren't you an ugly thing?" He walked around the pedestal, guessing the hidden compartment would be in the same location as the last. He found the likely spot on the base of the pedestal and tried to insert the key into several different shadowed crevices in the surface design. On the third try, the key slipped in. Jake gave a satisfied grunt and turned the key. As before, a solid click sound came from apparatus hidden within the pedestal and a small lid popped open. Jake reached in a pulled out a leather scroll.

Back in the Command Center, Jake unrolled the ancient document and laid it across the desk.

Shaded eyes to setting sun, a pillar leads to seas of sand. Dark and light will take you in, seek then life of green and blue.

"That seems straightforward enough," he said.

"A desert," said Mr. Griffin. "To the west."

"Life of green and blue. An Oasis."

"There is no desert anywhere near here, Master Jacob. To the west or anywhere else."

"Stay with me now, Griff. None of these Other Worlds are going to be near here. Not as the crow flies."

"Right you are, sir," Mr. Griffin said quickly, embarrassed.

"What I'm going to find to the west is a pillar that hides the gateway to this world of *seas of sand.*"

"The west is a very big place," said Mr. Griffin.

Jake plopped himself down into the chair. "Take the paths less traveled, I suppose; like the last time."

"That would narrow the search down a bit. The West Outland has several populated locations."

Jake thought about that. The last time anyone had seen Tobias had been at the temple. Had his uncle gone from the temple to this second Other World? Was this where he had disappeared?

He may yet find out what happened to his uncle.

He opened the desk drawer and brought out the handwritten map that he had taken with him on the trip to the Abandoned City gateway. There were numerous scribbles and lines on it, work done while walking the northern trails of the Outland, or sitting on a fallen log, or huddled beside a small campfire. He planned to transfer his notes to a more permanent document later, but for now he wanted to distinguish between the original map and what his observations were.

What if what was left off the map was a clue? Could there be a similar relationship in the West Outland? Mr. Griffin was skeptical, but he was willing to consider the possibility. He was learning that young Jacob Quigley had a bit of Master Tobias Quigley in him. He would do his best not to underestimate him again.

Jake waited another day before making a trip to the marketplace, giving his wounds a little more time to heal and himself time to regain some strength. He went on his own midmorning, wandering casually from booth to booth, purchasing an item now and then, some of which he planned to take on his next journey out, some he would store in the supply room for later trips.

In particular on this trip he sought clothing that would hold up well in a desert climate and fend off the sun and heat. He found a hat and boots that would do him better than what he had, and shirt and pants that would breathe as well.

He also found a water bag with a shoulder strap to supplement his belt canteen. He wondered why Tobias didn't have something like this in the supply room, and then it occurred to him that maybe he had them with him when he went missing.

Yet another indication that he might be on his uncle's trail.

Jake felt a tap on his shoulder and turned to find Meara smiling up at him.

"Good morning, Master Jacob."

"Good morning, Miss Gyles. What brings you to the marketplace?"

"I heard that you were here, and I remembered your suggestion that I join you on your next shopping trip."

Jake held up his packages. "I'm not doing too bad," he said.

Meara glanced at what Jake held in his arms and nodded. "I see."

"A rousing endorsement if ever I heard one."

Meara continued studying Jake's purchases, and from these she thought she had a good idea as to what Master Jacob suspected things might be like on his next trip. He could see in her expression that she was already making plans that included her. She said nothing of this, however. Instead, she looked casually about them and said softly, "I think you should come with me, sir." She started across the square without waiting. Jake had little choice but to follow.

She led him to a narrow passage between two booths set into one corner of the market square. The owners of both booths gave him hard, wary looks as he passed through. Meara didn't seem to notice or care, and held a thin, wooden door open for him. Jake stepped through and down into a short, dead-end alley that ran behind the row of booths.

Shut away from the marketplace, Meara pulled on a rope hanging on one wall and released it. Nothing happened.

"It should be just a moment," she said.

Jake nodded and took the time to look around. The alley was about eight feet wide and ran twenty feet from the steps he had taken to a brick wall at the far end. The walls on either side were made of wood panels of various sizes, shapes and colors. It all looked haphazard.

He was about to ask what they were waiting for when he heard movement and scraping noises coming from behind one of the panels. It shifted suddenly and then noisily slid aside. Jake saw a woman's hand gripping the side of the wood panel and pushing it open.

And then Mrs. Hodges stepped back into view.

"Ah," she said heartily, covering whatever surprise she might have felt. "Young Master Jacob."

Behind her was a windowless room cluttered with low tables and counters, all lit by several flickering gas lamps. The back wall was lined with shelves of ceramic jars. On a narrow side wall were hung cut vines and branches.

"Mrs. H?" Jake looked dumbfounded.

Mrs. Hodges looked over at Meara. "What is it you're bringing the Master here for, girl?"

"He'll be going out again, Ma'am. He'll be needing your sun cream and your special healing salve."

"Mrs. Hodges, what are you doing here?" asked Jacob.

"She's the village herbalist," said Meara. Mrs. Hodges had already turned around and was walking toward the shelves of ceramic jars.

"Her shop is hidden away in a secret alley, Meara."

Mrs. Hodges set the jar down on a round table in the center of the room. "Some of my methods… and ingredients… well, they are not entirely accepted by the more *conventional* of our citizens."

"Are you like a witch doctor or something?"

Mrs. Hodges laughed lightly. "Not exactly, young Master," she said, continuing about her work. "But I guess there are similarities."

"Well, what then?" Jake was having trouble believing that he had never seen this side of her. "Have you always… I mean, when I used to come here in the summer?"

"And my mother before me," she said, nodding sagely.

"I sometimes think she's a witch," Meara said, mocking a conspiratorial tone.

"Fine, fine, missy," Mrs. Hodges sighed. "Oh, I suppose I have more in common with witches than with herbalists."

"But... how come I never... did Uncle Tobias know?"

"Of course the Master knew." Mrs. Hodges had measured a small amount of something yellow into a bowl and was returning the ceramic jar to the shelf.

"Master Quigley often got supplies from Mrs. Hodges," said Meara.

"I am tolerated because I don't offer my services out where people are forced to acknowledge them. Most folks I get along with well enough because most folks don't come face to face with it." She set another jar on the counter. "Most folks convince themselves I'm nothing more than Master Quigley's cook and housekeeper."

Jake watched Mrs. Hodges as she calmly prepared the mixtures, looking much like she did when working in the kitchen back in the mansion. Meara talked with her, asking her normal, everyday questions as if all this was absolutely normal, everyday activity.

But they were in a hidden alleyway, and Mrs. Hodges was some sort of druid-like medicine woman.

Okay, exactly the kind of person Uncle Tobias would associate with...

Mrs. Hodges finished her mixtures and placed them into two fist-sized leather pouches. As Meara stuffed these into her shoulder bag, Mrs. Hodges went to a heavy wooden cabinet, lifted the latch and opened it. She took down a small metal urn and placed it on the table beside the cabinet.

"It's a bad sign, ya' know," said Mrs. Hodges, speaking over her shoulder. She was very carefully spooning a small amount of the contents into an oily pouch.

"Yes, Ma'am" said Meara. "I sensed their fear."

"You mean the wolves?" asked Jake. Being outside the loop made him feel very uncomfortable.

Meara nods in answer.

"What is it about them?"

"The Outland has a good many strange things, young Master," said Mrs. Hodges. She returned the container to the cabinet and brought the pouch to Meara. "I hope you don't have to use this," she said.

"Perhaps having it will be enough," said Meara.

"What is it?" asked Jake.

Meara stuffed the pouch into a side pocket. "Mrs. Hodges and my father came up with the mixture to fend off the wolves many years ago."

"There was little choice. It was the only way to stop them," said Mrs. Hodges.

"It has kept the peace for a long time, Ma'am."

"What is it?" Jake asked again.

"Monkshood," said Meara.

"That is but the catalyst," said Mrs. Hodges. "There are many plants in the Outland that can be used to harm."

"Whatever it is, the wolves hate it," said Meara. "They're terrified of it."

"The potion is death to them," said Mrs. Hodges. "It is quite dreadful."

"It's ugly," Meara grimaced.

"Why does it affect them like that?"

"They're not like us," said Meara.

They came through a gate... thought Jake. *Dragons and wolves and... what next?*

"The Outland is a very strange place, Master Jacob," said Mrs. Hodges.

You don't say...

Chapter Eleven

Jake stood at the edge of the clearing and carefully studied the perimeter, looking into every shadow encircling the grassy circle. Stunted trees and thick brush pushed in from all sides, but the weed-like groundcover blanketing the clearing kept the scrub-forest from engulfing the area.

A stone pillar stood in the center of the clearing.

"You did it, sir," said Meara. Jake nodded, continuing to scan the woods around the clearing. Twelve days earlier, Jake had tried his best to make Meara stay in the village, but in the end had relented. Truth was, he wasn't ready to take on the Outland by himself. Truth was, she was better at surviving out here than he was. And, truth was, she would be better at dealing with the wolf-like creatures than he.

But he would deal with any dragons...

Twelve days; it had taken them twelve days of mapping and surveying and choosing one path over another. They had stretched their rations out by foraging whenever they could, but they were nonetheless short on supplies. They had four or five days of rations left, and as best they could estimate, it was at least three days back to Serpent's Keep by direct route. That meant that he had two days at most to find a way into the gateway, search and discover the next artifact piece in some desert Other World, and return to the clearing.

Meara stepped into the clearing before Jake had a chance to start forward. She walked toward the center of the clearing, toward the pillar, and stopped two steps from the monolithic stone. She turned about slowly, seeking out any possible dangers.

Jake had stepped into the clearing and was walking the boundary, looking closely into the thick brush. There didn't appear to be any other way into the clearing.

One way in, one way out. That was good and that was bad.

"Two hours till dark," said Meara, looking overhead. "I'll gather up wood for a fire."

Jake nodded in silent acknowledgement, already drawn to the pillar. He was mumbling to himself.

Dark and light will let you in... Dark and light will let you in...

Shadows and light? Sun and night? Sun and shadow?

The last gateway needed a dragon to get him through; could this one need a dragon? How could dark and light involve a dragon?

Jake looked up into the sky. The canopy of ugly, twisted trees surrounding the clearing reached in from all sides, leaving a circle of sky above him not more than sixty feet across. Not much in the way of light. Shadows, though...

Dark and light...

How could the author of the scroll, whoever that might be, know what the vegetation would be like now?

He couldn't... so dark and light had to be something that would be around for a while; sun and earth and stone.

And dragons?

Maybe. But, again, what could dragons have to do with dark and light?

"What do you think, sir?" asked Meara. She had already stacked up a considerable supply of firewood.

"Not a clue," said Jake.

"You'll figure it out, sir." She was standing at the site where she intended to create a fire pit.

Jake reached out and rested a palm on the side of the pillar. It was cool and solid and rough to the touch. He ran his hand slowly across the surface, starting randomly and then laying out a methodical search pattern, feeling every crevice and bump.

He lost all track of time, and when he stood and backed away from the stone, having found nothing, he was surprised to notice that the clearing had fallen into heavy gray. It was after dusk and it would be dark soon.

And he was alone. Several stacks of wood lined one side of the clearing, and gourd-sized stones encircled a shallow fire pit. Kindling was prepared in the pit, waiting for spark to ignite it and get the evening dinner-fire going.

But there was no sign of Meara.

How long has she been gone?

The clearing and the surrounding forest was deathly quiet. It felt wrong to break the silence by calling out for her. Besides, he would feel foolish. There was no reason to suppose that anything was amiss.

For the moment, he would wait. He went to his pack and found the matches. He got the kindling going, and then fed the flames with heavier wood. The fire-bed ashed to hot coals. Jake found the small metal pot that they used to heat water, filled it and set it on what Meara called the *hearth stone,* a flat stone placed strategically in the fire pit; near enough to the edge of the pit to provide easy access, far enough in to sufficiently heat the stone and whatever was set onto it.

All the while, Jake continued to feed the fire with larger wood selected from the stacks that Meara had gathered together. He settled in beside the fire, poking at it with a sturdy stick, unable to concentrate on the pillar, unable to think about anything other than where Meara might be, what trouble she might have gotten herself into, and wondering what he should do about it. Call out? Go looking for her? Make a large bonfire to help guide her back?

He heard a noise from somewhere beyond the clearing. Standing, he turned and faced the mouth of the trail that emptied into the clearing.

One way in, one way out.

He subconsciously held the small fire-poker stick in front of him. He could see nothing. It was almost dark out now, and he had been staring into the bright flames of his campfire. *Smart move, Sherlock...*

"Good evening, Master Jacob," said Meara. Jake could just make out her silhouette as she came into the clearing. "Are you making any progress?"

"Where have you been?" he asked sharply; too sharply.

"I'm sorry, sir. I was foraging." Meara held up a line strung with two fish. "And then I found a creek."

"I'm sorry," he said guiltily. "I didn't mean to jump at you. I was afraid something happened. I thought you might be... I didn't know what to think."

"I'm very sorry, sir." Meara hurried to the fire. She let her foraging bag slide off her shoulder and knelt down. "I found some roots, some blackberries, and we can have fish tonight, if that's all right. It should help stretch our supplies."

"That sounds fine."

"I didn't mean to frighten you."

"Not frightened. Really. I was just concerned. It's okay. Just... let me know before you go off like that."

Fresh fish. After two weeks consisting mostly of dried meat and stale trail mix and some indescribable fibrous foodstuff that Meara had said was good for you and lasted weeks in a backpack, fresh fish sounded pretty good.

"Of course." Meara began preparing the fish for the fire. Jake looked back toward the trail. Night was falling fast, and the campfire was creating shadows that flickered across the encroaching forest.

In their twelve days in the Outland this trip, Jake and Meara hadn't come across the wolves, or any wild animals. The only threats they had faced had been losing their way and having to backtrack and make adjustments to the map, and at one point they had come up on an irate monk who was upset at having his 30-day wilderness solitude interrupted.

Dark and light will let you in...

What could that mean?

Dark and light… two separate things. The key to opening the gateway contains two components, one having to do with darkness, one having to do with light.

That sounded plausible.

While Meara put the fish onto the fire, Jake returned to the stone. He sat before it, stared at the flickering of shadows and light the campfire created.

Back to shadows again...

After a few more minutes of staring at the monolith, Jake heard Meara come up beside him and set a plate in his lap. He stared down at it, then up at Meara. She held a fork out to him.

Jake took the fork. "Smells great."

Meara went back to the campfire and served herself, then returned to sit beside Jake.

The shadows and the bright reflections continued to dance across the rough surface of the stone as the flames of the campfire rose and fell, flickered and licked at the air. It was as hypnotic as staring into the flames themselves and Jake found his thoughts and his concentration slowly feathering away.

"That one looks like a dragon's head," said Meara.

Meara's voice startled Jake. "What?"

"Right there." Meara pointed toward the stone, indicating a dark spot in the surface. "It looks like a dragon's head."

"Really?" Jake leaned a little to one side and turned his head slightly. It did look like a dragon's head, if just a little. It was about two inches across, and faintly resembled the profile of a dragon's head, mouth open and teeth bared, horns rolling back from the top of the head. It was a dark fresco, and in the shifting light of the fire, it looked like it was moving.

Dark and light will let you in...

"Do you see any more?" he asked. "Look for another one… a light one."

"There," she said, almost immediately, and pointed at a location up and to the right of the first. This one was about the same size, and of the same design, but due to the color of the stone and the reflections of the fire, this one was much brighter.

"I think you've done it, Meara." Jake stood and walked toward the stone. As he moved forward, he lost sight of the images. He had been looking right at them, but the images disappeared as his perception changed. He stopped, backed up, and caught sight of them again. He moved slowly forward, but again lost sight.

"I'll guide you, sir," said Meara.

Jake nodded and stepped up to the stone. Holding the palm of his left hand against the surface, Meara directed him down until he was holding two fingers against the dark dragon head. He pushed in on the image, but nothing happened.

"Take me to the second image," he said, and held the palm of his right hand against the stone. Again Meara guided his hand until it was over the light dragon head.

Jake pressed in on both images at the same time. He felt the stone beneath his fingers slide in a quarter of an inch.

Meara stood, sensing something different about the stone.

Jake stepped back from the stone as it began to shimmer and fade. The colors slowly disappeared and then returned as the pillar coalesced from a milky white cloud to a new shape—the same primitive stone archway as the last time.

Jake stepped over and picked up his pack, started toward the gateway. "Keep an eye on things, Meara," he said.

A deep, husky voice, definitely not Meara, came from behind him. "What is that?"

Jake stopped and turned sharply toward the voice. Meara was backing away from three ragged-looking men who had come into the clearing. Jake placed the palm of his hand on Meara's back as she neared him and she stopped.

"That twarn't here before, Eddie," said one of the men.

"No kiddin'," said Eddie. He looked warily at Jake. "So, what's goin' on here, buddy?" As he spoke, Eddie's two companions spread out, one in each direction. They stopped four paces from their leader.

"There's nothing going on," said Jake.

"Now that ain't true, mister." Eddie pointed sharply at the archway. "That wasn't there. There was a plain ole' stone there, no more'n this high." Eddie held a hand up shoulder high.

"Are you suggesting that I somehow removed this other stone and replaced it with this?"

"Don't you be gettin' smart with me," Eddie glared at Jake, and then moved his gaze slowly over to Meara. "You folks is in enough trouble as it is."

"That's for sure," said one of Eddie's companions. "They's in a heap a hurt."

Eddie visibly sized up the scene, returned his attention to Meara, and then finally spoke to Jake. "Now, sev'ral things is goin' to happen here. Nothin's gonna' change that. What you can help determine is how difficult each of 'em is gonna' be. Not that I mind partic'arly, but what say you make 'em easy?"

"I'd say that pretty much depends on what you have in mind, Eddie."

"Now ya see? You're already makin' things difficult. Yur givin' me lip."

"Eddie don't like it when ya' give him lip," said one of Eddie's flunkies.

"First up," said Eddie, pointing sharply again at the gateway, "is that yur gonna' tell me what *that* is and how ya got it here."

Jake slid his hand down Meara's back and took her hand. "It's a sculpture," he said. "Just something that I made."

"That don't look like no sculpture, mister."

Jake eased back toward the gateway, bringing Meara back with him. "Thank you," he said. "I tried to make it look like a part of the surroundings."

"It don't look like that, neither." Eddie stepped toward him. "Yur lyin'."

"That is possible, I suppose." Jake could sense that he was one long stride from the gate. He inched nearer. With Eddie moving steadily closer, Jake's backward steps looked defensive rather than a planned move toward the *sculpture*. There was nothing about the stone archway to indicate that it offered any escape.

"Oh, it's more'n possible," Eddie hissed. His mood was darkening. "You start talkin' true, or this gets ugly." Eddie pointed an angry finger at Meara, "And it gets real bad for her."

Alrighty then, time to go... Jake gripped Meara's hand hard and turned sharply toward the gate. *This better work, or we're going to look real foolish...*

Jake ran into the archway with Meara in tow. The world around him disappeared, replaced with a formless universe of gray that surrounded whatever it was that served as his own existence. A tiny point of bright light appeared in the distance. Just as he began struggling with the concept of distance in an indefinable universe without dimension, the pinpoint of light rushed at him and swept over him. Instantly, the universe exploded into white, and then the white turned to gray.

Jake knew that he was holding Meara's hand, and yet neither of them had a body; neither had any physical presence at all. He couldn't actually feel her hand, but knew that the two of them were connected. He knew also that he had to maintain that connection or he would lose her.

Lose her to what, or to where, he did not know.

Another tiny point of bright light appeared at the center of his vision. Again it rushed at him and swept over him and the in-between place they were in turned white. He had an infinitesimal moment to wonder what Meara was thinking about all this, and then there came the explosion of color and he and Meara were thrown into the Other World.

Chapter Twelve

Meara cried out excitedly. She was gripping Jake's hand so hard that he was afraid she might break his fingers. He managed to free himself and turned to face the gateway. Just as in the Other World of the Abandoned City, a stone archway stood silent and alone before them. It looked just like the one that he had just stepped through, just as the gateway to the Abandoned City had looked. And, just as before, this one shimmered and faded, the colors merging into a foggy gray. Within moments, in place of the archway stood a four-sided stone pylon, slate gray and smooth as glass.

"I think we're safe for now," said Jake. If the bandits had followed them into the gate, they hadn't made it. *Where would they be?*

"What happened to the gate!" said Meara in a panic.

"It's okay," said Jake. "Once we find the artifact, we can open it up again."

Meara stepped forward and rested a hand against the smooth pylon. "That was amazing." She was still trying to take it all in. Realization suddenly washed over her face and she looked uncertainly at Jake. "What if we don't find the artifact?"

Jake looked around at their new surroundings. The heat of twin suns beat down on a desert world of rolling sand dunes. The only feature that he could see was the glassy stone pylon standing beside them. "That would put us in a bit of difficulty," he said slowly. "Let's think positive, shall we?"

"Yes, sir." Meara saw the same featureless terrain that Jake saw, felt the same heat from the same twin suns. "Which way, sir?" she asked.

"Well," Jake turned about in a slow circle. There being no other indication, might as well go in the direction the gateway had pointed them. "That way," he said.

Meara looked in the direction he was pointing. It didn't look any different than any other direction. "Master Jacob? What are we looking for?"

"An oasis," said Jake. *Seek then life of green and blue.*

Meara looked at the meager supplies they had managed to bring with them. Jake had his pack; he had the canteen on his belt, but not the larger water bag. Meara hadn't had a chance to grab anything.

"We are short on food and water," she said.

"True enough," said Jake. "The oasis should give us both."

"Of course, sir." Meara squinted and tried to look further into the distance. Scrunching her eyes up didn't help.

May as well get started... Jake calmly started forward. Meara came quickly up beside him.

Walking across the fine sand was difficult. They quickly tired, but knew they had to push, since they had no idea how far they would have to go or how hot the day might get. The larger of the two suns was directly overhead, and its companion was right beside it. For all they knew, a day on this world might last many of their own Earth days, or even weeks.

They crested one dune after another, and at each Jake looked back along the path they were traveling. Two trails of deep footprints reached back to a dark speck on the horizon; the gateway home, should they ever find the artifact.

They had one canteen between them, and they used it sparingly. If they were to reach their goal, they had to drink to maintain their strength, but the thought of traveling this world with no water was terrifying.

What if we're going in the wrong direction? thought Jake. What if they were supposed to go in exactly the opposite direction? What if the oasis had been just over the first dune in the other direction, on the other side of the gateway?

Jake tried not to second-guess himself, but with each passing hour that became more and more difficult. He watched as the smaller of the two suns glided across the sky and eventually set directly ahead of them. The larger sun, the hotter of the two, moved much slower. It took several more hours before it followed the first below the horizon.

When the second sun finally set, they felt the difference almost immediately. The air cooled, making it easier to breathe. The sand beneath their feet began to cool; eventually cool enough that they were able sit comfortably, and when dusk had settled in they decided to take a break before pushing on through the mild evening. The comfortable temperature and the break to relax and have a quick meal of rations gave them a renewed energy. Jake hoped that it would be enough to get them to their goal before the heat of the next day.

With true darkness came an alien night sky and a strange splash of stars. The night grew colder and Jake found himself working to stay warm, exaggerating his movements to keep his blood pumping. Cold or not, however, their forced march was exhausting, and his effort to stay warm only made that worse.

They finally had no choice but to stop, at least to rest and regain some strength. They sat on the lee side of a dune ridgeline, out of the breeze that had been blowing for several hours. They were facing the direction of the pylon, looking back along the path they had taken on their day-long journey. Behind them, somewhere beyond the ridgeline, the oasis they sought was still hidden from them.

They ate more of their ration and washed it down with the last of their water. Unspoken between them was the knowledge that if they didn't find more water before the following midday, they were going to be in serious trouble. Jake tucked the empty canteen back into his belt and gave Meara a weak smile. She smiled back and looked again at the night desert in front of them. This wasn't a desert of dry earth and brush and cactus and scurrying lizards. This was sand. Sand as far as one could travel and as deep as a world; dunes that moved with the wind.

A huge moon began to rise up from the distant horizon. Moonlight streaked toward them, shimmering across the rolling terrain. The footpaths they had left behind shown as a dark band leading from the moon directly to them.

"The wind hasn't wiped our footprints away," said Meara.

"It will," said Jake. That breeze had been growing stronger by the hour.

"There's not much out here in the way of landmarks. Will we be able to find our way back?"

Jake didn't answer. He observed where the moon rose in relation to their tracks. He was about to stand, to suggest that they move on, when he thought he noticed a shifting of shadows several dunes away. "Look there," he said, nodding in the direction of their foot paths.

"I see it," said Meara. She stood and took two steps back, until she was standing at the highest point on the ridge. Jake continued to study the movement from his sitting position.

Meara spoke softly. "He's following our trail."

"Yes he is."

"What should we do?"

Trying to hide was useless. From the speed this newcomer was traveling, he wasn't on foot. Running was useless. A meeting was inevitable.

"Wait for him," said Jake.

"Yes, sir," Meara said softly. She unclipped the strap on the hilt of the knife on her belt. Seeing that, Jake opened a side pocket in his packet and took out the large knife that he had brought with him. He held it clumsily in his hand, finally slipped it into his belt at the small of his back.

The stranger crested the ridge of the near dune and formed a clear silhouette, the large moon serving as a bright backdrop.

"Oh, man," said Jake. *What the heck was that?* The silhouette disappeared as the stranger and his mount started down the slope of the dune.

"What was that?" asked Meara.

Jake was pretty sure the rider was human, but the animal wasn't any kind of horse that he had ever seen. The silhouette was of something low to the ground, legs splayed out to the sides, and a tail jutting straight out behind it.

Jake and Meara watched as rider and mount reached the bottom of the dune and started up the slope toward them, finally coming again into the moonlight. Jake stood and stepped back, so that he was standing directly beside Meara.

The rider was indeed human; a big man with a long bushy beard, brown shirt and trousers, high-top boots, and a large wooden staff comfortably at the ready. He sat in a leather saddle positioned far forward on a lizard-like dragon creature. The animal held its head high, studying the two humans that it was approaching. Its legs were short and powerful, keeping its belly and tail up off the sand, and it easily propelled itself and its rider up the slope.

Rider and dragon veered left as they neared Jake and Meara, reached the top of the ridge and turned and stopped. The human looked down on them, examined them, gaining as much information as he could before speaking.

"Chee han... don la pah," he said, clear and crisp. He waited for a response. The dragon looked to be waiting as well. After Jake's recent experiences with dragons, he had to assume this one had at least some rudimentary intelligence.

"I'm sorry," said Jake. "I don't understand."

"English?" asked the stranger, the word tumbling off his tongue as if seldom used.

"Yes. English," said Jake. "You speak English?"

"Who are you? Why are you here?"

Jake thought before answering. He didn't want to give this man any more information than was necessary to satisfy his questions. "I'm Jake. This is Meara. We are travelers."

"No doubt. That doesn't answer either question."

"As I said, I am—"

"Your names mean nothing to me."

The dragon stretched its head forward and looked closely at Meara, then at Jake. It snorted and grunted. At that, the stranger climbed down from the animal's back and came forward, staff in hand. He stopped within a staff's length of Jake.

"You are blood to Tobias Quigley?" he asked.

Does Tobias know everybody?

"My uncle," said Jake. "I am Jacob Quigley."

The stranger nodded, held the staff firmly at his side. "I am Nehman. I am Guardian."

Guardian? As Tobias was Guardian?

"I'm on a quest left to me by Tobias," said Jake.

"You gather the artifacts," Nehman stated flatly, "to make them again one."

"That's right," said Jake. *Okay... I think that's what I'm doing.*

"There are dangerous times ahead." Nehman looked up at the alien night sky. A disturbed expression swept across his face. "It is true? Tobias is lost to us?"

"I don't know," said Jake. *This man knows things...*

"My heart..." Nehman started, but could not finish. The dragon lowered its head and nudged him, made low grumbling noises. Nehman gave it a pat on the nose. "Yes, my friend. We must prepare for changing times."

"Can you help us?" asked Meara. "We must find the oasis and recover the artifact for this world."

"A three hour journey remains."

"We are traveling in the right direction, then?" asked Jake.

"Yes," Nehman looked at him curiously, as if Jake had asked a foolish question.

"I wasn't given all the information," said Jake. "I have had to be... creative."

"Ah," Nehman smiled. "Tobias' poetry."

Nehman said something to the dragon and it turned about and left, scrambling over the ridge and disappearing down the other side.

"I have sent him ahead," said Nehman. "I will take you to the oasis." He held a leather water bag out to Jake.

"Thank you," said Jake. He took a short swallow, handed the water bag to Meara, then reached down and picked up his pack. "Ready when you are."

Knowing they were only three hours from their goal, Jake and Meara were in better spirits as they set off, following the trail left by Nehman's dragon. Their guide set a steady pace, but one they were able to keep up with. This, coupled with the knowledge and excitement in knowing that they were heading in the right direction and within easy reach of the oasis, gave them the strength and endurance to withstand the increasingly cold night air.

"It doesn't get this cold back where you come from?" asked Nehman, seeing that Jake and Meara weren't dressed for desert nights. His own clothes, while not bulky, kept out the cold and wind. "Serpent's Keep, right?"

"Yeah. Serpent's Keep," said Jake. "We figured we were coming to a desert world; didn't really figure on cold."

"Most deserts are like this. Hot during the day, cold at night. I suppose the extremes might be greater here than some."

"Yeah, well... you know about Serpent's Keep?"

"Sure. Tobias' world. Primary."

"Earth."

"Primary. All gates lead to Primary."

That made some sense to Jake. At least, it fit in with what he knew and the experiences that he had. "And Uncle Tobias was the Guardian at Serpent's Keep?" he asked.

Nehman gave Jake another suspicious side-glance. "And Watcher of the gate that leads to the Rhetani."

"Like I said, I'm a bit in the dark on this. Uncle Tobias was my favorite person in the world, *any world,* and I had no idea that he was involved in anything like this."

"No one did," said Meara. "I've lived in Serpent's Keep all my life. My father was a good friend of Master Quigley."

Nehman nodded slowly, finally grunting out, "Tobias much enjoyed the people of your village."

Jake spoke quietly. "When he went missing, and was declared dead, I was given the estate and this cryptic message that I was to carry on the quest."

They walked in silence for a few moments.

"If he trusted the gathering of the artifacts to you," said Nehman, "then so do I."

"Do you know what happened to him?"

"Only that he was lost to us."

"Any idea what he was doing when he was lost?"

Nehman continued marching steadily forward, his face hard and eyes focused on the horizon ahead. Jake didn't think he was going to answer, and he didn't want to push too hard. Finally, Nehman cleared his throat. "A Rhetani had shown up on several worlds. I do not know how this could be, but it was so. There was much concern that they might find the artifacts and attempt to open the gateway to their world."

"But that's what *I'm* going to do."

"If the Rhetani open the gateway, they will gain a foothold in Primary. From there, they will have access to your world and to all the Other Worlds."

"But if I open the gateway, won't—"

"You will go through the gateway and close it on the other side—permanently."

Jake kept walking. "Oh," he said.

"But sir!" Meara started forward again, coming up quickly and taking Jake's arm.

Jake spoke to Nehman in a dead calm. "And that will keep the Rhetani in their own world."

"That's the idea," said Nehman. "With all the artifact pieces locked into Serpent's Gate, the Other Worlds will be closed to one another."

"Master Jacob, you can't do this," Meara pleaded. "You will be trapped with these... these *Rhetani.*"

Jake walked on in silence. So that was it. That was Tobias' mission, his quest, and he had bequeathed it to his nephew.

All the Other Worlds closed to one another...

"What about you?" Jake asked Nehman.

"Do not concern yourself with me."

The moon continued its slow trek across the night sky, until finally Jake found himself directly marching toward it. They trudged their way over one rolling dune after another, following the trail left by Nehman's dragon. They seldom spoke, intent on pushing forward, on reaching the oasis before morning.

Nehman stopped at a high crest and waited, and once Jake and Meara caught up to him, he pointed toward the moon, now just touching the horizon. There, silhouetted against the great white ball, was a grove of trees, half-hidden beyond several more dunes.

They lost sight of the trees when they descended into the sink between each dune, but the grove was all the nearer as they climbed up to the next ridge. At each crest the moon had sunk a little further into the horizon, until finally it was gone altogether, and the night turned black and the silhouette of trees disappeared.

They climbed the last dune in darkness. Nearing the top, Jake could see the tops of tallest of the trees beyond, and as they crested the ridge and started down the other side, he found himself surrounded by trees and bushes. Reaching the floor of the little valley, he felt soil beneath his feet rather than sand. The ground was covered in tufts of grass and hardy groundcover.

In the heart of the oasis was a hill of rock and earth. One side had fallen away, leaving a cliff twenty feet tall that jutted out and formed a high overhang. The overhang created a sheltering cover for a small pool inset at the base of the cliff. Resting beside the pool was Nehman's dragon. Its head lay on a bed of grass, one eye open and watching as Nehman brought the strangers to the pool.

They dropped their gear and Meara knelt down and drank from the pool. Jake looked around for some sign of the artifact, but could see nothing.

Nehman pointed toward the mass of vines growing in a shadowed recess in the cliff. "There's a door behind that growth," he said. "The artifact is in there."

"Will I have any trouble getting it?"

"That I would not know."

"You haven't actually seen it, then? You haven't been in there?"

"I had no reason."

Meara stood up and wiped water from her chin. "And you've been here how long?"

"Since the formation of the gates," said Nehman.

"But that was—"

"I have been here a long time."

Hundreds of years, thought Jake.

Nehman walked slowly over to his dragon. He held his hand out, palm down, and the dragon lifted its head until the man's hand was resting on the dragon's brow. Jake thought he could hear Nehman's voice, but couldn't catch the words. It seemed to be a personal exchange, so he turned away and spoke to Meara.

Jake pointed to a spot near the cliff and under trees where they could set up camp. It was near the water and looked like it would stay in shade most of the day. "I'm too tired to think clearly. We'll try for the artifact after we get some sleep."

"Yes sir," said Meara. She nodded toward Nehman as she picked up their gear. "Do you really think that he, you know…"

"Possible, I guess."

"But, hundreds... maybe thousands..."

The two of them carried their supplies toward the camp site. "People like Nehman and Tobias have sacrificed a lot for the rest of us, and no one will ever hear about it."

"But they could be immortal."

"Immortal or not, they've spent their lives standing watch, waiting for the unthinkable to happen. When it does, they fight, maybe die, in obscurity."

Meara stared at the Guardian of this world, watched as he looked after the strange creature that was his only companion. Such an unbelievable life he must have lived.

Jake made himself as comfortable as he could. It was still very cool, and would likely grow colder yet before the first sun came up. Despite the cold, and the recent experiences churning about in his mind, he fell asleep almost immediately.

He woke to the sounds of Meara preparing a meal. Sitting up, he looked around and judged the time to be midday. It was warm but not overly so. The oasis, the surrounding terrain, and the shaded grove in which they had made camp all combined to keep their immediate environment relatively cool when compared to the surrounding desert.

Meara was working over a pot hanging above a small cooking fire. Seeing Jake up and about, she told him that lunch would be ready in a few minutes. Nehman had brought her the pot and the ingredients for a stew from a cache that he kept at the oasis.

Jake had to wonder where Nehman would find food on a world such as this. But then, there was obviously a food source somewhere, as the man had been surviving here for a very long time.

Lunch was ready by the time Jake had finished cleaning up. Sitting beside Meara, he took the bowl offered to him and used the spoon to investigate the contents. He found meat, potato, and three different vegetables. It smelled good. He filled the spoon with broth and sipped it. A bit spicy, but tasty.

As he ate, he studied his surroundings in the daylight. The oasis was in a deep sink, surrounded on all sides by a high ridge. A layer of sand on the surface hid compact soil beneath. There were several groves of trees; some species that he wasn't familiar with.

They ate in silence for several minutes. The stew really was good. Jake wondered what the meat was. What animal around here served as a food source?

"Where's Nehman," he asked.

"I don't know. He left not long after giving me these supplies."

"He didn't say anything?"

"I don't think he interacts much with people," said Meara. "Talks to his dragon a lot, though."

Jake slid around until he was facing the cliff. An entire section was covered in thick vine, and according to Nehman there was a door somewhere underneath it.

"Don't suppose it's unlocked," he wondered aloud.

"I guess that would depend on what's on the other side, sir."

That wasn't very comforting. There had to be to be some defensive measure in place. Either the hidden door was locked, or there was some other protection inside.

So, do I want it locked or unlocked?

Jake set his empty bowl down beside him and stood up, walked determinedly across the camp and up to the cliff wall. The layer of vines covering the cliff was thick and they were tightly intertwined. It took all he had to pull apart a section of the vegetation, only to find that beneath it was only rock. He stepped to one side and tried again.

He found a dark, heavy door on the fourth search. Once found, he and Meara worked together to pull apart the thick vines and clear away an opening.

Carved in the center of the door was the symbol for this world's artifact. *A good sign,* thought Jake. Also on the door was a simple, heavy metal latch. Jake rested his hand on it and pushed down. It moved easily and Jake pushed in. The door glided inward an inch.

"It isn't locked," said Meara.

"No. It's not."

"Then there might be something in there," said Meara, "protecting the artifact."

"Yes. There might be. You wait here."

"But sir—"

"Do you really think you should go in alone?" asked Nehman, coming up behind them. Jake and Meara both jumped at the sound of his voice.

"Geez—" Jake said sharply.

"Pardon."

Jake took a moment to catch his breath, then turned back to the door. "All right," he said. "Okay... but stay behind me."

"Yes sir," said Meara.

"As you say," said Nehman.

Jake pushed the door open. It was dark inside. He was about to ask Meara to go get the lantern when he noticed a faint light at the far end of a long hall, as if sunlight was somehow filtering through into a subterranean room.

"Interesting," said Nehman, standing close behind Jake.

"If you say so." Jake stepped through the doorway, glad now that he wasn't doing this alone. There was an old, musty animal smell intermingled with the smells of dry earth and moldy vegetation.

"The temperature," said Meara. "It's comfortable in here."

Jake nodded, though it was too dark for anyone to see. He continued moving down the hall, unable to see the floor on which he walked. He could hear Meara and Nehman walking in step directly behind him. Far ahead, the filtered light drew nearer.

Jake thought he saw a shadow in the light and stopped. He watched and waited. After a few seconds, Meara whispered. "What is it?"

"I thought I saw something."

"What?"

"I don't know," said Jake. "Nothing." He started forward again.

The pungent odor grew stronger with each step.

"What's that smell," asked Meara.

"Dragon's nest," said Nehman.

Jake frowned. "I knew you were going to say that."

The tunnel emptied into a large, oval room with sloping walls and a high ceiling that was pockmarked with a dozen small openings through which sunlight streamed in like fuzzy laser beams. There were tunnel openings at three locations in the surrounding walls, each set about four feet above the stone floor.

On the far side of the room was a large bed of matted vegetation. Resting comfortably in the nest was a reptilian dragon, its large head resting on its hands. It grinned as it watched the three humans come into its lair.

"Welcome," it said. The word sounded foreign coming from the creature.

"Hello," said Jake. As he continued into the room. "I am Jacob Quigley. Nephew of Tobias Quigley."

"Blood," said the dragon. It lifted up its head.

"That's right."

"Not Tobias."

"Right again." Jake stopped in the center of the room. He glanced up at the holes in the ceiling, at the dark entrances to several exiting tunnels. Peripherally, he saw Nehman step to his right and Meara move to his left.

"You are most welcome here," said the dragon. "I have been a long time alone."

"I've never seen you on the surface," said Nehman.

"Seldom travel surface. All I need here." The dragon lifted one hand and casually waved it toward the tunnels. "Too hot, surface."

"It can get warm."

"Do you know why I am here?" asked Jake.

"Collect what Tobias left in my care."

"Is that going to be a problem?"

The dragon grinned broadly. "Why you think that, Jacob Quigley, blood of Tobias Quigley?"

"I don't," Jacob replied carefully. "From what I've seen, dragons are friends of Tobias."

"All respect Tobias Quigley, Guardian of the Artifact, Watcher of Serpent's Keep, warrior in battle against Rhetani."

Something is wrong...

Nehman took a step forward, standing now well within Jake's view. "The Guardians stand in defense of the Jahai," he said. Jake had no idea what Nehman was talking about, but it was clear the Guardian didn't like the look of things any more than Jake.

"Yes..." The dragon nodded its head slowly.

"Tobias Quigley has conferred the gathering of the artifacts to Master Jacob," Nehman continued. "Do you contest that?"

"I do not," said the dragon.

"Then will you assist Master Jacob?" asked Meara, stepping forward.

Jake watched the expression of the dragon. There was definitely something not right. The creature was an ally of Tobias Quigley, of the Guardians, of the Jahai, yet there was a devious undercurrent about this dragon. Jake didn't think this was going to end well.

The dragon cocked its head to one side and gave Meara another twisted smile.

"You should answer the lady," Nehman said coolly. He moved further to one side, putting more distance between himself and Jake. Seeing that, Meara did the same. There were three distinct targets rather than one.

The dragon cocked its head the other way, studied the three of them, and then looked directly at Meara.

"I have but one master," he said. He turned back to Nehman.

"How can a dragon serve the Rhetani?" Nehman asked sharply. He reached over his shoulder and pulled his sword from the scabbard strapped to his back. The dragon glanced only casually at the weapon, and appeared unconcerned by the accusation.

"Rhetani not master. I serve my heart, human."

"And yet you've given it over to the Rhetani?" asked Meara.

"Give nothing. We travel same path."

"You, my wayward friend, are a disgrace to the race of dragons," said Nehman. He took several more steps to the side and moved cautiously nearer. As he did, Meara slid the pack off her back and pulled her blade free, tossing the pack behind her. She stepped calmly forward.

"A pleasant diversion," said the dragon, lifting itself up and pulling its head back. Its legs were short and stocky, its chest wide and heavily scaled.

"It doesn't have to be this way," said Jake. He held his own knife loosely at his side, wanting to avoid a fight if possible.

"Your blood... the most sweet," said the dragon.

"What have we done to you?"

"Nothing at all."

Nehman moved so quickly that he was little more than a blur. The dragon saw him coming, however, and just as quickly leapt aside to avoid the sword thrust in under the creature's chin. It roared, swung about and pushed forward at Nehman, brought its head in low and tried to clamp its jaws around the man's legs. Nehman, instead of jumping back as expected, jumped forward and brought his sword down like a spike onto the dragon. He missed the head, instead burying a foot and a half of sword into the creature's neck.

Again the dragon roared and pulled back violently. The sudden wrenching knocked Nehman backward, bloody sword in hand. He staggered back several steps before regaining his footing.

Meara had rushed forward at the same time and plunged her blade into the dragon's shoulder. The beast twisted about and batted her aside; she flew back and struck the wall. The dragon lunged at her as she slid down to the floor, but before it could reach her Jake threw his knife at it, striking its belly as it began to rear up. Again the beast roared and clouds of dust rolled from the walls and the ceiling. It spun about angrily and rushed at him and Jake stumbled backward and fell to the ground as the dragon snapped at the air above him. It turned its head and looked down on him with one yellow eye. Its breath was hot and foul, but didn't have the same intensity of the fire-breathing dragons that Jake had recently come across.

"Blood die now," it said and laid a heavy, clawed hand on Jake's chest. The weight made it hard for Jake to breathe, the claws closed in around him and Jake could feel his bones bending and tendons tearing. He stared up into the eye of the dragon and saw a sparkle of insane glee. The dragon must have been harboring an intense hatred for Tobias for centuries and was now venting that hate on him.

Jake's arm was spread out to his side, pressed against the floor of the chamber by the weight of the dragon. He could feel the handle of his knife, the blade of which was buried in the flesh of the belly. Twisting his wrist, he managed to grasp the hilt and turned the blade, pushing it deeper into the monster.

The creature let out a shattering, blood-curdling scream and swung its head from side to side as it fought against the agony. It raised itself up, away from the source of the pain. Jake held tightly to the knife and it pulled free from the beast. Holding the weapon now in both hands, Jake struck up at the vulnerable belly. As he did, Nehman rushed in and pierced the dragon's neck with his sword. The animal shuddered, let out a hollow gurgling rattle, and dropped down onto Jake as several thousand pounds of dead weight.

He couldn't breathe, couldn't expand his chest and fill his lungs with air. He tried desperately to suck in thin threads of oxygen. Then he heard Nehman scrambling beside him, heard the man call out. "Hang on! Hang on!"

Nehman pressed his back against the body of the dragon and lifted it enough that Jake was finally able to crawl free.

"You hurt?" he asked. Jake sucked in three deep breaths, pressed his hands against his ribs.

Jake shook his head, turned and looked over the back of the dead dragon, over at Meara who was slumped down against the far wall. "Meara," he called, and grimaced at the sudden pain that webbed across his chest. He spoke more softly, "Meara. Are you all right?"

Meara lifted her head and nodded without speaking.

§

Nehman moved from one tunnel opening to the next and peered inside. He really couldn't see anything, but nonetheless hoped that there would be some indication, some sign, something to tell them which one would lead them to the artifact.

"These tunnels go on a ways," he said. "This may take some time."

"Maybe not," said Jake. In those few seconds when he had looked into the eye of the dragon, Jake had felt a connection, an understanding, and he had a sense of the workings of the tortured mind of the creature.

He nodded in the direction of the nest of the dragon.

Nehman grimaced. A dragon's bed had a rather unique odor to it. "Oh, I'd rather not," he said.

Jake gave a chuckle and suffered the pain for it. It would take a long time for the torn ligaments to heal. "I'll do it," he said, and started toward the nest. "My quest, after all."

"I'll help you, sir," said Meara.

"Oh, very well," Nehman moaned. "If it must be done."

They all moved up to the nest. It consisted of decomposing branches from the trees of the oasis, bits of fabric from old human clothing and bedding, soil from the tunnels, and sand from above. There was also a considerable amount of shed dragon skin and broken scales.

The artifact lay half buried in the heart of the nest, as a delicate egg that would never hatch.

"How did you know, sir?" asked Meara.

It was in his eyes.

"Sir?"

"He would not keep it anywhere else."

Chapter Thirteen

Jake, Meara and Nehman stood beside the closed obelisk, Nehman's mount resting nearby. Jake held the artifact, ready to use it to open the gateway. He turned to Nehman.

"You should come with us," he said, though he knew the man would not.

"I will remain here."

"You said it yourself... all the gates will close. Forever. This one included."

"I have been on this world for a very long time."

Jake and Nehman looked at each other for several very long seconds, during which time something seemed to pass between them, perhaps an understanding. Jake finally held out his hand. Nehman looked at it, and for a moment didn't seem to know what to do. Finally, however, the two shook hands.

Jake turned to the obelisk and inserted the artifact. There was only the faintest flicker, and then nothing.

"Master Jacob?" Meara looked concerned.

"It's all right, Meara." Jake removed the artifact. He looked back at Nehman again and gave a curt nod. Turning back to the gateway, he took hold of Meara's hand. "Whatever you do, do not let go of my hand."

Their passage through the gateway started out the same as previous crossings. Jake saw the familiar point of light in the distance. It came at him, grew to overwhelm his vision and was suddenly all around him, turning his world into white nothing.

And then it was different.

In that peculiar world of white nothing, Jake... *saw something...*

There was something in that nothingness... Faint images, shadows against the white, in the white, a part of the white.

Shadows of people.

Jake saw the faint silhouettes of several people.

The bandits?

And then it was past. The white turned to dull gray and he had the odd sense of falling forward. There was another point of bright light in the center of his vision. It rushed at him and over him and the gray turned to white, and then came the explosion of color and Jake stumbled out into the clearing in the Outland, hand in hand with Meara.

"Sir?" Meara asked anxiously steadying herself.

"You saw them?" asked Jake.

Meara nodded sharply. Jake let go of her hand and nervously rubbed his face with the flats of his palms.

So they had followed after them, before the gate had closed, and they had gotten stuck somehow in that in-between place.

This was bad. Nasty as they were... they were trapped—in that place.

"They followed us in," said Meara.

"They had no way out."

The supplies they had been forced to leave behind when they had stepped through the gateway were still in the clearing. That was good news, anyway. They would have food and equipment for the trip home.

"Come on," he said sharply. He was in no mood to hang around. "Let's get out of here."

They gathered up their supplies and made ready to leave. They could put a good distance between them and this clearing before nightfall.

Jake started to the mouth of the trail, and then slowed. His senses were picking up something. He couldn't think or voice what it was, but he knew that there was something... He stopped, turned his head and looked at Meara.

Meara was looking at the edge of the clearing far to their right. Jake continued turning and looked in the direction of her gaze.

Wolves...

"Not again." He watched as one wolf leapt out into the clearing and slowly stalked the perimeter. Glancing quickly at the way out of the clearing, he saw that another wolf was moving down the path, stopping as it reached the mouth of the trail.

Their way was blocked. They would have to deal with these wolves. Jake let his pack slide down from his shoulder and held it in his hand. Watching the lead wolf for any sign that it was ready to charge, he carefully reached in to pull his weapon free.

"Let me, sir," Meara said softly. She had already dropped her pack and was holding one of the leather pouches that Mrs. Hodges had given her. She held it up to the lead wolf. "Do you know what this is?" she asked the animal.

The wolf eyed the object in Meara's hand suspiciously, keeping to the edge of the clearing but continuing to pace. Meara held the small bag up for the other wolf to see. She turned then and held it toward the opposite side of the clearing. Only then did Jake see two other wolves crouched down in the shadows of the brush.

The lead wolf began to creep inward, moving closer with each traverse, one side of the clearing to the other, always watching Meara, watching her gestures, looking for an indication that she would make good her threat.

"He's not going to back down." Jake slowly raised his knife.

"You won't need that, sir." Meara used her free hand to pull open the leather pouch. At that, the lead wolf stopped cold in his tracks. Jake looked quickly at the others, and then turned back to the leader. All were tensely observing Meara's movements.

"You should leave now," Jake said to the leader. The wolf bared its teeth and silently snarled, didn't advance or retreat.

Meara pleaded with the wolf. "Whatever your reasons for breaking the truce, is it worth your lives? You cannot win this."

The wolf gave a long, low growl, but still did not move.

There was the faintest of sounds behind them, like a whisper of air. Jake froze, but Meara instantly went into action. She held out her arm, leather pouch in hand, and began to spin about. A cloud of deadly dust formed around her, expanding outward, reaching out toward the wolves that were rushing at her.

Meara was knocked backward, thrown off her feet by one of the wolves that found itself leaping through the cloud. Jake dropped to the ground and threw his weapon at it, striking it behind the shoulder just as it hit Meara; it was dead before the two of them hit the ground.

The other wolves had tried to turn away from the poison, but neither made it alive to the edge of the clearing.

Only the lead wolf, which had not charged, survived. Jake had rolled over onto his knees and turned toward it. He couldn't see it at first, but as the dust began to disperse he caught the silhouette of the animal as it moved in the shadows beyond the perimeter.

Meara pushed aside the dead wolf lying on top of her and climbed slowly to her feet. She grabbed the second leather pouch and held it high over her head.

She was letting the wolf know that she was ready for it, was waiting for it, and was willing to kill it should it follow them. Only when she was sure that she had made her point did she lower her arm, then wearily dropped to her knees.

"That's really potent stuff," said Jake.

Meara looked down at the empty pouch, nodded. "Yes, sir."

"What about us?"

"Not harmful to us. Only the wolves."

They are not like us.

Jake saw several birds in the brush, happily hopping from branch to branch.

They're not like any animal from this world.

"This clearing will be death to them for many days," said Meara. "It will settle onto the ground, will be active for weeks. A wolf kicks it up as it passes through, it breathes it in..." Meara stood up and walked over to her pack. She stuffed the now empty pouch into it and pulled the pack up to her shoulder. "I think I'm ready to go home now."

"Meara will be fine," Mrs. Hodges said consolingly. "In her brief life, she has had to face much worse."

Jake watched Mrs. Hodges busily moving about the kitchen preparing food for the midday meal. He was sitting at the kitchen island, a glass of iced tea and a small blueberry muffin in front of him, just as he had so many times as a child. The room, the woman, the atmosphere, all helped to soothe his tattered nerves. That at least was something. It helped. But his bruised bones and torn muscles and ligaments would take time, not ambiance, to heal.

"That's hard to imagine," said Jake. He thought about all that had happened on just this one trip. It was a miracle they had made it home.

"I can't speak to dragons and deserts," said Mrs. Hodges, "but missy has been dealin' with wolves and the Outland all her life."

Jake picked at the muffin, tossed a piece into his mouth. "I can see I missed a lot during my summers here."

Mrs. Hodges gave him a comforting side glance. "Now Master Jacob, why should a young cub like you have had to face such things? You warn't much more'n a baby."

"And an outsider at that."

"Oh, now—"

"I could hear it, even if you didn't say it."

"Young Master... most folks within the village walls have no idea of the goings-on in the Outland. And most that do, they choose not to face it or accept it."

Jake leaned forward and stared at his muffin. He studied it as if he might find something special about it. "What's with the wolves, Mrs. H?"

"I don't know what you mean."

"Sure you do. You have to know something. You came up with the potion to kill them."

"The potion wasn't my doing," Mrs. Hodges turned quickly to her vegetables, picked them up and tossed them into the sink. She turned on the water and started cleaning them. "Mister Gyles brought the recipe to me. I just mix the ingredients together."

"Meara's father was certainly a resourceful guy."

"That he was. Master Quigley himself aside, I doubt he came second to anyone else in Serpent's Keep."

"So... what did the resourceful Mister Gyles have to say about the wolves?"

Mrs. Hodges stopped her work, stared thoughtfully at the vegetables in the sink. "I do remember he once said... he said they were '*allied to an evil born of another land*'. Them's his words, as best I remember 'em."

"The Rhetani?" Jake asked. *What else could it be?*

"Didn't say. Don't know if he knew." She began cleaning the vegetables again. "He did say they came to the Outland millennia ago, and with 'em came all the malevolence that exists there." She smiled thinly, "Don't know if he meant that for true or was sayin' it for color."

Jake was still sitting at the counter long after Mrs. Hodges had left the kitchen; his iced tea gone, his muffin eaten. He was staring down at the empty glass when Mr. Griffin came into the room, on his way to the pantry.

"Good afternoon, Master Jacob." Mr. Griffin continued on toward the tall, narrow door.

Jake spoke up, still looking down at his glass. "Mr. Griffin. You remember that pistol I found?"

Mr. Griffin stopped and turned to Jake. "Rather an antique, if I recall."

"Do you think you could find some bullets for that thing?" Jake looked up from his glass and directly at Mr. Griffin. "In that *other* market of yours?"

"It is possible, sir."

Jake turned his attention back to his empty glass.

"Let's do that."

Jake couldn't sleep. For the third night in a row he wandered the mansion and its grounds late into the night, looking through the books in the library, studying the artifacts and maps in the command center, standing before the stone dragons in the Hall of Statues and silently asking each of them for some sign, some guidance. He still had no idea where his uncle might be, or what he might have been doing when he disappeared. There were certainly enough dangers out there, and it would certainly be reasonable to assume that Tobias had fallen victim to one of them, but Jake didn't think it was a simple as that.

Yes, the wolves could have turned on him, or the bandits could have gotten him, or one of the dragons.

He could have fallen off a cliff...

Jake didn't believe that it was any of those things. He believed that something specific about the quest had gotten him, had swallowed him up.

The quest...

Tobias hadn't collected any of the artifacts; that had been left to Jake.

So what had he been doing in those last weeks?

Jake stepped out of the dining room and into the main hall. Straight ahead was Mr. Griffin's room. He could see a sliver of light at the bottom of the door. Griff often stayed up late, making extensive use of the library.

Jake turned to go up the stairs. He decided that he might as well grab a book himself and settle in for another fitful night.

Instead, he veered left of the staircase and stepped into the shadow of the narrow hall beside the main stairs and came to the door beneath the staircase that led down to the basement. He seldom went down there himself, but he knew the staff stored extra supplies and equipment there. He had gone through the shelves and boxes more than once during his recent searches of the house.

Now, though, light coming from under the door had caught his attention.

*Oh, Mr. Griffin...*thought Jake. *What are you up to now?* He opened the door and stepped through, stood at the top of the landing and looked down the steep, narrow stairwell. He could see a small square of the basement floor at the foot of the stairs, but no movement, no shadows gliding across his vision.

He started quietly down the stairs, but not so quietly as to imply that he was trying to sneak up on the old man. Ol' Griff's activities might be completely innocent, and Jake didn't want to storm in on the man looking for a jar of peaches.

On the other hand, skulking about the basement in the middle of the night did seem a bit out of the ordinary.

Except... well, Jake was skulking, had been skulking about the place for three nights running...

The basement was divided into two sections. The first was lined with shelves stacked with large boxes of supplies used to replenish the containers kept in supply rooms upstairs. One shelf on the left held the overflow of Mrs. Hodges' canning.

Jake walked through the first room and into the second room filled with plastic-lined bins. To the left were the kitchen bins, to the right, inside a mesh cage, were the yard and garden bins.

Mr. Griffin was standing at the far wall. He had slid aside one section of shelf that lined the wall and was staring at the wooden panel behind it. The grain of the wood was twisted into great whorls and jagged designs.

"I believe that you will succeed in gathering together the artifacts from the Other Worlds, Master Jacob," said Mr. Griffin, speaking over his shoulder.

"I hope so," Jake said uncertainly.

"And when you do, what then?"

Jake stepped up beside Mr. Griffin, tried to see what the old man saw. "I'll use them to open the gate to the Rhetani."

"Where will you do this? Where is this very special gate to which Master Quigley served as Guardian?"

Jake suddenly shivered. "Here?"

"Would it not make sense that he would keep such a thing close at hand?"

Uncle Tobias built his mansion on top of the gate?

Mr. Griffin continued. "No one can remember when the estate was not here. No one can remember the village without this mansion."

"You think the mansion came first, and the village was built around it?"

"The gate came first."

Jake imagined Tobias Quigley, many hundreds of years ago, standing as Guardian over the gate that led to the world of the Rhetani, just as Nehman stood watch in the Other World of the desert. Only this gate, this obelisk in the heart of the Outland, was special. This Outland, serving as the fulcrum for all the gates, was special.

The conflict with the Rhetani had reached its zenith, and in desperation the gates had been closed, and the guardians had been put into place to watch over them.

Here stood Tobias Quigley, guardian at the center of the wheel, custodian to watch the Rhetani gate.

A keep to hold the Rhetani.

Serpent's Keep.

Mr. Griffin raised a hand and pointed at the wall in front of them, long hidden by the dusty section of shelf. "Do you see it?"

Jake looked closely at the panel. Hidden amidst the wood-grain patterns was a definite and familiar shape.

"It's one of the polygons." It matched the shape on one of the keys, and he knew to which statue the polygon belonged. "But, this can't be the gate."

"I believe there is a passageway behind this wall."

Jake moved his hand across the wood. It was cooler in the center, perhaps three feet across. "I see what you mean. There's air space beyond this wall."

"Perhaps a passage to the gate."

"So do we just tear down the wall?"

"I would guess that Master Quigley had a less invasive way of getting in, sir."

"Don't start getting cute with me, Griff," said Jake. He ran his fingers across the small section of wood formed by the polygon. "This feels different." He tried pushing it in, pulling it, twisting it, scratching it. Nothing he tried made any difference. "I'll bet this is the key, but I don't see how it works."

"May I? Sir?"

Jake stepped back, "Absolutely."

Mr. Griffin ran the tips of his long, bony fingers across the polygon. "I don't believe this is of the same material as the rest of the panel."

"Well, that's what I said. It doesn't feel the same."

"I don't believe it is wood at all."

Jake thought a moment. He gave a sudden, sharp nod. "It isn't the key... It's the lock."

He turned and started away. "I'll be right back." He hurried out of the basement and up to the front hall. He stomped up the main stairs to the second floor, thinking that there were times when this was a very big house.

He glanced quickly at the first statue in the Hall of Statues as he ran through and into the command center. He kept the ring of keys in the supply room. He found the one that he wanted as he quickly stalked back to the statue with the ring of keys held out in front of him.

Within the hidden compartment he found the scroll. He also found a bone dagger and the artifact.

Returning to the basement, he held up the artifact. "I do think I found our way in." He had left the scroll and the dagger upstairs.

Mr. Griffin stepped aside and Jake stood before the wall. He pressed the artifact against the polygon blemish on the panel.

He immediately felt a tingling, as if the artifact and the panel were somehow becoming electrically charged; perhaps a circuit was now completed. Jake heard a faint click and a door in the panel eased open an inch.

"Very good, Master Jacob."

"Thank you, Mr. Griffin." Jake stuffed the artifact into his pocket and pushed the door open. Beyond was a long, narrow hallway, most of which lay in darkness. "We're going to need light."

Mr. Griffin brought a lantern down from a nearby shelf. "Perhaps that would explain this, sir."

With the lantern lit, Jake and Mr. Griffin stepped into the hall. After thirty feet, the hall turned sharply right, and after another thirty feet turned left. Jake noted that there were no doors or other accesses. The hall was a tunnel. It was going to take them directly from the basement to the sole purpose for the access way.

Jake stepped into a room twenty feet on a side, and a ceiling that was at least twelve feet overhead. The walls were smooth and unbroken. There was no furniture; there were no objects of any kind.

But there was something set into the cement floor at the center of the room; a small inset in the shape of a hexagon. Jake knelt down before it and brushed his hand lightly over it.

"Look at this," he said softly, his words echoing in the chamber. There was a pattern inside the recess. The pattern divided the hexagon into six polygons. "This is it. This is how I open the gate to the Rhetani."

Restore the individual artifact pieces, restore the artifact to its original state... open the gate.

Mr. Griffin glanced around the empty room. "There is no obelisk like those you have described."

"Nor is there a dragon. Nonetheless, when the artifact is restored, the gate will make an appearance." Jake stood and studied the chamber. There was no telling how the gate might be hidden. "Maybe the whole room is the gate."

"Then we should use caution."

"I'll do that."

This was an important discovery, and Jake was excited. He was also terrified. This chamber, these bare walls, this cold stark floor, would be the last he ever saw of his world.

Chapter Fourteen

The owner and editor of the village newspaper had a pleasant face and manner, bright, inquisitive eyes, and from their few minutes of conversation Jake could assume a quick, sharp mind, though the man's thoughts seemed to jump from subject to subject at the slightest provocation.

Which might explain the condition of the office. The desk that separated the two of them was cluttered with paper and folders. The shelves that lined the walls were filled with haphazardly stacked books, binders and files.

Through the open door in the back wall, Jake could see a very old printing press dominating the center of the back room. The machine looked well taken care of, but the rest of the room looked to be in as precarious a state as the front room.

Jeb Rainey was very familiar with Tobias Quigley's trips into the Outland, as well as the recent excursions of the new Master Quigley. He agreed with Mr. Griffin's observation that Tobias' trips had been more frequent during his last few months, though he didn't know why. He had asked around a bit about what supplies Mr. Quigley had been taking with him on those trips, but the front-door suppliers revealed nothing extraordinary and his back-door suppliers revealed nothing at all.

"I of course looked into Tobias' disappearance, but in the end I found nothing."

"Did you go into the Outland?"

The editor smiled. "I limit my investigations to within the walls of the keep. I interviewed those in the village who would have been in the best position to know something."

"Such as?"

"Our constable, citizens on Gate Watch at the time, members of the Adventurer's Guild, and members of the Quigley Estate household."

"What's this Adventurer's Guild?"

"Ah, yes." Rainey's smile broadened. "The Guild. A rather odd assortment of self-proclaimed adventurers who purportedly seek out excitement and danger, but who for the most part sit around small tables in the Guild Hall and play Serpent's Ladder all day."

"So these guys don't actually go out into the Outland?"

"Some manage to tear themselves away from the Hall now and then. For a guide, though, you probably won't find anyone in the bunch as good as the one you've found in Meara Gyles. But, there are those among them with unique expertise, should you choose to take the time to meet with them." Mr. Rainey leaned over the paperwork covering his desktop. "Just remember to take all they say with a pound of salt."

The editor leaned back in his chair and gave a sage nod. He then gave Jake detailed directions to the hall, interspersing the instructions with tidbits of information on just about every building between the newspaper office and the guild, before suddenly leaning forward across the desk again and asking Jake what he was up to, if not searching for his uncle.

"That's pretty much it, Mr. Rainey. I'm simply trying to find Uncle Tobias."

The man smiled as if he had captured his quarry in a trap of words. "You don't believe that Tobias has passed on to the next life."

"Really don't know," said Jake. "I have doubts."

"Then where could he be?"

"If I knew that, I would just go there and get him." Jake stood and reached over the desk, shook the man's hand and thanked him. He wanted to get to the Guild hall and see if there was someone there whom he would be willing to have join him on his next trip out. He was serious about leaving Meara safely at home, but had seen the value in not going it alone.

He stood outside the newspaper office and tried to get his bearings. The air was damp and cool, and a thick gray fog lay over the village so that the rooftops were hidden and the streets took on the appearance of brick-lined, cobblestone tunnels.

"Hello, Jake!"

Jake looked in the direction of the voice and saw Sparta Vesper crossing the street and coming toward him. She looked as if she may have just finished up a long day at the café.

"Sparta," Jake put on a friendly smile. "How are you this afternoon?"

"Well enough." She came up beside him and stopped, folded her arms across her chest and took in the scene. "What possesses our newest citizen to stand out in the street on this dreariest of days? Lost?"

Jake indicated the newspaper office behind them. "Visiting."

"You know Jeb?"

"Nice gentleman. Friendly."

"And nosy."

"Tool of the trade, I suppose. How are things at the café?"

"Same. Always. You should drop in more often, Jake."

"I'll do that. Have some of that great coffee. Partake of much more than that, though, and I'll have to answer to Mrs. H. I'm walking a fine line as it is."

"Hodges?" Sparta's gaze took on a studied look. Jake could tell that Sparta was struggling with how much to say regarding the multifaceted Mrs. Hodges. She finally pasted on a careful smile. "She's one who'll be watching out for ya'. On that, you have no fear."

Sparta stepped closer and leaned in conspiratorially. She tried to look casual, but only managed to look more suspicious. "You take heed, though, Jake. There'll be those watching out for ya, and those just watchin'."

"How am I supposed to take that?"

"It means what it means. I may not be on the inside on most things, but I am close to the ground. There's some here that know more about the secrets of the Outland than others, and some what carry about with 'em dangerous secrets of their own."

Jake was growing increasingly irritated. "I don't suppose you'd like to point one or two of them out to me?"

Sparta was looking uncomfortable and anxious to move on. "You just mind what I say."

"How?"

She was already stepping away, backing into the street. "Very little happens in the Village without a reason, Jacob Quigley," she said, before turning and heading quickly away.

Jake stared after her in bewilderment, and after a few moments started more slowly in the same direction. He still wanted to check out the Adventurer's Guild before heading back home.

He took several wrong turns before finally finding the narrow side road that he had been directed to. He found an unmarked door midway down the long brick wall that spanned the length of the road and that the buildings behind it shared. As he prepared to go in, he saw a strange man watching him from the shadow of a recessed doorway on the other side of the street. The man's face looked weathered by time and events, and he stood slightly hunched over, as if standing straight would take too much effort.

Great... he thought. *Now she has me spooked...*

Jake opened the door and went inside. In the small foyer, a man stepped up to a counter beside an open double door, beyond which Jake could see a large room with half a dozen tables, half of them occupied with one or two men each.

"Can I help you?" the man asked.

"I'd like to go in, if that's all right?"

"Are you a member?"

What an asinine question... have you ever seen me before?

"Not at the moment, no."

"A guest, then."

"Yeah. A guest."

"Of whom?"

"Mr. Rainey suggested that I come here." He didn't need this. "Listen, if you're gonna make a big stink about it, I'll just leave."

"And you are?" the man arched one brow.

"Quigley," said Jake, quite ready to leave.

"I see." After a moment's hesitation, during which time the stuffy old turd gave Jacob Quigley a thorough look-over, he stepped over to the double door and waved his arm, bidding entrance. "You are most welcome, Mr. Quigley. Please consider yourself an honorary member of the Guild."

Jake entered the main hall without saying another word. Several of those inside glanced up at him, but most did their best to ignore the newcomer. All had no doubt heard the exchange and knew that there was someone attempting to enter and exactly who that someone was.

They would do their utmost to restrain their enthusiasm.

Jake walked casually over to the nearest occupied table. Two older men were playing a dice game. One of the men gave a gruff grunt and handed the cup and dice to the other. He put a score on a pad, spoke without looking up. "Mister Quigley. Have you ever played Serpent's Ladder?"

"Afraid not."

"You should try it sometime."

The second man spoke up. "But not now and not here."

"Don't be disrespectful, Madsen," the first man said sharply.

Madsen studied the throw of his dice. "We're in the middle of a game, Jeffers. I don't want to start over."

"Not a problem," said Jake. "I don't want to interrupt." Looking around the room, he noticed a man watching him from a corner table. When the man nodded a silent hello, Jake walked over and stood before the table.

"Good evening," said Jake.

"Good evening, Mr. Quigley," said the man. He nodded at the two men playing dice. "Ignore them. They've been unpleasant for forty years. I don't think they would know how to be otherwise."

"I'll try not to let it get to me."

The man leaned forward and held out his hand. "I'm Troy McLaughton." They shook hands, and McLaughton indicated an empty chair. He watched Jake pull out the chair and settle in. He had a friendly face, but there was an air of deviousness about him that Jake couldn't quite point to. "What brings you to the Guild, Mr. Quigley?"

"Curiosity."

McLaughton smiled. "A vital component in the character of the adventurer. That, and greed."

"Is that why you're in it, Mr. McLaughton? Looking to get rich?"

"It pays the bills," McLaughton shrugged, not taking offense. "But curiosity and excitement are just as important to me. At the moment, I'm quite curious as to what you are all about."

"Loyalty, honor, all that pompous, high-brow stuff."

McLaughton gave out a genuine, cheerful laugh. "Excellent," he said, nodding. "I like that."

"And just what is it that you do, Mr. McLaughton, when you're out there adventuring?"

"Tracking mostly. Guiding, some."

"You know your way around the Outland pretty well, then?"

"Are you looking for a guide, Mr. Quigley?"

"Just curious; like I said."

"So you did. I understand that Meara Gyles has been shepherding you around."

"We've made a few trips out."

McLaughton nodded slowly. "She knows her way around, so long as you stick to the more traveled routes."

"I have no complaints," said Jake.

"You lookin' to go beyond the more traveled routes, Mr. Quigley?"

"We've managed a few deviations on our own, and I may have plans for one or two more."

"Perhaps you could use a little more muscle."

"Meara has acquitted herself quite well in that regard, Mr. McLaughton." Jake studied the man carefully. "But, I wouldn't be opposed to bringing along a trustworthy sort, one who is familiar with the

Outland and able to respond appropriately, when faced with the unexpected."

"There is little out there I haven't seen, Mr. Quigley, and even less that I can't handle."

"Overconfidence is not a trait that I'm looking for in a travelling companion, Mr. McLaughton."

McLaughton gave a dismissive shrug. "Just stating fact."

"The opinion of someone who mistakenly believes that he has seen it all." Jake stood up. "Pardon my bluntness, but whatever you've seen, whatever you've encountered, you have yet to leave the park. I don't hold that against you. That is to be expected. But I need someone with some imagination."

Jake turned and started away. He had taken three steps when McLaughton sat up straight and called after him.

"All right, Mr. Quigley. You have my attention. How about I buy you a cup of coffee?"

Jake took a few more steps and stopped near the table of the two men playing Serpent's Ladder. When he looked at Jeffers, Jeffers gave him a knowing smile before rolling the dice.

Jake gave Jeffers a wink, turned back to look at McLaughton. "A quick cup, and then I really have to go. Mrs. H. will have my hide if I'm late for dinner."

Jake told McLaughton very little about his experiences other than those of the Outland itself, though he did allude to the fact that there was something more. He dropped hints as to creatures beyond the unique creatures of the Outland. All of this was to gauge the man's reaction and try to draw out specifics on what the man may already have seen.

He found that McLaughton had made quite a number of the trips into the Outland, and had crossed paths with the obelisks, though he saw them as ancient stone markers and did not discern their real purpose or power. And he had faced the wolves on several occasions.

He had also been to the ravine, and had seen the silhouettes of great flying creatures within the abyss. He had wanted to go into the ravine, but hadn't been able to at the time. He planned to return there one day.

He and Jake came to an agreement, a fair flat rate for services for five to seven days. With a deal struck, Jake told him that he sought a stone marker to the east, and from there a Dark Lake.

"I know the marker you're looking for, but there's no lake to the east, dark or otherwise."

"You show me the stone obelisk, Mr. McLaughton, and I'll show you the lake."

"You're the boss, Mr. Quigley."

Tomorrow, then," said Jake, standing. "East gate."

"First light," said McLaughton. He stood and they shook hands again. Jake turned and started across the room.

"Hah! Look at this Quigley!" said old man Jeffers, pointing to the dice on the table. Jake stopped and tried to make since of it. "Dragon's Tail, son. A tough roll to get."

"I see," said Jake.

"It should be worth more; don't you think?"

"I really wouldn't know."

"Sure you would, son," said Jeffers. "Sure you would."

Jake stood at the island counter in the kitchen stuffing supplies into his backpack. Meara stalked out of the room just as Mr. Griffin entered.

Jake spoke up without looking up from this packing.

"You here to give me grief?"

"Absolutely not, Master Jacob."

"I got enough from Meara."

"Mr. McLaughton is adequate, if not always fully aboveboard."

"I don't want Meara to get hurt."

"I understand."

"You don't agree?" Jake stopped his packing and looked curiously up at Mr. Griffin. "You weren't all that keen on my bringing her along before."

"She has served you well; but I fully understand your concern for her safety." Mr. Griffin took a long, cautious breath. "My own concern at the moment is for your safety."

"McLaughton will do."

"I believe it is specifically in regard to Mr. McLaughton that Miss Gyles takes issue."

Jake closed his backpack and lifted it from the counter. "He knows only what he needs to know to get me to the next obelisk."

"Of course." Mr. Griffin stood silent. Jake looked at him warily, sensing there was something else. Mr. Griffin took an awkward step toward the counter as he reached into his jacket pocket.

He brought out four bullets and set them on the counter.

Chapter Fifteen

The sandy soil formed a narrow strip of beach opening out to the dark lake. Jake and Troy McLaughton stood at the water's edge, looking out across the black, glassy surface to a small island out in the heart of the lake.

Dark, heavily shadowed forests encircled the lake. The sky overhead was a sooty grey.

This Other World was a dark, still place. It made Jake feel uneasy.

McLaughton had been good to his word, taking Jake directly to the gate. From the possible description that Jake had provided, McLaughton assumed that it could have been no other clearing in the East Outland.

Accessing the gateway hadn't been quite as straightforward.

> *Toward the birth of day and the birth of life. Walk the path of reflection and enter there, search then within the hidden world to which those above are blind.*

While the *birth of day* reference had brought them east, once the stone was found, Jake continually looked to the second line for the way to access the gateway. He just assumed there was something that he had missed when it came to the rest of the first line, and simply ignored it.

Once he forced himself to look at the *birth of life* reference as the possible key, the solution came, albeit with much difficulty.

He had noticed a concave recess set into the top of the stone, as if something that might be created by thousands of years of water dripping onto the stone and slowly creating a cup-like pocket. He had wondered about it, having not seen anything like it on the other stones that he had come upon. He had even tried pressing the spot, but nothing had happened.

Wasn't water supposed to be birth of life?

Jake took his canteen and poured water into the depression. He stepped back then and waited.

Nothing happened.

He stepped back toward the stone and looked into the depression. The water was gone.

Startled, he took a step back and studied the stone, looking for a sign that it was going to turn into the gateway. After a few moments, he saw something. He almost missed it, as he wasn't looking for it. He was looking for the mysterious change from solid stone to ethereal gateway.

There was a small dark spot on the face of the stone. He was certain it hadn't been there before. Moving nearer, he raised a hand and lightly brushed a finger across the spot.

It was damp.

Jake pushed in. There was a slight give. Jake stepped back and watched as the obelisk became a gateway to an Other World.

Now, as he and McLaughton stood at the shore of the lake, Jake felt drawn to the island beyond, but he wasn't sure how the text of the scroll could mean the island.

Walk the path of reflection could mean that they had to cross the water, perhaps even walk on the water.

"You figure whatever it is you're looking for is out there?" asked McLaughton, pointing to the island.

Jake nodded silently. He hadn't told McLaughton about the artifacts, the gateways or the scrolls. He hadn't even warned the man about the possibility of coming face to face with dragons, beyond telling him to watch out for unexpected obstacles that might stand in their way.

Meara had been very outspoken in her objections to Troy McLaughton, and it had been more than just leaving her behind in favor of the man. She knew McLaughton, mostly through reputation, and didn't like or trust him. He was going to find out about the gateways, about the Other Worlds, and about the artifacts. With such knowledge, he could become a dangerous man and a powerful enemy.

Jake didn't completely trust the man either, but had weighed the pros and cons and believed that he was making the right decision. McLaughton would be told only what was needed in order to help recover the artifact and return to Serpent's Keep.

None of this made Meara feel any better. He might not start out knowing very much, but in the end he would inevitably know way too much.

Staring out across the water, McLaughton stated that if they were going to get out to the island, they were going to need a boat. They split up, McLaughton heading north and Jake going south, agreeing to check back in a few minutes, boat or not.

Jake followed the shore for several hundred yards, having to skirt around thick brush a number of times but always managing to stay within site of the shoreline. He saw nothing, and, more ominously, he heard nothing. It was all deathly quiet.

Still, the air wasn't too hot or cold, wasn't too muggy, and the terrain was easily traveled. Despite some uneasiness that he couldn't quite shake, Jake was beginning to regret not allowing Meara to come with him. Particularly as he held the same misgivings as she did regarding McLaughton and the knowledge that he was going to come away with from this trip. He could cause trouble.

Jake returned to the beach to find McLaughton standing beside a small wooden boat.

"Nice work," said Jake.

"Found it tied to a little dock a couple of hundred yards up," said McLaughton. "I guess that means there's folks here after all."

Citizenry or visitors? Jake wondered. Or it could mean that there was a Guardian around, like Nehman. "We'll need to put it back, once we're done."

"If you say so." McLaughton held the bow of the boat steady and waved a welcoming arm, bidding Jake to climb aboard.

The journey out to the island was an eerily quiet, anxious one. Jake studied the water and the distant island as McLaughton worked the oars. The only sound was that of the wooden shafts of the oars twisting within the metal eyelets and the blades pushing easily into the water.

They appeared to be all alone; just the tree-lined shore, the lake, the island, the oppressive gray sky, and the two of them in a borrowed small, wooden boat.

And yet there were scurrying shadows moving about beneath the black, glassy surface of the water. They may have been nothing more than a trick of the eye as the boat glided through the water and the reflections of the low-hanging sky dancing across the mirror-like surface.

Jake thought it was more than that, but said nothing.

As they approached the island, the blackness behind the trees and heavy brush reached out to them and drew them in. Jake spotted an inlet and a clear stretch of shore inside it and directed McLaughton toward it. The air grew cool and damp and there was a strange heaviness about it.

Once the boat was secured, McLaughton took a moment to study their surroundings. The vegetation grew all the way to the water line on either side of them, and it was only where they had come ashore that there was any open ground at all.

"There," McLaughton said finally, pointing to a location in the tree line. Jake didn't see anything, but followed his guide. Reaching the brush that reached out from the trees, McLaughton pushed the bramble aside and stepped into the shadows.

The path, such as it was, led them inland, meandering in and around twisted trees and large, misshapen bushes. Again and again, McLaughton stopped and knelt down close to the ground to examine signs that would tell him if the nearly invisible trail led one way or another, or if the left fork or the right fork was the most used and hopefully the correct trail.

As they traveled, Jake struggled to hear a sound, any sound, that wasn't of their own making. He tuned out his breathing, his footfalls, and the brush of air against his eardrums as he walked. He tuned out the light footfalls of his guide.

What remained was silence. No animal noises, no rustling of a faint breeze through the canopy overhead. Nothing. It was as if this world wasn't there, that it was but a three-dimensional snapshot of a world from another time or place; it was as if they had stepped into a picture.

McLaughton stopped and waited for Jake to come forward. Without turning to acknowledge his presence, McLaughton nodded toward a large clearing ahead of them. In the heart of the clearing stood a small open temple; stone pillars at the corners supporting a flat stone roof.

"This what you lookin' for, Mr. Quigley?"

"Most likely, Mr. McLaughton." Jake looked around the clearing before stepping into the open. There was no movement, no sign of danger. He left the shadows of the trees and moved out onto the damp green grass that surrounded the little temple. Reaching the stone steps, Jake stopped and looked around again at the surroundings.

It was eerily peaceful. Well... the scroll did say to *walk the path of reflection...* and this would certainly be a quiet place to reflect; reflect on what, he had no idea. He turned and climbed the three steps up into the building.

The walls were open to the elements, with thick stone pillars standing at each corner, holding up a wide, flat roof. At the center of the roof was an opening in the shape of an oval, three feet wide and six feet long. The opening was directly above a large pool of water set into the center of the smooth stone floor of the building. The pool might have been kept filled by rainwater from overhead.

"Okay, you got me," said McLaughton. "I've never seen anything like this place before. Temples, yeah, but this... this is just weird." He walked along one side of the pool, studying the black water and the opening overhead. The pool was twenty feet long by eight feet wide, taking up a major portion of the interior of the temple.

Reflecting pool...

The phrase came unexpectedly into Jake's thoughts. He wasn't really sure what it meant or just what a reflecting pool might be. It was just a phrase that he had heard somewhere.

Walk the path of reflection...

Jake stepped up to the pool and positioned his toes right up to the edge. The length of the pool ran directly away from him. Looking down at the water, it was impossible to see beneath the surface. He could see his reflection and the reflection of the ceiling with its oval opening exposing the gray sky.

He had a thought, then. He stepped out into the pool, one foot, followed quickly by the other. McLaughton turned and started to call out, then snapped his mouth shut.

Jake was standing on the surface of the water. He paused several seconds and then took two short steps and stopped.

"It's only half an inch deep," he said. He stared down at his feet. He saw only himself looking back, and the oval opening in the roof beyond.

Walk the path of reflection...

He took another cautious step, stood now at the center of the pool. He felt something shift beneath his foot and there was a hollow grinding sound.

"Quigley?" McLaughton asked uncertainly.

The thin layer of water began draining away from the pool. Directly in front of him, a section of the floor of the shallow pool slid aside as an access to a narrow stairwell yawned open.

"Not bad, Mr. Quigley," said McLaughton, stepping out onto the empty pool. He gazed down into the black pit of the stairwell. "You figure on you and me going down there?"

"That's the plan."

McLaughton shook his head doubtfully. "Okay," he said. "I'll be right behind you."

"I appreciate that." Jake pulled his pack from his back and dug around for his hand lamp.

With the dull sphere of light pushing its way ahead of him, Jake cautiously worked his way down the steep stairs. The stairwell was just wide enough for him climb down without having to turn sideways, and once he was fully inside, just barely tall enough that he didn't have to hunch over. The stone walls were damp, the air held a stagnate smell, heavy with mildew.

Reaching the bottom, Jake stepped out into the room and found that the ceiling was just as low as the stairwell. His head almost brushed the wet, mossy ceiling.

Search then within the hidden world to which those above are blind.

Okay, Jake thought. *I'm searching...* He held the lamp out in front of him and turned about in a slow circle. The light reached out to only one wall, the others beyond the reach of the lamp. He was going to have to move back to the stairwell and then follow the perimeter. McLaughton grumbled something about following right behind him and Jake started out.

He found an open doorway in the center of the far wall, and after investigating the rest of the room and finding nothing else, returned to it. The hallway beyond was very narrow and in some places the ceiling was so low that he had to crouch down to continue. It twisted and turned and sloped down and then up and then down again. There were no side passages, though occasionally Jake saw small, round openings set high in the wall that he suspected might provide what little air there was.

The passageway began sloping upward again, this time at a fairly steep grade. After eight or nine steps, it turned right, continuing the same steep rate of ascent. Once he made the turn, he was able to see a dull glow up ahead. He slowed and turned off the lamp. Behind him, McLaughton quietly readied his pistol.

Jake stepped out into a round cavern, the centerpiece of which was a large, dark pool. The ceiling overhead was riddled with hundreds of tiny openings, and through them Jake could just make out the gray sky beyond.

"Man, what's that stink?" McLaughton scrunched his face against the onslaught of the smell of dragon's nest.

"Keep a sharp eye out," said Jake.

"For what?" McLaughton walked cautiously to the right of the pool and Jake walked to the left.

"Something resembling a dragon."

"A what?"

"Dragon."

"You're kiddin', right?" McLaughton asked anxiously.

Jake stopped beside a bed of decayed and dried water plants and damp soil set into a recess in the far wall. It looked vaguely similar to the nest that he had found in the desert. "One lives here."

"Yeah? Doubt that." McLaughton pointed up at the ceiling, speaking now in a harsh whisper. "Nothing bigger than a raven is gettin' through there. And as for the way we came, well, if it's coming and going through there, it's gonna be a mighty puny dragon."

Jake indicated the pool. "That's its way in and out," he said. "Amphibian." The statue in the Hall of Statues had in fact looked like it lived in water but could walk on land.

"You mean like a salamander?" McLaughton leaned out over the water and looked in.

"I'm guessing it's a bit larger than your garden variety salamander." Jake indicated the bedding. Turning his attention back to the pool, he thought about the last stretch of passageway they had travelled and the uphill climb. Considering that, and the visible sky in the ceiling, he figured they were back up to ground level. "I bet this connects to the lake," he said. "There's probably an underground waterway leading out to it."

"And this giant salamander of yours spends his days out there, and comes in here to sleep?" McLaughton was not quite convinced as to the whole dragon thing, but was growing slowly more concerned. He could think of more plausible explanations for all of this than dragons, amphibious or otherwise. Still, if any of what this guy was saying was true... "Then how about we find whatever it is you're looking for and get out of here before it comes back?"

"Excellent idea, Mr. McLaughton." Jake climbed up onto the creature's bedding and began digging around with his feet. McLaughton watched, grimacing at the smell emanating from the decomposing mulch that this mysterious animal slept on.

"What am I supposed to be looking for?" he asked.

"Smooth, flat polygon, a few inches across."

"Poly what?"

"A geometric artifact. Flat, about half an inch thick; polygon shaped, you know... rectangle with extra sides."

"What?"

"You'll know it when you see it."

McLaughton glanced around the cavern. There weren't a lot of places to hide one of these *geometric artifacts.* He wandered slowly about, looking into shadows, scratching at the dusty floor with his foot. All the while, he kept an anxious watch on the dark pool, expecting Quigley's mysterious dragon to make an appearance. "Ya' know, a serpent is snake. Dragons have legs."

"What?" Jake glanced up for a moment, returned to digging around the nest.

"Serpents and dragons aren't the same thing."

"I didn't say they were."

"But it's called *Serpent's* Keep, not *Dragon's* Keep."

"Dragons might not be serpents, but serpents are dragons," Jake said impatiently. "Dragons without legs."

"What?"

Jake stopped searching. It wasn't in the nest.

"Do you know all about dragons? Maybe the dragon at Serpent's Keep didn't have legs."

"There's a dragon at Serpent's Keep?"

"I don't know."

"Interesting," said McLaughton. He still thought this Quigley character was a bit bonkers. But... he was Tobias Quigley's nephew, and Tobias Quigley was into some pretty weird stuff. "So, if a serpent is a dragon, and a snake is a serpent, then is a snake a dragon?"

"I didn't say *all* serpents were dragons."

"Sure you did."

"I don't know. I'm not a dragonologist."

"A dragon-what?"

"I didn't name your village."

"I know that, but I thought you said—" McLaughton gave up and shook it off. He put his hands on his hips. "Your poly-whatever isn't here, Mr. Quigley."

Jake stepped down off the nest and took several steps toward the pool. He stopped at the water's edge.

McLaughton studied the man's face, then looked down into the water. A faint panic washed over his face. "Nuh-uh. Not me."

Jake sighed. "If it's not up here, it has to be down there."

"I don't care."

"I'll do it."

"You said it yourself. The dragon is in there."

"I thought you didn't believe in my dragon."

"I believe there's *something.*"

Jake pulled off his shoes and sat down, slid his feet into the water. At least it wasn't cold. He wouldn't die of hypothermia before getting eaten by a giant salamander. "Wish me luck," he said, and slipped into the water.

"Well, *duh.* You haven't told me how we're supposed to go back through that gate."

Jake grinned and let himself drop beneath the surface.

The water was dark but clear, and whereas from above he could see nothing, from beneath the surface he could see a fairly good distance. He wasn't able to see all the way across the pool, however, so he concentrated his efforts on the near side first, using his hands to push himself deeper and deeper.

There was no life visible in the water. The wall was rough stone with very few recesses. It was as eerily quiet in the water as it was in the woods of the island above. It made Jake nervous.

After going down twenty or twenty five feet, he returned quickly to the surface to catch his breath. He gave McLaughton a quick *'nothing yet'* and slid back under the surface again, moving to another section of the cavern pool.

On his third trip beneath the surface, Jake found a large tunnel opening in the wall about twelve feet down. Afraid at first that the as yet unseen dragon would rush out at him, he frantically pushed himself back and up, scrambling out of the water as soon as he reached the surface.

"What is it?" McLaughton leapt up and back, certain that something was going to come flying out of the pool at him.

"A tunnel," Jake said between deep breaths. "I found a tunnel."

"Yeah..." McLaughton looked at Jake with a puzzled expression. "Well you said the pool was connected to the lake."

"No. I think that's deeper down. This is different. This goes somewhere else."

"Your dragon has a summer cottage?"

Search then within the hidden world to which those above are blind.

"I'm going to have to go in there," he said.

"You be careful," said McLaughton, as Jake slid back into the water.

"I know," Jake smiled. "I gotta show you the way out of here."

"Exactly."

Jake slipped beneath the surface and vanished from sight, leaving McLaughton staring at his own reflection.

Jake quickly swam down to the tunnel entrance, stopped and stared directly into it, placing one hand on the rim of the opening to steady himself. He saw nothing but black. Realizing that he was either going to have to go into the tunnel immediately or return to the surface, he pushed himself into the darkness.

He propelled himself by pushing himself first off one wall and then the other, noting that the underwater tunnel was large enough to accommodate a dragon, albeit a slim one: long and sleek and amphibious; and capable of reaching out from the darkness and snapping up unwary intruders.

Half a minute into the tunnel, Jake considered turning back. He had no way of knowing how much further he might have to go, but did know how far he would have to go to get back to the surface. If he continued much further, he would have trouble making it out.

Just as the phrase *beyond the point of no return* came to mind, he thought he could see a faint glow in the water far ahead. He rushed forward, almost in a panic, hurtling himself towards the dull light. It grew slowly brighter, which encouraged him to continue pushing onward.

The underground waterway opened abruptly into a pool similar to the one that he had left behind, and he quickly swam up to the surface. After taking several moments to breathe in fresh oxygen, he looked about and glided toward the nearest bank.

He was in a cavern of sorts, though the dome-like roof had large, gaping holes opening to the sky. The interior was exposed enough that there were trees and brush growing in the cavern, and there was a groundcover of grass and weed over much of the floor.

There was no dragon, and no sign that a dragon lived there.

An alter stone stood near one wall. On it was a box similar to the one that Jake had found in the Abandoned City, and in the box was the artifact.

He suspected that if he had searched around enough in the caves of the Desert world oasis, he probably would have found an alter stone there as well, but in that world the dragon had taken the artifact and hidden it in its nest.

Finding an alter with a box containing an artifact in two different worlds was definitely a good sign. This gave Jake a commonality to look for once he was through a gate and had used the scroll to reach the location in the next Other World.

McLaughton was staring down at him as Jake surfaced once again in the main cavern. "You were gone a long time, Mr. Quigley," he said, reaching down to pull Jake out of the water. He sounded very relieved.

"Sorry about that," Jake sat at the edge of the pool and took a moment to catch his breath.

"Did you find what you were looking for?"

Jake pulled the artifact out of his shirt and handed it to McLaughton. He saw no reason to hide it from him. If the man had bad intentions, not showing him what he found wasn't going to stop him.

McLaughton looked unimpressed. "This is it, huh?"

"That's it."

"What's it do?" McLaughton tossed it casually back to Jake.

Jake stood and walked over to his backpack. "It's just one part of a puzzle, Mr. McLaughton," he said, stuffing the artifact safely away.

"Puzzle..." McLaughton said flatly.

"Yep." Jake lifted his pack and slung it over his shoulder. "How about we get out of here?" He wanted to get as far from the cavern as possible, as quickly as possible. While the artifact hadn't been easy to find, at least he hadn't had to do battle for it, and he would just as soon keep it that way.

They took the long, narrow passageway back to the stairwell and eventually climbed out and up to the temple. It was as quiet as when they had last been there, what seemed like days earlier but in fact had only been a few hours. Dark shadows lay over the scene, crawling in from the surrounding woods. Jake found the entire island creepy, and the temple clearing gave him the willies.

The walk back through the forest to the boat was long and overshadowed with the heavy sensation that something was about to happen; something bad... Jake and McLaughton hardly spoke at all throughout the entire return journey, and Jake was certain that his companion was fighting that same ominous sense of impending disaster. When they finally stepped out of the woods and onto the small beach, he had the odd feeling that they had somehow averted some great and horrible confrontation.

They silently pushed the boat into the water and left the island, grateful for their good fortune.

Then, halfway between the island and the shore, just as Jake was beginning to shake off the gloom and doom that he had been wrapped in, there was a surge beneath the boat and the smooth, sleek head of a serpent-like dragon rose up from the water directly beside them. The curve of its long neck undulated as the creature rolled its back slowly forward and backward, rising up and looking down upon the two humans in the tiny, wooden boat. It twisted its head and studied first McLaughton and then Jake.

"Greetings," it said at last, its calm voice as smooth and slippery as its damp, shiny skin.

McLaughton started for his weapon, but Jake held his arm. McLaughton gave a quick, questioning look, and then relented, though he didn't look happy about it.

"Hello," said Jake.

"What brings you uninvited to my water?" The cadence of the sentence curled as the curve of the neck rolled down from head to shoulder. The dragon wore the disquieting façade of a broad, slippery smile. It had observed the response of both humans, and had calculated various possible scenarios.

"We are on a gathering quest for my uncle, Tobias Quigley."

The dragon looked unsurprised and unimpressed. "I smell Quigley blood, human, but I see only you..."

"Tobias Quigley and I are of the same family; the same blood."

"Even if that be true, how does that give you the right to come unbidden into my home?"

McLaughton leaned close to Jake. "Talk isn't how we're going to deal with this, Quigley," he said harshly.

"Your companion is not of a friendly sort, is he, human?"

"My name is Jacob Quigley." *Was this dragon more articulate than the others that he had come across, or just more slippery with words?*

"Jacob Quigley," breathed the dragon. "I take seriously the responsibility given me."

"I understand your responsibility. The same as has been given to others I have met on my quest. They have seen and understood my duty, given to me by my uncle."

"The gathering..." the dragon said silkily.

"Yes."

"No," the dragon said suddenly and sharply, turning its gaze quickly away from the human. He sniffed the air noisily. "You have taken that which belongs to me. I will have it back."

"That's it," said McLaughton, and he pulled out his weapon. Jake struck McLaughton's arm and grasped the man's wrist.

"Stop it, you dolt."

The dragon held its chin high in the air, but turned its gaze askance down at the two humans in the boat. It carefully watched the interaction between them.

When Jake and McLaughton finally returned their attention to the creature, it gave a loud grunt-like *snuffing* sound, and then waited, no longer deigning to look at the intruders.

Jake stood slowly, careful not to tip over the boat. He held his hands out and spoke respectfully. "You have served well as Guardian of the artifact. I stand before you now and humbly ask that you allow me to fulfill my duty. Please, allow me to pass."

The dragon looked down at the human for a long time. Jake could hear the creature's breathing, the only other sound being the placid noise of the water thumping gently against the hull of the boat.

"Blood of Tobias Quigley," the dragon said at last, speaking in a slippery but formal tone, "You... and your unpleasant attendant, may pass."

The dragon slid beneath the surface of the lake so smoothly that there was almost no ensuing wake. Jake waited several moments before carefully returning to his seat.

"We can go now," he said.

"That was something," said McLaughton, putting away his weapon. He took hold of the oars. "I still think we could have taken it."

"It's on our side, Mr. McLaughton."

"Didn't look that way to me."

It was almost dark when Jake and McLaughton stepped through the gate and returned to the Outland, so they decided to make camp near the gate obelisk and start the trip back to the village in the morning. It was only a day's journey, and if all went well they could be home by nightfall the next day.

Once McLaughton had finished his inspection of the perimeter, he returned to Jake and sat down beside his gear. He pulled out his canteen and took a deep swallow, then watched as Jake got the kindling burning. "A cup of coffee sounds good about now," he said.

"We have enough for one more pot." Jake was starting the campfire in the fire pit they had used during their time spent in the clearing earlier; the days during which Jake had searched for a way to open the gateway.

"Okay," McLaughton sighed. "It can wait till morning."

McLaughton looked over at the stone as if reassessing a long-held belief. "I never knew the old girl had such a secret in her, Mr. Quigley. She surprised me."

"Come now, Mr. McLaughton... I wouldn't think that anything in the Outland could surprise you." There was just the slightest edge of sarcasm in his voice.

"Ah, my own words, back at me. Guess I deserve it." He gave Jake a studied look. "The other stones hold similar secrets, then?"

"I don't know about all of them."

McLaughton took a step nearer the stone. "Those things have been staring me in the face my entire life."

It was the middle of the night when Jake was awakened. The clearing was quiet, and was enveloped in a bluish glow. Sitting up, He saw that McLaughton had activated the gate and was standing mesmerized before it. Jake reached anxiously into the pocket of his backpack, was relieved when he found the artifact was still there.

He stood and approached McLaughton. "I wouldn't go in there," he said.

McLaughton spoke without taking his eyes from the glowing magic in front of him. "An amazing piece of work."

Jake stepped beside McLaughton, held the artifact out protectively. "Without this, you'd never get back."

McLaughton coolly watched Jake tuck the artifact into his shirt pocket. "Have you thought about the possibilities, Mr. Quigley? The opportunities that are opened up to you; and you alone know the secret."

"Not me alone."

"Where it counts, Mr. Quigley."

"As may be, Mr. McLaughton. But it's not about opportunity."

"It's always about opportunity." He indicated the artifact in Jake's pocket. "Of course, it doesn't really matter who knows, does it? Even if someone can figure out how to open a gateway, without an artifact, the specific artifact, it doesn't mean much, does it?"

"Depends on what that someone is after."

McLaughton silently agreed, then smiled and nodded in the direction of the open gateway. "How about letting me take a trip through and back?"

"I don't think so, Mr. McLaughton."

"What would it hurt? I'll be gone and back before you know it."

"It's not a toy."

"It's the greatest toy in the universe, Mr. Quigley."

Jake turned away from McLaughton and the gate. From past experience, he knew that if no one went through, the gate would eventually close on its own.

McLaughton reached out and grabbed Jake by the upper arm. "I think I'd like to go through." His tone strongly hinted that he was going to insist that he go through.

"Go right ahead." Jake tried to be just as stern. "I won't stop you."

"I'm going to need that little trinket."

Jake slowly shook his head no.

McLaughton softened his tone, but it came across more menacing. "I'll be right back... Mr. Quigley."

Jake looked down at McLaughton's grip on his arm, as if studying it. He looked up then into the eyes of the man.

"Stop and reflect, Mr. McLaughton. What do you think you're going to get from this one gate?"

"It's a start," said McLaughton, and with that he pulled Jake around and pushed him into the gate, holding onto him as he followed him in. Once inside, as they rushed toward the Other World of the Dark Lake, McLaughton dug into Jake's shirt with his free hand, and the two of them began to wrestle for the artifact.

Jake suddenly realized that McLaughton planned to strand him in the Other World. With the artifact in hand, he could reinitialize the gate and return alone. Once back in Serpent's Keep, without Jake to hinder him, he would no doubt attempt to locate the other artifacts that Jake had already gathered.

Jake absolutely could not let that happen.

He gripped tightly to the artifact; he brought up his right leg and, leaning back, put his foot against McLaughton's chest and pushed.

McLaughton's grip on Jake was broken.

Troy McLaughton just disappeared. He didn't fade away. He didn't slowly drift out of sight. He simply vanished.

Jake had entered the gateway first. He was the directing entity to the other side. So long as McLaughton held onto him, they could pass through together. Without Jake, McLaughton was lost somewhere in the in-between place. Jake didn't know what that meant, only that it had happened before to the marauders that he and Meara had confronted at another gate.

Jake knelt down beside the hexagon pattern in the floor of the Serpent's Gate room and set the latest artifact piece into place. He stood then and looked down at the partially completed artifact.

Mr. Griffin stood near the doorway to the hallway that led back to the mansion basement.

"I trust Mr. McLaughton was helpful?" he asked.

"Very subtle," said Jake. "Yes, he was helpful. No, I shouldn't have taken him."

"I'm very sorry to hear that." Mr. Griffin walked to center of the room and looked down at the pattern in floor. Three pieces were now in place.

When Jake had returned to the village alone, the guard on duty had not been the same person who had let them out a few days earlier, but he had known that Jake had left the village with Troy McLaughton and so asked about him. When hearing that McLaughton would not be returning, the guard had simply nodded and told Jake that he would need to check in with the sheriff.

The sheriff listened calmly and dutifully took down the facts, as Jake had described the incident. He glanced up from his paperwork at the mention of wolves, but chose not to press the matter. He no doubt suspected that McLaughton had attempted to move in on whatever Jake was doing and had paid the price, but for now it seemed that he would remain silent. An attack by wolves would do for now.

"Will he be a problem?" asked Mr. Griffin.

"No." Jake stated flatly and started toward the hall. "Mr. McLaughton won't be a problem."

Mrs. Hodges said little during dinner, but Jake could tell that she knew what had happened. By that time, most of the village must have known. Sheriff Smith had probably only informed those that needed informing, but they had no doubt told a few, and those few had told a few... and then of course there was the guard at the gate. He may not have known the facts, but he knew that Troy McLaughton wasn't coming back.

Jake had insisted on eating in the kitchen rather than the dining room, and regretted it. Mrs. Hodges' silence as she hustled about the room made him uncomfortable. It wasn't that he felt guilty about what had happened, nor did he think that she blamed him for it, but the whole thing had changed him and maybe that change had altered his relationship with Mrs. Hodges.

Later, as he lay awake in bed, unable to sleep, he thought about how this latest trip out might have gone if he had taken Meara instead of McLaughton. Certainly it would have taken longer to find the gateway, and McLaughton had definitely helped as they searched the paths on the island. And he wouldn't have liked for Meara to have had to face the dangers they had faced. He wondered whether he would have acted differently in the confrontations had Meara been beside him instead of Troy McLaughton. Would that have changed the outcome?

He had no idea what he was going to do on his next trip into the Outland.

Chapter Sixteen

Jake could barely make out the figure of the monk. A heavy fog was rolling through the forest and the trail ahead quickly faded into the wet mist. The robed man maintained a brisk pace, faster than Jake wanted to travel, and he had to stop and wait for Jake at each fork in the trail to ensure that Jake didn't get lost.

That was just too bad. Jake was walking as fast as he was willing. If the monk didn't like it, he could leave him behind. Jake had made this trip to the temple before and he could probably find his way again.

And after all, the man had come looking for him, not the other way around. That was surprising in itself, and Mr. Griffin had literally been at a loss for words when the monk had shown up at the mansion asking for Jacob Quigley. He had been even more taken aback when the monk had asked Jake to accompany him to the temple.

The guard at the West Gate had been just as surprised. The temple monks only rarely came to the village, usually for supplies they couldn't produce themselves or acquire elsewhere. They never came looking for residents of the village, and certainly never sought them out in order to escort them back to the temple.

So it must have been important.

So the monk could just slow down. Jake would walk at whatever pace he wanted and would get there whenever he got there.

The open clearing in front of the temple was shrouded in the same shifting mist as the rest of the Outland, and the tall temple spires reached into low, gray clouds that blanketed the world. The monk moved smoothly through the fog and stopped at the foot of the steps.

Standing at the top step was another monk, whom Jake recognized once he drew near.

"John," he said. He didn't really know what John's role in the temple was, but he thought of him as Peter's assistant.

"Hello, Master Quigley. It is good of you to come."

"My curiosity got the best of me. Your man here wouldn't tell me anything."

John nodded to Jake's escort, who silently climbed the steps and went into the temple. Once the monk had gone inside, John said softly, "Master Peter is most anxious to speak with you."

"What about?"

"That would be for Master Peter to address." John turned to the door. Jake gave up and climbed the steps. Once inside, John led him through the narrow hallways to the library. He left him there, stating simply that Master Peter would be with him shortly.

The library was much as it had been the last time he had been there. It smelled of ancient paper and old glue, and there was a golden glow emanating from the lamps. Jake went to one of the tables and casually turned the pages of several books that were stacked there. The words were of a language that he was not familiar with, and he closed the books one by one.

"Brother Jacob," said Peter, coming into the room. He closed the door behind him. "Good of you to come."

"So I hear."

"I hope it wasn't too much trouble." Peter moved to one of the larger tables, waving a hand for Jake to follow and sit in one of the high-back chairs.

"Not at all," said Jake.

"Good, good." Peter sat down, placed his arms on the table and clasped his hands together. He wore a genuine smile on his face. "You have been a busy man, Brother Jacob."

Jake shrugged in answer.

"Oh, come now, don't be modest. I have been kept apprised of your journeys into the Outland."

"Oh?"

"And all is going well?"

"Well enough," said Jake. He chose not to speak of the Other Worlds or of the artifacts. If the leader of the monks already knew of the Other Worlds, then he had chosen not to tell Jake of them during his last visit; and if he didn't know of the Other Worlds, then Tobias had chosen not to tell the monks, and there had probably been a reason. "Master Peter, you didn't bring me all the way out here to ask about my walkabouts."

"No, no, of course not." Peter stretched to his left and grasped a very large, very old book that was sitting on the table. He slid it in front of him and placed both hands flat on the leather cover. "This is a collection of narratives put down by the founding members of our order. They were written in an ancient, nearly forgotten dialect that was used, quite frankly, to keep those within the order *in the know,* and those not in the order *in the dark.*"

Jake indicated the shelves around them. "Many others in this... dialect?"

"Some of them very important works." Peter softly patted the ancient book in front of him. "As such, the necessity of learning the language."

"And what did you find this time that you think I need to know?"

"Yes," Peter raised a finger and pointed down at the book. "An interesting passage, considering your quest."

Jake visibly stiffened at the word *quest.* Peter leaned over the book and slowly nodded.

"It refers to a labyrinth. It is quite cryptic, and does not speak to specifics, other than to say that it lay in the path of a great quest."

"You believe that this quest is my quest?"

"I do."

"But how? I mean, if this thing was written hundreds of years ago—"

"Millennia ago, actually."

"Then how could the author know—"

"Brother Jacob... there is much that I do not know, but I can say with absolute certainty that the events of the distant past blazed the trail you now travel. Those who participated in those events knew the events in which you are now involved would occur."

Given all that had happened since his arrival at Serpent's Keep, Jake could no longer completely discount such a thing. And, considering the preparations that had been made at the time the gate to the Rhetani had been closed and the artifacts had been scattered to the Other Worlds, the people back then had indeed anticipated the events surrounding the gathering of them up again.

Okay, I can accept that they knew at least some of what would be faced by the person who would one day gather the artifacts.

"So, this labyrinth... I haven't come across one yet, so it must be something I have to look forward to. Where is it?"

"From what I can infer through my translations, I believe that it is not of this world," said Peter. He studied Jake's face for a reaction, but saw none. "There is also have a phrase that translates to something like '*The labyrinth lay beyond the way and in the path, and must be navigated*'."

Jake frowned, but said nothing.

"You will have to face this. It must be navigated."

"So I gather," said Jake. Somewhere beyond one of the gates, between the obelisk and wherever an Other World artifact was hidden, would be some sort of labyrinth. What made Jake anxious was that the writer of this manuscript had seen fit to document this. Up to now, all he had needed to know had been on the scrolls hidden away in the pedestals of the dragon statues. What made this different?

"And there is this," said Peter. He pulled a sheet of paper from the inside cover of the book and slid it across the table. On the paper, someone had recently drawn a diagram. Jake had only to glance at it to recognize it as one of the artifact symbols. "This image was annotated in the margins beside the text. There was no explanation."

"This will help," said Jake. He would be able to combine the information of the labyrinth with the scroll belonging to the statue that bore this symbol. He looked up from the paper and gave a gracious nod. "I appreciate this, Peter."

Peter slid the heavy book aside. "I have no doubt that we are all dependent upon the success of your undertaking."

"Of that I am increasingly certain."

It was a rare warm afternoon in Serpent's Keep. Jake and Meara sat at a table in the plaza across the way from the estate. An old map was spread out between them. Meara pointed to a location on the map.

"The North Highway is about two hours beyond the Farm. Take that west; it should get you where you need to go." The Farm was known to everyone in the Village. Most of their food was grown there. This highway, though, was new to Jake.

"I like the sound of that," he said.

Meara looked up at Jake. "It is still Outland. There will be dangers. There are some who prey on those traveling the highway."

"I've had to deal with bandits all over the Outland. How will this be different?"

"It won't. And the North Highway will get you there faster."

Jake sensed movement behind him and turned to see a man carrying a long flame-rod. He was moving from pole to pole along the plaza's main walkway, lighting the gas lamps. Only then did Jake notice that dusk had fallen. It would be dark soon.

He turned back to look at the map, then at Meara. "Thank you for your help, Meara."

"You should know that near the end of the North Highway, where you leave the highway, you'll be entering rough lands. That part of the Outland is probably the least hospitable you'll find out there."

Jake studied the map, noting where he had marked his departure from the North Highway. He had the used the hand drawn diagram given him by Peter to locate the next scroll. He had it memorized.

The winding path leads north and west, through and beyond well travelled trails. See the face that is seldom seen, find south and east to get you through.

The first line could very well have referred to where Jake would leave the highway, the path through the rough country that Meara referred to. The second line... in the past the second line was usually a clue as to how to open the gateway. But this time? Jake really had no way of knowing.

Once he got through the gateway, somewhere between the obelisk and wherever the artifact was hidden, lay the labyrinth.

"Please, Master Jacob," pleaded Meara. "You need to take me with you."

"We've already been through this." Jake's thoughts continued to pull first in one direction, and then another. He spoke then as if to himself. "There's something odd about this one. Up to now, all that I've needed I've found on the scrolls. This one is different. Why this warning from some ancient temple text?"

"Sir, everything about this trip says that you can't go alone."

"Everything about this trip says that I *have* to go alone."

"Sir—"

"I go alone."

The road from the village to the farm was well-defined from many years of use by wagons loaded with supplies and food. The first part of the trip was familiar to Jake, as he had taken the north route out of the village on his first expedition into the Outland. Early on, however, where on the previous journey he had veered east, this time he continued north.

It was midday before he reached the Farm; a vast expanse of cultivated fields spreading out to his right, the dirt road running along the western edge of the cleared land. It had been cut out of the forests of the Outland, with the road that he walked serving as the boundary between wilderness and agriculture.

The Farm was as much a part of the village as the marketplace; this was where the village got its food, with only very little coming from the *outside world.* The land looked well-tended, though he didn't see anyone out in the fields. There was a cluster of buildings in the heart of the Farm, but they were too far away for Jake to make out anyone.

It was all a bit too quiet, and at first he assumed this was the reason for the uncomfortable feeling that he had about the scene. Then he remembered having the same sensation back when he was on the island in the middle of the Dark Lake; there was no sound, no movement; it was like a picture, like a painting made by someone who didn't really know what a farm was like. Everything was right, and yet something was wrong.

However intently he studied the scene before him, Jake could not figure out what it was about the place that made him ill at ease, but he knew that the next time he sat down to a meal, he was going to look more closely at what was on his fork.

It took a long time to get past the Farm. It was a big place, with a lot of fields growing a lot of different crops. He noted that all the while he had been walking past those fields, there hadn't been so much as a breeze blowing across the wheat, the corn, the tomatoes, the potato plants. The world was still.

About two hours beyond the last field, Jake found the North Highway running east to west. It was sixty feet wide, smooth and straight; a hard, flat surface was covered in a low, yellow-green grass. He suspected that there might be something artificial just underneath the groundcover, but didn't take the time to investigate. He turned west and started down the center of the wide road.

He had been traveling only a few minutes when he saw a shimmering far on the horizon that eventually formed into the silhouette of someone or something coming towards him. It took another quarter of an hour or so before he could make out that it was the figure of a man leading a horse and wagon. As it drew nearer yet, he could see that the wagon was empty.

"Hello," said Jake, when the man was finally close enough that they could speak in a normal voice. He kept moving toward the stranger, and the man continued to lead the horse forward.

"Hello," the man said cautiously. A large rifle was cradled in his arms. He had probably brought it down from the wagon when he had first glimpsed Jake.

When they were twenty feet apart, Jake stopped and waited. The man continued slowly for another few steps and then he too stopped.

"You heading for the Farm?" Jake asked.

The man nodded. "Heading there," he said.

"A nice place. The Farm, I mean."

"I like it."

Jake indicated the road behind the man. "Any problems?"

"Been no problems to now. You should be all right."

"Good to hear," Jake said, nodding. "Ways to travel yet."

The man shifted his weapon and gave the horse a light tug. He started forward again. "Good luck to you," he said, with little emotion.

"Yeah," said Jake as he watched the man pass by. "You too." *Nice talkin' with ya...*

He walked the highway throughout the afternoon. The forests of the Outland pushed up close to the highway most of the way, though there were occasional clearings and small meadows along the roadside. An hour before dusk, he came upon a small group of people that was gathered in one of the clearings. They had made camp and had started a small cooking fire. The two men in the group stood as a wall between Jake and the camp. Behind them, several children ran over to a woman who may have been their mother. Another older woman sat near the fire and ignored the commotion.

"Waddya want?" asked one of the men, cold and firm, but not overly snippy.

"Not a thing," said Jake. First the man with the wagon, and now these guys... Maybe there was real cause to be nervous when traveling the highway. "Just passing by."

"We ain't got enough to share."

"Not asking," said Jake. He started walking. "Be seein' ya."

The men stood unmoving, their eyes fixed on Jake's every move as he passed by.

"Good luck to you," said one of them, with as little emotion as the man with the wagon had spoke hours before.

"Yeah," mumbled Jake, not caring whether they heard him or not. "You too." *Nice talkin' with ya...*

He found the trail that he was looking for just before the sun went down. Wider than most that he had come upon in the Outland, it led away from North Highway just after the highway began to narrow. If what he had seen on the map was correct, the highway itself would end another mile to the west.

Jake followed the trail for a thousand paces before moving off to a small clearing on the left, where he set up camp for the night. He cleared away much of the brush around the perimeter, exposing those shadows that could hide someone or something that might try to creep up on him, then gathered kindling and firewood. He made a small campfire and prepared a light dinner. Afterward, settled into a comfortable spot near a bed of warm coals, he had some quiet time to think on things.

Despite the nervous manner of the folks that he had met that day, his hours on the North Highway had been trouble-free and there had been no sign of danger. Highwaymen may yet jump out of the dark at any moment, but up to that point it had been a peaceful day. Still, he would let the coals die out and let the cool night close in on him. He probably should have eaten a cold dinner, but he hadn't exactly hidden his arrival in the area and his small dinner fire had probably not given anything away that hadn't already been given.

He thought about Meara and regretted, yet again, not bringing her with him. But he believed that leaving her back in the village had been the right thing to do. The dangers yet to come were very real. This, he knew. If his attention was directed to her safety and not to the goals of the quest, and it would be difficult to do otherwise, then he was more likely to make a mistake. And if, despite all his efforts and all her ability, something were to happen to her, he would never forgive himself.

Yes. Leaving her behind had been the right thing to do. Despite her knowledge and expertise, her strength, and the fact that at that moment he felt very alone and very vulnerable, leaving her behind had still been the right thing to do.

And still he wished that he had brought her.

Chapter Seventeen

The journey from the trailhead at the North Highway to the clearing with the obelisk had been as difficult as he had been led to believe. The trails were narrow and twisted and overgrown, when he could follow them at all; the forest was dark and heavily shadowed, the trees misshapen and gnarled and ugly. The sounds that emanated from the dark were chilling and ominous. It all seemed... haunting.

The clearing, when he finally found it, was obvious. A great stone stood in the center of an open area that seemed to push back against the encroaching forest, rather than the forest pushing in on the clearing. The ground was covered in a mulchy layer of dead leaves and twigs and other decomposing vegetation.

As Jake stood before the stone, the great obelisk loomed high over him, its shadow laying over him. He calmly tossed his gear aside and quietly circled the clearing and surveyed the perimeter. He cleared away brush and began preparing his encampment, glancing now and again at the obelisk.

> *The winding path leads north and west, through and beyond well traveled trails. Seek the face that is seldom seen, find south and east to get you through.*

The *winding path* had brought him to the clearing. He wondered now whether the *face seldom seen* was a clue to opening the gateway or to locating the labyrinth. Perhaps the *find south and east to get you through* reference referred to locating the labyrinth.

More likely, the entire second sentence referred to opening the gateway and the labyrinth was not referenced at all in this scroll text.

Once camp was set up, Jake sat before the small fire and studied the pillar. When the coffee was ready, he poured a cup and walked slowly around the stone, cup in hand, studying the ethereal images formed by the changing shadows. The world was as quiet as ever, and he found himself easing peacefully into the oncoming dusk.

He eventually returned to the fire and prepared a small meal using the standard rations. After dinner, once the sun had fully set, he studied the surface of the stone with only the light of a flickering torch to bring out the shifting images. From past experience, Jake had learned that he needed to be patient when seeking the key to these gateways. He now thought nothing about giving it up for the night and settling in to sleep.

Perhaps the answer would show itself in the morning. After all, the scrolls weren't meant to prevent him from accessing the gateway, but rather to aid in overcoming the precautions put into place to prevent anyone from inadvertently opening a gate. It had to be assumed that if someone had recovered the scroll from the Hall of Statues, and had arrived at the correct, corresponding stone pylon, that the individual had some inherent right to access the gateway. Because of this, the scroll needn't be too cryptic.

The morning found Jake staring at the stone.

Face seldom seen...

Find south and east...

The side of the pillar facing southeast? But how is that *seldom seen?*

Jake didn't get up from his place near the fire. He had already checked the southeast side of the stone a number of times and had found nothing.

His thoughts returned to the original assumption that the *face* reference meant the face of a dragon. Somehow, some way, dragons always seemed to be involved.

But he saw no image of a dragon, or a face of a dragon...

If not a dragon, then what was meant by the *face seldom seen?*

The sun's rays spidered through the trees and daggered across the clearing. The stone pillar took on new life as shadows and light danced across its surface. Jake watched in fascination, hoping for some sign, some clue that might lead him to the key.

A quick reflective glint flickered momentarily and was gone. It had appeared at about eye level, and if he hadn't been looking at exactly that spot on the stone, he wouldn't have seen it. He stood, staring at the location, leaning to one side and then another, lowering his head and raising it. A flash of light came and went several times as he changed perspective, and he moved slowly toward the stone, never losing sight of the position on the surface.

There was a spot on the rock's surface, several inches in diameter, that was smooth to sight and touch. He rubbed at it with two fingers and found that the surface almost shone. He wet his fingers and rubbed at it again.

It was almost like glass. Leaning forward, he saw his eye reflecting back at him. He leaned his head back a few inches and saw himself reflected in the small, mirror-like surface.

A face seldom seen...

People seldom saw their own faces, and back in the time the scroll was written, people likely saw themselves much less often than they did now.

Jake pushed in on the blemish. Nothing happened. He frowned, furrowed his brow and stared harshly at the spot. He was certain this was the key.

But there had to be more to it. Over the centuries, someone could easily have spotted this shiny spot in the stone, rubbed its surface, and even pressed on it.

Find south and east to get you through...

Jake took a step back and slowly let his gaze move down the stone and to the right, south and east from the face seldom seen. There were several likely candidates, several circular dark or shiny blemishes in the stone that might serve as the second half to the key.

He held two fingers lightly against the mirror-blemish, reached down with his other hand and placed two fingers over a dark, raised knob of stone. He pushed in on the two locations at the same time.

He heard and felt nothing. He gave it a few moments, and then moved on to a second thumb-sized blemish, again raised to form a slight knob. Again he pressed on the two locations at the same time. Again there was nothing.

On the third try, however, this time a dark spot set into a slight dimple in the stone, Jake felt a slight click and release against his fingertips, felt a slight give in the stone. He stepped back six steps and watched the now familiar transformation from ancient stone pillar to shimmering gateway.

Moments later, Jake stepped out of the gateway and into another clearing. This one was surrounded by an even darker forest than the one he had left behind. A damp, pungent smell pushed in from all around him. Overhead, the sky was a dull gray with low, black clouds that hung unmoving above him. Far in the distance, a castle of menacingly tall walls stood on the crest of a high hill, silhouetted against black sky and blacker clouds. Somewhere between the clearing and the castle, Jake should find the labyrinth. Considering the gloomy atmosphere of this Other World, he wasn't looking forward to it.

Noting there was only one path out of the clearing, Jake steadied himself and started forward. Once he left the clearing, the trees and bushes and shadows of the surrounding woods quickly closed in. The barely discernable trail was little more than a narrow footpath, probably used only rarely by the occasional small animal. The path wound its way through the forest, fading into and out of existence as the underbrush and groundcover reclaimed it for the forest floor.

Jake knew the direction that he had to go, so whenever he lost the trail he trekked through the woods, managing to pick it up again each time before growing too concerned, relying on the trail to eventually point him to the entrance of the labyrinth. If the monks' scroll was correct, bypassing the maze would mean losing the artifact. Going through the castle's front door wouldn't be enough. The labyrinth was the only way into the castle that would get him to the artifact.

As the day crept toward dusk, the shadows stretched further across the forest floor, making it even more difficult to see and follow the trail. He found himself doubling back more and more as he followed false paths that led nowhere. Finally, coming into an open area, surrounded by short, scrubby trees and with a clear sky overhead, he decided to stop for the night. He dropped his pack in the center of the clearing and quickly set about to make the site a camp.

He cleared the perimeter, gathered kindling and wood, and prepared a spot for a campfire. It was dark before Jake had a fire going and he was able to heat his rations and make coffee. He settled back then and ate his meal. He tried not to stare into the flames, knowing that it would blind him to any possible movement in the darkness, but campfires were made to be watched. That's just what people did.

Jake felt very alone. He realized that he was probably further from home than any human he had ever known. Serpent's Keep was out of the way, but this, this was real isolation.

No one knew where he was, and even if they had known, there was no way to reach him if something happened. If anything did happen, he had no way to ask for help.

This would be a very bad place to have something go wrong.

Had Uncle Tobias been somewhere like this? Had he been alone, far away in some distant Other World, unable to reach out for help, when something went wrong?

As the fire began to die down, the cool dampness crept in on him. In defiance of whatever might be watching from the shadows, he added wood to the fire and moved in closer. He stared in at the glowing coals building up at the base of the flames and tried to push away thoughts about where he was and what he had to do, but this world had a way of seeping into his bones and crawling into his thoughts.

A movement overhead caught his attention and he lifted his head in time to see a shadow move across a half-moon that was peeking through the clouds. As he watched, the shadow came back across the moon again, this time much larger.

Whatever it was, it appeared to be getting closer.

Jake stood and stepped around the fire so that it was behind him. He looked not directly at the bright moon but a few degrees to one side. He watched as something flew towards him, casually drifting one way and then another, occasionally passing in front of the moon. It was big.

It was a dragon.

Passing directly over the clearing, its wings blotted out the sky. It had a long, thin neck that supported a large head that it held high. Its tail slid smoothly from side to side as it shifted direction. Jake turned about as it passed over, watched as it turned to the right and gained altitude. It flew full circle and came back for another pass, dropping altitude and coming in just above the treetops. Coming in to one side of the clearing, it turned slowly and studied the scene of the campsite and of the man standing beside his small fire.

It turned away again and glided casually upward. Jake heard and felt the pounding as it began beating its wings in slow powerful strokes. It climbed higher and disappeared finally into the clouds. Jake waited for a full minute for it to return, and when it didn't he eventually sat down again in front of his fire.

Was this dragon a guardian, like others Jake had come across, or did it serve as the eyes of someone else?

Either way, for good or for bad, Jake's presence in this Other World was known.

The massive steel door was set into the side of the hill. Jake estimated that a person twice his height could walk through without having to lower his head.

Or a big dragon...

The trail that he had been following continued on to his left, winding its way around the hillside, and he assumed right up to the front door of the castle another half a mile ahead. If he hadn't been advised otherwise, he would certainly have taken that route. It sure seemed easier, and safer, than trying to get through this ominous door and on into whatever dangers may lurk beyond.

He stepped up and placed his hands on the door. It was smooth and cold to the touch. His right hand slid down to the heavy latch. It didn't appear to be locked, and it looked like it was probably the kind of latch that was accessible from both sides.

I can come and go as I please?

Jake pushed down on the lever.

It didn't budge.

Empowered with an unreasonable sense of confidence coming from he knew not where, Jake lifted himself up and pushed down hard; and then a second time. The mechanism within the door came free and the latch released.

Here goes...

The hinges howled as he pushed the door inward, shattering the silence of the world outside and alerting anyone or anything inside that someone had been foolish enough to enter. He stopped when the door was open enough that he could squeeze through. Poking his head in, he saw that the chamber within was in absolute darkness.

Naturally...

He had already pulled his pack off in order to squeeze through the narrow opening. He scrounged around within it until he found the hand lamp. Holding this in one hand, his backpack in the other, Jake stepped sideways through the open doorway.

There was a hollowness to the sound of his footsteps, but he could sense that the walls on either side were close by. The ceiling was beyond the reach of the sphere of light from his lamp. Beneath his feet, the floor was stone.

The air smelled dank and stale.

Old...

The entire world had an overwhelming impression of age about it, much more so than any other world that he had been to; this was a very, very old place.

He crept slowly forward in the dark. He occasionally sensed, and even rarely could see, side passages. He stopped at each one and listened, but heard nothing. After traveling for some time, the tunnel that he was in emptied into another that ran left to right. Again he stopped and listened. Again there was no sound.

But there was a faint breeze. When he turned his head he could feel it against his cheek. It was very light, but it was definitely there, coming from the left. He turned and followed it. He didn't know whether it would take him where he wanted to go, but at least it was something. It provided a reason to choose one direction over another.

Coming to another fork, he again followed the barely perceptible breeze.

And then again.

He eventually found himself in a large square chamber, only to discover that he had reached a dead end. He searched it thoroughly to make sure there wasn't a hidden door, an object, perhaps the bedding of some animal. He thought that he could smell something animal-like in the chamber, and maybe there had been something there at some time in the past. Now, though, it was an empty room with one way in and one way out.

He retraced his steps and took the first side passage that he came to, and then again. In this way, he came up on several dead ends, some leading to empty rooms, others simply ending. There may have been some secondary access, such as a hidden panel high on a wall, but he could find none.

Several hours into his search, he had yet to find a way through the labyrinth. He grew increasingly anxious and began to pick up the pace.

He almost didn't see the pit in time.

It was little more than a dark shadow on the floor in a passageway filled with dancing shadows that were continually chased by the sphere of light created by his small hand lamp. His right foot hung over the open air above a deep darkness. He sensed more than saw the emptiness beneath him, his muscles tensing and his mind racing to respond to this unexpected situation. His heart beat six times before he could pull back and he dropped to the ground, sitting heavily on the stone floor.

Oh, man...

He let his backpack slip off his back, then scooted around and crawled forward on his hands and knees, keeping the hand lamp in front of him. He reached the lip of the pit and stopped. Moving the lamp from left to right, Jake could see that the passageway had widened and the edges of the pit reached the walls on either side of the tunnel. Holding the lamp up and forward, he couldn't see across to the other side.

Jake stood slowly. He turned his head from side to side.

The breeze he had been following seemed to come from the pit.

Oh, man... he thought again. *And I bet there's something down there...*

He couldn't hear anything; he didn't sense anything.

This was an obstacle that, by design or by circumstance, he would need to overcome in order to reach the castle and the artifact.

He moved to his right along the edge of the pit until he reached the wall of the passageway. Holding the hand lamp out, he sought for some way around the pit. There was nothing. There were no handholds or footholds that he could use to get past the pit.

Moving over to the left wall, he could see a few places that he might be able to grasp onto, a few places to put his feet, but it looked very precarious.

He knelt down and looked again into the pit, this time studying the pit wall for a possible way down.

Maybe...

Jake took a long, shaky breath.

Oh, man...

He stood and returned to his pack, put it on and tightened the straps. Back at the lip of the pit, he mapped out his first few footholds and handholds, then clipped the hand lamp to one of the pack straps, turned, dropped to his knees and slid himself over the edge.

He found the first foothold, and then the second. Pressed tight against the rough rock wall, he carefully slid his left hand down and found the handhold that he knew to be there, then did the same with his right. Secure, he eased himself down and sought out another foothold. He began working his way down into the pit, working mostly in the dark but for the faint light that spilled out to his left from the lamp clipped to the strap near his shoulder.

He slipped only once, and recovered with little more than minor scratches to his palms. It was a long, painfully slow climb down, but eventually his left foot touched bottom. He didn't trust himself at first and carefully tested the ground beneath him before bringing his right foot down and turning around.

The light shone on a tunnel entrance leading away from the bottom of the pit. It was just tall enough that Jake wouldn't have to crouch, and was narrow enough that the light from his lamp would be able to reach both side walls.

Before moving nearer the tunnel, he glanced up. The darkness had swallowed him up; he couldn't see the opening of the pit. Looking again at the mouth of the tunnel, he stepped forward. In all likelihood, this was what he had been looking for, and whatever might lay ahead, he had no intention of going back.

Once in the tunnel, a new smell quickly overwhelmed the constant background odor of dank and damp that he had grown accustomed to. It was a musky smell, and Jake was immediately reminded of the dragon dens that he had been in lately. He wondered if the flying dragon that he had seen earlier lived down here. If it did, it certainly didn't use this tunnel. There would need to be a much larger access.

He continued forward, lamp out in front, its yellow glowing sphere of light pushing its way down the tunnel. The passageway twisted and turned, but there were very few side tunnels and none beckoned him away from the main path. It was a long, winding passage from the pit to… where?

Following a slow arcing curve, Jake stopped and stared at the tunnel ahead, the right wall disappearing beyond the bend. He turned off the lamp and let his eyes adjust.

There was definitely a lessening of the dark; the black was not quite as black. He was certain that he could see the curving wall in the darkness.

Leaving the light off, he crept cautiously forward, holding his free hand out in front of him, keeping the lamp in his other hand with his finger on the power switch, ready to turn it back on in an instant. As he continued around the curve, the darkness continued to grow less so. Beyond the curve, once the tunnel straightened, Jake could clearly distinguish a square grey shadow in the distance, as if the passage was taking him into the light.

As Jake continued ahead, the grey square slowly grew, slowly brightened, until at last he stepped through the grey and into a high-ceilinged chamber; one large section of the roof was open to a late-afternoon sky. Visible through this opening, the great, dark castle rose above a sheer cliff, looming high overhead, silhouetted against purple and black clouds.

In the chamber, the dragon sat on a low ledge at the far wall, its wings folded atop its back, watching the human step slowly into its lair. Its eyes were sharp and clear, and somehow sad.

Jake walked into the center of the hall and stopped. He bowed his head respectfully. "Hello," he said. "My name is Jacob Quigley."

"Human."

"Yes." Jake spotted a small wooden door a dozen feet to the left of the dragon. It probably led up to the castle.

The dragon sniffed the air, leaned its head forward and looked more closely at the human. "I…" he examined Jake. "*know...*"

"Tobias is my uncle," said Jake. "I am blood of Tobias Quigley."

The dragon pulled its head back and settled in again. "I am Guardian."

His uncle must have had a lot of respect for these dragons. He had selected them and they had served as Guardians for a very long time.

"Tobias has sent me on a quest to gather together the artifacts." He pointed to the door leading up to the castle. "May I pass?"

The dragon studied Jake a moment. "You see... *Little Ones?*"

"I don't understand."

"Little Ones," it said. "You see?"

"I'm afraid not." *Were these 'little ones' like those that he had come upon in the Abandoned City?*

"Not see them..." said the dragon. "Not heard them... Long time."

What did the dragon mean by long time? Weeks? Months? Years? Hundreds of years?

"I'm sorry," said Jake.

"You find," said the dragon after a long, studied pause.

The labyrinth? I don't want to go back in there...

"I saw nothing in there."

"You find." The dragon showed no sign of aggression, but it sat only a dozen feet from the door to the passage leading up to the castle. "Then you pass."

"But—"

"No pass."

Jake looked at the door, then looked behind him at the tunnel entrance leading back into the labyrinth. If he wasn't going to fight his way past the dragon, then he was going to have to go back in the labyrinth and see if he could find these Little Ones. But if they really weren't in there, or if he just couldn't find them, then what?

"All right," he said. "I find."

"You find."

Jake had tried to keep a map in his head of his journey through the labyrinth, tossing out the misdirected routes he had taken, should he have to return the way he had come. There had been only a few side tunnels between the dragon's chamber and the pit, and he hoped that he would not have to go beyond the pit in his search.

The first side tunnel led Jake into a confusing maze of passageways that continually turned back on each other, bisected one another, occasionally dead-ended, and in its center opened into a large, low-ceilinged chamber. There were some signs of it having been occupied in the distant past, or at least been visited by some creatures, but nothing had been there for many years.

The second side tunnel took him into a maze that looked to be a mirror image of the first, with a similar central chamber. Again there were signs that the *Little Ones* had been there in the past, though Jake doubted they had actually lived there. There was no indication of it being a den.

The third side tunnel started similar to the others, but Jake quickly noted that there were far fewer branching passageways. This sector wasn't nearly the maze of the other two.

He also noted an odor in the air, not as strong as the muskiness of the dragon, similar but more intense than the smell he had picked up near the central chambers of the other sectors. *A den long ago abandoned?* Possibly.

The light from his hand lamp revealed the walls curving away from the entrance into the chamber. Stepping cautiously into the room, his footsteps echoed away from him and into the dark. He could tell that the room was big. Glancing up, he saw that the glow of the lamp didn't reach the ceiling.

The air was warm and heavy, which surprised him considering the size of the chamber. He would have thought it would have been fresher. The fact that it was as stale as it was meant that there was no flow, which probably meant the only exit was the way he had come.

The silence was as oppressive as the darkness. If there was something alive in the room, it was very quiet; sleeping or waiting?

If there was something sleeping in the room, he didn't want to surprise it. If there was something waiting for him to pass near, then it already knew that he was in the room.

"Hello?" he called out. The sound of his voice reverberated in the chamber. He listened carefully for a reaction, a scurrying, a scratching on the stone floor, anything. There was nothing.

Quiet as a tomb...

Five paces into the room the lamp shone its light on something laying on the floor. He stepped very cautiously forward, his outstretched arm holding the hand lamp toward the object.

It was a skeleton; reptilian or something very like it. Jake had no doubt that it was one of the little ones. Kneeling down beside it, Jake studied the old bones. The skull had been crushed, and a leg bone had clear markings of trauma, as if struck by a staff or sword. Jake mumbled under his breath. *What happened to you, boy?* He stood and held the lamp out. He could see other piles of bones within reach of the lamp's light. Moving to each, he found that each had signs of trauma.

These creatures had been attacked.

He found the remains of what he took to be their bedding, long since decomposed to dust, lining the curved walls. Near one of these, he found the skeleton of a very different animal.

This one was human. The clothing had long ago gone to dust, the flesh and muscle was gone, leaving only the bones to hint at what had happened so long in the past.

Humans had come into the chamber and attacked the *Little Ones*; provoked or not he had no way of knowing. Perhaps the *Little Ones* had confronted them out in the labyrinth and had been chased back here to their den. Maybe the humans had come into the labyrinth looking for them. But whatever the reason, the creatures had been slaughtered in their lair.

Other than the remains of the one human, his body left behind by his companions, there was nothing else in the chamber to provide any further clues as to what had happened. Jake would have to return to the dragon and explain that the Little Ones it so desperately missed would never again be coming out of the labyrinth; that they were dead, that they had been killed by humans.

§

Jake saw the pain in the dragons eyes as he told it what he had found. He had considered lying to the great creature, saying that he had found nothing, or telling it that he had found the den and the remains of the Little Ones, but hiding the fact that humans were somehow involved, but in the end he had told the truth as best he knew it, describing the scene exactly as he had found it.

"Thank you, blood of Tobias," said the dragon.

"I am sorry—"

"I afraid that what you find."

Jake wondered if the dragon had already known what had happened, but had needed verification in order to have resolution. Had it been involved in some conflict or confrontation a long time ago? Had a band of humans run into the dragon's lair after having killed the *Little Ones*, only to then be killed by the dragon? The dragon would certainly have made the connection between the appearance of the humans and the subsequent loss of contact with the little creatures.

Jake had been afraid that the dragon would associate him with those other humans and seek revenge, but he had chosen to tell the truth nonetheless. He had felt an obligation to do so.

The dragon had its own sense of honor. It spoke stoically. "You pass."

Jake nodded in acknowledgement, approached the dragon and the heavy wooden door beside it. He pushed down on the thick metal latch and pulled the door open. Glancing a final time at the creature on the ledge, he stepped into yet another passageway.

This passage went straight into the mountain for a hundred paces. Jake stopped at the foot of a staircase of stone steps. It spiraled steeply within a cylindrical shaft that reached up into the castle hundreds of feet above. It took him ten minutes to climb the stairs to the door at the top of the shaft, the yellow glow of the light from the hand lamp pushing up in front of him all the way.

He was afraid that the door would be locked and that he wouldn't be able to go any further, but he found a simple latch and pushed down. The hinges screeched noisily but the door opened easily enough.

The room beyond was oval in shape, with a single narrow window and no other obvious access. In the center of the room was a wooden chair and table. On the table was a box similar in appearance to the others that had held artifact pieces.

Ignoring the box for the moment, Jake went to the window. It was a thick glass pane set into a wooden frame, with no curtain. It looked out over the dark forest, beneath which must lay the underground labyrinth that he had navigated. Pressing his face against the glass and looking directly below him, he could just make out the dragon's lair, but couldn't see any details.

He turned his attention back to the room. A leather map hung on the wall beside the door. On it were the details of the labyrinth; the dragon's lair, the den of the Little Ones, the central chambers of the other sectors, the pit, the maze of the upper labyrinth beyond the pit.

Also detailed were the trails of the dark forest beyond the labyrinth, including a path leading from the castle's front door all the way back to the gateway.

Then there should be a way out of the room and into the castle.

Jake turned quickly at the thought and studied the curved walls that enclosed the room. The wall opposite the door was the only one that could have a room on the other side. This room in the top of the tower could actually be two.

The wall was a mix of stone blocks of different shapes and sizes. At first glance, there was no indication that any one of them would give way and provide him with a way out. Besides, if it had been as simple as that, then someone on the other side could have as easily gotten in, and the whole point had been that the only way in was by way of the dragon.

From past experience with the gates, he knew that these things weren't overly complicated, and weren't meant to keep people out but rather to prevent inadvertent access.

With each, there had been several layers to access. The first layer was the assumption that if someone was there and was seeking access, that person had knowledge of the gate (or door) and knew there was something to be sought after.

Jake knew of the artifact, knew of the gates, and had gained knowledge from another source as to the whereabouts of this gate. He had discovered the gateway, found a way to open it using knowledge from the scroll, and had passed through.

In the second layer of protection, the person attempting access had to have acquired knowledge from another source that would indicate that the person should have access. In this case, Jake had found that he would have to travel the labyrinth to get to this room. He also had to have successfully made his way past the dragon.

Now that he was here, what knowledge would he need to have brought with him that would serve as the key to this hidden door?

Jake stared at the wall, standing as stoic and as silent as he had at every gate that he had faced.

With each gate, the answer had been hidden levers and catches within the stone. Jake gave a mental shrug. Well… it would make sense that the same would be true for a door in a wall; perhaps more so.

He studied the features of the wall. As he noted before, it consisted of an array of differently shaped stones of all sizes. Studying the mortar and grout that held them in place, he saw no obvious sign as to the edges of this hidden door.

What knowledge had he brought with him that justified his entry?

He looked again at the individual stones.

The shape of the artifact?

He knew the shape of the polygon for this Other World, for this artifact.

Jake began systematically examining each stone in the wall. It took him half a minute to find a stone with the same shape. Stepping forward, he pushed it.

Nothing happened.

Of course nothing happened. It had never been so simple at the gates, either. There was usually a pair.

He found the second stone three rows down. He stepped forward again, reached out and pushed them both simultaneously. There were two satisfyingly loud clicks as something fell into place within the wall.

And yet no door appeared. Jake pushed and pulled and nothing happened. He stood back and studied the wall again.

The two stones were definitely hinges of some kind; of that he was certain. So what was it that he had missed?

Hinges in a door...

A doorknob?

Jake scanned to the right of the hinges. Midway up between the hinges, about three feet to the right, just about where a door knob would be, Jake saw a rectangular stone about six inches wide and two inches tall. He took a step forward, reached over and pressed in on the stone.

The stone gave a fraction of an inch and there was another click as the latch within released another lever. Jake stepped back and watched a section of wall silently slide open, revealing an empty room beyond. He stood tensed and ready, should something come through. Not until he felt fairly certain that there was no imminent threat did he relax enough to gather his things together. He went over to the table then and opened the box. The artifact was there. Picking it up, it felt cool and heavy in his hand. He tucked it safely into the side pocket of his backpack, zipped the pocket shut, and looked back at the opening in the wall. Filtered sunlight shone through an unseen window and gave the room beyond a bright gray glow. From where he stood, he could see only the same stone floor and curved walls that looked as though they were continuing on from the room that he was in.

He walked through the opening in the wall. The room he entered had one window, as had the hidden room he had just left. Instead of a door, however, there was a hole in the floor near the far wall, through which Jake could see stone stairs descending into darkness. Looking back at the wall that he had come through, he could see that the hinge stones didn't have the shape of the artifact as they had on the other side of the wall. He pushed the door shut and returned to the stairs, pulling out his hand lamp as he strode across the room.

Starting down, he found himself growing increasingly uncomfortable. The light was reaching beyond the curve of the stairwell and he was afraid it might alert someone to his presence before he knew they were there. He didn't want to trod down the stairs completely in the dark, so he finally compromised and held his free hand in front of the lamp. This lessened the light, if only a little, while continuing to illuminate the steps directly below him.

He had only traveled downward a quarter of the distance that he had traveled coming up through the other staircase when he came to a door. It had a lever-style door handle, and it wasn't locked. He would have been surprised if it had been. Why lock an interior door leading from an empty room with no other obvious access?

Jake stepped out onto a mezzanine. The wide landing looked down onto a grand hall that appeared to serve as a kind of main room for the castle. Jake ignored the doors on the second floor and took the treacherous, narrow stairs down to the first floor. His footsteps echoed in the hollow chamber as he walked across the main hall towards the massive set of doors that had to be the front door to the castle. Tall, narrow windows were set high into the front wall and let in the gray light that seemed to permeate this Other World.

Jake stopped in the middle of the huge room.

Another light, brighter and painting a yellow glow across the floor, was coming from somewhere else, somewhere other than the front windows.

He turned and looked at an open set of doors to his left. From where he stood, he could see chairs and tables of dark wood, an area rug covering the cold stone floor, and drapes hanging on the far wall. Light was streaming through the open doorway and into the front hall.

Jake felt cold creeping up his back, yet his skin burned hot.

Someone is in there...

He stared dumbly in the direction of the other room, watched the narrow section of the room that he could see, knowing there had to be someone in there.

The strange thing was, all Jake could think of was that he was breaking into someone's house and that he was going to get caught... he was going to get in trouble...

Oh, man...

He had to go over and see what was in there. What if he went all the way back to Serpent's Keep and found out later that there was something in that room that he needed? All he had to do was walk over and pick it up.

Oh, I really shouldn't do this...

He took one step toward the open doorway.

A shadow moved across the floor of the other room.

Oh, man...

Jake lowered his backpack to the floor and pulled out the small sword that he had used against the dragon in the Desert world.

He really had to look into upgrading his weaponry...

Stepping up to the open door, he slid to one side and carefully pushed it the rest of the way open. The room beyond looked like a study or a sitting room of some kind. Several oil lamp fixtures hung on walls, each shedding a soft golden light into the room. A small fire burned in a large, stone fireplace. A small, strange looking man sat in a high-backed wing chair near the fireplace, set in such a way so that the man could see both the fire and the door. Shadows danced across his face as the flames of the fire actively flickered above the glowing wood and embers.

"You are *his* blood," said the man. His voice was a soft hiss. The tone was cold and precise. His mouth worked in a peculiar way, as if the act of speaking was an unfamiliar and unsavory activity. "I can smell it on you."

"I am Jacob Quigley."

"Of course you are."

There was a movement behind the man's chair; a shadow reached out across the floor. A moment later the head of a creature appeared, peering around from the back of the chair, looking anxiously at Jake, seemingly frightened at this intruder. The creature was perhaps three feet tall, the head was large and thin, faintly reptilian, thick skin, eyes set wide on the sides of the head. Three fingers slid around the edge of the chair, long thin claws.

Jake eyed the creature cautiously but tried to maintain an air of calm. "Cute pet."

"Not amusing."

Jake shrugged absently. "Nice place ya' got here."

The man said nothing.

"Been here long?"

"A thousand years, give or take." If the man expected a reaction from Jake, he didn't get one. Jake had seen and heard too much to be surprised by much of anything. What he wondered, though, was whether this man knew of the secret room and of the artifact. He would have to watch himself and not give anything away.

"Yeah," said Jake. "Just you and the dog, then?"

Again the man said nothing.

"Must get lonely," Jake continued. "What made you choose such an out-of-the-way location?"

"Out-of-the-way doesn't begin to describe it, young Mr. Quigley."

"So what keeps you here?"

"I didn't have much of a choice in the matter. Circumstances dictated my sanctuary."

"Ah... there's a lot of that going around."

"You, by contrast, have managed to get around quite a bit."

"Not so much."

"Now that's just not true, Mr. Quigley. You have visited a number of... *out-of-the-way* locations as of late."

"Oh... well... if you want to count *those.*"

"And you have acquired a number of souvenirs."

"Mementos," said Jake. There was a faint rustling sound and he saw the creature hiding behind the chair stretch its neck and twist its head to get a better look at Jake.

"They don't belong to you."

"You gonna tell me they belong to you?"

"I shall see that they get into the proper hands."

"Thanks just the same."

The man didn't sound in the least surprised. "What Quigley did was wrong. He had no right to shut down the gates. One man doesn't have the right to isolate entire races to a single universe, or to a single world."

"And you are going to correct that..."

The man nodded sagely. "And prevent you from committing an even more egregious wrong than the evil perpetrated by Tobias Quigley."

"He saved worlds and all of the people in them from the Rhetani. As for me, I fully intend to follow Tobias' wishes. You will find that I am not easily stopped." Jake wasn't quite as confident as he sounded, but he figured that he may as well go down with a little dignity.

"You have no idea who I am."

Jake didn't like the sound of that. Still, he did his best to hide his anxiety. "Would it make a difference?"

The man smiled thinly. He leaned his head back, rested it against the back of the chair. "My name is Marcus," he said. "Your uncle and I arrived in the Outland together."

Human, then. Kinda hard to tell...

"We got swept up in the whole mess between the Jahai and the Rhetani."

"You were friends?" asked Jake.

"Comrades," said Marcus precisely. He lost his smile. His glare was unnerving. "He gave up everything for the Jahai. That wasn't enough. If it had been, at least it would have been something I might expect of Tobias. No. No, martyrdom wasn't enough. He had to drag the rest of us down with him, to pull us into a cause that we did not believe in, one that—well…" He let his commentary fade.

So how did you end up here, Jake wondered. He was afraid to ask. Tobias had probably stranded him here after this guy tried to do something really bad.

"How can defending worlds against the Rhetani be wrong?" he asked, finally.

"The Rhetani will bring only good," Marcus said crisply. "I will not argue this with a simpleton."

"No problem, I'll just be leaving, then."

"I don't think so."

"What you think is not my concern."

"It should be."

The continuing calmness in Marcus' voice and manner was unsettling. The man just sat there, relaxed, the fire in the fireplace sending its flickering shadows across his face.

"I'm leaving," said Jake. "Not you, not your little friend there, can stop me."

"My friend?" Marcus paused, looked at Jake as if for the first time. "You *are* in the dark. Do you know anything at all about what you've gotten yourself into?"

"I manage to pick up what I need to know."

"You stumble blindly and clumsily along, with no knowledge as to the true purpose behind your task or the consequences of your actions."

"I understand that the Jahai believed the Rhetani were a threat," said Jake, defensively. "Tobias believed the Rhetani were dangerous enough that he shut down the gates to stop them. The dragons, at great sacrifice, joined Tobias to serve as Guardians."

"The dragons," Marcus leaned forward and hissed, "*are* the Jahai."

Jake stared dumbly at the man. He was at a loss for words. This was completely unexpected.

Marcus shifted back again in his chair. "A dozen species spread across four habitable planets, not bound as others are bound, not limited to a single, crowded world."

"This somehow gives the Rhetani the right to conquer other worlds? Other races?"

"The Rhetani will free worlds from squalor and childish conflict. They will spread their civilization for the benefit of everyone." Marcus turned his head and fixed a sharp glare at the small creature that peered around the chair and looked side glance at him. "The Jahai shut away what they cannot control, imprison what they fear."

"They sent you here?"

"I came of my own accord," Marcus said dully.

"If you—"

"This is the only world where they will let me live. I remain safe so long as I remain here. I am under threat of death should I leave."

"Wow… you must be a nasty sort."

"My only crime is that I do not share the same beliefs as the Jahai."

Jake nodded silently. So the creature behind the chair must serve as the eyes of the Jahai, ensuring that Marcus remained in his prison. But, even if he hadn't been under watch, how could Marcus leave? Wouldn't he have needed the artifact to open the gate?

Another thought occurred to him. If it was true that Marcus had been here a thousand years, how could he know the things he knew? And wasn't the language of a thousand years ago different than the language spoken now? He sounded very contemporary.

"And you've been here…"

Marcus managed to smile again. "I could not get very far without this little monster raising the alarm, now could I? I could kill it, I suppose, but that would raise as big a stink as leaving."

Jake looked at the creature peering around from behind the chair. "It doesn't appear to have any qualms about my leaving."

Marcus said nothing, did not acknowledge Jake's comment. He calmly watched Jake turn away and start again toward the door. As he reached it, Jake heard a mechanical click. He knew the door had been locked.

"Unlock the door, Marcus," said Jake, not turning from the door.

"Give me the artifact."

"Not gonna happen."

"Then you and I shall keep each other company. I am of a patient disposition."

"I am not." Jake slowly turned away from the door. Dropping his backpack, he held his short sword at the ready.

"You *are* a primitive creature, aren't you?"

"I am whatever I have to be," said Jake.

"You are too ignorant to know what that really means, young Quigley."

Jake moved forward, came within sword's reach of Marcus. "You will let me out of here."

"Or what?" Marcus didn't look as though he was someone being threatened with a sword. This made Jake uncomfortable. Everything about this man made Jake uncomfortable.

"Since starting on this little quest, I've had to do some things I didn't like doing. This would be just one more."

Marcus was unimpressed. "I've waited a thousand years for someone to bring the artifact down from the tower. You're not leaving this room until you take it from your pack and set it here on the table beside me."

Jake looked over at the small table next to the chair. There was nothing on it, as if it were waiting for the artifact to be placed on its smooth surface.

He turned his attention back to Marcus. "Now, you know I'm not going to just hand it over to you. What is it you really want?"

"I want the artifact."

"You can't have it." Jake turned away from the man in the chair, looked carefully around the room. He knew that Marcus knew he wouldn't just run him through with the sword. He knew that Marcus knew that he wasn't going to just hand over the artifact. So what was going on? And what were his options?

"What's your game?" he asked.

"I do not play games, Mr. Quigley."

"Now that's just not true," said Jake, throwing the man's earlier statement back at him. "I may be a primitive creature. I may not know what I've gotten myself into, and I may even be totally in the dark on one or two things. But I know when I'm being played."

Marcus started to say something, but Jake turned suddenly and lifted the sword, dropped it quickly down onto the table. The moment the blade made contact with the image of the table, Jake found himself rushing through an electrified version of a gate passageway. The unexpected rush of light and warped vision made him dizzy and he stumbled forward the moment he came out on the other side.

The room that he found himself in was the same room that he had left, and yet somehow... more real, more substantial. He turned quickly, readied himself against an attack by Marcus.

Marcus remained in his chair, calm, almost serene. "Welcome, young Quigley."

"Okay... I'll bite. What's going on?" Jake took a step away from Marcus, studied the room around him. Everything was the same, even the fire that was burning in the fireplace. The Little One was still hiding behind the chair. The door, leading who knew where, was closed. "Where am I?"

The air smelled different. It was cleaner, fresher.

This was definitely a different world.

Marcus smiled, said nothing.

"The room that I was in," Jake spoke softly, quietly. "It wasn't real. Or rather, what I was seeing wasn't the room I was in. I was seeing a projection of *this* room."

"Close. Think of this as a side door to the gate system that you are familiar with. There are a few of them around. Their capabilities are limited, but they can be useful."

"Where are we?"

"The same universal plane as that of the castle. Different location on this world, and a different time. I suppose you could argue that the room in the castle and this room we are in now share the same space in some multidimensional sense; one being just a touch out of phase with the other."

"And you can go back and forth—" Jake waved his arm at his surroundings.

"Between the castle and this despicably pleasant little prison of a community? No. No, I'm afraid that without the artifact, the functionality of the side door is even more limited."

Jake nodded somberly. He had the artifact in his possession, so once he had placed himself into a specific location within this *side door*, he was brought through.

What do I have to do to get back?

He could see nothing that would indicate a gate, side door or otherwise, but since passing the blade of his sword through the image of the table had brought him here, maybe it would send him back.

Marcus saw Jake surreptitiously eyeing the side table. "You would never make it."

"Pardon?"

"I am much more agile than I look."

"Actually, I think you look quite fit for a thousand."

Marcus rose from his chair as Jake moved slowly to one side. He stood between Jake and the table. "You'll like it here, Mr. Quigley. There are a lot of folks here just like you; primitive, ignorant, blind to the truth of the universe."

Jake was through bantering back and forth with this peacock. He said nothing, took another step to his right, forcing Marcus to move to his left in order to maintain his position between Jake and the table.

As Marcus eased to one side, Jake noticed the Little One inch its way cautiously out from behind the chair. He thought at first that he was going to have to deal with the two of them, but the manner in which the creature moved and the way that it positioned itself out of the line of the sight of Marcus indicated otherwise.

"No more amusing quips, Mr. Quigley?"

Jake slid half a step more to the right. Marcus casually repositioned himself, as if he just happened to be moving in that direction.

"You know," Marcus held a finger to his cheek and put on a mock-thoughtful expression. "I think there's a young lady here in town that you might fancy. Her family is a bit thick on the protocols, but then they are about five hundred years behind what you are accustomed to."

The Little One continued to cautiously move in behind Marcus, ever watchful for any sign that the man was going to turn around. Jake kept his eyes directed to Marcus' face, but watched the shoulders for any indication that he was about to move on him. The Little One was at the edge of his vision. Whatever it was up to, Jake was ready to take his cue from it.

So when it leapt up onto Marcus' back, shoving the man forward and knocking him to his knees, Jake dove forward, arms outstretched, and reached for the table. His hands were disappearing into the surface even before Marcus' knees touched the floor.

When Jake came through to the other side of the gate, he continued his fall forward and landed face down on the floor. He realized with a start that he hadn't come through alone. He rolled over and scrambled backward, his sword in one hand pushed out in front of him.

The dragon creature had somehow managed to jump from Marcus and onto Jake in time to catch a ride through the gate. It sat down and eyed Jake curiously. Jake, seeing that he wasn't in any immediate danger from the creature, looked quickly around the room to ensure that Marcus hadn't come through as well.

He and the Little One were alone in the room.

It was dusty and rundown and not anything like he had thought it to be when he had first entered it earlier. It had somewhat the same dimensions, and had furniture in somewhat the same locations, as the room Marcus had lain in wait for him.

That thought brought Jake quickly to his feet. He wanted to get out of that room.

§

Jake pulled open the castle's front double-door and stepped out onto the large porch landing. Wide concrete steps led down and away from the main entrance to the castle, spilling out into a clearing at the edge of the dark forest. From the high landing, Jake could just make out the trailhead that emptied into the clearing. He knew from the map he had found that this trail would take him all the back to the distant clearing that held the gateway.

The sky was slathered in wide swaths of purple and black and deep, dark blue. He couldn't tell what time of day it was, and had no idea how long he had been on this Other World. He knew only that he was very tired and that the trail between the clearing at the base of steps below him and the clearing with the gateway was a long, winding one.

He turned at the sound of claws on stone. The small creature came out of the castle and sat now beside him. It looked up at him, an anxious expression on its face.

"Hello there," said Jake. The creature gave a series of low, soft groans that could have been a greeting or a plea. Jake nodded at the castle doors behind them. "Doesn't he still need watching?"

The creature didn't answer. It continued to look up expectantly at the human.

Suppose not, thought Jake. *Not any more...*

He turned his gaze back to the black expanse of forest, above which the heavy sky hung, ever threatening. "Hey, I know someone who's gonna be real glad to see you. You up for a walk in the woods?"

Jake sat before a small campfire in the same forest clearing where he had previously seen the dragon flying overhead. It hadn't taken them nearly as long getting here as the underground route via the labyrinth and the tower, but it was dark before he had managed to set up camp.

Little One lay nearby, curled up near the fire. It was sleeping, and seemed quite at ease with the whole situation.

Jake sensed something then, and looked up at the night sky. A silhouette passed in front of the alien moon. He looked over at the little creature. "We have company."

Little One opened its eyes and looked at the human, but didn't move. It took in a deep breath and let out a contented sigh.

Chapter Eighteen

Mr. Griffin came into the sitting room and stood in the center of the oval area rug. Jake was sitting in one of the chairs, an elbow on the arm of the chair, his cheek resting on the knuckles of his left hand. He was staring at the small fire flickering hypnotically in the fireplace. He was deep in thought, and while his senses registered that Mr. Griffin had come into the room, his brain had not yet acknowledged the fact.

"Master Jacob," Mr. Griffin said at last, and waited then for Jake to respond.

Jake lifted his head from his hand but kept his attention directed on the fireplace. "Hey, Griff," he said.

"Mrs. Hodges insisted that I inquire as to your health, and to your state of mind."

At that comment, Jake turned to look at Mr. Griffin. "What?"

"I have been informed that you ate very little of your dinner, and very little of your lunch. That is not like you." Mr. Griffin pursed his lips and raised his brow. "So I have been informed."

"Nothing to worry about," said Jake. "Kinda tired; not much of an appetite." He had returned home from his trip to the Other World of the Castle on the Hill just that morning. This latest expedition had been a particularly exhausting one, both physically and mentally, and he was going to need some time to rebound.

"I shall relay your assurances to Mrs. Hodges," said Mr. Griffin. "I do not believe that they will be considered acceptable, however."

Jake smiled halfheartedly and set his head back against the high-back chair. "I'll grab a snack later. Perhaps that will ease her mind."

"I doubt it." Mr. Griffin turned and started to leave. As he reached the door, Jake called out to him and asked him to stay. Mr. Griffin turned about and took several steps back into the center of the room. Watching the young man's face, he could see that Jacob was having difficulty either sorting out some issue that he wanted to discuss or was having a hard time broaching a subject.

"So... how's Meara?" asked Jake, clearly avoiding what he really needed to talk about. "She was pretty upset about me leaving her behind."

Mr. Griffin had become increasingly concerned that the young lady had grown far too familiar with Master Jacob of late. "She understands her position," he said coolly.

"I was only thinking about her safety."

Mr. Griffin gave a sharp, abbreviated nod. "Of course."

Jake hardened his voice. "I have one artifact piece left to find; one more Other World to travel to. It's pretty clear now that way too many people know more than I do about what's going on. Some of those people would like for things to turn out differently than Uncle Tobias had in mind."

"Yes, sir."

"Now that we're so close..." Jake looked again at the fire. "It's dangerous, is all."

Mr. Griffin waited, seeing that Jake still wasn't finished. There was the matter of whatever it was that young Mr. Quigley really wanted to talk about.

"I figured something out," Jake said finally. "I don't think that Tobias was a thousand years old."

"Is that so?" Despite evidence that pointed to Tobias Quigley's apparent activities in the distant past, he never seriously believed that the Master was immortal.

"I think that Tobias and Marcus came to the Outland a thousand years ago and discovered the gates. They previously discovered a side door gate on some other world and traveled from the past to the present time, and then returned to this world through a main gate."

"Confusing, but plausible."

"I'm betting Nehman was with them."

"And while Master Quigley may have been born in the past, and fought the Rhetani in the past, he spent much of his life in our time, perhaps preparing for the return of the... *the Rhetani.*"

"The dragons, the *Jahai*, joined with Tobias and they stood watch these thousand years as Guardians." Jake looked away from the fire, looked up at Mr. Griffin. He took a long, noisy breath. "And something else..."

"Sir?"

"I don't think the Serpent's Keep gate is a primary gate."

"Sir?"

"I don't think our gate downstairs is a main gate. It doesn't look like a main gate, you don't access it like a main gate, and it just doesn't *feel* like a main gate."

"One of those side door gates?"

"Yeah," Jake said, almost surrendering.

"A side gate to the Rhetani?"

"Yeah..."

"I see. If I understand correctly, these side door gates lead to other locations on the same world, but in a different time."

"That's right."

"Master Jacob, you are saying that the Rhetani come from our world, but from a different time."

"I know. Not from the past, as Tobias did. If they had come from the past, we would have known about them. The Rhetani... are from our future."

Mr. Griffin stared numbly at young Mister Quigley. While Jake had had time to try and at least begin to sort out what this might mean, it was brand new to Mr. Griffin. What was there to say to such an idea?

"Yes, sir."

Jake gave a sympathetic smile to the old man. "Kinda my feelings on it, too."

Mr. Griffin looked for some sign that the conversation was finished, and when he could discern nothing one way or the other, he simply gave a brief, sharp nod and backed away.

When Jake was again alone in the sitting room, he turned his gaze back to the fire. It had died down during his conversation with Mr. Griffin, and if not rekindled soon and provided with more wood, it would quickly become only a gray bed of faintly glowing embers.

He remained in his chair, watching the flames slowly subside.

Whatever the truth about the gates, about the Rhetani, or about Tobias, Jake still had one more world to visit. He had little doubt that he would find the last artifact. Once he recovered the piece and set it into place, he would come face to face with the most frightening part of the quest, and the component that he felt the least certain about.

Exactly what was he to do once he crossed over into the world of the Rhetani, wherever that world might be? How was he to close down the gate for good?

Chapter Nineteen

The stone obelisk stood near the far side of the clearing, near the foot of one of the largest trees that Jake had ever seen. The great tree towered above the clearing, over this entire area of the forest and the river that cut through these West Outland woods. The stone itself was larger than the other pylons that he had seen, but other than that there was really nothing very unique about it, nothing to distinguish it from any large rock in the Outland; yet it drew from Jake the same feeling that all the gateway pylons had. There was something about it that radiated an atmosphere, an invisible aura. This was definitely the next gate to the next Other World.

Meara dropped her small pack onto the ground and walked towards the stone. Despite all his protestations, in the end Jake had relented and allowed her to come with him.

Allowed? His concerns about her safety aside, Meara's presence was an asset that could not be ignored. He probably had a better chance of succeeding with her along.

"I never really thought much about these stones," said Meara. She stood before the pylon, drawn to it. She placed a hand on it.

"Why would you," said Jake. "I mean, rocks, right?"

"Gateways to other worlds."

"Other universes," said Jake. "Alternate planes... other Earths..."

"All of it right here in the Outland, Serpent's Keep at the center of it all."

"Now that doesn't much surprise me."

Meara turned to look at Jake. "I've never known anything but the village, and the Outland."

"Prepare yourself, Meara. Your world is not normal. The village is not normal, the Outland is not normal." Jake pointed at the big stone in front of them. "And *that,* most definitely, is not normal."

Meara gave Jake a gentle smile. "I'm glad you came, sir. To Serpent's Keep, I mean. I'm sorry about Master Quigley, but I'm really glad that you came."

"It has been an experience." Jake let his backpack slide off his shoulder and let it drop. He looked around the clearing as he spoke. "I wouldn't have missed it for the world, so to speak."

"Thank you for letting me come this time."

"Completely selfish, I assure you. Chances for success seem greater with you than without you." said Jake. He glanced up at the sky. "Let's get settled in. It will be dark soon, and we may be here a while."

Jake decided to wait until the next morning before exploring the pylon, but the quiet evening gave him time to reflect on the verse on the scroll.

On the western bank stands nature proud, reaching high and broad. Within lay the path to kin of its kind, and there the ancient dwells.

He let that rest quietly in his thoughts as he sat before the fire, the obelisk a black shape just within the reach of light of the flames.

It seemed to Jake that in this case the message told him where to look and what he would find when he crossed over, but not how to open the gateway. If that was true, then he was going to have to rely on observation alone. He would have to use his past experience with the other pylons to help him find his way in.

When he woke in the morning, he found Meara standing by the stone, studying its features, brushing her hand over its rough surface.

"So much hidden beneath," she said. "And she's beautiful, in her way. I think that what lives within her brings something out in her."

Meara smiled thoughtfully, walked slowly about the stone. The great tree growing at the edge of the clearing began to cast an early morning shadow across it. "That tree and this stone have been together a thousand years," she said.

"At least," said Jake. He leaned his head back in order to see the full height of the tree. "She probably watched this stone get placed here." Even as he said the words, he began to wonder whether there was more to it than that. Everything about this gateway seemed to point to trees or forests, one way or another, and to ancient trees in particular.

Perhaps the scroll verse had a double meaning.

...reaching high and broad. Within lay the path...

Jake stepped away from the stone, stood with his back to the great tree. He stopped and studied the features; let his mind make what it would of the whorls and faults and peaks and shadows. Meara continued pacing around the rock, passing between it and Jake every half minute or so.

After several minutes had gone by, Jake took another two steps back and again let his mind wander across the face of the rock.

On the western bank stands nature proud, reaching high and broad. Within lay the path to kin of its kind, and there the ancient dwells.

Jake turned about sharply and looked at the tree. It was indeed very, very old. It had been old when the scrolls had been written.

It stood proud. It reached high and broad.

Within lay the path to kin of its kind...

Within the stone, or within the grandmother of every tree in the forest?

In the past, he had specifically ignored everything that grew, could change, or could die.

But in this case...

Jake walked slowly toward the tree, lifting his gaze carefully upward as he did so, taking in the features of the deeply crevassed bark of the trunk from the ground on up, until by the time he reached the base he was looking straight up.

"Master Jacob?" Meara was standing behind him. She had to step aside when he started to walk backward, still studying the gigantic trunk.

"We may have been looking in the wrong place."

"You think the way in is through the tree?"

"I think that this tree was expected to be around for a very, very long time."

Would they take such a chance? Perhaps not if it was growing where he come from... but here, in the Outland?

"There," he said.

Twenty feet up, a patch of bark was twisted into misshapen whorls around a gray patch a foot across. Jake ran forward and leapt up onto the trunk, grasped onto the bark and began climbing. The deep crevasses provided easy handholds and footholds and he quickly reached the spot.

Hidden deep within the bark was stone. It was rough, but flat. Jake reached in and laid his palm flat against it. It was cool. He pushed against it, but nothing happened.

It was never that simple. It almost always required two points.

He asked Meara to step back and study the trunk on either side of him, to search for the second pressure point, the key that would release the gate. But she saw nothing. Frustrated, Jake returned to the ground and stood with her.

It had to be there, and it had to be within arm's length of the first. In the past it had on one occasion required a dragon, but it had never required two people. Jake was counting on that rule applying.

The bark...

What if the bark had grown over the second pressure point? After all, it almost completely covered the first.

Assuming the two locations were side by side, within a few feet of one another, Jake climbed the tree again, this time with the small hand hatchet they used to cut firewood. Giving himself a strong foothold and holding tight with one hand, he used the hatchet to pry within the bark crevasses on either side of the first position.

"Don't hurt it," pleaded Meara.

"I'll do my best, Meara."

It took only a few minutes to find the second stone. He quickly tucked the hatchet into his belt and repositioned himself. It was awkward to place both hands into the bark and push at both stones, but it didn't take as much pressure as he had imagined.

He heard the sound of the gateway opening behind him.

The Other World they stepped into was beyond anything that Jake could have expected, or could ever have imagined. They were enveloped on all sides and from above by oversized vegetation, great broad leaves and branches and trunks many times larger than anything he had seen before.

It took a moment for them to realize that they had come out of the gateway not onto solid ground but onto a branch unbelievably massive and hundreds of feet above the floor of a vast rainforest. Looking behind him, Jake saw that the gateway they had traveled through, closing now and reverting to its quiet state of ancient pylon, was set into the trunk of an alien tree the diameter of a large house.

"Sir," Meara said calmly. Her hand was still in his from their journey through the gate, her grip tightening now.

Jake turned back and saw that there was movement in the leaves beyond that created by the faint breeze that was drifting through the canopy. There were faces in the leaves, and arms and legs. There were people huddled in the vegetation, moving slowly, eyes staring out from the shadows, watching the two strangers that had stepped through the gateway.

A small man climbed down onto the branch eight feet in front of Jake and Meara. He wore a leather poncho that reached midway down his thigh and was tied at the waist. His feet were covered in soft, pliable leather that no doubt helped him to move more easily about in the trees. His skin was light and his brown hair hung loose and long.

He took a step forward, his gaze moving casually from Jake to Meara. After a moment, he turned away, lifting an arm and waving for them to follow him. He walked effortlessly along the branch, looking back only once to see if they were coming.

As soon as they began moving, the others in the surrounding vegetation began climbing out onto the branch and followed after them. Most, men and women, young and old, were dressed similarly to the first, though a few wore only shorts and shoes, and one wore an open vest and calf-length trousers. Most had the same brown hair, though there were variations both lighter and darker, and Jake noticed one that had hair almost the color of straw.

They were led to a planked deck some thirty feet wide and twice as long. The wood was worn smooth from years of constant use. There were no rails; the edges of the deck were abrupt, stopping at living walls of green leaves and twisting branches.

There were openings in the leafy walls, however, and through these accesses rope bridges connected the deck to the decks of distant trees. As they approached one of these rope bridges, Meara slowed and finally stopped.

"I don't think I can do that, sir," she said flatly.

Jake looked from her to the bridge. Wooden planks a foot wide, set end to end, served as the base of the triangular shaped structure, two thick ropes set chest high serving as hand rails.

"You don't want to stay here, Meara," said Jake.

"Can I?"

"That's crazy. I thought you came on this trip to help me."

Meara stared coldly at the bridge. The far end was hundreds of feet away, lost in the shadow of the canopy. It bowed in the center from the sheer weight of rope and wood.

The man leading them stopped six paces out and looked back. He gave an encouraging nod, waved again for them to follow. Jake smiled apologetically and turned to Meara. He tried to reassure her that everything would be all right.

"Do you want me to go first?" Jake asked.

"Yes," Meara said quickly, and then abruptly, "No." She walked around him and onto the bridge. Their guide grinned and turned about and started forward again. Meara ignored him, staring down at her feet and taking it one step at a time.

Jake waited until Meara was well out onto the bridge before following after her. He could feel every step she took reverberate back to him and knew that she must also be able to feel his steps. He was careful to keep his distance and make each footfall as soft as possible. Before long, however, he felt the footfalls of others, and the bridge began to bounce and vibrate.

Looking behind him, Jake saw that a handful of the others had begun to follow. The remainder stood on the deck and watched the strangers slowly and clumsily cross the bridge.

Meara tensed and held tightly to the rope rails, but stoically continued forward, keeping silent her fears.

The deck they came to was much like the one they had left. The exception was that one of the open accesses in the walls of vegetation led to an elevator rather than a bridge. It had a wooden floor six feet on a side with a post at each corner supporting an open framework overhead. Attached to this framework was a set of ropes and pulleys.

A single rope set waist high connected each post and served as a rail. Their guide unhooked the rope and stepped inside, waited for Jake and Meara to climb on. Thankfully, he set the rope back into place before the others could join them. Jake thought that it was crowded enough with the three of them, especially considering the feeble appearance of one thin rope as a rail.

The elevator jerked slightly and started downward. The guide did nothing, which meant that someone somewhere was working the block and tackle and easing them, rather quickly Jake noted, to the ground.

The world grew darker the further they descended, with only narrow shafts of light boring through the canopy and providing what light there was. The air had a dampness to it, and an earthy, musky smell.

Three men were waiting at the bottom when the elevator softly touched the floor of the rainforest. One reached out and unhooked the rope, pulled it aside and waited for the passengers to step off the elevator.

Their guide led the way again, with the new escort following behind. The ground was soft and mulchy, the gigantic trees hundreds of feet apart, each eighty to a hundred feet in diameter. The thick canopy was high overhead, with only the occasional opening allowing in the light.

On their march to wherever it was they were going, Jake saw only one other elevator, but he suspected that all the trees were connected by bridge and silently wondered whether they would have traveled the entire distance in the canopy if their guide hadn't observed how uncomfortable Meara had been with the first bridge crossing.

After more than an hour's march, they came out onto an open expanse of wide, rolling terrain, in the center of which sat a primitive village of dozens of wood and grass huts. The huts surrounded a set of wooden community buildings that encircled the community square. Set in the heart of the square was a large, raised platform. The platform was empty but for a single, overly-large wooden chair.

The man sitting in the chair was dressed as all the others, but he nonetheless had a look about him that declared to anyone who approached that he was in charge around here. He watched in pretentious silence as Jake and Meara were led into the square and up to the edge of the platform.

"Hello," the man said calmly.

"You speak English?" asked Jake.

"What is... *English?*" asked the man.

"The language you speak," said Jake. "It is what we call English."

"I speak what I speak," said the man, bored with the subject. "I am Seshan, leader of this village."

"I am Jacob Quigley. This is Meara Gyles."

"You came through the gate."

"That's right," said Jake. He had hoped that invoking the name of Quigley would have sparked some reaction, but it hadn't. "We are on an important—"

"Few come through the gate," said Seshan, cutting him off.

That's good to hear, thought Jake. "We seek an artifact," he said.

At that moment, a great shadow glided across the platform. Jake looked up in time to see a winged dragon just as it reached the tree line and disappeared from view. After a few moments, it returned and circled above the village.

Jake looked back at Seshan. The leader wasn't looking at the dragon, but at the newcomers. Glancing around at the crowd that had gathered around the platform, he found as many people were watching them as were watching the dragon.

They are used to the dragon. They do not fear the dragon.

"A friend of yours?" asked Jake.

"He is curious about your arrival."

The dragon hovered above the platform, spun slowly in a tight circle and came delicately down beside Seshan. It was long and sleek, with smooth, shiny skin and a long neck. It settled in, wings pulled up and back. It turned its head and stretched it out slightly.

"Quigley, but not Quigley," it said.

"I am Jacob Quigley. I am the same blood as Tobias."

The dragon pulled its head back and straightened. "Yes," it said, having deduced as much and apparently satisfied with that deduction.

"Are you guardian to the artifact on this world?" Jake asked.

"Guardian," it said, then looked questioning at Meara.

"I am Meara. I help."

"My uncle has tasked me to gather together the artifacts," said Jake.

The dragon lowered its head to be closer to Jake. Being on the platform, it was still towering above him. "Not good," it said quietly.

"No. I don't think so."

"You close gate to Rhetani?"

"Yes."

The dragon breathed softly, looked at Meara and then again at Jake. It slowly raised its head, studied the crowded plaza, and then turned to Seshan, who had been quietly listening to the exchange.

"Get artifact," the dragon said to the tribal chief.

Seshan nodded, stood and walked to the edge of the platform. He waited until he was certain that he had the attention everyone. "We go to retrieve the artifact," he said.

"You know where it is?" asked Meara.

The dragon had stepped to one side, giving itself enough room to spread its wings. It leaned forward and pushed itself up and away from the platform. Within moments it was once again circling the village, and then disappeared beyond the trees.

"We know," said Seshan.

"We were once one tribe," said Seshan. He was walking beside Jake and Meara, a few paces behind several of Seshan's people. Further ahead, lost in the shadows of the forest floor, others scouted the way, ensuring the safety of their leader and their guests. Seshan used a tall walking staff, and from the way he handled it, Jake suspected that it could as easily be used as a weapon.

"What happened?" asked Meara.

"Long before my time, or that of my father, there was disagreement about our loyalty to the Jahai."

"Some didn't believe in their purpose?"

"The virtue of the obligation had faded with time. But for the presence of the guardian, no one had seen or heard from the Jahai for generations. There was only the dragon and the artifact. On the other side, there was the threat of the Rhetani. The legend of their power and ruthlessness, rather than fading, had grown."

"Strange the way that works," said Jake.

"Contentment breeds complacency, while fear festers," said Seshan. "It is the way of things."

Rather gloomy way of looking at things...

"Some began to question the wisdom of defending the artifact against such strength," Seshan continued. "Some wondered aloud why we were tasked with such a responsibility."

"But isn't the dragon the guardian?" asked Meara.

"Tahan is guardian. We serve Tahan."

Jake wondered what that meant, but chose not to pursue it. It may have been as simple as assisting the dragon in protecting the artifact or as dangerous as a dragon-worshiping cult with ritualistic sacrifices. A good subject to avoid.

"Did these others of your tribe turn against the Jahai, or from the obligation?"

"They await the return of the Rhetani so that they can hand to them the artifact."

"They have the artifact?" asked Meara.

"Tahan said to let them go. This is why we are vigilant in our watch of the gate. So long as we control who enters our world, it is not necessary to possess the artifact. Let them keep it safe until we have need of it."

Makes sense, I guess... thought Jake. Much better than both sides continually fighting to regain and hang onto something that neither side would need for centuries, if ever.

"There is going to be a fight then," stated Jake.

"We will take possession of the artifact."

When Jake stepped out of the trees, there were already dozens of others running across the grassy field, racing towards a similar group that was rushing out of a village much like the one they had just left.

He started forward, but Seshan took hold of his arm and held him back. "My people will take care of this," he said.

Meara, already several paces ahead, stopped and looked back over her shoulder. "We should help."

"This is our task," Seshan said firmly. "Leave us to it."

Meara looked anxiously at the two groups, now only moments from clashing. She turned desperately to Jake.

"Sir?"

Jake reluctantly shook his head.

A shadow swam across the grass then, racing towards the two groups about to do battle. The dragon was suddenly down in their midst. It grasped one of the second group by the shoulders and continued its forward momentum, dragging the small man backward towards the village. His feet left the ground, the dragon beating its great wings and gliding slowly upward. The man was six feet off the ground, kicking his legs frantically and pulling at the claws that gripped his shoulders, when the dragon released him and turned away, rising quickly in a circling arc. The man continued in the direction he had been carried, until finally crashing into the side of one of the village buildings.

In the center of the open plain, the two groups had met and were fighting hand to hand. Angry cries and screams of pain and desperation reached across the expanse to Jake, Meara and Seshan. There was the sharp rattling of metal on metal, the softer pounding thumps and crunches of body blows, of clubbed weapons against flesh and bone.

All the while Seshan stood placidly, hands clasped behind his back, waiting for his people to complete their task so that he might continue with his.

The dragon circled around and dropped in again, knocking two of the enemy to the ground before grasping a third. This time, the man's body was used to club several more to the ground as he was dragged and lifted, before finally being hurled against the side of the building.

The dragon then swung around over the village itself, and Jake watched as it dropped again and again down amongst the buildings. From his vantage point on the other side of the field, he couldn't see what the dragon was doing, but he had his suspicions.

The artifact must be right in the heart of the village.

Seshan spoke matter-of-factly. "Tahan will make certain that it isn't taken away before we can get to it."

The fight lasted only a few minutes. A number of Seshan's people were hurt, some seriously. More of those from the other village were hurt, and some had been killed; many more scattered into the surrounding forest, and a few returned to the village in an attempt to make a final stand and carry on the fight. The dragon targeted those that dared to come near the artifact.

As Seshan approached the village with Jake and Meara, he ordered that those who stayed inside their homes were to be left unharmed. Those who showed themselves were to be dealt with.

Seshan had prepared for this moment his entire life. As they walked through the village, Jake remained a pace behind him, allowing him to lead the way to the central compound and the small temple that held the artifact.

Tahan the dragon was perched atop the structure, a simple building six feet on a side and twelve feet tall. A heavy wooden door filled most of one side, a large crossbeam locking it in place.

Seeing the shape and design of the structure, it became clear to Jake why the dragon hadn't been able to get the artifact without Seshan's help.

There were a dozen or more of Seshan's people in the compound. Others moved through the village in small groups, ordering the villagers to remain in their huts.

One of Seshan's men lifted the crossbeam and another pulled open the door. Seshan stood in the doorway, took one step inside and lifted the box from its stand. Stepping outside again, he held tightly to the box. Above him, the dragon shifted uneasily.

"Our obligation is fulfilled," said Seshan, handing the box to Jake. "My people will return you to the gate, that you can continue the fulfillment of your own."

Jake took the box and nodded somberly. He really wanted to open it up and look inside, but it was clearly not the time. Once the ritual was satisfied and he was on his own...

"We go," Seshan announced to his people.

Jake and Meara were quickly led out of the village and into the forest, a large group moving out ahead of them, a slightly smaller group following up behind. Jake could occasionally see the shadows of figures pacing them on either side.

Those they had taken the artifact from would know that Jake would be heading for the gateway with it. Their escort was obviously aware of that and took extraordinary measures to protect them from ambush. The route back seemed random and very roundabout, but the defensive perimeter surrounding Jake and the artifact was strong and alert.

After several hours march, the rays of sunlight that pierced through the canopy were beginning to gray, angles shifting so that they seldom touched ground. The group approached a tree that dwarfed the other great trees of the forest. A maze of walkways, elevators, small buildings, ropes and guy wires, enveloped the massive trunk, winding their way upward to the forest canopy overhead. Lanterns set in place at stepped locations all the way up the trunk gave a haunted glow to the scene. There was a flurry of activity at the base of the tree, a number of the lead travel party scurrying about preparing for the ascent, others already in elevators or on walkways and on their way up.

"Wow," said Meara.

"The Great Tree," said their guide. "Our Gathering Place."

"It's amazing."

"It is our main access to the canopy."

The guide indicated that they should continue to the tree. They followed a well-traveled path between two roots that gradually closed in on them from either side, each rising up far above Jake's head. An elevator waited for them at the base of the tree. Two of their escort stood beside the elevator, a man and a woman, and the woman held the gate open for them. Once the guide and his guests were inside, the woman followed them in.

The elevator started its steady climb upward toward the canopy. It hung on a rope and pulley system six feet from the trunk, its rough bark with crevices deeper than a person's arm. Jake and Meara, looking outward, couldn't take their eyes off the scene that was spread out below them. Beneath the Great Tree was a vast open area with fire pits, long tables, pole lanterns, raised wooden platforms for musical bands, dancing, speechmaking and ceremonies.

Our Gathering Place...

As they rose higher, the guide indicated some of the defensive stations that were set up throughout the area. Some were on the ground, but most were set in the trees at stepped elevations; some had one person, others with two and even three.

The positions were probably more heavily fortified for occasions such as this. He couldn't imagine maintaining such a high human resource all the time.

The elevator came to a sudden, violent stop.

Their escort and the guide grabbed Jake and Meara by the shoulders and pushed them to the floor of the elevator. Looking through the rails, Jake could see the flickering arches of arrow trails tracing from positions in the neighboring trees toward the canopy above them, others to the ground below.

Above them... The enemy had waited until just the right moment to make their move. If they could force the elevator, with Jake and the artifact inside, to plummet to the ground, those waiting below could grab and run.

But those above had to get to the block and tackle, and those below had to get through the defenders protecting the Great Tree.

The elevator shuddered, dropped several feet and began to rock. After a few moments, it slowly settled into its new position.

"I'm not feeling too well, sir," said Meara.

In all the excitement of getting the artifact and seeing the Great Tree, Jake had forgotten how terrified Meara was of heights.

"I know that feeling," said Jake. "Let's trust our friends here to get us out of this and back home."

Meara stared directly ahead at the trees on the far side of the Gathering Place. "Yes, sir."

The elevator shook and began to fall, this time plummeting downward with no signs of stopping. Jake heard the snapping and whistling of lines suddenly free. He grasped a rail with one hand and Meara's wrist with the other. A moment later, the elevator stopped abruptly and Jake heard wood crack. The floor of the car slammed at his knees and his head jerked down and snapped back up.

Their guide took hold of his arm and pulled him to his feet. "Get ready, please," he said, then turned about and opened the gate facing the trunk of the tree. He easily jumped the six feet to an opening in the trunk. He ran a plank out, and the woman escort took hold of one end and set it into place. She turned to Jake, stepped back out of the way.

"Quickly now," she said.

Jake nodded and moved quickly to the plank. It was six feet from the elevator to the safety of the tree. Their guide, waiting within the tree, was reaching out to him. Behind Jake, the woman now had a firm grip on Meara's arm.

Three short, shuffling steps and Jake was across. Turning about, he could see that Meara wasn't going to make it quite as easily as he. When the elevator had dropped, it had dropped a considerable distance, but looking down, he could see that it was still a long way to the forest floor.

Meara saw that, too.

"You can do it, Meara," said Jake. "Three feet up, or a hundred, the plank's the same width."

"Not nearly wide enough, sir."

"Please," said the woman holding her arm. "We must move quickly."

Meara nodded quickly. She was standing at the very edge of the narrow wooden foot bridge. "I know that."

Jake put one foot out onto the plank and reached out. Meara had only to lean forward and she could just about take hold. "Come on, Meara."

Meara nodded again. She took a deep breath and slid one foot cautiously out. The woman holding her arm moved up directly behind her. She cupped Meara's elbow in the palm of her hand. Meara eased forward, reached out and grasped Jake's outstretched hand. She slid forward again, now midway across the little bridge.

The fighting far above them continued, but the sounds were much fainter now that they had dropped so far. Jake wasn't sure why he glanced up when he did, perhaps an inner sense of impending danger, but he did, and just in time to see a body hurtling down towards them. A victim of the battle that was going on in the canopy, the poor man was now little more than a missile rushing directly at them.

Jake didn't take the time to sort the situation out. He had Meara's hand in his, so he gripped it tight and pulled, leaning forcefully back. Meara cried out in panic, and the woman holding onto her arm froze in surprise.

Jake fell backward and inward, landing on his butt, holding tight to Meara. She was dangling half in the tree, half out.

Jake saw the falling body strike the elevator, shattering it. Its remnants hung precariously by its guy wires, spinning wildly. The makeshift bridge fell, and the woman who had been helping Meara fell with it, lost from Jake's line of sight a moment after the collision.

"Oh, god..." Meara muttered shakily. "Oh, please..."

"I have you," said Jake, and he slid backward, pulling her with him. The man inside the tree immediately rushed forward to help.

Meara quickly turned and looked back out, still sitting.

"What happened?" she asked.

"There was... *debris,*" said Jake.

"What happened to—"

"She didn't make it."

"We need to hurry," said their guide.

There was a shaft within the trunk of the tree beginning at the landing they were on and disappearing in the darkness above them. The chimney was about four feet in diameter, with a ladder running along the wall. The guide led the way, with Meara and Jake following.

After a few moments climb, what light that seeped in from the opening below was blotted out, and the sounds of the conflict faded with it. Jake could see nothing above those climbing directly above him. He found himself in near-absolute darkness, with the only sounds being that of the breathing of his companions and their movement on the wooden rungs of the ladder.

After what seemed an eternity, but was in fact probably no more than a couple of minutes, they stepped up and out onto another landing within the tree. The guide looked out an opening similar to the one they had entered below. He said nothing, instead moved to the chimney shaft and climbed up onto the ladder.

Before following the others, Jake went over to the opening and looked out.

They were probably a hundred to a hundred and twenty feet above the destroyed elevator. Looking up, they had at least that far to go before they reached the canopy.

"Please, sir," the guide called down. Meara had already started up the next section of ladder, leaving only Jake on the landing.

Jake gave a silent *okay* and went to the ladder.

Midway up this next section, Jake began to hear the sounds of the skirmish going on in the canopy. There were angry voices, shouted orders, and the sharp cracking sounds of wood striking wood.

Reaching the top landing, Jake found there were half a dozen people defending the access, though there was no immediate fighting going on there. They stood ready, defensively, while the sounds of one-on-one conflict came at them from all around, from within the leaves and branches that lined the perimeter of the wooden platform that served as a porch-like structure beyond the opening to the shaft.

As soon as Meara and Jake were both on the inner landing, the entire team moved forward, hurrying quickly across the platform and through an opening in the vegetation.

The path through the canopy was well defined from many years of use. Those leading the way moved easily and confidently, as if they had traveled this way a thousand times.

As with their original journey through the canopy, Jake occasionally saw the flittering movement of scouts scuttling through the shadows on either side of the main troop.

It was as he watched one of these flitting shadows that he saw something.

The shadow was there, and then it wasn't. It hadn't disappeared through normal movement, as he had come to expect. This shadow looked like it grew larger for just a moment and then dropped from sight.

"Something's wrong," he said softly.

The guide, now following behind him in the group, spoke just as softly. "Yes... keep moving."

Jake could feel it. There was a growing tension amongst the entire group. They all knew that something was wrong.

The man traveling in front of Meara turned about suddenly and threw himself over her, knocking her to the surface of the large branch on which they were traveling. Seeing this, Jake dropped down to one knee, only to be smacked from behind by the body of the guide, knocking him face down. As he was thrown forward, he heard the singing of arrows as they filled the air around him.

Only after he was face down on the branch, the weight of the small man pressing down on him, did he feel the hot stinging of the arrow in his side. As he lay there, he began to feel a dull ache in his gut, a warmth under his shirt. He felt uncomfortable, and tried to shift position. When he did, though, sharp streaks of fire raced out from the location of that dull ache.

"Hey," he grunted. "You gotta get off me."

The guide gave no indication that he was going to get off Jake.

"No, really. You need to get off me. I've been shot."

"I know," said the man.

The rustling of branches and leaves and the cracking of wood came from all directions. Voices echoed throughout the canopy, unintelligible to Jake but clearly communications between comrades.

Jake's protector rolled to one side, rose to one knee and lifted Jake up by his left arm. Another pair of hands lifted him by his right. Looking ahead, he could see that entire troop was up and moving, with Meara directly ahead of him.

They traveled quickly. Sounds of activity continued to push in from both sides, but it all seemed fuzzy to Jake. The world around him blurred and he moved only because he was being carried along with the group.

At several points along the way they crossed wooden decks and then quickly returned to the pathways along the branches.

They stepped out onto another wooden platform and stopped. The troop gathered together, guards taking stations at the several access points. Jake was led to a bench and he carefully sat down, strong arms guiding him down.

"How are you, sir?" asked Meara, sitting down beside him. A middle-aged woman sat down on the other side and began tending to his wound.

"I'm fine," said Jake. Everything was still a bit fuzzy, but now that he was able to rest, things were beginning to clear. He felt really, really tired.

The woman tending his wound pulled out the arrow without warning. It was like an electric shock and Jake almost passed out.

"Sir?" asked Meara.

"Fine," said Jake, this time more hushed.

Their guide approached and stood directly in front of Jake. "How are you doing?"

"Fine," Jake said firmly.

"That is good."

"How much further?" asked Meara.

"Two platforms, yet," the man answered. He looked again at Jake. "We have a rope bridge to cross. Are you up to it?"

"No problem." Jake held up his arms and let his doctor wrap his torso with a wide cloth bandage.

"Very good," said the guide. "We leave as soon as you are ready." He turned and began giving directions to the others of the team. The doctor finished her work and pulled Jake's shirt back into place. Jake slowly stood up, letting Meara help him and using her for support.

Keeping his balance on the rope bridge required that he use stomach muscles that he hadn't realized he had, and this put pressure on the wound, which in turn made him move clumsily as he worked his way across.

They reached the tree with the gateway set into the trunk. The site was heavily defended, shadows within shadows moving within shadows. Jake brought out the artifact and stepped up to the obelisk. As with all the obelisks, there was a place to insert the artifact and open the gateway.

Jake was studying the stone when the world around him exploded in movement and sound. A visual rush drew in on him as men and women frantically fought to get through the defenders and reach Jake. Several men closed in to protect him. Meara stood directly beside him, torn between helping him search for the recess in which to place the artifact and guarding him against any who would approach.

"The dragon," she said suddenly, almost under her breath. Looking away from the stone, Jake followed Meara's gaze. She was looking down a pathway through the canopy. The dragon, crouching low, its wings folded back tightly along its back, was rushing forward along the top of the heavy branch. It struck aside several attackers before reaching the open clearing.

Jake had to force himself to turn away from the sight of the dragon and continue searching the surface of the obelisk. Behind him, the dragon roared, raising its head as much as it was able in the confined space. It struck at the attackers that had made it into the clearing, several of whom fell from the canopy, disappearing into the darkness below.

Jake found the location on the stone and hurriedly put the artifact into place. The change was immediate. The obelisk blurred and the image of it transformed, becoming vaguely transparent. The area took on a bluish glow.

Behind him, the dragon swung around angrily and swept its claws across a group of attackers. Some of their arrows had struck home, burying themselves beneath the creature's scales, and a web of burning pain was enveloping it. It rolled one eye in Jake's direction and saw the open gateway. It knew that it had accomplished its task. It laid its head back and let out another great roar, this time a proud call to all in its charge.

Jake stuffed the artifact into his pocket and took Meara by the hand. He caught sight of their guide and they gave each other a curt nod.

Jake and Meara stepped into the gateway.

"What are *you* doing here," said Meara. She was looking at a figure standing at the edge of the clearing, leaning against a tree. She obviously knew the man, and didn't much like him. Jake thought he recognized him, as well. He was pretty certain that this was the same man that had been standing outside the Adventurer's Guild; he had the same weathered appearance and hunched over stance. He looked as though the years of a lifetime had beaten against him.

"You know this guy?" Jake asked. He and Meara stood beyond the gate, both cautiously eyeing the man. Jake heard the gate close behind him.

"Karl Brogen," said Meara. "Weasel."

Karl Brogen tilted his head back and stared at Jake from under a heavy brow. He gave a dull, tired smile. "So, boy... you think you're something special, eh?"

"As a matter of fact, I find myself to be less special every day," said Jake.

The man snorted. "Yeah, well, you got that right. You're *nothin'*."

"I certainly appreciate you coming all this way to confirm that."

Brogen look wearily at Meara. "You're as annoying as your father, missy."

Jake took several slow steps closer to Brogen. Every step was a spear in his side. "What brings you out here, Mr. Brogen?"

"You don't know what you're doing, boy. I don't hold your ignorance against you, but you're on the wrong side. If you had the facts, you'd understand that."

"I trust my uncle's judgment."

"Now *that* I do hold against you. How can you trust someone you don't even know?" Brogen pushed away from the tree and stepped toward Jake. He relied heavily on a tall staff. "Up to a few weeks ago, d'ya have any suspicion at all that he had been involved in any of this?"

"I don't feel the need to justify my actions to you."

"Yeah? What do you know of the Rhetani? D'ya know when it came face to face, the Jahai crawled back to their worlds and left the likes of Tobias Quigley to do their dirty work for 'em?"

"How about we get back to *my* question, Mr. Brogen." Jake wasn't going to let Brogen's ranting get to him. "What are you doing here?"

And just what is your part in all this?

Brogen grinned. The man wore Meara's opinion of him well. There was something very unpleasant behind that face. "I've been watching you, Quigley," he said. He tapped a crooked finger against his temple. "I am the eyes of the Rhetani."

Jake felt cold, but did his best to hide any emotion. "And what is it that your masters have you watching for?"

"Not my masters, boy. I side with the Rhetani because they are in the right." He brought back just a hint of the smile. "And because they will win."

This guy sounds an awful lot like Marcus. They must have gone to the same school...

"Sorry, but I'm just not seeing it," said Jake.

"Blind as well as ignorant."

"If you're involved, there's money in it somewhere," said Meara.

"Oh my, yes... Nothing wrong with being well paid for services rendered."

"My uncle needed no reward to do what was right," said Jake. "Neither do I."

"Tobias was a pompous fool. There was never any reasoning with him."

Definitely in Marcus' class, thought Jake. *How many of these old guys are there?*

"I doubt you'll find me any more accommodating than my uncle."

"I don't find you much of anything at all," Brogen growled. "Now give me the artifact."

"Really... just like that..."

"It wouldn't do you any good," said Meara. "Not all by itself."

"Do you think I don't know where the Rhetani gate is? This is the last artifact. It is all that I need."

"Not gonna happen," said Jake. He had barely finished the statement before Brogen lifted and swung his staff. It came in at a level arc, blisteringly fast, and struck Jake across the shoulder. The force knocked him off his feet and to the ground; the sharp, burning pain was mind-numbing, radiating out from his shoulder through his entire body. Brogen moved in quickly before Jake could clear his head enough to react, stood over him and brought the end of the staff down hard onto his chest.

Meara leapt into the air and struck Brogen with a body blow before he could raise the staff and bring it down for a final strike. Both sprawled face down onto the ground and rolled. Jake scrambled aside and frantically dug into his pack, came out with the pistol. He brought it up in both hands, turned and aimed it in Brogen's direction.

Meara was crawling to one side, but Brogen was already on his feet and swinging his staff. It struck Jake across the wrists and knocked the pistol across the clearing. Brogen started to swing again, but this time Jake managed to grab hold of the staff before there was much force behind it. He pulled it around and he and Brogen found themselves struggling in each other's grasp, the staff between them. The exertion tore through the wound in his side. It felt hot and wet beneath the bindings.

Jake was surprised at how strong the man was. His appearance was very deceiving. Beneath the ragged clothes and disheveled look was a tough, aggressive, brawny fighter. He was beginning to think that he might lose the fight when he heard the shot. He felt Brogen tense, and at first thought that the man had been shot.

"Stop," Meara called out sharply. "Right now. I won't say it again."

Jake pushed himself away from Brogen, letting him have the staff for the moment. He turned his head and looked toward Meara. She was standing three long strides away, pistol raised and pointed toward Brogen.

"Drop the staff, Brogen," said Jake. "I don't want Meara to have to shoot anyone. Not even you."

Brogen was looking angrily at Meara. He gave a side glance to Jake, shoved the staff away from him and stood. Meara took a cautious step back. Jake stood and walked to Meara, careful to stay out of her line of sight to Brogen. He held out his hand for the pistol. When she ignored him, he spoke softly to her. "Rope in my pack."

She handed him the gun and went over to their gear.

Brogen grinned thinly. "You think you can get me back to the village, boy?"

Jake took one step toward Brogen, slowly shook his head.

It took Brogen a few moments to realize what Jake was thinking. When he did, his expression hardened. "You can't leave me here, Quigley."

Jake didn't respond. He was too weak. Brogen must have sensed that, too. He could see Meara out of the corner of his eye. She was kneeling beside the backpack.

Brogen hurled himself at Jake. Jake just managed to lift his weapon before Brogen was on him and the two of them flew backward. Brogen wrapped himself around Jake. When they struck the ground the weapon fired. Jake felt a burning at his belly and thought that he had been gut shot. He quickly realized that it was the flash from the exploding gunpowder. He twisted his hand and pulled the trigger. From Brogen's reaction, Jake was certain that he had been hit. Brogen fought desperately to get at the pistol. Jake fired again.

§

Mr. Griffin opened the front door and hurried down the steps. Meara was half-carrying, half-dragging Jake up the front walk from the gate. He could hear Jake mumbling under his breath.

"I'm all right, I'm fine... okay, okay..."

Once inside, as they started toward the stairs, Meara made to drop the backpack before beginning the climb.

"No... no," Jake mumbled. *The artifact...*

"Get Mrs. Hodges," said Mr. Griffin.

Meara looked torn. She didn't want to leave him, not after all she had done to get him this far.

"I will get him upstairs," said Mr. Griffin. "Get Mrs. Hodges."

Meara stepped away and Mr. Griffin started up the stairs with Jake.

Jake wasn't about to be parted from the artifact. He forced Mr. Griffin to stop and held his hand out for the backpack. Mr. Griffin let out an impatient sigh and nodded to Meara.

Meara followed Mr. Griffin and Master Jacob up the stairs. "I dressed the wounds as best I could," she said.

"I'm sure you did just fine, Meara. Once we get upstairs... Mrs. Hodges."

"Yes, sir."

Chapter Twenty

Jake opened his eyes. The ceiling above him seemed strangely unfamiliar and yet somehow he understood that he should know it.

He laid his head to one side.

I'm in my room...

He heard the words in his head and the thought made him feel safe and warm. It took a few moments for the realization to catch up: Not his room back home in the real world...

Serpent's Keep... I'm home...

He heard a very faint rumbling noise and rolled his head to the left. Mrs. Hodges was asleep in the chair beside him, a book lying open in her lap. She was snoring softly. Looking around the room Jake saw his backpack sitting on top of the dresser. His situation came rushing back at him.

He had the last artifact. With it, he would be able to open the Serpent's Keep gate. *The Rhetani gate...*

Jake was certain the gate was a side door, and it would take him to this very same world, but in a different time, just as the gate inside the castle had taken him to Marcus. The Rhetani were in Jake's world in another time, though he had no idea how or why. What he did know for sure was that it would soon be his home, for once he permanently closed the gate, there would be no way for him to return.

He couldn't clear his mind enough to bring any of these thoughts into focus, but they wouldn't go away, either. They swam in a blurry sea of words and images until he finally fell back into a restless sleep.

When Jake woke the second time, Mr. Griffin was sitting in the chair, book in hand, oil lamp turned down low and illuminating the pages.

"Hey, Griff." Jake's voice crackled as he spoke. He tried to clear his throat, realized that his throat was dry as old paper. Mr. Griffin lowered his book, reached over and picked up a glass sitting on the side table. He half-filled it from a metal pitcher and handed it to Jake.

"How are you feeling, Master Jacob?"

Jake took a cautious sip from the glass, then took a longer, deeper drink and let it slide soothingly down his throat.

"I think I'll live." He handed the glass back to Mr. Griffin. "How's Meara?"

"Quite well. Concerned as to your health."

"And how is my health? Technically speaking."

"Your ribs are bruised, but not broken. Burns from the gunpowder flashes should heal with only minor scarring. The arrow did some damage, and you lost some considerable amount of blood."

"Sounds scary."

"Mrs. Hodges has significant experience in this area."

"Good ol' Mrs. H."

"Yes," said Mr. Griffin. "As to your follow-up care, you are being treated with medicinal herbs, both topically and internally."

"Cool," said Jake. He laid his head back.

"You will recover, Master Jacob."

"Cool," he said again. His strength was fading, but he felt that he was being drawn back into sleep not so much because he was weak but rather because his mind wasn't yet ready to face both the past and the future. He returned his attention to the ceiling. After half a minute, he closed his eyes. Tiny explosions of light flickered against his eyelids, as if a strobe was flashing above him.

§

Jake wandered along the high-walled fence that bordered the back perimeter of the estate. Trees and shrubs were strategically positioned around the grounds, giving the property the look of an enclosed private park. The walls that surrounded most of the estate prevented him from seeing the village beyond from ground level, but the sound of the villagers bustling about their midday activities reached into the estate and was as warm as the rays of the noon sun that pushed against his face. He turned his face up to the clear, bright sky, closed his eyes and let his skin turn hot, let the healing warmth work its way deep into the flesh and bone and muscle.

Turning from the sun, he continued his walk along the wall. The heat that had gathered within the stone throughout the morning now pulsated outward. He wore a loose baggy shirt that hid the bandages beneath, the slight breeze helping to cool him. The wooden cane that he used bore much of his weight and eased much of the pressure.

Jake's thoughts were continually drawn to the last remaining action that he had yet to perform in the quest given him by his uncle. He had the last artifact. All he had to do was put it into place and the Serpent's Keep gate would open. That would be it. Whatever had happened up to this point in the quest, whatever he had done, whatever he hadn't done, once he opened the gate, there would be no more choices to make, no more decisions to wrestle over. He would step through the gate and do whatever had to be done to close it forever.

A major, life-changing event if he ever knew one. There would be no returning to life as normal. If he survived, all that he had known—people, places, maybe even the warmth of the sun, all would be gone.

The words from the final scroll came unbidden into his mind.

The heart of the serpent cannot be seen, yet its powerful beat sends life to head and tail. To close its eyes, the aim must be true.

Jake hadn't liked the sound of that. The thought that he might have to kill something as the final act in a moral quest turned his stomach. Yet, the words had the ring of killing in them.

And there had been the dagger that he had found in the hidden compartment with the scroll; a dagger with a blade made of bone.

There was no real reason to think so, but he believed the bone had come from a dragon. A Jahai bone?

Meara came up beside him and moved into step as he continued walking.

"Master Jacob? Mrs. Hodges would like you to come in now. She has soup ready."

Jake had worked his way around the side of the house. He stopped and leaned heavily on his cane. From here, he could see the front gate.

"Sir?" Meara urged.

Meara stood silently beside Jake, waiting for him to head inside, ready to follow him. Watching him, looking at his face, at the way he stood, she realized that he had changed since first arriving in Serpent's Keep. He had aged far beyond his time here, and more than that, his experiences had worn him down. They also seemed to have changed the way he responded to the world around him. She could see it in his eyes. They weren't just sad, they were... mournful; but also careful.

"I think I'll go for a walk," he said suddenly.

"But... sir... Mrs. Hodges..."

"I'll be back later." He started around toward the front of the mansion, in the direction of the gate.

"But... but Mrs. Hodges... she has soup."

Jake stood across the street from the café. He watched the people passing in front him, going about their business. A few looked curiously in his direction; a few nodded to him in silent greeting. A few spoke, offering him *good afternoon.* With each, he smiled and offered a *good afternoon* in return.

The café looked fairly busy. That was good. He started across the cobblestone thoroughfare, reaching the door at the same time as the banker. He remembered Mr. Dante from another visit he had made to the café.

"Ah, Mr. Quigley. Here, let me get this for you." The man opened the door to the restaurant and stood to one side.

"How's business, Mr. Dante?" Jake stepped through the open door.

"Never so busy as to keep me from lunch, yet well enough that I can afford it." Mr. Dante followed him in.

Once inside, the short, chubby man moved around Jake and hurried through the half-filled room to his own personal table, which waited for him against the far wall.

"Good afternoon, Mr. Quigley," said Sparta. She approached Jake, coffee carafe in one hand, cup in the other. She indicated an empty table. "Glad to see you up and about."

"Thank you, Miss Vesper." Jake took the two steps and sat down. He leaned back in the chair. "I think I'd like to start with some of that great coffee, if you please."

Chapter Twenty One

Jake stared down at the collection of artifacts already set into the concrete lattice design in the floor. All the pieces but one were there. The empty space that remained had exactly the same shape as the artifact he held in his hand. It was smooth and hard, cool to the touch. It was heavier than he would have expected had he not had experience with the other artifact pieces.

Jake could feel his heart pounding against his ribs. He was short of breath, dizzy; the air in the room around him was hot and didn't seem to have enough oxygen.

Get it over with...

He stepped forward, knelt down and set the artifact into position. As he stood and stepped back, the grinding sound of stone rubbing against stone filled the room, the hollow reverberations echoing in the chamber until it was a physical pressure pushing against him, vibrating deep into his bones.

The floor beneath the reconstituted artifact emblem began to rise; from below rose the gate, a set of slender stone-like pillars capped by the completed artifact.

Once it had risen waist-high, energy started to crackle within the gate and fire-like threads danced from pillar to pillar. As the gate continued its slow ascent, the energy within it grew brighter and hotter and more intense.

Mr. Griffin came out of the long tunnel and into the chamber, keeping his distance from both Jake and the rising gate.

"Hey, Griff," said Jake. He tried to smile. "I guess I'll be seein' ya."

"It has been a pleasure, Master Quigley."

Jake nodded a silent thank you, turned back to the gate just as the grinding noise stopped. The only sound now was the crackling of electrical energy, which grew suddenly louder. The heart of the gate began to glow, growing brighter and brighter.

All sound stopped suddenly with a dull thud. Set in the heart of the gate, within the pillars and four feet above the ground, was a shimmering blue sphere two feet in diameter. As he watched, the sphere began to expand, slow and steady.

"Perhaps you should move back into the tunnel, Mr. Griffin," said Jake, not taking his eyes off the growing sphere.

Mr. Griffin backed silently into the tunnel. A moment later he turned at the sound of someone running down the long, narrow hallway, held out his arms in time to catch Meara.

"Master Jacob!" Meara cried out, struggling against Mr. Griffin's grip.

"It'll be all right, Meara. This is what I was brought here to do."

He turned his attention back to the gate. The sphere had grown large enough that it had swallowed up the pillars. Images began to form in the swirling, ethereal mist within the sphere. He couldn't tell what the images were at first, but as the sphere continued to expand, the shapes within it continued to take form, to solidify.

The outer perimeter of the sphere crept outward until it was just inches from Jake. The top vanished into the ceiling, the bottom into the floor.

In place of the gate, with its pillars and cap and base, furniture materialized within the chamber: chairs, tables, lamps. From his experience with the *side door* in the castle, Jake knew that he was seeing a room and objects not in the chamber beneath the mansion, but from some other place, some other time.

If this side door of the gate system was like the other, then crossing over should be a simple task. The other gate had required that he have the artifact in his possession and that he move to a certain location within the room. He had done that by reaching for the table beside the chair that Marcus had been sitting in: the first time with the sword, and the second time by dropping his hand through it.

In this case, the center of the chamber itself was the artifact, hidden now, held above the unseen pillars of the gate. Would stepping into the center of the room be enough?

The outer edges of the sphere quietly swallowed him up. He was fully inside the room, though he knew that he was still in the underground chamber beneath the mansion.

Mr. Griffin and Meara were still visible, though from his perspective, Jake saw them standing not at the entrance to the tunnel, but in an open doorway leading to another room. They took another step back, beyond the doorway, safely outside the influence of the chamber. As they did, Jake lost sight of them.

He looked systematically about the room.

> *The heart of the serpent cannot be seen, yet its powerful beat sends life to head and tail. To close its eyes, the aim must be true.*

The walls were covered in light-colored paneling; the hardwood floor was covered in a scattering of area rugs, one large, a handful of smaller. There were several electric lamps sitting on side tables beside stuffed chairs.

A single window looked out over the rooftops of a small, quiet mountain village containing a cluster of buildings with steeply sloping roofs.

None of what Jake saw gave any indication that the scene came to him from a dark, distant future.

The only other door into the room opened and two humans came in, one man and one woman. They were of average height and weight, looked to be in their late thirties or early forties. Their hair styles were rather normal, nothing *futuristic* or otherworldly bizarre. They were dressed in pants and shirts, cotton in appearance, again rather normal.

Jake wondered if he had somehow misinterpreted what he had learned over the course of the quest.

"You must be Jacob," said the man. He spoke English with no discernable accent; at least none that Jake could hear.

"And who are you?"

"We do appreciate what you've done, Mr. Quigley," said the woman.

"Yeah? Who is *we*?" Jake was growing increasingly uneasy with the situation. He had found himself in a number of similar conversations since starting this quest, and not one had turned out good. He began studying objects in the room. One would cross him over.

"We are not the enemy, as some have made us out to be."

Jake turned his attention full to the woman. "You work for the Rhetani?"

The woman gave a patronizing smirk; the man gave a hearty laugh.

"Oh, dear," said the woman. "How you have survived up to now must be an absolutely marvelous tale. Should we have the time, perhaps we can explore it together."

"Sure. No problem." Jake again eyed the furniture, the objects on the furniture, the window, the world beyond. He suspected the small, round table in the center of the room, which was also in the center of the chamber, to be the key to crossing over. He wasn't quite ready to test that theory, though. Once he was on the other side, they would be able to get to him, so before he made the attempt, he wanted to know exactly what he would have to do in order to permanently close the side door.

After that, they could do with him what they wanted. He didn't think it would be pleasant, but at least the sacrifice would have been worth it.

If he crossed over and then failed to close the gate, the connection will have been established; and since the artifact was now a permanent fixture of the gate, they would be free to cross over into his time.

Be very, very careful...

"I apologize, Mr. Quigley," said the man. "But your question was... unexpected."

The heart of the serpent cannot be seen...

"Jacob," the woman held her arms outstretched. "We are all Rhetani."

sends life to head and tail...

What? Jake couldn't help but be startled, and it showed. *What did she mean by that?*

"Just what were you expecting, if I might ask?" asked the man.

"I know that you are in our future. I know that you want to use the side door to access the gates."

"Yes, we are in your future," said the woman. "As such, we can see what you cannot."

"And you want to use the gates to control the universe."

"Look at us, Jacob. Do we look like monsters?"

"Maybe a little," Jake mumbled, continued to search.

The heart of the serpent cannot be seen...

"Oh, come now..."

Jake turned his attention back to the woman. "The Rhetani are human?"

"Of course we are." She wore a soft, gentle, albeit patronizing smile. "Centuries from where you are now, a great leader will unify humanity. The Rhetani were born from that magnificent unification."

I don't like the sound of that...

"And you would spread that unification?"

The woman's face was aglow. "Across time and space and universal plane."

The heart of the serpent cannot be seen, yet its powerful beat sends life to head and tail. To close its eyes, the aim must be true.

"Apparently not everyone wants to be unified," said Jake.

"We're not some religious cult, Quigley," said the man. "The Rhetani aren't about forcing beliefs on anyone."

Just obedience, thought Jake. He had almost said it aloud, but stopped himself in time. He didn't want to get into philosophical or political discourse with these two. And he didn't really think they were carrying on the discussion in some righteous attempt to convert him to their way of thinking.

They were trying to ease him into lowering his guard enough so that they could control the situation when he crossed over.

Jake, on the other hand, wanted only to ensure the situation didn't get any more complicated before he could figure out what needed to be done the moment he crossed over.

The Rhetani are human? Jake wished that he hadn't heard that. It only distracted him from the issue at hand.

At some point in the future of Earth, *his* Earth, humanity will be unified by, dominated by, some government body referred to as the Rhetani. What form of government will this Rhetani take? From where will it come? Political organizations could start from most anything.

Jake tried to shake all such thoughts from his mind. If he accomplished his task, and if he survived, he would have all the time in the world to discover the answers.

To close its eyes, the aim must be true.

Did he have to strike at something?

He again looked quickly about the room, half involuntarily. The man and woman watched him quietly. They had to know what he was doing, but they didn't seem concerned. Did they know that he had faced this situation before, with Marcus?

How could they know? Marcus would have no connection with this gate.

But then, they had known who Jake was. How did they know that? They were from the future... Certainly some information had to have made it across the centuries.

His mind began to swim in a sea of questions. Again he forced himself to push aside such thoughts for later.

The heart of the serpent cannot be seen, yet its powerful beat sends life to head and tail. To close its eyes, the aim must be true.

Did he have to strike at something that could not be seen?

...its powerful beat sends life to head and tail.

The connection would be established once he crossed over. The gate, the side door, would be in both locations; that included the completed artifact, which was directly overhead, directly above the center of the gate, directly above where the woman now stood, beside the small, round table.

The chamber under the mansion that Jake stood in had a low ceiling, easily reachable by simply raising his arm.

The room that he was looking into appeared to have a higher ceiling, but Jake had a hunch that was illusion, or at the very least, the artifact was hovering at the same height in both locations.

He turned his head and looked in the direction of the now unseen Mr. Griffin and Meara. He raised a hand in farewell, at the same time reaching for the bone dagger that he had tucked in his belt in the small of this back. He turned about and stepped into the world of the Rhetani.

Jake moved immediately to the small table and swept the bone dagger through the shiny surface. As was the case with the other side door, Jake found himself hurtling through an electrified version of a gate passageway. Despite the fact that he knew what to expect, the rush of vertigo and lightheadedness sent him reeling. He fought to hold himself steady so that he wouldn't stumble when he crossed over.

And then he was there. Jake quickly turned the dagger about in his hand, held it firmly in the grasp of both hands, and thrust it upward directly over his head.

He felt it strike home, bone dagger against the unseen artifact latticework; the blade struck against solid surface at first, then slipped in as if guided, pushing through a thick, dense, yet yielding barrier.

And the world that he had just stepped into appeared to explode in a sudden blast of light, everything vanishing in a wash of pure, bright white.

And then it all returned.

Nothing moved. The world was motionless, as if caught between one second and the next. The Rhetani couple, the clouds in the sky outside the window, an insect in mid-flight several feet in front of him, all were absolutely still.

And Tobias Quigley was standing in the far corner of the room.

"Hello, Jake." There was a cloudy gloominess to the words.

"Uncle Tobias?"

Tobias took the three steps across the room. He had a smile on his face, but it was a sad smile. When Jake moved forward to give his uncle a hug, Tobias held up a hand for him to stop.

Jake stopped short. He looked around him more carefully. "What's going on?"

He noticed then that the artifact was now visible, hovering above them, seemingly with nothing holding it in place. There was no sign of the gate that had risen from the chamber floor and upon which the artifact lattice rested. The dagger was gone, and the individual artifact pieces had merged together to form a single object with a design on the face depicting the pieces from which it was born.

"You did good, Jake." Tobias walked around Jake and had a close look at the couple standing unmoving in the room.

Jake nodded at them. "You wouldn't know they were evil by looking at them."

"They see only what they have painted," Tobias sighed. "The reality of their words is unknown to them, and is quite unknowable."

"Where are we, Tobias? I know we're not in their world, and I know we're no longer in ours. Mine."

"True, and true."

"And this doesn't look like the in-between place between gates."

"True again." Tobias put on a genuine smile. "The gates allow us to travel to alternate universal planes. To do so, we travel through what you call the 'in-between' place. It has no location in any physical sense."

"But these side doors," Jake urged. "They don't take us from one plane to another. They take us to another time on the same plane."

"Exactly so. And while they are a part of the gate system, you don't cross that in-between place when using one of these side doors."

"So, we're in... like, the door jamb?"

"In order to get from one time to another time, we must step *out of time*, through the... door jamb."

Jake's head was spinning. Very little of what he was hearing made any sense, but he understood enough of it to believe what he was hearing. He tried to push it to the back of his mind, to let it sort itself out on its own. "Okay, so... how did *you* get here?"

Tobias drifted from the Rhetani couple to the open window and studied the scene. The motionless clouds looked as though they were being pushed by a strong breeze in real time. He held a hand out, palm to the world, and closed his eyes.

"I can almost feel the wind." Tobias said. He let out a cheerless sigh. "Each plane has several of these side doors. None cross to other planes, but they are connected to others on the same plane."

Jake had understood that, on some level, from his experience with Marcus. It was only one more step to understanding what Tobias was saying. "You're in some other door."

Tobias turned about then and stepped back into the center of the room. He came face to face with the woman. He moved to within inches, looked directly into the bright blue eyes.

"She's heartless, you know," he said. "She doesn't realize it, but she is. Her obsession made her that way."

Jake had seen a lot of that as of late. He said nothing.

"There is a very fine line between obsession and fanaticism." Tobias was moving in and out of a number of different lines of thought. "Mania, manic, maniac..."

Jake wondered how long Tobias had been lost in this place, alone, with only those thoughts to keep him company. "Are you all right?"

The man turned away from the woman then, let out yet another heavy sigh and looked directly at Jake. "Two of my comrades, Marcus and Janice, turned against the Jahai. Until recently, both had been safely isolated, each on different planes and in different times. Janice managed to get free. We are not totally without means, and Janice was probably the smartest of us all."

"In spite of her misguided loyalties?"

"If our adversaries were stupid, there wouldn't be much of a problem, would there?"

"Would sure make things easier."

Tobias had already moved his mind onward. "Because of a stir of activity, I had begun preparations to collect the artifacts. When I heard that Janice was on the loose, I knew that I first had to stop her. I was afraid that she might use the side doors to reach the Rhetani."

"An alternate time in our world?"

Tobias nodded. "Our world has three side doors: my time, your time, and the time of the Rhetani. The only gates to the Other Worlds lay in the time of Serpent's Keep. Your time."

"You were afraid that she would find a way to bypass Serpent's Keep and go directly to the Rhetani?"

"Janice and I struggled—that side door is forever closed."

"You couldn't make it back out?"

"There was no other way. Closing that door was a simple matter."

"But how did you get there? Marcus couldn't travel the gates. He couldn't get through the side door."

"The gateways, the artifacts... they are not magic, Jake. It is technology. Technology that can be known. That is the reason for the guardians. Discovery was inevitable."

"But—"

"I had pulled apart the gateway system, scattered the components to the Other Worlds, but I had to maintain some method of monitoring what was going on."

"You have a way into the in-between place, but you can't go to other side..."

"I kept a back door into the non-plane, what you call the *in-between* place, but even I can't cross over without an artifact. Without the technology underlying the artifacts, no one can cross over from one world to another."

"Janice found your back door?"

"She created one of her own, or something like it. She was able to enter the non-plane, and control her travel within it. If she ever managed to find the side door of the past, the one that we had originally come through, and then had found a way to use that door to reach the Rhetani, then sooner or later they would have found a way to reopen and exploit the gateways."

And so Tobias had been waiting for her. Jake was curious about what had happened, but it didn't really matter, and it sounded as though Tobias had told him as much as he was going to.

Whether Janice was alive or dead, whether she was trapped in the past or in some non-place, the fact was that Tobias didn't believe she was a threat. Not any longer.

And besides, now that Jake had permanently closed off the only access to the Rhetani, none of it mattered. Tobias had given Jake the time that he had needed, and now the task was done.

And that thought brought to the forefront what had been rumbling around in the back of Jake's mind from the moment that he had thrust the bone dagger into the reconstituted gateway machine.

"Uncle Tobias?"

Tobias was looking once again at the humans-turned-mannequins. "I didn't know what was going to happen to me once you closed the gates. I don't exist in the physical sense. Now, neither do you."

Tobias indicated the scene around them. "It wasn't until you used the key, the bone dagger, to lock the gateway system, that I had any reality. Until that moment, I had no sense of smell or sight. Or rather... I suppose my senses were there, but there was nothing to see, nothing to hear."

"What happens now? What's going happen to everyone?"

"Everyone else is fine, Jake." Tobias nodded in the direction of the Rhetani couple beside him. "By now, they've realized what has happened, that all is lost, and they've gone to tell their superiors."

"But, they haven't gone anywhere. They're right here, frozen in time."

"Jake, you know what has happened and yet you don't comprehend. You know that you can't trust your eyes, and yet you let them draw your conclusions for you."

Tobias held a hand in front of him, studied it closely, distracted for a moment by some other thought process going on in his mind. He rubbed his fingertips together, studying the sensation, continued to speak.

"There is your time, and there is the time of Rhetani. Both exist, both are real. The place we are in now, this *non-plane,* has no time, has no reality. It doesn't exist. In spite of that, up until a few moments ago, a misnomer in itself, it continued to flow along with those realities.

"But when you entered the key and shut down the gateway system, we were... left behind. What you see is that instant of time, of their time, that moment when you thrust the dagger up above your head."

"Oh, man..." Jake mumbled, barely audible.

"I'm so sorry, my boy."

"Oh, man." Jake had been certain that he would cross over to their world, to their time, and would live or die in some future land.

This isn't living or dying.

Tobias turned to face the Rhetani couple. "Our sight is a snapshot of a moment already past. Sound is only that of our own voices. Touch..." Tobias moved his hand toward the chest of the motionless man. It disappeared beneath the man's shirt. He pulled it back. He turned to Jake, held his hand palm out. Jake cautiously lifted a hand. Their palms touched, their hands pressed together.

"I guess that makes sense," said Tobias. "I can hear you, I can see you. I can smell coffee on your breath."

"But... if we don't exist..."

"Where we are doesn't exist, and therefore, to be here, in this non-plane, we cannot exist. The paradox is that we don't exist, and yet we... *are.*"

Jake swallowed hard, realized that he had swallowed hard and immediately tried to comprehend the fact that he didn't really exist and hadn't actually swallowed at all.

"Do you have a way out of here?"

Jake could see that his uncle wanted desperately to tell him yes, that he did indeed have a way out. After a few painful moments, in a non-place in which moments didn't really exist, Tobias shook his head.

"Not that I can think of at the moment."

"Oh, man."

Chapter Twenty Two

Mr. Griffin stepped into the empty chamber, the sounds of his footfalls resonating off the concrete walls. He knelt down before the octagon-shaped design set into the floor. He rubbed his hand lightly across the smooth surface.

The individual artifacts were gone. Now, inset within the cold, smooth concrete floor, was an emblem, a pattern composed of what the artifacts once were.

"The gate, that room." Meara stepped out of the tunnel. She had a slightly dazed look on her face. "I don't think I much liked those people."

Mr. Griffin rose to his feet. He felt as though his age might finally be starting to catch up with him. "I don't believe you are going to have to concern yourself about them, Miss Gyles."

"Then you think that—"

"I believe that young Master Quigley has completed his quest."

Meara tried to feel happy about that, but couldn't. She had liked Jacob Quigley, and he had certainly brought some excitement back into this old mansion.

"I hope he's all right," she said.

"The boy has always proven most resourceful." Mr. Griffin offered a consoling smile. "I am certain that whatever predicament he finds himself in, he will undoubtedly find his way out again."

Mr. Griffin stood beside Meara and took her gently by the arm. He turned her toward the tunnel entrance and the two of them left the chamber that for millennia had held Serpent's Gate.

~ end book one – Serpent's Keep ~

| 2 |

Serpent's Keep Two - the Six Temples

Chapter One

The small room held a narrow cot and a tiny side table. There was an unlit oil lamp on the table, the only light in the room coming from a small, square window that was set high on the wall. In the wall opposite the window was a heavy wooden door bound with iron straps and hung on iron hinges.

Jacob Quigley was asleep on the cot under a drab-green blanket. He woke slowly and rolled onto his back. He opened his eyes and stared blankly up at the ceiling. He blinked, rubbed his face and looked sharply again at the ceiling.

He recognized that ceiling.

He pulled the blanket off and sat up, looked curiously about the room. He was in a monk cell in the temple.

The temple. Jake was home.

That's impossible. How can I be home?

He stood up, shrugged a sore shoulder and looked again about the small cell. His jacket was hanging on a hook beside the door. He looked down at his clothes then. He was wearing the same clothes that he had been wearing the last he could recall.

He found his boots under the cot, put them on and tied up the laces. He went to the door then and pushed down on the heavy, iron latch. The door opened easily and he stepped out into the hall.

Jake was definitely in the temple. He was home. Serpent's Keep was less than a day's hike away.

He had no idea how he got there. The last thing he remembered, he and his uncle Tobias had come out of a gateway side-passage and had just started across an empty world of drifting gray fog.

What happened?

He followed the narrow hall to the wider corridor that ran the length of this wing of the temple. Reaching the front foyer, he met Brother John and another monk just coming in through the front door, both dressed in plain, heavy monks' robes.

Brother John gave his companion a nod of dismissal and turned to Jake.

"Brother Jacob," he said with a patient smile. "It is good to see you up. How do you feel?"

"Confused," said Jake.

John indicated the passage directly ahead and they started into it.

"I'm sure it will all sort itself out," he said as they walked.

"Uh, huh," said Jake. "How did I get here?"

"I couldn't say," said John. "Are you hungry?"

Jake realized then that he was. "A bit, yes."

"This way, then." John guided Jake into the dining hall and to a nearby table. The hall was nearly empty, with lunch just finishing. John caught the attention of a monk standing at the small buffet who was beginning to clear things away. The man nodded and began preparing a plate for Jake.

"I'll let Master Peter know that you're up and about," said John.

"All right," said Jake. "And he'll know how I got here?"

"He has been eager to speak with you."

Jake noted silently that John had avoided answering his question. He watched him leave the hall and then gave a polite smile to the monk bringing his plate and a glass of water.

"Thank you," he said.

The monk nodded in reply and returned to clearing away the buffet. Jake ate in silence. After several minutes he found himself alone in the hall. He had finished his meal and was taking his plate to the return window when Master Peter came into the room.

"Ah, Brother Jacob. Welcome home." Peter was in his sixties, but despite his graying hair could have passed for a man much younger.

"Thank you, Master Peter." They shook hands, and then Jake stepped over to the buffet table. He refilled his glass from a water pitcher. "I must tell you, I'm surprised to find myself here."

"Is that so?"

"Yes." Jake stared at his water glass, set it down on the table beside the pitcher. "I don't suppose you can shed any light on how I got here?"

"Very little, I'm afraid." Master Peter indicated the nearest table and they sat down facing one another. "I was in fact hoping that you might regale and enlighten me with tales of your adventures these past seven months."

Seven months...

"Seven? Really?" Jake hadn't realized that so much time had passed in the worlds outside the passageways. It certainly didn't jive with his internal calendar.

"Seven months and a handful of days," said Peter. "Miss Meara Gyles told us of your sacrifice in closing the gates, though she had no doubt that we would one day see you again."

"I had enough doubt of my own for everyone," said Jake. "And I have no idea how I ended up here."

"We found you unconscious on the front steps," said Master Peter. "Near sunset last evening."

"And Uncle Tobias?"

"Tobias?" asked Peter. "You've been with Brother Tobias?"

"We've been traveling the side-passages," said Jake. "Last I remember, we came out of a passage... we were in a landing..." Jake frowned, struggled to remember. He looked up at Peter. "Tobias and I were together."

"I'm sorry, Jacob. You were alone when we found you." Peter managed a smile then. "I am pleased to hear that Tobias is alive."

"Presenter of good tidings," said Jake tiredly. "That's me."

"These *side-passages...* they are related to the gateways, I assume?"

"Kind of," said Jake, shrugging. "They are very limited in where they go, and until recently each was confined to a single world."

"I see." Peter looked thoughtfully at Jake. "And they didn't shut down when you closed the gates?"

"Only the main passages closed. Good thing. I found Tobias at a landing between side-passages."

"Fortuitous, indeed."

"Janice," Jake said suddenly.

"Excuse me?"

"Tobias' nemesis, you might say; more so even than Marcus. She is more of a threat, for sure."

"And she—"

"We think she's creating them," said Jake. "Passages."

"Such a thing is possible?"

"Honestly, I don't know. Even Tobias can't say for sure, but something is happening. Janice knows the science of the gateways better than anyone alive, enough to make her dangerous."

"And she is out there now?"

Janice had been trapped in the side-passages when Jake shut down the gates. The Other Worlds were now isolated from one another, and even the side-passages were supposed to be limited to their individual worlds.

"She's looking for a way out," he said. *And a way to reopen the gateways.*

"You found a way out," said Peter. "Clearly. You are here."

"Clearly? Apparently, at most." Jake grew retrospective. When he spoke again, his words were distant. "Tobias and I had come onto a landing. It was empty... I heard something; like wind. A strange wind. And then... then I was here."

Master Peter reached out and placed a hand on Jake's arm.

"As you have returned to us, I am confident that we will soon be enjoying the company of Brother Tobias." Peter stood then, rested his hand heavily on Jake's shoulder. "You are welcome to stay as long you feel need. We will talk again."

"Thanks," said Jake. "I'll be heading to Serpent's Keep in the morning."

"Of course." Peter gave Jake a final pat on the shoulder and started away. "I'll see you at dinner. I would hear more of your adventure."

Jake stepped out of the trailhead and approached the wooden west gate, set into the rough stone wall that enclosed the village of Serpent's Keep. He pulled on a metal ring, listened to the peal of the bell on the other side of the wall. Several moments later he heard the voice of the guard on watch.

"Can I help you?"

"Sure can," said Jake. "Jacob Quigley. I'd like to get inside, please."

"Jacob Quig—" There was a long hesitation. "Are you sure?"

"Um... pretty sure..."

Another long hesitation, and then Jake heard the wooden beam slide aside and the gate opened.

"Sorry," said the young man on watch. As a member of the Citizen's Watch, he was unarmed and dressed in civilian clothes. "You took me by surprise, Mister Quigley."

"Oh, I hear ya'," said Jake. He mumbled over his shoulder as he started down the alleyway, swathed in shadow. "I'm still gettin' over the surprise myself."

Reaching the main thoroughfare, he stopped at the corner and took in the sight. It was early evening, and it was quiet at this end of the small village. The main gate was a short distance to his right, the heart of the village to his left. There was a small group of people gathered outside the café several hundred yards into the village.

He crossed the avenue and started up the street, walking into the village proper, He passed the park plaza and turned into the narrow side road where the Quigley Estate waited.

The gate wasn't locked. He took the walk and the steps up to the front door. The door was locked, and he lifted and dropped the door knocker. He stared at the dragon knocker and waited. It was almost a minute before the door opened and Mr. Griffin stood looking down at him. Only the briefest of emotion washed across Mr. Griffin's face, then the man's mouth and eyes locked into their more familiar state of formal dispassion.

Or at least he tried.

"Master Jacob," Mr. Griffin said calmly. "I am... pleased... to see you."

"You and me both," said Jake. He pointed inside, past Mr. Griffin. "Um..."

"But of course," Griffin said quickly, stepping back and to one side. "My apologies."

Once inside, with the front door closed to the world outside, Jake looked about the room, quietly absorbing the comforting atmosphere of the Quigley Estate.

He turned about and gave a contented sigh.

"No place like home, Mr. Griffin," he said. "I never thought I'd see the old place again."

"There was never a doubt, sir."

Jake looked side-glance at Mr. Griffin. "Really?" he asked doubtfully.

Griffin now managed a trace of humor. "Miss Gyles wouldn't allow it."

"That sounds like Meara," said Jake. "So I'm not dead then?" His uncle Tobias' death had been declared in much less time than this.

"Presumed only," said Mr. Griffin. "There was nothing official."

"Good. I bet the paperwork to bring me back would have been a nightmare. Which reminds me... have you seen Uncle Tobias?"

The question managed to startle Mr. Griffin. "Should we have? Is he—"

"He is." Jake indicated that they should head into the kitchen. Once there, he set about getting a glass of water, sat then at the island counter as he ate fruit from the bowl.

Fresh fruit; in their travels these past months, food choices had often been limited. They ate what they found, any extra they carried with them for the scarce times to come.

There had been more than a few of those.

No need to bring that up just now. He took another bite of the apple, told Mr. Griffin how he had found Tobias after closing Serpent's Gate, how together they had found and then began traveling side-passages. They spent months following the trail of Janice while always on the lookout for a way out of the passages.

"And so you have. What of Master Quigley?"

"The last thing I remember before waking up at the Temple was stepping out of a side-passage into a gray, empty place, and Tobias was right beside me. I think I heard something, like wind... but I can't be sure. Next thing I know, I'm waking up in a monk cell. Peter says they found me on the front steps."

"And no sign of Master Quigley..."

"Nope."

Mrs. Hodges came in through the back door. Seeing Jake, the expression on her face changed from anxious to delight.

"So it's true then!" she exclaimed.

"Hey, Mrs. H." They met in the middle of the kitchen and hugged. Mrs. Hodges stepped back to get a better look at Jake.

"Word is all through the village... young Quigley has come home." she said, still smiling broadly. "Wasn't sure to believe it, but here you are."

"Yes, Ma'am."

§

The tall double-doors opened ahead of Tobias Quigley and he stepped through and into the large audience chamber. The strong scent of dragon filled the great hall, the walls to either side lined with every species of Jahai, the varied inhabitants of the four habitable planets of the Jahai system.

Tobias continued down the center of the chamber, walking steadily past the dragons and on toward the raised wooden platform at the far end of the room. Tobias was in his late fifties, with rugged features and bushy salt and pepper hair.

He reached the platform and looked up at Natan, the Jahai ruler. Natan was of the Bentai Jahai. The Bentai were much more humanoid in physical appearance than other Jahai species. Natan was just a head taller than the average human, with sloping shoulders, a large head and protruding snout. He had extraordinarily long fingers ending in curved black claws. As most Bentai, he was dressed in an open leather vest and a calf-length skirt.

"So good to see you, our friend Tobias Quigley," said Natan. His voice was smooth, his words clear and precise.

Tobias gave a slight nod, briefly held out his palms. "Dear friend Natan, sovereign guide of the Jahai."

Natan held out a clawed hand, turned it palm up and then drew it back. He rested the hand on the arm of the heavy wooden throne. At that gesture, Tobias took a step forward, stood now directly at the base of the platform.

"I thank you for your welcoming salutation," he said.

"It has been many cycles since you last walked this hall, friend Tobias."

"Due to circumstances rather beyond my control, friend Natan," said Tobias.

"So I understand. I was pleased when I heard that you were yet among us." Natan looked aside, lifted a hand and gave a signal to a Jahai standing just off the platform, another of the Bentai. He turned again to Tobias. "Come sit with me. We have much to discuss, I should think."

Tobias stepped up onto the platform as a chair suitable for humans was brought up and placed beside Natan's throne. Tobias sat in the chair, made himself comfortable and looked about the chamber. The Jahai in the hall had begun to settle back into their stations, seeing that Natan and Tobias would likely be in quiet conversation for some time.

As was often the case when friend Tobias Quigley visited.

"My feelings go one way and then another, Tobias," said Natan. "To close Serpent's Gate, to seal it for all time; to isolate our worlds, all worlds."

"We suspected the day would come, Natan."

"Perhaps we did. Yes, perhaps we did."

"I do understand."

The conversation drifted then to the Rhetani, the threat that had caused the closing of the gates. The Rhetani had always been there, had been the reason for originally dividing and dispersing the artifacts.

And then the threat had become more imminent. The Rhetani would bring all the worlds under their control.

The conversation then fell to matters more immediate.

"Janice is out there still," said Natan. It was an observation more than a question.

"That she is," said Tobias. "We have been following her trail."

"You and your blood," said Natan. "Jake."

"My nephew, yes."

"You will find her; you and your... *nephew.*"

"We must."

"What will you do with her, friend Tobias?" Natan asked calmly. "How can we help you?"

Tobias had trapped Janice in a side-passage landing long ago, back when he separated the gate into individual artifacts that he then scattered across the Other Worlds.

He had hoped that she would exist there for all time. But she had somehow managed to gain her freedom, had brought together others of the Rhetani in her search of the artifacts, threatening all worlds. To defend against this threat, Serpent's Gate had been sealed, forever isolating the Other Worlds from one another.

It was now feared that even that had not been enough. Janice had abilities beyond any human, beyond any Jahai.

"Janice needs to be rendered harmless," said Tobias.

Natan nodded slowly. "A secure confinement."

"Yes," said Tobias.

"I understand," said Natan.

Tobias stepped away from the Grand Hall, the massive doors closing behind him. The central plaza of the sprawling Village of the Dragons was open and spacious, surrounded by large structures that were set in amongst towering trees; beyond these to either side, great cliffs rose high into the sky.

The village was a sprawling community of large, stark, cavernous structures surrounded by a forest of massive trees and an open forest floor. It was one of only a few sites with hub landings, central locations reached by several side-passages.

Yet Tobias should not have been able to get to it from any passage that he and Jake had traveled since the closing of Serpent's Gate. The fact that he was there was at odds with everything that he knew of the side-passages.

Taking this, with his recent experiences, with the disappearance of young Jake, and with the disquieting news that Natan had just given him at the close of their conversation, all made Tobias more than a bit anxious.

Chapter Two

After a good night's sleep in his own bed and a delicious breakfast prepared by Mrs. Hodges, Jake spent a few hours in Tobias' library and in the hidden command center. He had no idea what he was looking for, rather hoped that it would jump out at him and cry out *here's what happened to you, Jake!* to be quickly followed by *here is how you find your uncle... yet again.*

Actually, he just wanted a clue. Such had happened before. He needed to know what the first step was. After that, the second step would show itself.

He found nothing.

Late morning, Jake left the estate; he wandered first across the road to the town park. About a dozen people were gathered around a group of picnic benches. It looked like a family gathering. After watching from a distance for a few minutes, he left the plaza and started up the main thoroughfare.

There were quite a few villagers out and about. Most gave Jake a smile and a nod, several wanted to stop and say hello and welcome him home. He didn't know most of them, but they recognized him.

He found Meara's mother at her booth in the marketplace, where she sold kitchenware and assorted utensils. He didn't know her very well, had really only spoken to her a couple of times, but she apparently knew every detail of his journeys into the Outland and the Other Worlds. She had been kept fully up-to-date by Meara.

Mrs. Gyles also had been certain that they would see Jake again, having been so advised by her daughter.

As for Meara, she was going to be upset that she had missed his return. It was only then that Jake found that Meara was at the Farm, where she worked several days a week, necessary to supplement what she earned working part time at the Quigley Estate. She wouldn't be back in the village for several days.

Jake thanked Mrs. Gyles and wandered toward the exit of the marketplace. It was close enough to lunch that he decided to drop in to the cafe.

Entering the restaurant, he saw only one other patron. Jake gave a nod when the man looked up from his bowl of soup, then headed toward a table in the middle of the room.

"Jacob Quigley!" Sparta hurried from behind the counter. Jake braced himself as she reached him and gave him a powerful hug.

Well that was odd. They hadn't been on hugging terms before his disappearance.

"I heard you were back," she said.

"How are you, Sparta?" he asked awkwardly.

"Oh, you know," she said with a shrug. She indicated the nearest table, waited for him to sit down. "What can I get for you? It's on the house."

"That's very nice of you. Whatever's the special is fine," said Jake. "So long as there's no peas."

"You got it," Sparta said, grinning. She started away. "Coming right up."

Jake managed to relax then, called out to Sparta. "And how about some of that great coffee?"

"Absolutely, Jake."

Sparta gave Jake's order to Wallace and quickly returned with a cup and the carafe. As she poured his coffee, she began detailing the theories that folks had on what had happened to Jake and where he might have gone. From what he could tell, Meara had accurately described how he had disappeared when closing the gate, and had glowingly noted Jake's sacrifice. The theories as to what had happened next went all over the place, but they usually involved barren landscapes and feral creatures of the night.

Sparta was called away in mid-tale when a pair of customers entered the cafe. She returned a few minutes later with a bowl of soup and a small plate with two biscuits.

"The special of the day," she said. "And no peas."

He was halfway through his soup when Sheriff Smith came in. He worked his way to Jake's table, catching Sparta's attention before giving Jake a friendly smile.

"Mister Quigley. Mind if I sit down?"

"Not at all, Sheriff." Jake set his spoon down, picked up the last of a biscuit and tossed it into his mouth. "I recommend the soup."

"Perhaps I will." The sheriff slid the chair out and sat down. "I'll be having lunch a bit later."

Sparta returned with coffee. "How are you today, Sheriff?"

"I'm doing just fine, Sparta." He watched her fill his cup. "Thank you."

Sparta refilled Jake's coffee, gave him a wink and left the table. Jake lifted his cup to the sheriff.

"And the coffee is as good as I remember," he said.

"It is fine, at that." The sheriff took a cautious sip. "I understand you've had yourself quite the adventure. And you found your uncle, I hear."

"And you may also have heard that I've misplaced him."

"Not in quite those words. Still, great news that he's alive and kicking."

"The last I saw," said Jake. *He was right beside me...*

"You'll be going out again to find him, I imagine."

"Just as soon as I have an idea where to start looking."

"I'm sure that'll come." The sheriff gave a friendly grin. "You did it once before."

"I had clues before. Lots of 'em."

"Oh, I expect the clues will come soon enough." The sheriff gulped down his coffee and stood up. "Well, I just wanted to welcome you home and let you know that we're glad to see you back safe. And we're mighty grateful for the news about Tobias."

"Thank you, Sheriff," said Jake. "And my uncle's death certificate?"

Sheriff Smith gave Jake a sharp nod. "Not to worry. City Hall is already on it."

The sheriff passed Mr. Dante on his way out of the café, the bank owner arriving right on schedule for his daily lunch break. Seeing Jake, the banker stopped on his way to his traditional table along the back wall. After the briefest of welcomes, he advised Jake to drop by the bank at his convenience. While Mr. Griffin had never allowed young Master Quigley to be declared dead, there were nonetheless a few papers to review regarding the estate's ongoing financial arrangements.

Jake assured him that he would drop in later, at which Mr. Dante gave a deep bow of the head and continued on to his table.

Tobias approached the sturdy, circular building that was sitting to one side of the central plaza of the Jahai village. A pair of heavily muscled Thrauhm dragons stood watch, one to either side of the tall, wide opening that faced the plaza. The dragons shifted slightly at Tobias' approach, bowed briefly in acknowledgment and let him enter unchallenged.

The floor of the inner chamber was compact dirt. There were no windows and no other doors, and the chamber was empty but for a circle of six daises standing in the center of the room. A square stone, about twelve inches on a side, rested on each of the six platforms. Each stone was engraved with its own unique geometric symbol.

Tobias circled the daises, glancing at the symbols engraved on each *passage stone*. He found the one he wanted. He reached out and placed a hand on the stone.

He was immediately enveloped in blinding, empty white, awash in a rush of light and warped vision. He had been expecting it of course, but the onrush of the side-passage thread nonetheless made him dizzy and he stumbled forward when he came out on the other side.

He stood in a large clearing, a dais similar to the one he had just left standing nearby. The clearing was surrounded by a thick forest; towering cliffs rose hundreds of feet to either side. High above, seen between the tops of the cliffs, the midday sky was pale blue.

He was standing on the floor of the Great Ravine.

He shouldn't have been able to reach the Great Ravine directly from the Village of the Dragons. The village resided in a side-passage landing on another world entirely. Prior to shutting down the gates, the passage stone would have taken Tobias to another time and place in that Other World. In the past, it had always been three distinct steps to get from there to here, and that had been back when Serpent's Gate had been open.

Yet here he was. Natan had said this was so. The physical laws regarding side-passages made it impossible for it to be so. Something had changed. Something *was changing*. Someone was messing with the laws underlying the web of the universe.

The Jahai had identified a number of similar impossible and yet very real alterations to the universe over the past months. Tobias had direct experience with such occurrences, the most recent being when he and Jake had been separated, his nephew vanishing before his very eyes.

Janice was doing something very bad and it was shattering the universe.

The Farm was a sprawling two hundred acres of agricultural landscape surrounding a cluster of barns and assorted buildings. To anyone traveling the dirt road that ran alongside the western perimeter of the farm, the scene gave an impression of a still-life painting. Very little moved, very little changed.

In the heart of this still-life, Meara was helping tie down the tarp of the last in a line of four wagons that had been loaded with vegetables destined for Serpent's Keep. She and the others of the small work crew worked in silence, which only intensified the atmosphere of an *otherworld* that lay eerily over the farm.

Meara looked up from her work to the hollow, resonating sound of wooden wheels, iron axles and jostling sideboards. In the distance, a caravan of empty wagons was approaching, traveling up the road bordering the farm.

It was another work crew coming to harvest and pack vegetables and fruit to take back to the market.

The manager of the village Farm came out of one of the buildings and walked past the line of loaded wagons. He stood in front of the first and waited for the arriving caravan.

Charles Victor was a tall, slender man in his early sixties. He had been managing the farm for thirty years, and before that had been a fulltime farmhand. He had lived on the farm his entire life.

The lead wagon turned off the road and into the farm, and the caravan worked its way toward the compound. The man leading the caravan let the empty wagons continue on as he stepped aside to talk with the farm manager.

Charles smiled at some comment made by the wagonmaster. He looked briefly in Meara's direction before turning again to his conversation with the new arrival.

Their conversation finally finished, the wagonmaster followed after his caravan and Charles walked back to Meara.

"I expect you'll be eager to start back, Meara," he said. The comment was almost cheery, something Meara seldom saw from the farm manager.

"What's going on?" she asked.

"Your friend has returned."

"Sir?"

"Jacob Quigley."

"Master Jacob?"

"And if the rumors are to be believed, young Quigley found Tobias out there somewhere, though for some reason he didn't return with him." Charles looked up and down the line of fully loaded wagons. Catching the attention of the caravan's lead wagonmaster, he gave the go-ahead hand signal, looked again to Meara. "You have a safe trip back, Miss Gyles."

Dusk had come to the Great Ravine. Dark shadows crept out from the thick forest of evergreen and into the expansive clearing. Flying dragons appeared in the black hollows of cave openings set high in the cliff walls and leapt into the airspace above the forest canopy, drifted out above the treetops.

Tobias sat amongst a small gathering of dragons in the heart of the clearing. Many of the twelve species of Jahai were present, including several of the more humanoid Bentai dragons. One fed wood into a campfire in the center of the gathering. Tobias suspected the fire was for his benefit, as he knew campfires were rare in the ravine. While he had never put the Great Ravine on any map, he had visited there many times. It served primarily as an outpost for the sleek Lynhaur dragons, one of the flying Jahai, and was a landing with a minor side-passage gate to a landing in the distant past.

Looking about at the gathering now, he wondered aloud at the number of Jahai species that were present.

"We feel a disruption in the web," said one of the Bentai. "Many are anxious."

"Some have come to bear witness," said another.

"Some are not here by choice," said a third. "The threads were not intended to bring us here."

"Though all stand watch against what may come," said a dragon of the Thrauhm species, with strong reptilian features.

"I understand your unease," said Tobias. "I too have felt the disturbance."

"Why would the closing of the gate create such disruption in the passages, Tobias?" asked the Bentai dragon.

"It would not, my friend," said Tobias. "It did not."

"The Rhetani?" asked another.

"I fear so."

"Alone here... was sad," said a large, heavyset dragon. He had been trapped here when the Other World gates had closed, had not been able to return home. "Apart from brothers and sisters. Sad. This different. Worse than sad. Feel bad inside. This... bad."

New threads had been born from the disruptions of late, their origins unknown, and many were afraid to travel them. There had been stories.

And then most recently the story of Tobias and his travels with his nephew, their separation. Tobias mentioned as much.

"Was here," one dragon stated, unaccustomed to human speech.

"Excuse me?" Tobias wasn't sure what he had meant by that.

"Was here," he repeated. He lifted a clawed hand and pointed to the edge of the clearing. "Was there."

"You did not know?" asked one of the Bentai. "You were not told?"

"Apparently not, my friend," said Tobias. "To what are you referring?"

"Jacob Quigley, blood of Tobias, was found at the edge of the clearing. When we could not revive him, he was taken to the Temple to be cared for."

Chapter Three

Jake stepped out the door of the Adventurer's Guild and into the narrow side street. He started in the direction of the main thoroughfare. It was late afternoon, and the air was beginning to grow cool. He stuffed his hands into the pockets of his light jacket and pushed on.

The streets were lined with lamp posts, the lights mostly gas but there were also a few electric. The scattering of electric lights were already on. Jake passed a man standing beneath one of the gas lamps, lifting a rod to the globe. He gave Jake a mumbled '*good evening*' before lighting the lamp and moving on to the next.

Jake had spent the past hour at the Guild, talking with members about nothing in particular, hoping to catch some bit of news that might be a clue as to what he should do next. Perhaps someone had seen something in the Outland, heard of some strange sighting or event; perhaps the sudden appearance of a slightly graying, middle-aged gentleman...

As he had found during visits to the Adventurer's Guild in the past, most members, despite the guild's name, seldom actually traveled beyond the walls of Serpent's Keep. What tales were to be heard were often wild rumors with little fact underlying them, or were oft-repeated stories of adventures from long ago.

In the end, Jake left the Guild with no more than he had going in.

He did have an idea forming in the back of his mind that he would need to think on further... something born from his earlier journeys into the Outland. It wasn't much, but it was all he had. With nothing else to go on, it was better than waiting around for something to happen.

He was pulled abruptly from his thoughts when someone called out to him.

"Young Quigley." A small, thin, graying man crossed the street. Jake recognized him.

"Mason, isn't it?" Jake had crossed paths with Mason before. The man hadn't seemed to be quite all there the last time they had spoken, but several of Mason's observations had suggested that he may see more than folks gave him credit for.

"A brief word, if that's all right, Mister Quigley."

"Of course." Jake looked wistfully down the pedestrian thoroughfare in the direction of home. He started walking, leaving Mason to fall in line beside him. They passed a few villagers who were out and about; the lamp lighter continued to work his way down the street.

"You are recently returned, I understand," said Mason.

"That's right," Jake said cautiously. The last time they had spoken, Mason had scolded him for taking Meara into the Outland. He wondered what he could possibly have done wrong now.

"You traveled the threads with Master Tobias."

"That's right." He wondered at Mason using the term *threads.* Jake had found that it was the way the Jahai usually referred to the passages, both primary and side. His uncle Tobias used the term.

"And what be your plans now, young Quigley?"

"Pardon my bluntness, Mason, but how is it any of your concern?"

"I only be concerned for your well-being, sir." Mason stopped, reached out and took Jake by the arm. "There be wrong out there. Things be very wrong."

"What do you mean?" asked Jake.

Mason studied Jake's face. He saw something there.

"You saw it, I bet," said Mason. "You be a witness, I bet."

"What do you know of it?" asked Jake. Could Mason know something of what had happened, of how he had been separated from Tobias? How he had ended up at the steps of the Temple?

"There be cracks in the world, Jacob Quigley," said Mason.

"How so?"

"You've seen it. Things ain't right, and they be gettin' worse." He placed a hand on Jake's chest. "You know what I say be true. I sense it in you."

Jake took hold of Mason's wrist and pulled his hand away.

"What do you want, Mason?"

"You have to fix it, Quigley. You have to fix the world."

"Yeah? And how do I do that?"

"That be your path, sir."

"Right. Thanks for that," Jake frowned. For just a moment, he had thought this crazy old man knew something. "And what about your concern for my well-being?"

"It is your spirit that is in the shadows, my friend."

Standing in the mansion's main foyer, Jake took a moment and let the evening quiet of the house work to soothe him. Mrs. Hodges had no doubt gone home soon after dinner, and Mr. Griffin was probably settled into his room. He had a small suite just off the foyer to the left of the staircase.

Jake took the stairs to the second floor. His exchange with Mason had left him unsettled and he wasn't ready to go to his room. He instead continued on down the hall and stepped out onto the second floor deck. It opened out to the west, providing a scene of the village below, the west wall, and the Outland beyond the wall. Night had come. The criss-cross of streets within the village glowed with the street lamps and curtained lit windows.

A minute later Mr. Griffin came out onto the deck behind Jake. He hesitated briefly before stepping up beside him. He stood silent, noting that Jake was lost in thought.

"Good evening, Mr. Griffin," Jake said at last. He continued looking out past the village to the dark, heavily shadowed Outland beyond the wall.

"Good evening, Master Jacob." Griffin had heard Jake come into the mansion and had followed after him when he realized that Jake hadn't gone to his room.

"It's nice out," said Jake.

"It is."

They both stood quietly taking in the evening for some time.

"I missed this," Jake said finally.

"Yes, sir." Mr. Griffin paused a moment. "You'll be leaving, then."

Jake grinned at that. Nothing got by good ol' Griff. "Day after tomorrow."

"I see."

"I have to get supplies together."

There was another long pause. Mr. Griffin let out a calm sigh.

"Mrs. Hodges observed that you didn't eat much of your dinner before going out," he said. "She prepared a snack for you before leaving for the evening. It's waiting for you in the ice box."

Jake spent the next morning gathering supplies, including rations of dried fruit, cheese and bread, jerky. He also allowed himself some fresh vegetables. Returning to the hidden command center off the mansion library, he packed an essentials kit, a first aid kit, and some extra clothes. He included the maps that he had drawn during his previous journeys into the Outland before shutting down the gate.

With everything ready to go, he stowed his gear and headed out of the command center. Coming into the library through the hidden panel, he found Meara sitting in one of the two chairs, waiting for him. She stood and put on an awkward grin.

"Where are we headed, Master Jacob?"

"Meara?" Jake closed the panel and stepped into the middle of the room. He was about to give her a hug but stopped short. Mr. Griffin had long ago made clear the separation between the master of the estate and staff.

"Yes, sir," said Meara. "It's great to see you."

"It's good to be back," said Jake. "I heard you were out at the Farm."

"That I was. I came back as soon as I got word." Meara's smile broadened. "So, when do we leave?"

"We?"

"You don't expect to do this all by yourself, do you, sir?"

Jake sat on the edge of the other chair, waiting for her to return to her seat.

"You don't even know what *this* is," he said then.

"To find Master Quigley, of course."

"That's the goal, yes, but—"

"That's good enough for me, sir."

"I see." Jake sat back, looked over at Meara. To be honest, he would feel better with her along. He may have more experience in the threads, but she was still the expert when it came to the dangers of the Outland. "We're heading for the Ravine."

"The Great Ravine?" Meara sounded genuinely surprised. "You mean, with the flying dragons?"

"It's the only place in the Outland that I know of where I can see something of the Other Worlds without having to step through a portal. We saw dragons there, and dragons aren't from around here."

"Right, sir." Meara managed a grin. "It should be fun."

Tobias moved off the trail and entered a wide clearing. The sun had set half an hour earlier and night would come soon to the Outland. He surveyed the shadows that were closing in on the clearing as he tossed his backpack aside. Satisfied that nothing was lying in wait for him, he began gathering dry branches and twigs from the surrounding forest. Once he had a small campfire going, he brought out the makings of his dinner. It would be a simple meal of soup and bread; what he really wanted was a cup of coffee.

Minutes later, sitting before the fire with coffee in hand and soup heating, Tobias felt an uncomfortable tingling throughout his body; the sensation of cobwebs brushing across his face, his arms. He lifted his gaze, looked across the clearing into the shadows of the surrounding woods.

Nothing...

Whatever it was, it wasn't coming from there.

Tobias set his cup down and stood up. He turned from the fire, looked about in all directions. He glanced up at the sky then. It was gray and growing darker.

But there was something odd about it. The color was... wrong. It was hard, like a shell. It sat over the world like a metallic dome, shining smooth.

Tobias moved out of the clearing and out onto the trail. He looked in both directions, then let his gaze slide slowly back to the sky. The color tinted the world. A heavy, hollow silence pushed in on him.

The world about him exploded then in shattering bright blue, a thousand cracks spiderwebbing across the dome; the landscape around Tobias burst blue and white, all shadows vanishing and revealing the underworld of the forest floor.

The white rushed in on Tobias, and in that white were flashes of images of people and places and landscapes, images from many worlds bleeding into this one.

And then it was gone. The bright was pushed back as shadows rushed back out from the surrounding forest, eating the white and the blue, snaking in and around trees and bushes; gray splashed across the sky.

The world was as it had been, with dusk quickly giving way to dark.

Tobias looked again up the trail, turned and looked down-trail. He looked up at the sky. The first stars were already beginning to show. He looked off-trail, back into the clearing. The flames of his small campfire flickered and danced.

Expect the soup is about ready...

Chapter Four

Mrs. Hodges stepped out of her booth and into the short back alley, bringing her wire basket cart out with her. Hers was the only booth in the alley, which ran behind several of the public booths up in the market plaza proper.

She slid the wood panels of her booth closed, set and clicked the padlock, then took the several steps up to the narrow access door that opened to the marketplace.

It was mid-afternoon, and there were only a handful of customers wandering from booth to booth. Mrs. Hodges started in the direction of the farmstand at the far end of the plaza. She needed to be home in time to prepare supper, though once again she would be cooking only for herself and Mr. Griffin.

She was worried about young Master Jacob; home only a few days and now off again, no doubt getting himself into all sorts of trouble. The boy was very much like Master Quigley, continually facing down danger in one righteous cause after another.

She stopped briefly at Mrs. Numidia's booth along the way. Her friend sold tools and other items handmade by her husband, the village blacksmith. Mrs. Hodges seldom had need for such items, but the two women got along well and Mrs. Hodges' less than reputable herbalist activities had never bothered Mrs. Numidia the way it did some of the other villagers.

She excused herself after a few minutes and continued on to the farmstand. The man behind the counter had returned from the farm with Meara, and so considered himself on the inside regarding all the news of Jacob Quigley. Mrs. Hodges smiled patiently and nodded at all the right times, managed finally to break away after purchasing several days' worth of fruit and vegetables.

She passed Mrs. Gyles' booth on the way out. She had hoped for a brief word with Meara's mother, but the booth was already shut down for the day. She continued on out of the marketplace and moved out into the main thoroughfare.

Walking through the village, she met Mr. Dante as he was coming out of his bank. He was on his way to an afternoon meeting with a young man seeking a business loan. They were getting together at the café for coffee.

The café was just about a second home to Mr. Dante.

Mrs. Hodges was about to comment on what she believed to be the young man's considerable integrity when the sky overhead suddenly turned a bright, explosive blue, sending Mr. Dante's face aglow. It lasted only a moment, and then all was back to normal.

"Oh my," said Mr. Dante. "Peculiar weather we've been having these past few days; eh, Mrs. Hodges?"

"Strange indeed," Mrs. Hodges said warily. This wasn't right, and it had nothing to do with weather.

Mr. Dante managed an uncomfortable smile.

"On my way, then." He gave a slight bow of the head. "Please give Mr. Griffin my best."

"I will, Mr. Dante," said Mrs. Hodges. "I certainly will."

Mr. Dante hurried on, leaving Mrs. Hodges to follow along after, pulling her wire basket cart behind her. She only managed another dozen steps when she heard someone call her name. She stopped and looked behind her.

"Hello, Mason," she said.

Mason looked anxious; not unusual for Mason.

"Mrs. Hodges."

"Is everything all right? You appear troubled."

"That I am, ma'am. A bit and then some."

"Is that so?" They started walking, Mrs. Hodges pulling her cart behind her.

She and Mason had been friends for more than thirty years. They had never moved in the same circles, and Mason had found himself isolated from most in the village these past years, but Mrs. Hodges and Mason had a shared history. They often passed the time in pleasant conversation.

"Did you see what happened a few minutes ago?" he asked.

"I did. Would you know what that was?"

"It's a sign," said Mason.

"How so?" Mrs. Hodges stopped and turned to look directly at Mason. Something had him rattled. "A sign of what?"

"Young Jacob didn't heed my warning. Now I fear the worst."

"In what way?" asked Mrs. Hodges. "We've talked about this before, Mason. You're not making yourself clear."

Mason grumbled to himself. He knew that much of his awkwardness with his fellow villagers was due to his inability to clearly articulate his thoughts.

He had spent so many years alone.

"There's bad happening in the passageways, ma'am," he said.

"The passageways are closed," Mrs. Hodges stated flatly. "Jacob closed them when he shut down Serpent's Gate."

"The gates are closed, that's for true, but there's threads seeking worlds, more and more by the day."

"How that can be?" asked Mrs. Hodges. "Mason, passageways can't exist without gates. Even side passages need landings."

"There be a power out there, Mrs. Hodges. I see it. There be cracks in the world. I don't know how or why, but I can see it. You know me. You see I speak true."

Mrs. Hodges did at that. Mason saw things, felt things, sensed things. The problem was, his visions often meant something wildly different than what he saw. They may be based on reality, but not necessarily his reality.

This time out however, it seemed clear. Whatever may be causing it, there was *bad happening in the passageways.*

From the signs, the village itself might be in danger; perhaps the world.

Mrs. Hodges placed a comforting hand on Mason's arm. "We'll just have to trust in Master Jacob, Mason. There's not much else we can do, so far as I can see."

Mason wasn't much comforted by that.

"Cracks in the world, ma'am," he stated firmly. "Bad happenings. Bad, bad happenings."

Jake and Meara were sitting near their campfire, their gear stacked nearby. The flames from the fire sent shadows dancing across their faces, and behind them, across the wall of trees that surrounded the small clearing. They had finished their evening meal and sat silent now with cups of coffee in hand.

They had followed Jake's hand drawn maps since leaving Serpent's Keep, and by his reckoning they were about a day from the Great Ravine. The journey had so far been uneventful.

Meara broke the silence and asked not for the first time about Jake's time *out there,* after he had closed the gate. Jake hadn't spoken very much about his experiences in the passageways, the '*threads*' as Tobias often referred to them, the name the Jahai used. He had told her of finding Tobias, of their escape from the landing once a thread had unexpectedly formed, but little else. Now, as he stared into the glowing embers of the campfire, he found himself drawn back there, to those ethereal threads.

"We moved from landing to landing," he said distantly. "We never knew where we were going to end up, nothing being what it should be. Threads appeared and vanished. Some of the worlds were incredible, but most were empty."

"Were any of them like the Other Worlds we went to?"

"No," he sighed. "Nothing like those."

The Other Worlds had been variations of their own world. The landings that Jake and Tobias had visited while trapped in the side passages had for the most part been unearthly, in many ways unreal. Only occasionally had they found themselves on a world that was in any way familiar, and where they could replenish supplies.

Jake looked up from the fire, which was slowly dying down to glowing coals. He took a swallow of his coffee, looked at Meara. "So... how did you spend the last seven months?"

"Me?" Meara gave a tired shrug. "I dusted furniture, swept floors; picked vegetables... scary times."

"Sounds like it," said Jake, trying a thin smile. He took a last swallow of his coffee. "We'll be at the ravine tomorrow, another day to get to the entrance."

"Should be fun, sir."

"It could be quite a letdown for you, after picking tomatoes."

"I'll try not to expect too much, sir."

It was late; the world was quiet, the Quigley Estate asleep. Tobias was in the kitchen, sitting at the island counter eating a sandwich. A nearby oil lamp provided the only light.

He sensed movement in the shadow of the open doorway leading to the rest of the house. He took a bite of his sandwich, spoke without looking up.

"We're running low on mustard." He set his sandwich down on the plate and took a long drink from his glass of milk. "And milk."

Mr. Griffin wasn't sure how to respond.

"I'll let Mrs. Hodges know, sir."

Tobias picked up his sandwich then and took another bite. "Are you hungry?" he asked. "I'll make you a sandwich."

"No sir. Thank you." Mr. Griffin stepped fully into the kitchen. He was carrying a small club. "I heard noises; I came to check."

"Good man." Tobias finished his sandwich. He took another drink of his milk, looked over the rim of the glass at Mr. Griffin. The man hadn't changed at all. "I missed you, Griffin. Can't tell you how much I've missed you."

"Yes sir." Mr. Griffin leaned the club against the wall and took another step nearer the counter. "It is very good to see you, Master Quigley."

"You too, my dear friend." Tobias finished his milk, set aside his glass and plate. "I don't suppose you've seen my nephew?"

"Come and gone, sir. Looking for you."

"Is that so?"

"I believe he's headed for the Great Ravine."

"Of course," Tobias grumbled. He rested his arms on the counter, clasped his hands and frowned. Deep lines formed on his forehead.

"Is everything all right, sir?" asked Mr. Griffin.

Tobias had traveled first to the Temple, gotten news on young Jacob before returning to Serpent's Keep. Maybe if he had come straight to the village, as he had first considered...

"One of us is going to have to stop and let the other catch up," he said.

Chapter Five

Jake and Meara reached the wide ledge overlooking the Great Ravine in the late afternoon, shortly before dusk. The ravine was hundreds of yards across, a thousand yards deep, and ran east and west as far as the eye could see. The walls of the ravine were steep and the floor was hidden beneath a canopy of dark forest and darker undergrowth. At this time of the day there was no sign of the flying dragons that Jake knew to inhabit the Great Ravine.

There was a circle of stones near the back of the ledge, evidence of Jake and Meara's campsite from their previous visit there. Meara set about making the fire pit ready as Jake searched the perimeter for kindling and firewood. Once they were settled in, with their camp organized, they returned to the edge of the precipice and waited.

Come the dusk and the quickly darkening gray of the ravine, they began to see shadows skimming above the canopy below. Large, black silhouettes, gliding silently, created darker shadows that danced in the treetops beneath them. There were only a few at first, but as they watched another and then another appeared, dragons coming out of their cliff-wall dwellings to fly above the black forest of the chasm.

Jake and Meara watched until it was too dark to see, then returned to their campfire near the back of the ledge. They ate a light dinner and then settled in for an early night, wanting to get an early start the next morning.

They left the ledge just after dawn, as soon as it was light enough that they could see where they were walking. They followed along the edge of the ravine for most of the morning before the terrain forced them to move into the woods. Without a trail, they continued downslope, eventually finding an animal trail that wound through the thick undergrowth and eventually brought them again to the ravine's edge. The chasm was much shallower here, at most a third as deep as further up-ravine, and the forest canopy that hid the ravine floor was much closer.

Continuing east, the trail they followed led them steadily downhill, the ravine growing steadily shallower, the forest-covered floor seeming to rise up to meet them. They came out into a wide clearing in late afternoon.

The mouth of the ravine was on their left, half-hidden behind a wall of tall, thick brush. A large stone, five feet high, irregularly shaped, four feet wide at its widest, stood in the center of the clearing. It had at one time been the pylon that when opened had become the gateway to one of the Other Worlds.

Now it was just a stone.

Jake couldn't help but reach out and lay a hand on the granite. It was cool to the touch.

Meara watched from a distance.

"Memories, Master Jacob?" she asked.

"You could say that."

Meara looked in the direction of the mouth of the Great Ravine. A dragon had come out of there the last time they were here.

"Me too," she said, hardly more than a whisper.

Jake turned from the stone. "What say we make camp, start into the ravine in the morning?"

The great trees were spaced dozens of feet apart, many of the massive trunks eight to ten feet in diameter. The thick green canopy overhead nearly blotted out the sky, creating a permanent twilight beneath. The floor of the ravine was deep with mulch from centuries of falling needles and decayed branches. The only undergrowth was the occasional giant fern or cluster of salal, leaving much of the forest floor open.

Jake and Meara travelled up the heart of the ravine throughout the morning, with only the sound of their breathing and their muffled footfalls breaking the ominous, heavy silence of the forest. Despite the ravine being in his own world, in his own time, Jake thought it an alien place, more alien than any world he had visited since first arriving at Serpent's Keep and beginning his quest... now so very long ago.

They came upon a small brook at what Jake guessed to be about midday. They stopped, filled their canteens and ate from their rations. As they rested on the bank, filtered streaks of sunlight reached down to them through the canopy, creating sparkles of glitter on the surface of the meandering stream as it slowly worked its way past them.

"It's so quiet here," said Meara, not for the first time. "Not just quiet. It feels empty."

"At least we don't have to worry about wolves or bandits," said Jake. They had experienced both during their travels in the Outland the previous year.

"Then why don't I feel any safer?"

"I can't imagine." Jake looked calmly about them, into the shadows of a forest like he had never seen before. The quiet wasn't absolute. There was the hollow rippling sound of the brook, but that somehow made the enveloping silence all the more ominous.

He straightened and prepared to stand. "We should get at it. Best we get wherever we're going before it gets dark."

"How much darker can it get?" mumbled Meara.

"I'm guessing quite a lot."

They slipped back into their backpacks and started out again. They followed the stream until they found a narrow spot to cross. Several hours later the forest ahead shone just a little brighter. Drawing nearer, they could see that the trees here stood further apart.

They stepped out into a large clearing.

It wasn't completely open overhead, but the canopy was much thinner here, letting in what light there was. Evening wasn't far off, and the sky was already beginning to gray. Jake could just make out the dark mouths of caves set into the sheer walls of the ravine rising up to the sky.

Directly ahead, three dragons sat on a row of short pillars; flying dragons, their wings tucked back along their sides. The one in the center raised its head up and back, then forward, all while watching the two humans step into the center of the clearing.

Only when Jake and Meara were within easy conversation distance did it speak.

"You are welcome here, Jake, blood of Tobias."

Jake stopped two paces from the dragons, Meara beside him.

"You were expecting us?"

"Know you," the dragon said haltingly. "Watch you come here."

Jake looked back the way they had come, traveling up the ravine from the canyon mouth. He turned his attention back to the dragons. The two sitting to either side remained silent, though attentive. The dragon in the center appeared to be the leader and the speaker of the group.

"You better now," it stated very matter-of-factly.

Better now? What did he mean by that? Did these dragons know something? Did they know anything about how Jake ended up at the steps of the temple?

"Um... yes. I am; much better." Jake took another half-step toward the line of dragons. "Do you know of when I was *not* better?"

"Yes." There was a change in the dragon's expression, but Jake couldn't tell what it was or what it might mean. He knew from his previous encounters that all the dragon species were very intelligent, but that many were limited in how they could express themselves and how their emotions were reflected on their faces.

If they knew what happened to Jake, might they know what happened to Uncle Tobias?

Tobias was much better at understanding and reading the dragons than Jake, but then Tobias had spent a lifetime with them. If only he was here now...

"Have you seen my uncle?" he asked. "Tobias Quigley. Is he... *better?*"

"Tobias Quigley not hurt."

Okay. That sounds promising...

"Do you know where he is?"

"You better now. You fix."

"Fix? Fix what?"

"Threads bad. You fix threads."

Meara leaned nearer to Jake. "What does he mean? *Threads?*"

"The passageways," said Jake. "The dragons call them threads."

"Yes," said the dragon. Dragons had keen hearing. "You fix threads."

Dragons were always asking him to fix things.

"Okay. I will," said Jake. "But first I need to find Tobias. I find Tobias, together we'll fix the threads."

The dragon lifted his head high, looked down at the two humans. His expression changed yet again. It might have been humor; a smile or a smirk.

"So said Tobias Quigley," said the dragon.

Tobias held the small backpack open on the stool and began transferring food and other supplies from the kitchen's island counter into the pack. It was an hour before dawn, and he planned to leave Serpent's Keep well before the sun came up.

Mrs. Hodges was standing on the other side of the counter. She was wrapping a brick of cheese in a cloth. "It's a shame you can't spend a few more days with us, Master Quigley."

"I feel the same, Mrs. Hodges," said Tobias. "I do so miss our evenings at the card table."

"Canasta just isn't the same without you."

"I promise a long stay at home once we get back, dear lady."

"I look forward to that." Mrs. Hodges handed him the wrapped block of cheese. She wore a thoughtful smile. "You know, sir, young Jacob isn't all that different from you; when you were his age."

Tobias finished packing, began tying down the straps. "My memory has a hard time reaching that far back, Mrs. Hodges."

"I don't believe that for a second." Her warm smile faded. "You be careful, sir. You and the boy, both."

"That we shall, Mrs. Hodges." Tobias lifted the pack and slipped an arm into one shoulder strap. He held the other arm out across the counter and took Mrs. Hodges by the hand. "I'll be back before you know it."

Janice walked across the rooftop deck through a network of walkways and raised garden beds; she stood at the very edge. The building reached hundreds of feet up from an empty, desolate plain below into a metallic-orange sky that hovered over this strange world. She lifted her gaze outward, pushed her thin frame against a stiff breeze. She appeared as a well-kept middle-aged woman, a smooth complexion but for the slightest onset of wrinkles at the corners of her sharp blue eyes. Her hair was full, fell to her shoulders, brushed back now by the wind.

She lifted a hand and pushed it out against the scene before her. This world before her was hers; all hers, to do with what she would.

Her image flickered briefly, as if shifting out of and back into existence. She lowered her hand, paused; she waited; her form solidified. She raised her hand again, hesitated... she rubbed her fingertips together. In the distance, near the horizon beyond the plain, there came explosions of light and color; silent flashes, as of cracks in the universe.

Another flash then, blinding, erasing the sky and the plain and the rooftop deck.

Janice was strapped in a standing frame, her eyes closed. Wires and plugs were attached to her head and her arms. Her expression was terse, her countenance tense. She appeared older, grayer, more weathered than the Janice on the rooftop. There was darkness in her countenance, an emotional shadow over her face, and when she opened her eyes there was intensity, resolve.

Her assistant stood at the monitoring station beside the standing frame. Martin was a short, squat man with disheveled hair and ill-fitting clothes. He pressed several keys on the monitor's key panel, turned to Janice and began disconnecting her from the equipment.

"It went well?" he asked, setting the lines onto a nearby tray.

"It did not," said Janice. Her words were cold. She stepped out of the standing frame. "We'll have to reset and try again."

"The location was very precise," said Martin.

"Perhaps, but something went wrong. I could feel it from the start." She looked sharply at her assistant. "I slipped out for a moment. It was all I could do to maintain presence."

"How is that possible? Janice, the plane emanates from you."

"I know that, Martin," she said icily. "I created it."

"Of course," said Martin, bowing his head. He stepped aside and Janice moved to the monitor. She began reviewing the data, and after several moments brought up a code window.

It had taken her years to get free from the landing that Tobias had trapped her in, recreating from scratch an access to the ancillary threads. Since then she had worked unceasing to find a way out of the secondary planes and back to primary. This work had involved the repurposing of numerous secondary and tertiary threads. None had as yet given her access to the primary web.

She was certain that she was getting close. A number of the threads had actually breached the primary web, if only for a fraction of a second. These had caused some disruptions in the web, and on occasion had generated fractures, some of which yet remained.

Nonetheless, this gave her optimism. Success would come.

For the moment, she remained trapped in these infuriatingly restrictive side passages and landings. But once she reached the primary web, she would find her way to Serpent's Gate. Once she had access to that, the Rhetani would spread truth and stability across the universe.

And Tobias would be unable to stop them.

Chapter Six

Jake and Meara were escorted to a small encampment a short distance from the main clearing. There were several small structures, obviously made for human use, and a permanent campfire pit. A small supply of firewood was stacked nearby.

The dragon that had guided them there told them that one of the structures was for sleeping, another contained supplies. They were free to replenish their own supplies as needed. If they chose to start a fire for cooking or warmth, they should keep it small.

The dragon informed them that they would be escorted back to the main plaza in the morning and then left the two humans to their evening.

The sun had set sometime earlier, and it would be fully dark soon. Meara began building a fire as Jake explored the dwellings. By the time he returned to Meara, she had the fire going.

"What now?" she asked.

"We have something to eat and then get a good night's sleep. I guess we're out again in the morning."

"To this Village of the Dragons?"

It had been suggested they go there to wait for Tobias, after which together they would 'fix the threads'.

"It looks that way," said Jake. "And I can't think of a better option."

"We could stay here."

Jake knelt before the fire, nodded in the direction of the plaza. "They seem pretty keen on sending us to this village of theirs."

Jake had never been to the Village of the Dragons, though Tobias had mentioned it in passing once or twice. If he understood correctly, it served as a sort of hub for a handful of side passages within the web.

It had been stable until recently. But according to the dragons, a number of new, not so stable threads had formed and attached to the village. This was causing disruption everywhere.

Which was why Meara wasn't completely sold on the idea of taking a thread there.

"It'll be fine, Meara," said Jake.

"Right," grumbled Meara.

"I'm sure it'll be fine. Really. They wouldn't send us through if they didn't think it would be fine."

"Right," she said again.

They fell silent, spoke only sporadically as they prepared and then ate dinner. Afterward, they spent some time sitting quietly at the fire before settling in for the night.

The dragon returned in the morning and they were escorted back to the main clearing. Dragons didn't appear to be all that big on the concept of mornings, and there were only a handful of them about. One stood at the edge of the clearing near a raised dais and was waiting for them. Their escort moved to one side as Jake and Meara approached.

On the dais sat the small passage stone.

"Safe journey," said the dragon. "You are expected."

"Yes," said Jake. "Thanks."

"Right," said Meara.

The dragon moved further aside and waited. Jake took Meara's hand, gave her a playful wink. He reached out and placed his free hand on the stone.

They were enveloped in the familiar empty white, awash in light and the onrush of warped space. It lasted for several seconds, and they stumbled out on the other side.

They found themselves standing inside a circular room. Behind them stood a circle of six daises similar to the one they had just left. The floor was dirt; there was no furniture, there were no windows and only one tall, wide opening that would be large enough for the largest of dragons.

"See," said Jake. "No problem."

"Uh, huh."

They approached the opening and stepped outside. A pair of Thrauhm dragons stood watch to either side of the opening. Both glanced down at the two humans without turning their heads. One gave a slight welcoming nod.

"See? We're expected," mumbled Jake to Meara.

"Uh, huh," said Meara.

They were looking out across the open central plaza of a sprawling village. All along the perimeter of the community were large, stark cavernous structures set in amongst the enclosing forest. To Jake's left was a building that was much larger and more substantial than the others.

A number of dragons from many different species were moving about the Village of the Dragons. One of the Bentai species stood a few yards in front of the new arrivals, watching patiently, his hands clasped in front of him. He bowed his head and raised it again.

"Welcome Jake, blood of Tobias." He then acknowledged Meara, "Welcome, companion of Jake."

"Meara," Meara said coolly.

"You are welcome here, Meara."

"Thanks." Meara had never seen a Bentai. They were eerily humanoid in appearance. She was a bit taken aback.

"I am Khol. I speak for Natan, leader of the Jahai. He wishes you to be comfortable during your stay."

"Thank you, Khol." Jake looked around the plaza. Several of the dragons milling about were looking back at the two humans. "I don't suppose Tobias is here."

"He was with us only days past; not now." He turned and started across the plaza, walking in the direction of a small structure with a human-sized door and two small windows. He was clearly expecting them to follow. "We hope this dwelling suits your needs. It is similar to dwellings for Tobias Quigley."

"I'm sure it will be fine."

Khol indicated a box sitting on the ground beside the door. "We have provided food for humans."

"Thank you."

"Do you expect Master Quigley soon?" asked Meara.

"I cannot say. We have sent word out that you will be here."

Two days later, in early midmorning, Jake was escorted to the Grand Hall for an audience with Natan. Entering the chamber and approaching the raised wooden throne platform, he was surprised to find Tobias standing before the Jahai leader. He had heard nothing of his uncle arriving in the Village of the Dragons.

Tobias gave Jake a simple hello nod as his nephew stepped up beside him. He turned his attention to the leader of the Jahai.

"My friend Natan, I introduce Jacob Quigley, my nephew."

Natan silently acknowledged the introduction as he studied the young human Jake.

"You are welcome here, Jacob Quigley, nephew of our friend Tobias Quigley."

"Thank you," said Jake. "I am honored to be here."

"Yes." Natan turned his attention back to Tobias. "The journey that you would undertake is a dangerous one, our friend. But I agree. It may be the best of the few options that are available to you."

"The greater the chance for success with my nephew as traveling companion. With your permission, we will depart in the morning."

Natan turned again to Jake. "Words of your deed have reached this hall, Jacob Quigley," he said. "Tobias is wise to seek your companionship. You will attend him."

"Of course."

Natan turned a final time to Tobias. "Success to you, our friend Tobias Quigley."

"Thank you, friend Natan. We will seek an audience upon our return." Tobias stepped back, turned about and started away from the throne. Jake gave several uncertain nods to Natan and quickly followed after his uncle.

Stepping outside, he stood next to Tobias.

"It is good to see you, uncle," he said.

"And you, nephew." Tobias started across the open plaza. "You and Meara are staying in the huts?"

"It is where they put us." Jake stepped in line and they continued across the square. Tobias made a halfhearted attempt at conversation about the two of them getting separated, about following after one another. He told Jake that Mrs. Hodges sent her best.

His mind seemed to be elsewhere.

Meara was sitting at the campfire outside the huts. She stood when they approached.

"Master Tobias!"

"Meara, my dear." Tobias reached out and warmly took Meara's hand in both of his. He reached out then and pulled her close, gave her a warm hug.

What would Mr. Griffin have to say about that?

"Tobias, what's this journey we're going on?" Jake asked.

"Yes, yes... to it, then." Tobias indicated the short wooden stools of the permanent campsite. He sat and they sat opposite the small fire from him. "We are going to see the Ancient Guardian."

"Okay. And just who, or what, is the Ancient Guardian?"

"He was the first of us, as his title would suggest."

The first of us... Jake had never thought of Tobias as one of the guardians. He had just assumed that role fell to the Jahai dragons.

"He sounds like quite the fellow," said Jake.

"Rather," said Tobias. "It was while on my way here that I realized a visit to the Ancient Guardian may be the only way to resolve our dilemma."

"Your pal Janice does seem to be advancing her plans apace."

"So you've noticed."

"We have."

"And this Ancient Guardian can fix things?" asked Meara.

"I am hoping that at the very least he will be able to point us in the right direction," said Tobias. "It is believed that he was responsible for the gateways and the web underlying it all."

"That's good enough for me, sir," said Meara.

"Um... Uncle Tobias?" Jake held up a hand, raised a finger. "Your friend back there; Natan. He hinted as to possible danger on this journey."

"Quite so." Tobias gave a long, loud sigh. "To reach the Ancient Guardian, we must travel what the Jahai refer to as the Dark Path."

"The Dark Path..."

"So it is called."

"And it is dangerous?" asked Meara.

"So it is said," shrugged Tobias. "Not the word I would use."

Chapter Seven

Khol led them out of the Village of the Dragons just after dawn, their departure witnessed by a handful of solemn Jahai, the majority of the village residents still asleep. They followed a wide but little-used path away from the village; Jake saw that some of the branches of the encroaching vegetation had recently been cut back. After several hundred yards, they came upon a tall, wooden double-gate that blocked the trail. A weathered fence stretched away from the gate in both directions, disappearing into the brush on either side.

Khol stepped off the trail beside the gate and waited.

"What now?" asked Meara, to no one in particular.

"So it begins," said Tobias.

"The Dark Path? Here?"

"Successful journey to you," Khol gave a slow nod. "I can go no further."

"We thank you for your help, friend Khol," said Tobias.

The Jahai dragon gave another curt nod in response, stepped back another step and again waited.

"And so." Tobias looked to Jake and Meara. "Shall we?" indicating the gate.

"Right, sir," said Meara.

"Ready when you are, uncle," said Jake.

"Lead on, then," Tobias urged.

Jake stepped forward and lifted the wooden crossbar. He pushed the gate inward and walked through. Meara followed.

Tobias turned to Khol. "We will see you upon our return."

"One will stand watch awaiting that return, our friend Tobias Quigley."

Tobias followed the others through the gate. It closed slowly behind him; came the sound of the crossbar sliding back into position.

The trail ahead quickly narrowed; the brush on either side was tall and full, the forest beyond the brush stood dark and eerily quiet. The gray sky overhead lay heavy over the landscape.

The three walked single file, Tobias moving out ahead and leading the way.

"What now, Tobias?" asked Jake. "How far to this Ancient Guardian?"

Tobias shrugged a shoulder as he walked. "I haven't a clue, dear boy; I've never been here before."

"But I thought... what you said... I thought you'd met this guardian."

"Oh yes." There was the hint of something more, but Tobias left it unsaid. He looked briefly back at Jake. "We have not spoken since he took up residence here."

"Sir?" Meara piped up from the end of the line. "We don't know what's ahead?"

"That's nothing new for us, Meara," said Jake. "When have we ever known what we were walking into?"

The gateways... the Other Worlds...

"That's certainly true enough," said Meara.

"I'm afraid I don't know anyone who has gone through the gate," said Tobias. "But there are said to be several, shall we say, *situations...* between the gate and where the Ancient Guardian dwells. However, despite what Natan alluded, there is nothing to say there is actual danger involved."

Jake looked back to Meara. "See? Just like old times."

Tobias couldn't help but offer a final observation. "Then, there is nothing to say there is not."

Meara tried to sound upbeat. "It should be fun, sir."

Three quarters of an hour passed in relative silence, with only the occasional comment about a gray sky that only slightly lightened, or the dampness of the encroaching vegetation that threatened to swallow up the trail.

Coming around a bend in the trail then, they approached a primitive milestone marker that was set alongside the trail. The stone was about a foot tall, and while there were no markings on its face, it nonetheless didn't look natural. It had the look of having been shaped, albeit a very long time ago.

Further up the trail, a few yards beyond the milestone, a faint shimmer lay across the path, as of a micro-thin sheet of water being brushed by a faint breeze.

"What's that?" asked Meara.

"Well, well," Tobias stated matter-of-factly. He stepped forward past the milestone. He stopped a pace before the barrier, reached out and lightly tapped at it with two fingers. There didn't look to be any reaction. He studied his fingers, rubbed the tips with his thumb.

He looked back to Jake and Meara. He gave a wink and a slight smile. He turned forward and stepped calmly through the shimmering wall. He continued another two steps, stopped.

He looked about briefly, then waved for the others to come through.

Jake didn't feel anything as he walked through, not as he had when he traveled the gateways. Once on the other side, however, he noted a change in the air; it felt slightly warmer and dryer. And the smell was different; less musty, less mulchy.

But the main difference he noted was the view before them. They definitely were not where they had been a few steps back.

The forest ahead thinned, with the trail opening out to a wide expanse of low, grassy hillocks with occasional clusters of squat trees; here and there were narrow bands of brush that likely followed rivers or streams.

And beyond the plain, a castle was just visible set midway up a steep mountainside. The stone walls of the structure were as dark as the mountain itself.

"My friends," said Tobias. "I believe that is where we need to go."

"Looks simple enough, sir," said Meara.

Jake sighed doubtfully. "I'm thinking not."

"Sir?"

"There are those '*situations*' that Uncle Tobias spoke of."

"Right," said Meara. "Those."

"Off we go then?" Tobias said brightly.

"Yes sir," Meara said tentatively.

"Lead on, uncle," said Jake.

They followed the trail out onto the plain and the rolling hills and started toward the mountain with the castle on the horizon. There was no wind, not the slightest breeze, and the eerie quiet of the forest they had left behind followed after them, surrounding them. Colors faded, leaving only varied shades of gray.

They traveled until the grays darkened and they sensed dusk was nearing. They made camp along the bank of a wide stream, collected dry branches and twigs from surrounding brush for their fire.

The mountain was a dark silhouette in the distance, disappearing into the black as night fell. Tobias, Jake and Meara sat close by the campfire. The crackling sound of burning branches echoed out into the darkness beyond the reach of the firelight.

Jake couldn't help but be reminded of his other travels across the landscapes of other worlds. How many times had he sat before a flickering campfire, under an Other World sky?

Surreal worlds with dragons flying overhead, dark silhouettes set against bright moons...

He looked up from the fire, looked in the direction of the castle set into the mountainside, hidden now in the dark.

"How can we be sure he's still there?" he asked, not so much a question as an observation.

Tobias glanced in the direction Jake was looking, turned back to the fire.

"I don't suppose we can," he said. "'cept, no reason to think he's not."

They reached the edge of a deep gulley and followed the worn trail that ran along the rim for most of the morning. Vegetation grew thicker here, even more so down in the gulley itself, which looked to be the remnant of a streambed or wash; Tobias suspected it may fill during a heavy rain.

The trail eventually veered away from the gulley, disappearing into tall scrub brush. As the trail continued the way they wanted to go, they followed it in.

Several dozen feet into the brush, the trail straightened and widened. Set alongside the trail was another milestone marker. The trail beyond the stone didn't look any different than the trail behind them; and while the marker looked much like the last one, there was nothing to indicate a barrier like the one they had passed through earlier. There was no shimmering, transparent wall; the terrain up-trail appeared normal.

Tobias moved ahead without saying a word. Jake looked back once at Meara, then followed after his uncle. He glanced as the marker as he passed it, took three steps further and stepped up beside Tobias.

He heard Meara come up behind them.

"Oh my," she said. The terrain had changed. They had definitely passed through a barrier.

The mountainside castle was still visible, but the landscape directly ahead was now foothills covered in tall yellow grass and scattered groves of old, gnarly oak trees. The sky was dark gray, and Jake couldn't tell if it was morning or afternoon.

Which made him wonder... *is the time of day here different than it was a minute ago?*

Tobias continued to lead the way forward. The path led directly to the first hill, then turned right and took the slope gradually up to the rise. They passed twisted, brownish gray trees, faded yellow grass and thorny bramble brush.

As they approached the ridge, they began to see the tops of what looked to be broken building spires rising up from the basin on the other side of the hill. Coming up over the top, the gentle downslope fell away to a thinly wooded forest of oak and alder and evergreen, looking much as the Outland they were familiar with. In the heart of the woods they could see the ruin of a cluster of interconnected-buildings, now little more than the jagged outlines of broken walls.

The trail they were on led switchback down the hillside and then straight to the ruin. As they drew nearer, they could see stone stairs leading up to what had no doubt at one time been double doors but was now an opening leading to a foyer with no ceiling or walls. The shard remains of tall, broken spires rose on either side of the stairs, now empty towers.

Meara climbed the stairs and stood in what remained of the door jamb.

"This looks a lot like…" she started thoughtfully.

"Like the Temple?" finished Jake.

"Like the Temple," finished Meara.

The similarity to the temple in the Outland near Serpent's Keep was striking. The basic design was evident here. The wall foundations, tower remnants, it was all here; including the surrounding landscape.

"Yes," said Tobias. There was a deeply melancholy look about him. He was clearly disturbed by the site of the temple ruins. "There were a number of temples, on a number of worlds."

"Uncle Tobias?" asked Jake. "Are you all right?"

"Of course, Jake." Tobias attempted a weak smile. "I was unaware that one such temple was here on the Dark Path."

It doesn't make sense...

"All right," Jake mumbled uncertainly. He looked about at the ruin. *What had happened here? Neglected, long ago abandoned? Or something more ominous?*

They left the stairs and walked cautiously among the ruin. There were rotted wooden beams among broken stone and chunks of concrete, rusted handmade nails, and not much else. Rooms and halls were identifiable by the wall foundations and the jagged gaps where windows once looked out on temple grounds. They could see where the monk sleeping cells had once lined narrow hallways.

The sound of scraping stone came from the other side of the broken wall ahead of them, rubble scrabbling onto the ground. A silhouette appeared above the top of the wall. A dragon settled there, looked calmly down at the three humans. It was of the sleek Lynhaur species; colored in multiple shades of green and brown, with powerful hind legs, slightly smaller front legs. Its leathery wings were folded back along its sides.

Tobias looked up at the dragon, studied it a moment, and finally smiled.

"Friend Lamal," he said. "What are you doing here on the Dark Path?"

"Tobias Quigley," said the dragon. Human speech did not come easily to Thrauhm dragons. Lamal shifted his position to gain a better perch on the wall. "Not Dark Path. Pelonar."

Tobias considered, hesitated. *This is the temple on Pelonar?*

"I see," he said, reflectively.

"Tobias?" asked Jake.

Tobias gave a thank you nod to Lamal, turned to Jake and Meara. "This temple ruin isn't on the Dark Path. We are on Pelonar."

"Yes, but..." Jake started, stopped. He thought back on their journey so far, the markers, the barriers. "I think I understand," he said.

"Yes?" Tobias asked.

"Yes."

"Well, I don't," said Meara. "At least I don't think I do."

Jake looked from Meara to Tobias. "If I have this right, the Dark Path is a single thread, but it passes through landings on a number of worlds."

"Precisely," said Tobias. "The thread itself exists on its own plane, and as we move along the path, we pass through each landing."

Meara indicated the mountain in the distance. She spoke to her understanding of what her companions were saying. "The Dark Path, and the castle, are on their own world," she said. "The landings are here, and yet they are not here. They sit along the thread."

"Exactly."

"And we see the castle whether we're on the Dark Path or in a landing?" There was some doubt in her tone.

"Um... yes. That's true. It is, after all, the Dark Path."

"Yes sir," said Meara. She was willing to accept the explanation because Tobias accepted it.

Tobias turned his attention back to the Jahai. "We journey the Dark Path, my friend. We would seek an audience with the Ancient Guardian."

"I have seen the shadows. You would undo what is being done."

"We are going to try, friend Lamal," said Tobias. He thought to himself... *we search for direction from the First of us.*

The Jahai looked away from Tobias, looked to Meara and Jake.

"I'm Jake," said Jake. How many dragons had he faced along his last quest? *I am blood of Tobias...*

"I know. Jake," said the dragon. "You help... *uncle.*"

I am blood of Tobias...

"That's me," said Jake.

"I'm Meara," Meara said snidely. She had also faced more than a few dragons. All in all, she thought they were very honorable; they were also more than a bit full of themselves.

"Meara," said the dragon. "Help Jake."

"Right."

The dragon let his gaze drift back to Tobias. It again shifted position, adjusted its perch on the top of the broken, jagged wall. Small bits of stone and gravel fell away as it settled back down.

"You pass now. You go," said the dragon. "Dark Path."

Chapter Eight

The castle was no longer visible through the tall trees of the sprawling forest they had entered hours earlier. Now working their way up steep terrain, the trail wound and switch-backed, the path occasionally so steep that Jake and the others were forced to grab onto exposed tree roots that grew across the trail in order to pull themselves up.

Clambering over yet another large root, they stepped out onto a level stretch of path. Sections of old wooden fencing lined one side of the trail. After a few dozen yards they came around a bend in the trail and up to another milestone marker.

Jake looked for some sign of a barrier across the trail. "I don't see anything."

"As before," said Tobias. "Onward, nephew."

Jake led the way, continuing past the marker. He sensed passing through the barrier, but didn't see much difference on the other side. The air was just as damp as before, and what sky he could see above the treetops was just as gray.

Once the others had come through the barrier, they continued up the trail. After a short distance it switch-backed and began to climb again. Another switchback and the trail leveled out.

Ahead, a small, rustic cabin was set along the side of the trail where the path widened. As the three of them approached, Jake saw an old man sitting in an old rocking chair on the wooden porch. Asleep beside the man was what Jake at first took to be a dog.

They approached the cabin, stopping a few yards from the steps to the porch. The old man said nothing at first, moved not at all as he quietly studied the new arrivals. The animal sleeping beside him shifted, lifted its head and opened its eyes.

Jake realized then that it wasn't a dog, but something like a Little One, a small dragon-like creature similar to what Jake had come across in the Other World of the Dark Castle.

Jake grinned and winked at the Little One. The creature tilted its head and studied Jake. It blinked its eyes several times.

The old man leaned forward in his chair, placed his elbows on his knees and clasped his hands. His words were soft and unhurried.

"Hello, folks."

It was a quiet morning in the Village of the Dragons, as was normal. There was a hint of mist in the air as the dew evaporated and drifted from the surrounding vegetation and across the plaza.

Khol came out of the Grand Hall, having been in an early-morning meeting with Natan. Much of the discussion had been about the ever-increasing disturbances in the web despite the closing of the gates to the Other Worlds. There had also been some speculation as to the fate of Tobias Quigley and the humans' journey along the Dark Path.

Khol was about to step away from the great doors of the Grand Hall when something out in the plaza caught his attention. There was a shimmer of light in the air, the faint fog whorled and was shunted aside. An area eight feet across in the center of the plaza blurred and went out of focus.

A shadow formed in the disturbance, and a moment later Janice stepped out, stepped forward. She frowned darkly and looked about the plaza. Two other humans followed her out of the disturbance and stood behind her.

Janice ignored Khol by design; she stood waiting, almost as if waiting to be welcomed. The portal behind her faded.

Khol walked across the plaza, stopped several paces from the humans.

"Janice," he said, betraying no emotion one way or the other.

Janice glanced briefly at the human-like dragon, said nothing and let her gaze again drift across the village.

"Your presence here is unexpected," said Khol.

"I seek Tobias."

"Tobias is not here."

Janice looked sharply then at Khol. "What has the old man been up to?" she asked.

"I would not know."

Janice looked away dismissively. She silently noted that a number of Jahai, some of them of the heavier species, several others like this humanoid-looking Bentai dragon standing before her, had begun to warily approach.

"I would speak with Natan."

"I'm sure you would. Unfortunately, he is otherwise occupied."

"Advise him of my arrival. I have no doubt that he will want to see me."

"I have no doubt that he is already aware of your presence." Khol stood unmoving.

Janice's expression hardened. "I see. A low-level functionary seeks to rise above his station."

At the human's cold tone, two of the nearer Jahai moved up to stand beside Khol. They took no overt action, but the unspoken statement was made.

The two humans behind Janice responded in kind and moved up to stand beside her. She, however, wasn't about to give this Jahai the satisfaction of intimidating her. She calmly raised a hand, silently indicating that her companions should step back.

She gave Khol a gentle smile.

"It is of little consequence," she said. "I wished only to present myself in audience to your leader upon my arrival in this, his fair community. Please... would you pass along my salutation?"

"As you wish."

"Very well, then." Janice turned from Khol. Her escort moved aside to allow her to pass. She took several steps and slowed. She stopped and looked back.

"The Ancient Guardian..." she said softly, almost but not quite a question.

"What about him?" asked Khol.

Janice smiled thinly. She saw no reason to pursue it further.

"Yes... of course," she said. "I will see you again, Jahai."

She turned from Khol a final time and walked away. Khol watched as Janice raised a hand in front of her and appeared to rest her palm against something he could not see. The air before her shimmered and for just a moment Khol thought he could see something beyond the portal, a small room with furniture or equipment that he did not recognize. It faded as Janice and her companions stepped through.

Khol and the dragons standing beside him were alone in the plaza of the Village of the Dragons.

Tobias placed a foot on the first step, looked up at the old man on the porch.

"Good afternoon to you, sir," he said. "How are you this fine day?"

The old man leaned back, his chair creaking painfully. He scratched at his chin, looked to Jake and Meara, and then back to Tobias.

"I'm doing well enough. I thank you for asking." His tone wasn't overly friendly, but not totally unreceptive either. He was waiting to see where things went. He looked again to the others, again to Tobias. "Yourself?"

"Just fine," said Tobias. "We've been on the trail a spell. Our canteens are getting a bit light. Could you spare some water that we might refill them?"

The old man leaned forward again to the creaking of the chair. He pointed to a hand pump beside the cabin.

"Help yourselves," he stated flatly.

Jake could have sworn the pump hadn't been there before. Meara had the same thought.

"That's downright spooky," she said under her breath, though loud enough for the others to hear.

"I hear that," agreed Jake. He took Meara and Tobias' canteens, went to fill them along with his own. He wanted to be off to one side to better keep an eye on things, to be ready in case things turned unpleasant. He had grown accustomed to things turning unpleasant.

"I don't expect you get much company dropping in," said Tobias.

"You expect right," said the old man. He indicated the Little One beside him. "It's just me and Buddy, most of the time. Kinda prefer it that way, to be honest."

"Oh, I can appreciate that, sir. I surely can." Tobias could hear the water pump screeching as Jake worked the handle. "We'll be on our way just as soon as Jacob over there finishes filling the canteens."

"Don't want you taking offense," said the old man. He settled fully back into this chair. "More comfortable in the quiet, is all."

Meara wondered at the old man's curious choice of words.

"You've been here a long time?" she asked. "On the Dark Path?"

"I don't know from *Dark Path.* Home is home."

Beside the chair, the Little One slowly stood and stretched. It moved up nearer the old man, sat on its haunches and looked directly at Meara. It blinked, cocked its head, straightened. The old man reached out without looking away from the humans, rested a hand on the little dragon. Meara thought she could hear a low, rumbling purr.

"What's his name?" she asked.

"He never told me," the old man said, very matter-of-factly. "I just call him Buddy."

"Sounds about right," Jake grumbled as he returned to the others, handed Tobias and Meara their canteens. He had heard cryptic comments like that in every world he had visited on his quest.

"I thank you for your hospitality, kind sir," said Tobias. He slipped his canteen into its holster. For him, the comment hadn't been cryptic at all. It in fact said a lot. "We'll be on our way."

The old man looked down at the Little One, who appeared to be studying the humans. The dragon rumbled contentedly. "So you shall," he said.

With that, Tobias started away.

Jake took a step to follow, then hesitated and turned back to the old man. "Is there anything we should be watching out for up ahead?"

The old man continued to look down at the Little One. "Wouldn't know. Never been there."

"Right," sighed Jake. "Thanks." He and Meara followed after Tobias.

"He wasn't very informative for a Guardian," mumbled Meara.

"He wasn't the Guardian," said Jake.

Master Peter stood near the short wall enclosing the roof of the Temple's east tower. His hands clasped behind his back, he watched the strange, twisting, spiraling cloud formations in the distance. There was an odd musty smell in the air, drifting in the slight breeze that was brushing across his face. Peculiarly, it reminded him of the old scrolls in the library.

He heard the access door open behind him. Brother John climbed up onto the roof and walked over to stand beside him.

"Brother John." Peter nodded welcome while continuing to look out across the Outland.

"Good afternoon, Master Peter." John studied the sky. "It's not natural," he said.

"No," agreed Peter. "It is not."

Half a minute later, as they watched, the clouds quickly dissipated. The color of the sky returned to a late afternoon steely blue.

"They are more frequent," said John. "Whatever *they* are."

"And more severe," said Peter. "And while I have not noted any destructive effects here, I am reminded that we are not all that there is."

"Yes sir." John looked about the tower roof, out then to the surrounding forests of the Outland. He glanced once and again to Master Peter while never looking directly at him. He looked forward again and quietly cleared his throat.

Master Peter gave the hint of a smile. "What is it, John?" he asked.

"Nothing really," said John. He stumbled through his next words. "Just that we, I… I could not help but notice that you have been spending a lot of time locked away in the library these past days. A lot of time, even for you, sir."

"Have I?"

"Yes." John hesitated. "Master Peter, some have wondered if perhaps your research is related to what has been happening of late... the weather."

Peter turned slightly, let his gaze drift across the treetops of the Outland. Far in the distance, a thinning of the trees showed where the Village of Serpent's Keep was located, less than a day's walk from the temple.

"Brothers will gossip," he said at last. "It is easy to lose oneself when delving into the ancient scrolls."

"Of course, Master. I do not mean to pry." John struggled for a way out. "The ancient language can be quite demanding."

"Translation can be problematic, to be sure." Master Peter turned then to look directly at John. "Have you ever considered the original purpose of our brotherhood, John?"

"We exist but for one purpose, Master Peter. We bear witness to the good and the bad of humankind, that we might answer when called upon."

"Well spoken, Brother John," said Peter. "And just how might we bear that witness, isolated from humankind as we are in this temple?"

"If we are not apart, then we are part, by the very nature of such, and we would lose all objectivity."

"Yes, yes," Peter sighed. "In any event, your response, while well stated, does not actually address the question of the *origin* of our order, or specifically, of the Temple."

"Oh. I see." John was clearly confused. He didn't see. He wasn't completely clear as to the question. "I am sorry. I don't know how to answer."

"Yes," said Master Peter. "No need to apologize, John."

Again the two grew silent, each lost in his own thoughts, each letting his gaze drift out across the Outland. Peter eased out of the silence then, his question spoken softly.

"Have you ever wondered that our order has but one temple?" he asked.

"Such has not occurred to me before now."

They watched then as dark, misshapen clouds began to form once again on the horizon.

"Hmm..." Master Peter sighed.

Jake used the side of his foot to push dirt over the small campfire, riling up the glowing coals and sending a puffy plume of smoke into the damp, early morning air. Meara was kneeling a few yards away as she stuffed her few supplies into her small pack.

Their camp was in a grove of apple trees that had long ago gone wild. Tobias was standing a dozen yards from camp, was little more than a shadow near the edge of the grove. Jake came up and stood beside him.

The early dawn sky was quickly brightening. Tobias was looking out across a grassy plain. Jake followed his uncle's gaze. Half a mile away was a silhouette in the predawn light; a solid mass running several miles left to right.

"Is that a wall?" he asked. It was difficult to judge from this distance, but it looked to be twelve to fifteen tall.

"It looks like it," said Tobias absently.

"Was it there before?" Jake had stood at this very spot the night before and hadn't seen anything out there. But it had been dark.

"I expect so. It doesn't matter. It is now." Tobias took a long, deep breath. He was ready to move out. He looked back toward camp. "Let's get our gear."

A warm breeze brushed across the calf-high grass, creating an eerie whispering sound. In the distance, beyond the wall that still lay ahead, the mountain and its castle faded in and out of view as something fog-like drifted before it, between whatever lay ahead and the mountain on the horizon. It was a gray, swirling haze that itself faded in and out, as if one moment real and the next imaginary.

Approaching the wall, they saw that it was constructed of tightly fitted stone, twelve feet high and running left to right as far as they could see.

Directly ahead was a narrow opening in the wall.

"Well, that looks very much like an invite to me," said Tobias, leading the way.

Passing through the opening, they found themselves in a maze of stone walls, each wall tall enough that it made it difficult to use the sky or the world beyond the labyrinth to maintain any sense of direction. Jake insisted that he could do it, so Tobias and Meara quickly allowed him to take the lead.

In a true maze, direction wasn't always your best friend. What Jake tried to focus on was any sort of pattern. This wasn't the first maze that he had come across. There had been the labyrinth below the castle in one Other World and the storm drains beneath the abandoned city in another, just to name two. As a result of his past experiences, he thought himself not bad at navigating such things.

When it came to labyrinths, the whole concept of direction was often used to intentionally mislead. However, you eventually had to get from here to there. Jake understood that much. He also knew that labyrinths were usually designed in patterns, frequently interconnected clusters of mini-labyrinths. He soon found that to be the case with this maze.

Actually, this maze wasn't all that complicated. Jake quickly figured out that the secret to this one was not to overthink it.

It was almost twenty minutes before Jake began hearing faint grumblings from his companions following behind him; a few minutes more and the grumblings began to grow more vocal.

"Master Jacob," Meara started.

"Just up ahead," said Jake, his confidence waning hardly at all. "Not far now."

"Yes sir." Meara silently noted that there was no sign of an exit up ahead. "I'm sorry, sir. I'm not one to doubt, I know that I could do no better, but I can't help but be just a little concerned."

"Not to worry, Meara," said Tobias. "I'm sure Jake will lead us out soon enough."

"Yes sir." She looked back behind them, at the intersection they had just passed. They had just crossed their own footprints.

Rations low, and at best a few days of water.

They might die in here.

Jake noticed then sunlight on the ground ahead, near the next bend. Coming around the corner, it was a straight shot to the opening in the perimeter wall, and clear daylight was streaming in.

He wore a growing smile the others couldn't see, and he breathed out a barely concealed sigh of relief. He stepped through the opening and out of the labyrinth. Several steps out, he sensed that something was wrong, though he didn't know what that wrong was. He slowed, took several more steps. He stopped.

He didn't want to look back.

"Hey guys?" he mumbled. There was no answer. He waited. "Oh, boy."

He had no choice. He looked back over his shoulder.

Yep. There was no one there.

"Oh, geez... not again."

Jake turned fully around.

"Oh, geez," he said again. The opening into the labyrinth was gone. He stepped back to the now solid wall. He pressed a hand flat on the stone, hoping that it was illusion, hoping that the opening was still there. He rubbed his palm against solid stone.

The opening had been a portal, and at the moment that portal was closed.

He turned slowly away from the wall, faced outward then, across an alien landscape. It was a flat plain covered in clusters of low-growing gray vegetation. The sky was a colorless dusk.

The castle was much nearer, its mountainside a purple silhouette sitting high on the near horizon.

Tobias and Meara stepped out of the labyrinth, following Jake through the opening. Ahead of them was a flat plain covered in clusters of low-growing gray vegetation. The castle was visible in the distance, set against the mountainside on the horizon, appearing eerily closer.

There was no sign of Jake.

"Sir?" Meara asked anxiously.

"Yes," Tobias stated flatly. "So I see."

Chapter Nine

Mrs. Hodges had spent the afternoon in her back alley booth preparing several orders of her herbal mixtures. There had been an increase in requests for her services of late. It was difficult to ignore the atmospheric disturbances, if they could be called that, and many of Mrs. Hodges' fellow villagers were growing increasingly anxious. Most of the orders were for her calming potions, but there were a surprising number of requests for various first aid mixtures and even a few defensive concoctions as citizens considered the possibility of having to abandon the village for the Outland.

She had to wonder at that, as whatever was happening was obviously not exclusive to the village. What was happening here was happening everywhere.

And really, if it came to that she doubted that many of her friends and neighbors would survive long outside the walls of Serpent's Keep.

Her walk home from the marketplace was quiet; those she passed along the way weren't in the mood for conversation; so much the better. Rounding the corner from the main thoroughfare and looking down the side street, she noticed a figure dressed in heavy monk's robes standing across the road from the estate's main gate, near the entrance to the park.

She stopped at the wrought iron gate of the Quigley Estate and looked across at the monk. She recognized him then.

"Master Peter," she said. "It's been a while."

Peter took that as a sign of welcome and started across the road. They met halfway. "Good afternoon, Mrs. Hodges. Yes, ma'am. It has been several years, at least."

"What brings you to the village?" she asked as they shook hands.

"I was hoping to talk with you."

"With me?" Mrs. Hodges and Peter had a history going back a very long way, but they didn't really know each other very well. Their past relationship was tied to events from long ago and to a handful of shared acquaintances.

"If that is all right with you."

"Of course it is."

It was a pleasant afternoon, and even the intermittent disturbances had eased up some. Mrs. Hodges indicated the park and they walked back to the open gate. The park was empty, as it had been for days as people chose to remain in their homes as much as possible. Mrs. Hodges and Peter worked their way along the winding walkway and settled in at the first table.

She considered starting with small talk, instead got right to it. "What can I do for you, Peter? I assume it has something to do with what's happening..." she pointed a thumb up at the sky.

"In a roundabout way, yes." Peter grew thoughtful. "How to begin..."

Mrs. Hodges waited without comment.

"As you are aware," Peter started again, "our sanctuary is fortunate to have an extensive library, replete with a number of very old volumes."

"I may have heard something to that effect." Of course she had. Though seldom seen by any but the resident monks, the library at the Temple was renowned for its collection of volumes and ancient scrolls.

"Yes, well..." Peter hesitated, continued then, though seeming now to shift direction. "I have recently had cause to reassess the circumstances of our order."

"Oh... I see. The Temple? The brotherhood?"

Peter had spent a significant portion of his life in that musty library. He had spent years hovered over ancient scrolls, deciphering and translating and interpreting the meaning of very cryptic works written in ancient, obscure, sometimes dead languages. But due now to the events of the last few years, he had found reason to revisit many of the most ancient of those scrolls, seen now under the light of a shifting perspective. His translations took on new interpretations.

"Rather surprising, really," Peter wondered aloud. "As inquisitive as I most certainly am by nature, and always have been, the origin of our brotherhood was something that I seldom questioned. I suppose I falsely equated the founding with the purpose, and I let it go at that."

"And now?"

Peter looked directly at Mrs. Hodges. His focus seemed to shift again. "Do you know what Tobias is up to?" he asked.

"I seldom know what Master Tobias is up to," she said matter-of-factly. When she saw that Peter was waiting for more, she went on. "Other than trying to catch up with young Master Jacob, I do not. You can be relatively certain that whatever the two of them are doing, it has something to do with your *roundabout reason* for being here."

"I believe that, and more."

"What do you mean?"

Peter wasn't sure what he meant. He wasn't sure what it was that he knew, nor what he understood of what he knew. He didn't really know how to apply what he believed he knew to the real world.

The real world...

That was almost funny. It wasn't the real world that he was trying to understand. It was rather some bizarre ethereal landscape that Tobias Quigley had travelled for centuries, perhaps millennia, and that Peter had only just become aware.

"There were originally six temples," he said softly. "Six temples, scattered across six worlds, or planes of the same world, whatever that means." He shrugged. "The translation is fuzzy on that; planes of existence, and either different flavors of one world, or similar but different worlds. I'm not sure."

"Ah, you are not sure, but it all reads differently now that you know of the gates."

"And the planes and threads and doors and all that." Another shrug. "Interpretations change, Mrs. Hodges. They evolve. On the one hand it becomes less cryptic, on the other much more confusing."

"I can see how." Mrs. Hodges frowned. "But I don't see how any of that connects with any of what's going on."

"From what I have been able to decipher, I believe that whoever created the gates also created the temples; I just don't know why. I also believe the temples were at one time interconnected, bound... by something."

"You mean physically?"

"I don't know," he said. They had been bound together in some way, but he didn't have any more than that. He suspected that the relationship between the temples had at one time been strong. He was fairly certain that though the temples and the gates had been created by the same entity, they had not been placed on the same worlds.

Except for his own temple and the master gate. Serpent's Gate. That had to mean something. Yet from what he had been able to interpret, his temple had been considered an isolated outpost among the line of temples.

Was there an actual relationship between his temple and Serpent's Gate? If so, was the isolation of his temple from the others tied to that relationship?

The afternoon was growing late, the sky was shading from blue to bright gray. And Peter hadn't gotten any answers. Though, to be fair, he wasn't sure that he had asked an actual question. Certainly not the right question.

He wasn't sure that he knew what that question was.

"What is it you want, Peter?" asked Mrs. Hodges. "Why are you here?"

Peter leaned nearer Mrs. Hodges. She thought she could see a growing desperation in his eyes.

"I don't have it right," he said. "I'm missing something. Our origin. The temples. Something doesn't fit, and it's important. I know it is. I need to talk to Tobias."

"And you think it has something to do with what's happening."

"It may not be related at all. But that is not what troubles me."

"Right. The temples. The six temples."

"Translating the ancient script is imprecise at best. And the original words put to scroll were cryptic to begin with. With my greater awareness of what lay out there, the reinterpretation has left shadows in what I see. There is something incomplete in what I see. I am missing something important."

"You think Master Tobias has the answer?"

"Or he has the question. If he does not, he needs to find it.

Tobias and Meara had been walking for several hours. The world around them was flat and dry, mostly desolate with occasional islands of gray vegetation. The sky overhead was a cloudless, dull, dusky gray. It never changed, never growing darker, nor brighter.

There was no sound, no wind, no movement but for the two humans walking across the barren landscape. The walls of the labyrinth were now far behind them, the silhouette of the mountain range ahead sat low on the near horizon.

They stopped near a small cluster of short shrubs. Meara brought out her canteen and took several long swallows. As Tobias looked curiously around them, an increasing sense of unease weighed on him. He didn't like the feel of this place. It was more alien than any world he had visited, and he had visited a lot of worlds.

He reached out and took hold of a leaf of the nearest bush. It was triangular shaped, pale gray, with thin brown veins. He rubbed it between his fingers. It didn't feel real. None of this felt real.

Meara slipped her canteen back into its belt holster.

"We would have seen him by now, sir," she said. "If he were here."

Tobias let go of the leaf, looked ahead, across the plain in the direction of the mountain and the castle. There was no sign of Jake, but that didn't mean that he wasn't here. He could be here, just not the *same* here.

They had watched him vanish, disappearing before their eyes as he stepped out of the maze ahead of them and onto the plain. This plain.

They had followed Jake immediately after exiting the labyrinth, but he was gone.

Tobias was certain that whatever landing Jake had traveled to, he was still on the Dark Path. And if Jake was still on the Dark Path, then the castle would likely be before him, as it was for Tobias and Meara.

"He's here, Meara," he said. He indicated the castle set into the mountainside. "That's where we'll find him."

Traveling back to the Temple after his visit with Mrs. Hodges, Master Peter found himself walking the trail in the dark. He had no interest in spending the night in Serpent's Keep, and he had traveled the Outland at night more than once over the years. The trail running between the village and the Temple was well-traveled and he was quite familiar with it.

Still, even this part of the Outland, between village and temple, could be a dangerous place, all the more so at night. Shadows that kept to the woods during the day crept out onto the trails at night. Peter did his best to keep a watchful eye on his surroundings.

And yet his mind did begin to wander. His conversation with Mrs. Hodges had given him little so far as answers, but it did cause him to reevaluate what information he had brought with him; the origin of the brotherhood and the six temples in which the brotherhood resided; the real purpose of the brotherhood; the cryptic words written on ancient scrolls in all-but-forgotten languages; the library itself.

The night air grew cooler. The animal sounds emanating from the shadows of the forest beyond the trail slowly transformed as creatures of the dark replaced the creatures of the day. A partial moon had already risen and had begun to spread a silvery light across the path in front of him.

Peter did feel ill-at-ease, if only slightly, despite his own self-reassurances, and he grew all the more wary and a bit more watchful.

A strange sensation then; it crept up slowly until it was almost overwhelming. Physical, and yet not. It pulled at him, wore at him, frayed at the edges of his mind. As it spread, he fought to push it away as something unreasonable. But it kept coming back. It stayed with him then. He wasn't sure what it was at first, but it stole into his thoughts and seeded there, the meaning and the imagery growing steadily clearer.

It was as if the world in which he walked wasn't his world at all.

His pace quickened. He would not rest, could not rest, until he was safely within the walls of his temple.

Jake stood with his back to the small campfire. The thick, shoulder-high bushes encircling his campsite shimmered in the firelight, shadows and light dancing among the branches and leaves. Beyond the camp, the vast plain spread out across the landscape in all directions beneath a black night sky filled with sparkling stars.

The silhouette of mountain range on the nearby horizon was a different shade of dark than the sky or plain, and the castle set into the mountainside shone with the glow of the partial moon that was hanging in the sky just above it.

Jake estimated he would reach the castle the following day, this assuming that he got an early start in the morning and there were no unplanned side trips through unexpected portals. He hoped to find Tobias and Meara waiting for him there. He had no doubt that wherever they were, they traveled the Dark Path, and that meant the castle was before them as well.

Jake had been traveling alone for almost two days, ever since stepping out of the labyrinth and starting across the plain. In a strange way it reminded him of his earlier journeys in the Outland and into the Other Worlds. Meara had been his companion on some of those journeys, but he had traveled alone on several of them. He had been hardly more than a boy then, was not much more than that now. And though he could honestly say that he now had a lot more experience, it was equally true that he knew as little about what he was into on this journey as he had known about the portals and the Other Worlds back then.

He stared at the castle in the distance. It seemed almost near enough that he could reach out and touch it. He actually had to hold back lifting a hand.

Tomorrow. Tomorrow he would have answers. He hoped that his uncle and Meara would be there, but with them or alone he would soon stand before the Ancient Guardian.

Chapter Ten

Meara ate the last of her biscuit, washed it down with coffee. She moved away from the fire and stood at the edge of their small camp. Morning was coming, the eastern horizon growing lighter. The mountain range was much nearer, was showing clearer and brighter with the coming dawn. She estimated they should reach the range by nightfall.

Assuming the path from here to there was a straight line, which wasn't something that they could count on.

"Tonight you figure, sir?" she asked.

"Perhaps," said Tobias. He took a last sip from his coffee. He used his foot to push dirt over their dying fire. "Perhaps tomorrow morning."

Meara continued looking to the mountains, to the castle. Was Jake seeing what she was seeing? Was he near the castle? Was he already there?

Her brow wrinkled, a frown forming as a recurring thought pushed to the front of her mind.

What had been the purpose?

She glanced back to Master Quigley, turned again to the mountain range.

"Sir? I don't understand. What good was the quest, Master Jacob gathering the artifacts and closing the gate? He sacrificed so much."

Tobias took a step from the smoking embers, toward Meara. His gaze went past her, out to the plain and beyond, to the horizon.

"It was absolutely critical, Meara. Critical. Closing Serpent's Gate closed the Other Worlds to Janice; closed the worlds of the Jahai to her, as well."

"Pardon, Master Quigley, but isn't she going wherever she wants? Isn't that why we're going to talk to the Ancient Guardian?"

"Oh, not so, my dear." Tobias turned back to the camp and began packing their gear. "The worlds of the gates are quite different from the threads that she is now traveling. The Other Worlds of the gates offered a special access to the planes of the universe; so the Ancient Guardian is said to have designed them. Any worlds or landings that are now accessible across the web of threads are isolated, or are otherwise limited by time or physical presence."

Tobias' last words trailed off. He stared down at his pack, full now and ready to close.

"Sir?" asked Meara.

Tobias had to admit, if only to himself, that he had been surprised at Janice's ability to move from one set of threads to another. She appeared to be creating new threads, or repurposing existing threads, connecting planes and worlds and landings that had up to now been totally distinct from one another.

It didn't look like Janice was yet fully capable of directing her formation of these new threads, but Tobias believed that it was only a matter of time. And until then, she was creating serious disruptions in the fabric of the universe.

Tobias picked up their gear, handed Meara her backpack as he started from camp.

"What say we get this day started," he said.

Martin helped Janice step down from the standing frame and guided her over to the stool. Her face was pale, almost gray, her breath feathered and light. This had been a particularly difficult transit, as they usually were when the thread that she repurposed had to support not just her but an escort as well. It didn't matter that the thread was temporary, perhaps even collapsing behind her.

The frustration on Janice's face was visible through her gray countenance. This was her third attempt to reach the Dark Path since her visit to the Village of Dragons. Martin had doubts that Janice, despite her expertise, would be able to reach those planes of the web in which the Dark Path resided.

Janice herself had no such doubts. Her reach had only extended further since escaping the landing in which Tobias Quigley had imprisoned her. She believed that her increasing thread expertise would eventually get her to the Dark Path.

And to Tobias.

Martin handed her a glass of water that was supplemented with a number of nutrients. She took a long drink and gave the glass back.

"Thank you, Martin."

"You can't keep up this pace, Janice." He set the glass on the nearby table. "The next trip or the one after will be one way."

"Don't be so dramatic."

"With each return you are in worse condition than the return before. It's not worth it. He is not worth it."

Janice slid off the stool, using Martin for support. She started toward the door.

"We'll try again tomorrow."

"Janice, please. Two days. At least give it two days."

Janice reached the door. She ignored his pleadings. "I'll be in my room. Wake me for dinner." She held onto the door jamb and looked back over her shoulder. "I need to know what he knows."

She continued into the dimly lit hall without another word, briefly resting a hand on the old wood panel of the opposite wall.

Martin sat on the vacated stool and frowned at the now empty doorway.

Sure, Tobias may have information that Janice wanted, but Martin was certain that she could get by without it. Janice was the scientist, Tobias was not. She knew the web like no one else, excepting perhaps the Ancient Guardian himself.

Martin suspected that Janice may have an underlying fear that Tobias Quigley might again manage to derail the campaign to bring the universe under the blessed umbrella of the Rhetani.

And that Janice would not abide.

§

Khol's meeting with Natan had gone about as he had expected. Despite recent threats to the web, the leader of the Jahai had in the past repeatedly declined to return to the home world system.

He declined to do so yet again.

The location of the Village of the Dragons had been determined by the location of the hub of threads underlying the site. There were only a few dozen threads in the entire web. Some of those threads, though nowhere near all of them, intersected at several key locations within the web. The Village of the Dragons was one such hub. It tied together a number of important locations of the web, and had been the reason Natan had made this the administrative seat of the Jahai.

But conditions were growing more unstable by the day. Disturbances in the web, having subsided for a time, had returned and were increasing in frequency. The Village of the Dragons was becoming more isolated within the web, and Khol feared that should the situation continue to deteriorate, Natan could be forever cut off from their home system. Threads were not the gates of old, and their routes through the web had been extremely limited to begin with. The more threads that were lost, the more isolated the village became.

Khol stood outside the Grand Hall. There was a small group of dragons standing in the central plaza, all looking up at the sky.

A shattered dome hovered above the world, a spiderweb of thin orange cracks spreading, continuing to slowly spider across the dark gray shell. This continued for another minute as Khol watched. Then, at three points directly overhead, small blue spots formed. These quickly grew, eating at the gray.

An explosion of color then as bright blue suddenly swept across the sky. The gray was abruptly gone, and the world was again as it should be. A single faint wisp of cloud began to form. It drifted as it slowly expanded.

A group of five dragons, all of the sleek, flying Lynhaur species, came out of the Roundhouse, the building that housed the passage stones. They were returning from another journey into the threads. They were exploring each of the threads that emanated from the hub, this their third trip. As they neared, Khol could see that the news was not good.

The village was increasingly cut off from the other landings in the hub, and the hub from the rest of the web. They would soon be all alone.

The five Lynhaur dragons gathered before Khol and the leader of the group stepped out in front of the others.

Khol would be sending them out again, this time into the Dark Path. They must find Tobias and his companions. Tobias must be made aware of recent events.

Chapter Eleven

The front hall felt cool after days of the warm, dry air of the open plain. The room was wide, the ceiling two stories high. A central staircase led from the ground floor up to an abbreviated mezzanine. There were no windows. There were several doors on the main floor, one on the mezzanine.

A handful of narrow tables made of old wood were set along the walls, the only furniture. An old, musty smell emanated from the rough stone walls. There was something very ancient about the room, which was fitting considering the resident of this castle.

Jake walked from the heavy front door into the middle of the front hall. The castle was disconcertingly quiet. He ignored the stairs for now, chose the nearest ground floor door. The hallway that he entered was narrow, the ceiling low, the walls made of the same gray stone as that of the foyer. He passed by a number of open doors, all leading to empty rooms.

Rounding a corner, he saw the shadow of a figure hovering near the next bend. It disappeared beyond the bend as Jake approached. He continued down the hallway and rounded the next corner.

The figure was waiting at a wide archway at the end of the hall, the flickering golden light of a lamp hanging on the wall revealing the man's face; pale skin, dark eyes and heavy brows. He was human, of average height; he wore a heavy brown robe.

Jake stopped midway down the hall. The man's expression didn't change. The dark eyes reflected the light of the lamp as shadows brushed across the face.

The man lifted a hand then, waved for Jake to follow before turning and disappearing around the corner. Jake followed, stepped through the arch and turned down the next hallway; three more steps and he entered a large foyer.

Several hallways emptied into this room. The figure stood before a set of heavy double doors, looking back at Jake, his hands resting on the wooden door handles. As Jake crossed the room and approached, the man pushed down on the handles and pushed the doors inward.

Jake entered a round chamber, forty feet across, with russet-brown stone walls and a domed ceiling. To the left, two high-backed chairs with side tables were set against the wall; a set of French doors just beyond the pair of chairs led outside. Light spilled onto the chamber floor from the doors' inset windows.

Jake was alone, the guide nowhere to be seen. The main feature in the room was what at first looked like a thin curtain of water, four feet across and seven feet tall, that hung midair in the middle of chamber, two feet above the floor. The threshold membrane was half an inch thick, shimmered and sparkled. Jake stood within arm's length of the feature, what he assumed to be a portal. He could see nothing within it, but felt a cool breeze coming from it and pushing against his face.

The French doors opened and a tall, slender man came into the room. He had a thin face, startlingly bright eyes and smile, and long, salt-and-pepper hair. He was wearing loose pants and a long-sleeved shirt, soft shoes.

He was wiping his hands with a cloth hand towel.

"Sorry to have kept you waiting." He almost glided into the room, the doors closing behind him. "I lose track of time when I'm gardening."

"Not a problem," said Jake. There was more than a hint of confusion in his tone.

The Ancient Guardian indicated the portal. "Do you like my magic mirror?"

"Magic mirror?"

"Nah," said the Ancient Guardian, grinning. He stood on the other side of the portal. Jake could just make out the outline of the man. He saw him lift a hand, and a moment later Jake saw a village beyond the threshold. Figures were moving about in the central plaza. Dragons.

"A window," said the Ancient Guardian. Another wave of a hand. The image changed. It was another village, this one on an open plain, the sun high in the sky.

Another wave of the hand and the portal membrane again took on the illusion of a thin, watery curtain. The Ancient Guardian stepped around the feature and moved up beside Jake. He indicated the nearby chairs and started toward them, again wiping his hands with the small towel.

"It is good to finally meet you, Jacob Quigley," he said.

This really wasn't what Jake had expected. He nonetheless tried to keep the growing doubt out of his voice. "Are you the Ancient Guardian?"

The Ancient Guardian smiled as he tossed the towel onto a side table.

"Call me Aldwyn. Please."

"Aldwyn."

"Thank you."

Jake's guide reappeared, coming in through a narrow door a third of the way around the circular chamber. He was carrying a silver tray with a teapot and two cups.

"Thank you, Corwin," said Aldwyn.

Corwin set the tray onto one of the tables, turned half about and gave a slight nod. He picked up the hand towel and left the room as quickly and quietly as he had arrived.

Aldwyn poured tea, indicated one empty chair as he sat down in the other.

"Friend Jacob Quigley. What have you been up to?"

§

The edge of the plain pushed up against the rolling hills that quickly gave way to the steep side of the mountain. The castle was set into the mountainside, appearing as if it had always been there. It was as dark and ominous as the surrounding landscape, its smooth surface shimmering in the fading light of the setting sun.

It was obvious to both Tobias and Meara that they wouldn't be able reach it before nightfall, and decided to spend a night in the lower hills and make their way into the mountains and then on to the castle in the morning.

For Meara, it was maddening to have to stop for the night when they were so close. It had been an uneventful trek across the plain and they had made good time. The nearest hills were no more than half an hour away. But they were both exhausted, and they didn't feel it would be safe to head into the mountains in the twilight.

Something made Tobias slow his pace, his footfalls easing, his steps shortening. Something was brushing at his mind, leaving a faint imprint that slowly faded.

He stopped then. Meara came to a stop beside him. She gave him a questioning look.

He turned about, looked back along the path they had been traveling. There was nothing; only the open plain as far as the eye could see.

And then... a rippling in the air, a disturbance some hundred feet or more back along their path. Something was forming, coalescing, hovering just above the ground, several feet across.

"A portal," said Meara.

Tobias said nothing, took a step toward the portal, a second step. He stopped.

Janice... he thought to himself.

The portal struggled to come into existence. Tobias felt its presence, a hot prickly sensation on his skin, on his mind. There was a smell in the air, like electricity running along too-thin wiring.

Tobias took several more steps toward the disturbance. Meara followed cautiously beside him.

The portal began to fade, the rippling in the air to smooth.

Gone then, Janice appeared in place of the portal; she was down on one knee, the fingertips of one hand resting on the surface of the hard ground. She slowly lifted her head as Tobias approached. Her skin was pale, waxy, her eyes set deep in gray.

"You don't look at all well, my dear," he said, managing to sound casual. Meara stood beside him, looking down on the kneeling stranger.

"I've been better," said Janice. She rose deliberately to her feet. Only then did she realize she had come through alone. She hoped her two escort were safely back at the lab and that they hadn't gotten lost in the thread.

She struggled to keep her thoughts from showing on her face. She looked over at Meara, then back to Tobias. There was no sign of Tobias' nephew, Jacob Quigley.

"D'you lose the kid?" she asked.

"He lost us." His brief smile faded. "Is your presence here by chance or intended?"

"I have been looking for you."

"Is that so?" Tobias took a short step closer to Janice; she took a stumbling half step backward; he retreated back a step. "Your efforts are clearly coming at great cost, Janice. To what end?"

"No cost is too great in the service of the cause."

"The glorious Rhetani resolution? To spread acquiescent sunshine across all the universes?"

"Do not mock, Tobias."

"What do you want, Janice?"

She visibly ceded then. "I need your help."

Well, that is certainly unexpected...

"That you would need my help I find unlikely. That you would seek out my help in any event I find most unlikely indeed."

"And yet here I stand before you."

"Yes. Most curious," said Tobias. He paused a moment. "And just what form might this help take?"

"A map."

"A map?"

"The web. The primary landings. The secondary threads."

"You expect me to help you build a new gateway system?"

"I will get there. You have to know that I will get there."

"Will you? Look at the disruptions that you're causing, Janice. You're tearing the web apart, the very fabric of the universe."

Janice was growing noticeably weaker, her face increasingly gray.

"It doesn't have to be so, Tobias," she said tiredly. "With a map…"

"I have no map. Had I such a map, you have to know that I would never help you."

"No one was as close to Aldwyn as you," said Janice. "Other than Aldwyn, no one was as involved in the gateways."

"The gateways were but a small component of the web, Janice. You more than anyone—"

"I know the science. You know the design."

"I do not. Is this what brought you here?"

"We were friends once, Tobias. You, me, Marcus, Nehman, all of us." She nodded toward the castle. "Even Aldwyn. Comrades all, bound by honor."

"Bindings pulled apart by fanaticism and a twisted sense of what it means to be honorable."

"That is unfair, Tobias. The path of the Rhetani is noble and just."

"It is cultish religious extremism and so far beneath you, Janice."

Came the sound then of a number of leathery wings beating at the air. Meara saw shadows drift across the ground about them, skim over Tobias and the strange woman. She looked up, saw the silhouettes of five flying dragons set against the evening sky, circling overhead.

"More company," she said.

Thunder of dragons, Tobias thought to himself. *Traveling the Dark Path?*

"An unexpected turn of events," he said. "The second in an hour."

Meara brought her gaze back to Janice.

"Chance or related?"

Janice's response was to Tobias. "I suspect their purpose is as mine."

"To see us."

"The eminent Tobias Quigley." She took a step back, and another. She kept a close eye on the young woman who was standing next to

Tobias. She had the uneasy feeling that if given the chance, the woman would attack, would try to stop her from leaving.

Meara meanwhile watched with a cool, steady gaze. Janice raised a hand, holding up two fingers. Behind her, a portal began to form. The effort shown on Janice's face, draining color, draining what energy she had left to her. She took another step back, moving nearer the still-forming portal.

Meara stood unmoving beside Tobias; he nonetheless reached out and took her arm.

Janice looked at Tobias.

"This cannot end here, Tobias. Your refusal to see the truth will lead only to ill." She stepped back the rest of the way into the portal. The portal quickly dissolved, taking Janice with it.

With Janice gone and the portal closed, the dragons overhead circled a final time and then descended to the ground. They formed a circle around Tobias and Meara.

The leader stepped forward.

"Tobias Quigley," he stated firmly. To Meara then, "Companion."

"Meara," she grumbled.

"Yes."

"Your presence is most unexpected, friend," said Tobias.

"We enter Dark Path. We travel Dark Path. We find you."

"And so you have," said Tobias. "It must be important."

"Khol want Tobias Quigley know, Village of Dragons alone soon."

Tobias considered the meaning of the statement. "The threads?" he asked.

"Threads go."

"I see," said Tobias. He turned to Meara. "Time is not our friend."

"We must get to the Ancient Guardian," said Meara. "We must find Master Jacob."

Tobias turned again to the dragon. "Thank you, friend. You may return to the Village, your mission complete."

"We watch."

"We'll be fine, friend. Thank you."

"We watch."

Tobias considered, nodded agreement.

"Of course. You watch." He looked to Meara. "A walk in the dark after all, my dear."

It was early afternoon in the village of Serpent's Keep, and the day was pleasant. There were only a few wispy clouds in the blue sky and the midday sun was bright and its rays warm. Mrs. Hodges was sitting at a bench in the park opposite Quigley Estate, just finishing a light lunch. There were a number of others in the park, some sitting at picnic tables, others lounging out on the lawn, all enjoying the day.

The world had calmed down of late. There hadn't been a disturbance in several days and people were again daring to come out of their homes and into the daylight.

With lunch over, Mrs. Hodges decided to take a walk before returning to the mansion. She left the bench, followed the walkway around the park, taking a moment now and then to stop and say hello to folks that she passed. She eventually left the plaza through the entrance that opened out onto the main thoroughfare.

The village main gate was to her left. The double-gate was open and even at this distance she could see Mason standing just beyond. His back was to the gate, his attention on something outside the village.

She considered leaving him to his solitude, but her own curiosity got the best of her. He was obviously drawn to something out there and with all that had been happening, and it might be something that she would want to know about.

Walking through the open gate, she acknowledged the one guard standing watch and stepped up beside Mason. Ahead of them, a dusty dirt road wound its way across a sparse landscape of scrub oak, thorny brush and dry grass. She didn't see anything to warrant Mason's focus. He was just staring at the emptiness that was spread out to the south of the village.

"Good afternoon, Mason," she said.

"Ma'am." Mason said without turning to look at Mrs. Hodges.

Mrs. Hodges looked thoughtfully at the narrow road leading away from the village. She had never traveled that road. She had lived in Serpent's Keep her entire life, and other than a handful of trips to the farm to the north she had seldom left the village. She knew that to be true for most of the citizens.

"I sometimes forget how isolated we are," she said.

"Ma'am," Mason said again, distantly.

Mrs. Hodges looked back over her shoulder, back into the village. Okay then... she might as well get back to work. "Well..." she started.

"Our isolation may be greater than you know," said Mason.

"Oh, I don't know about that, Mason. I'm thinking we're pretty isolated."

Mason turned to her for the first time. "There hasn't been a bus arrived from the outside in months."

"Is that really so unusual? Visits from the outside have always been rare."

"The last bus to come to the village was the one that brought Jacob Quigley."

That startled Mrs. Hodges. How could that be so? Jacob had returned to Serpent's Keep not long after Tobias' disappearance. It had been the reason for Jacob coming home. It had been the start of his quest for the artifacts, his travels into the Other Worlds.

Several years ago, at least.

"That... is curious," she said.

"This is not right, Mrs. Hodges. This is most definitely not right."

Where are you going with this, Mason?

"Mason," she started cautiously. "What are you trying to say?"

Mason indicated the open landscape before them. "I don't think the outside is out there anymore."

It was a bizarre suggestion, and very much something that Mason would say. At the same time, if anyone but Mason had said it, Mrs. Hodges would have immediately dismissed it as crazy. But Mason saw things no one else saw. He didn't always see things as they were, but there was usually something there.

Mrs. Hodges felt a numbness spreading throughout her body. She felt cold and hot at the same time.

"Mason?" she prompted.

Mason turned and looked at her, yet wasn't looking at her. There was something distant in his gaze. He turned again to the world out there, to the world that wasn't there.

Mrs. Hodges looked again at the dusty road that wound through the landscape south of Serpent's Keep.

Where did it go? What was out there?

"I should probably get back," she said. "A lot of work to do..."

Mason said nothing. Mrs. Hodges backed away from him, turned about and walked past the man standing watch at the gate, continued into the village. She walked through the park on her way back to the estate. It was even busier than before, as more couples and more families came out of their homes to picnic in the afternoon sun.

Despite the sights and sounds of villagers out enjoying the day, Mrs. Hodges felt very alone. She returned warm greetings and smiling faces with barely an acknowledgment. She reached the park's north entrance and stepped out onto the side street, the Quigley Estate across the narrow road.

Mr. Griffin was standing on the front porch, his hands clasped in front of him, his focus up and past Mrs. Hodges.

She opened the wrought-iron gate and walked up to the front steps.

"Good afternoon, Mr. Griffin." She climbed the steps and stood beside him. She turned and tried to follow his gaze. There was nothing to see.

"Mrs. Hodges," he said softly. There was nothing more.

"I had an odd conversation with Mason a bit ago," she said at last, mostly to fill the quiet space, and perhaps to push unsettling thoughts out into the open.

"Did you?" He didn't sound all that interested.

"I did," she said. "Most odd."

"Yes..." Mr. Griffin said absently. "To be expected, I suppose."

Okay. He had a point. It was Mason, after all.

"I guess so," she said, but doubted that she would be able to let it go. This had been different. Beyond odd, this had struck a nerve. She had sensed real truth in Mason's vision. Yes, it could still mean just about anything, and yet Mason's words had managed to draw her in.

I don't think the outside is out there anymore...

Mrs. Hodges looked side-glance at the stalwart figure standing beside her; a silent presence, preoccupied. *What is he doing out here?*

Mr. Griffin seemed to read her thoughts.

"The mansion is acutely quiet of late, Mrs. Hodges."

How curious. She and Mr. Griffin often spent weeks looking after an otherwise empty estate. Such was the way with Master Tobias, and later with young Jacob.

"They will be home soon," she said.

Mr. Griffin pushed his chin out, drew it back in. "I sense..." he started, then took a long, deep breath. "I am uncertain."

"I am not," Mrs. Hodges said decisively. "They will be home soon. Meara has chores."

Chapter Twelve

After a brief walk in the garden, Jake and Aldwyn returned to the chamber through the French doors. The conversation to now had been light, drifting from one unrelated topic to another with no real direction. Aldwyn had done most of the talking, clearly enjoying having someone new to talk to.

The subject returned to Janice as they circled the window portal in the center of the chamber. The issue of Janice had come up several times during their stroll in the enclosed garden.

"Serpent's Gate and its associated gateways cannot be reopened," said Aldwyn. "Janice knows this. She instead seeks to overlay the sealed passageways with a gate system of her own. With a new system in place, she would open all the universes to the Rhetani."

The Rhetani; a cultish society from Earth's own future. Given the opportunity, their control would spread from their home world and their time to all worlds and all times... to all universes.

Janice was intent on creating that opportunity.

"Can she actually do it?" asked Jake. "Can she make a new gateway system?" From what Jake understood, Janice's abilities, as extensive as they at first appeared to be, were limited. He was given to believe that while she was creating portals, they were limited in scope, time and worlds, and were often temporary. A gateway system to replace Serpent's Gate would cross universal planes and time, would span the entire web of the universe.

"She is quite resourceful, and her abilities are evolving," said Aldwyn "But understand, she is not actually creating new threads. The web has all the threads that it will ever have. Janice is acquiring existing threads and is attempting to repurpose them in order to construct a gateway system."

"That is possible?"

"I do not think so. And almost certainly not one of the scope that Janice is attempting."

"But she thinks she can."

"She is obsessed by her purpose. Such is the failing of the zealot." Aldwyn stood before the portal. "I believe the greater danger, by far the greater danger, is the disruption that is created by her efforts. She is tearing apart the web of the universe. Worlds are being thrown into chaos, landscapes laid waste; entire planes are being set adrift."

Entire planes set adrift...

"Can't you stop her?"

"I cannot. I am forever bound to this place." Aldwyn held a hand out to the window portal, palm out as if resting it against the thin veil between planes. "My vision is far, my reach limited." He turned then to look at Jake. "But you can, Jacob Quigley. And that is why you are here. Is it not?"

Despite their concerns about traveling rough, uneven and unfamiliar terrain at night, Tobias and Meara set out in the early evening and traveled until it was too dark to see. They rested then for several hours, ate from their rations, and set out again when the half-moon rose and spread silvery light across the world. The rolling hills had hours earlier given way to steeper terrain, and with the moon glow they were able to follow the seldom-used trail that wound its way up to the castle.

They approached the castle several hours before sunrise, the half-moon already sinking to the horizon. The night air was cool, and there was a bit of a breeze. High above them, they could just make out the silhouettes of the dragons circling overhead. As they watched, the dragons turned back one by one, heading back along the way of the Dark Path.

Tobias and Meara took the stone steps up to the heavy front door, made of dark wood, black metal bands and large hinges. The door opened as they took the last step.

A middle-aged man wearing a heavy brown robe waited for them in the center of the front hall. He nodded welcome as the door closed behind them.

"Master Quigley," he said calmly. "It has been a long time."

"That it has, Corwin." Tobias gave a warm smile. It held the hint of nostalgia. "A distant time in a faraway land."

He indicated Meara. "This is my traveling companion, Miss Meara Gyles."

"Miss Gyles." Corwin nodded a second welcome, then looked again to Tobias before turning toward one of the hallways. "This way, please."

They followed him down one hall, then another. Meara wanted to ask Tobias how he had come to know this man in a castle at the end of the Dark Path, but each time she started to speak up, their guide looked back to urge them on as he rounded one corner and then another corner.

They came into a small foyer. Across the room was a set of double doors. Passing through, they entered a round chamber with a domed ceiling. The main feature was what looked like a portal hanging above the floor in the middle of the room. Jake and the Ancient Guardian were sitting in a pair of chairs near French doors.

Corwin silently dismissed himself with a curt nod of the head, leaving Tobias and Meara to cross the room on their own. Jake and Aldwyn stood at their approach.

"Friend Tobias," said Aldwyn. He smiled at Meara. "And this must be Meara. I trust your journey wasn't too difficult."

"Not too bad," said Meara.

"Good, good." Aldwyn turned back to Tobias. "Tobias, we weren't expecting you until later this morning."

Tobias told of their exchange with Janice, then of the arrival of the Jahai, of their fears regarding the disruptions in the web. With that,

Tobias and Meara had decided to travel the night, to reach the castle as soon as possible.

Aldwyn took the news without comment, then walked the several steps toward the window portal. Tobias followed along beside him, leaving Jake and Meara to wait by the chairs. Aldwyn told Tobias that he had been witnessing the disruptions and shared the concern of the Jahai.

Watching Tobias and Aldwyn in quiet conversation near the portal, Jake saw two old friends getting together after a long time apart. Meara saw it, too.

"I think they were closer than Master Tobias has let on," she said.

"Aldwyn told me they were as brothers," said Jake. He shrugged. "We talked. We've been up all night anticipating your arrival."

"So you knew we were coming..."

"Aldwyn sees much."

"I must say, he is not what I was expecting," said Meara.

He hadn't been what Jake had been expecting, either. But after spending a day and a night with Aldwyn, the Ancient Guardian could have been no one other than Aldwyn.

"Aldwyn was the first human to meet the Jahai," said Jake. He sounded rather retrospect. "They accepted him as one of their own; he lived among them for a time. He told me that he admired their integrity and their moral character. It was he who founded the Guardians when Tobias separated Serpent's Gate and scattered the artifacts across the Other Worlds."

"He really is ancient."

Jake looked about the chamber. "The castle is a place out of time," he said. "And so, therefore is he."

They watched Aldwyn turn from the portal and place a hand on Tobias' shoulder. The Ancient Guardian smiled warmly and said a few more words, then the two of them walked back to Jake and Meara.

"I so wish we had more time, my friend," said Aldwyn, speaking to Tobias while looking at the entire group. "But as has been stated, time is short."

Tobias agreed. "Perhaps when our task is completed, time for a true visit, you and I."

"Perhaps," said Aldwyn, but there was little behind the word. He looked to Jake. "Jacob knows the path you must take. His spirit is strong, and I am certain all will be well in the end."

They stood at the top step, the castle's large front door quietly closing behind them. The sky was brightening, with dawn now only minutes away. The air was still cool.

"He told you what we had to do; right, sir?" asked Meara.

"That he did," said Jake. "Apparently, it is possible to isolate a part of the web from the rest of the web. So he says. Once we do that, Janice will be trapped there, the rest of the web safe."

"Pardon, sir. Didn't Master Quigley trap Janice once before?"

Tobias held his face to the first rays of the rising sun. "The landing on which she had been confined yet remained a part of the web," he said. *It should have held her forever. I underestimated her abilities...*

"I'm supposed to cut away part of the web," said Jake. "Whatever trouble Janice manages to stir up will be kept there."

"Right, sir," said Janice. "And how do we do that?"

"Simple. I travel a thread and close it at the other end. That should separate a small section of the web."

"And that's where she is?"

"So I'm told."

"Pardon again, Master Jacob, but isn't that what you did last time?"

"I would argue that it wasn't a thread the last time, but yeah, pretty much the same."

Tobias shook his head. "The closing of the gates prevented the Rhetani from accomplishing their goal."

"And so Janice is trying to create a new system," said Jake. "Aldwyn doesn't think she can, but her attempt is trashing the fabric of the universe."

"Yes sir," said Meara.

The thread that Jake needed to close was one of the handful of threads that made up the hub underlying the Village of the Dragons. It was the only thread that connected a small segment to the rest of the web. It had to be closed at the far end in order to permanently sever that segment. If the thread was closed at the hub, the thread would remain a part of the isolated section and could theoretically be reattached to the web somewhere else.

"Okay, so you travel the thread, close it on the other side," Meara stated.

"Right."

"While you're on the other side."

"Right."

"Just like last time."

"Pretty much."

"Except, it sounds like there won't be any coming back this time."

"It looks that way."

For Tobias, there was something more, something about that isolated location in the web. It would be more involved than what Jake had been led to believe.

Typical Aldwyn.

"I'll take care of this, Jake," he said. "When we get back to the village, you and Meara head on to Serpent's Keep."

"No sir," said Jake. "Aldwyn was clear. This one is on me."

Tobias glowered for several moments, his eyes focused on the sunrise.

"Very well," he stated at last. "But you won't be going alone."

Chapter Thirteen

Khol walked across the central plaza toward the Grand Hall. The sky overhead was pale lavender, the shadows in the surrounding forest beyond the buildings of the village were tinted a grayish purple.

There were very few Jahai about. Their changing world was making them increasingly anxious and most would just as soon stay under shelter.

He entered the building, walked across the front hall and passed through the open double doors into the audience chamber of the Grand Hall.

Natan was seated on his throne, talking with a small group of Bentai Jahai who were standing at the foot of the platform. Khol stepped to one side in the hall and waited. Several of the larger Thrauhm dragons were slumbering along the wall.

The conversation ended and the group of Bentai started down the center of the chamber. One gave Khol a long, slow half-bow as they passed. They closed the double-doors as they left.

Khol approached the throne. Natan stood and stepped off the platform as Khol neared.

"What news, my friend?" he asked.

"Such news as we have is more grim this day than the last, more grim still than the day before."

"The threads?" Natan began pacing thoughtfully back and forth in front of the platform.

"Another is lost to us," said Khol. "Those that remain do not always lead to where you expect."

Natan briefly looked side-glance at Khol in silent response.

"Natan..." Khol steeled himself for his next statement. "Again, we should consider the journey home. I fear the path may already be lost to us."

The way home had always been a series of primary threads and side passages. The route was now all the more circuitous without the main passages.

Natan stopped his pacing. He stared out across the hall, though what he was looking at was worlds away.

He slowly turned then and looked broodingly at Khol. He gave a grumbling sigh and shook his head as he took the steps up to the platform.

"No, my friend." He rested a clawed hand on the arm of the throne. "Whatever our isolation here may be, it is nothing as that of the home worlds. If we are to continue to serve, in whatever limited capacity may remain to us, we must stay here."

Khol hesitated, then acknowledged with a respectful nod. "Yes, Natan."

Natan shifted about and sat again on his heavy wooden throne.

"To those of our brethren whom you are able to reach, call them to us," he stated. Natan didn't like the thought of Jahai being forever stranded alone in far off lands should the frayed web be forever pulled apart. They had lost enough with the closing of the gates. To lose these few side passages as well would remove all hope of those in outlying lands to return here to the Village of the Dragons, worse yet to return to the home worlds.

"Yes, Natan." Khol straightened, turned about and started away from the throne.

"Khol," Natan called after him.

Khol stopped and turned about. "Sir?"

"Tobias Quigley."

"I shall escort him here immediately upon his return."

Natan nodded, leaned back in his chair. Khol waited.

"Friend Khol," Natan stated at last. "We shall get through this."

"Yes, Natan." Khol accepted the dismissal, turned about again and left the hall.

Brother John opened the door to the library and quietly entered the room. The walls were lined floor to ceiling with shelves of old volumes; midway down the room an entire section of the wall was covered with a honeycomb of diamond-shaped compartments stuffed with scroll tubes.

Master Peter was sitting at one of the tables in the middle of the room, his back to John. A lone lamp illuminated an unrolled scroll that was spread out across the table before him.

John walked around the table and stood facing Peter. He waited in silence. It was some time before Peter sensed a presence in the room. He looked up from the ancient scroll.

"Yes, John?" he asked blearily.

"Master Peter," John said softly. "My apologies."

Peter struggled to come out of the misty world that he had been wandering around in; how long, he had no idea. He stretched and leaned back in his chair.

"Not at all, John. What is it?"

"If you have a few moments, sir, I would like to show you something."

"Of course," said Peter. When after a few moments John had yet to show him anything, Peter grasped that he was meant to follow John to whatever it was that he intended to show him. He slid his chair back and stood up. "Lead on then, Brother."

They left the library and started down the hall toward the front of the temple. There was no one about. The halls, rooms and cells all were dark but for an occasional night lamp glowing low. Peter hadn't realized that it was so late. He had been in the library all evening and likely half the night.

They reached the foyer and John quickly stepped ahead and opened the front door. The night air that pushed into the room was cool and refreshing. Peter stepped outside, John right beside him. They moved out onto the porch and stood at the top step. Ahead of them, the open space in front of the temple was dark, empty. The forest beyond the clearing was pitch black.

Peter was about to ask what it was that he was meant to see when he chanced to glance up at the night sky.

Something wasn't right.

The stars had lost their sparkle. They looked... smeared. And they all had an odd color to them; almost lavender.

"Well, that is certainly peculiar," said Peter.

"Do you see it, sir?" ask John.

Peter suspected that he was meant to see more than smeary stars. "See what, John?"

John gave a nod to the sky. "There, Master Peter; between us and the rest of the universe."

"I'm sorry, John. I don't see—" Peter started, then stopped.

Yes. He did see something. There was a film, a shell... something. There was indeed something up there, hovering up there, somewhere between the temple and the stars.

"What is that?" he asked, not expecting an answer.

"A bubble," said John. "We're inside a bubble. The temple, the Outland... we are inside. The rest of the universe... is outside."

Peter took a few moments to study the strange occurrence. The filmy bubble wasn't completely transparent, which was why the stars appeared smeary and off-color. He couldn't tell how much of the world it enclosed, but looking closely, he did see a very gradual curve to the shell. The tall trees encircling the temple prevented any real examination of the sky near the horizon.

Brother John interrupted his thoughts. "Master Peter? What should we do?"

"What do you suggest, John?"

As he asked the question, Peter saw John's face suddenly take on a glow, which quickly spread to the entire porch, the clearing and the forest. Looking again to the sky, Peter saw that the shell had grown opaque, was shimmering a bright, very pale violet hue now shadowing the world.

It faded then, slowly, leaving behind the filmy shell, which itself then slowly dissipated. The stars returned, sparkling against a clear black night sky.

To all appearances, all was as it had been.

"I'm off to bed, then," said Peter. He managed to sound a lot more perky than he felt. "It'll be morning before you know it. Eh, John?"

JohPa was of the Bentai Jahai. He was young, still had quite a bit of growing to do; at least another few inches. Even for a Bentai, his facial features were less reptilian, more humanoid than many of his brethren. His eyes were set closer together, his snout was almost petite.

He stood just off-trail near the gated entrance to the Dark Path. He absently scratched at an itch at the back of his head, sighed a noisy, bored sigh. He had been standing there for two hours, and had another hour before he was due to be relieved.

The world around him, the world around the entirety of the Village of the Dragons, was bathed in an unsettling gray with a tint of some color that he didn't recognize. He had never seen such a color. There was no such color.

He glanced up at the shell of sky. Yes. It was most unsettling.

He scratched again at the itch.

A sound came from the gate; wood striking wood, three times. JohPa stepped onto the trail and to the gate. He lifted the wooden crossbar and moved aside. The gate opened and the humans came through.

"Thank you, friend," said Tobias.

"Welcome, friend Tobias Quigley, and companions," said JohPa. He watched as one of the companions closed the gate. He then replaced the crossbar before stepping past them and led the way back along the trail into the village. Along the way he heard the humans commenting to one another about the changes to the sky, the odd color... and the ominous silence.

Yes, thought JohPa. *Unsettling.*

Khol was standing in the village center, as if he had been expecting Tobias' return.

"Welcome, friend Tobias," he said. He spoke then to the entire group. "I am pleased that you return safely."

"Thank you, friend Khol," said Tobias. He looked curiously about the village, at the sky above that seemed to be pushing down on them. "We are pleased to be back."

"The answers you sought?"

"Our journey was successful."

"Again, I am pleased." Khol looked to the young Jahai. "JohPa, escort our friend Tobias to Natan."

JohPa gave a curt bow of the head in response and started in the direction of the Grand Hall, leaving Tobias to follow after him. At the same time, Khol indicated that Jake and Meara should follow him in another direction, to the human quarter of the village.

They looked from Tobias to Khol.

"Okay, then," said Jake. He and Meara fell in step behind Khol and they started across the plaza. "Is everything all right here, Khol?"

"Everything not all right, Jacob Quigley," said Khol.

Chapter Fourteen

Martin poured another cup of coffee and leaned back against the counter. He took a sip, looking over the rim of the cup at his small lab: a well-organized mess; a cluster of tiny, well-lit islands of work tables in a sea of subdued lighting and shadow.

His life was slowly being eaten away, here, in this room; twelve to fourteen hours a day, seven days a week, week after week, month after month.

He wanted to go home.

Martin had joined Janice and the others on their divine mission to bring all into the way of the Rhetani; all worlds, all times, all universes, all to be embraced by the guiding hand of the Rhetani.

Unfortunately, those who would challenge the cause had managed to shut down the gates. Martin found himself alone, isolated on a world and in a time not his own. For how long, he did not know; perhaps for years. And then Janice, escaping a prison of her own, had found him and brought him here.

Again he served the cause. Now, however, it was sometimes difficult for Martin to draw the line between their actions and the purpose. What he was doing was necessary if Janice was to again reach out, to connect, and to bring all into the way; and yet…

Week after week, month after month...

A figure stood in the doorway; a silhouette, backlit by the light from the hallway beyond. Janice came into the room, worked her way through the work tables to the standing frame set against the back wall. She rested a hand on one of the frame's arm supports.

"You grow weary of this, Martin," she said, without looking at him. "I understand."

"I admit that I long to go home, ma'am."

"And yet there is the purpose."

"Yes, ma'am."

Janice turned then to look at Martin. She wore a slight smile.

"You are faithful, Martin. You would not abandon the cause, nor me."

"I would not."

Janice looked side-glance at the standing frame, her hand still resting upon it.

"I too miss home," she sighed. "I sometimes fear that the cause, the mission, will forever keep us from returning. If that be so, it is the sacrifice we must accept."

"It has been such a long time, Janice. Can we be certain the wants of the council are unchanged?"

Janice's expression grew hard. "The Way does not change."

"Of course not. But the means by which we might serve the needs of the Way may have."

Janice stepped away from the standing frame, slowly moved across to the nearest table. She was still very weak from the most recent series of passages through redirected threads. Standing now in the half-shadow between work stations, her sallow face was all the more striking. She used the table for support.

"Our path has been set for us, Martin," she said. "There are no alternative paths for us. We have no choice but to follow what has been given us. Our journey home, should we one day be so fortunate, lay on the same path as the purpose. We cannot reach the one without the other."

Martin held tightly to his cup. The coffee was already turning cold.

"Yes, ma'am," he said haltingly. He knew that however Janice's observation might be true, so too was what that meant should they fail. The very actions they were taking could very well forever close that path to them. The Way, and home, might both be lost to them.

The very fabric of the universe may well be coming apart as key threads were pulled free; threads that Janice had pulled free in order to repurpose. Events were now taking shape on their own, acting on their own, beyond Janice's control, beyond Janice's vision.

What might be happening out there of which they knew nothing?

Janice continued to use the table for support, looked back across at the standing frame. "You have input the data?"

Martin set his coffee cup on the counter behind him. "I have."

"Good." Janice pursed her lips, sighed. "Perhaps..."

"Ma'am?"

Janice frowned, pushed away from the table. She turned to the door. "Tomorrow, Martin. Tomorrow is fine."

"Yes, ma'am. All will be ready."

Jake circled the small campfire and sat on one of the three wooden stools. He picked up the long stick on the ground beside him and used it to poke at the coals glowing at the base of the flames.

Dusk had come, and the strangely tinted gray that enveloped the dragons' village was growing darker. The flickering light of the fire was reflected in the encroaching dark mist.

Jake glanced up at a figure approaching from the direction of the village, looked back then to the fire and waited. Meara came into the light of the fire and sat on the stool beside Jake. She had taken a walk after their evening meal, had been gone for quite a while.

"It sure is quiet," she said. "Eerie."

"They're spooked," said Jake. Dragons liked the dusk. It was their favorite time of day. With the recent sunset, the village should be bustling with activity, both on the ground and overhead. Yet there was hardly a dragon to be seen.

"Them and me both, sir," said Meara. The words faded into the surrounding quiet. They both drifted into their own thoughts, mesmerized by the flickering orange and red of the fire, the pulsating glow of the underlying coal.

They were startled back to the real world when Tobias was suddenly standing before them on the other side of the campfire.

"Uncle Tobias," said Jake. "You missed dinner."

"I can fix you something, sir," said Meara.

"No, no. Quite all right, my dear." Tobias took a seat on the last of the three stools. "I may have a bite later."

They waited for Tobias to say something more, to tell them of his meeting with Natan. He said nothing, quietly stared into the fire.

"Tobias?" Jake prompted finally. "How'd it go? You were gone a long time."

"Yes," said Tobias. "There was much to discuss. Natan is quite concerned."

"We gathered as much," said Jake. "We managed to get a few words out of Khol."

"Of course." Tobias nodded thoughtfully.

"Things are getting worse, aren't they, sir?" asked Meara. "Khol mentioned the threads. He said that Natan is calling everyone home."

"True, true," said Tobias. "A most difficult task, I'm afraid. What with the issue with the threads, reaching their brethren is proving problematic."

"Is there anything we can do?" asked Meara.

"We keep going," Jake stated.

"Exactly so," said Tobias. "We push on. A night's rest, and we continue on in the morning. Which means we'll need to be up well before dawn." Tobias looked up from the fire, out to the night that was quickly coming. He could see nothing; it would take time for his eyes to adjust after the light of the campfire. "It is quiet this evening."

"That it is," said Jake.

When Meara came out of the hut early the next morning, Tobias and Jake were already up. Tobias was putting a few final items into his backpack, while Jake was eating from a block of cheese. He tore a piece from the block and handed it to her.

Jake knelt then before the campfire and poured a cup of coffee from the metal pot that was sitting on a hearth stone.

"Coffee?" He held the cup out to her.

Meara took the cup and nodded a silent thank you. She took a bite from the cheese, took a sip of coffee. She looked about; at her companions, at the row of shacks, at the dark shadows that were beyond the reach of the firelight.

This was it. In a few minutes they would follow a side-passage to some distant landing, a thread to another world, and Jake would cut that thread free. They would in all likelihood be trapped forever in the other world. She would never see home again. She would never see her mother again.

If she really believed that, Meara was certain that she would be much more afraid than she felt. She was anxious, but not overly so. That was because somewhere deep in her heart she believed they would find a way home, a way back to Serpent's Keep.

After all, Jake had done it before. When everyone said that Jake was gone forever, she had known that he would return. And he had.

Why should this time be any different?

She ate the last of her cheese. Jake handed her a piece of bread.

"Are you ready?" he asked her.

"I am." Meara ate from the bread. "I just have to get my pack."

Tobias stood with his own backpack in hand. He slipped it on. "Let's not dawdle, then."

"Yes sir." Meara ate the last of her bread, washed it down with the last of her coffee. She went back into the shack to get her gear while Jake put out the campfire.

Ready then, they left the human quarter and started across the village's central plaza to the Roundhouse housing the passage stones. Two dragons stood watch outside the wide opening, even at this early hour. They said nothing, made no move, as Tobias, Jake and Meara went inside.

Tobias and Meara moved off to one side, let Jake approach the circle of six daises that were standing in the center of the room, each podium with its own passage stone. Each was the key to a unique thread in the hub that underlay the Village of the Dragons. He walked the circle, looking at the geometric symbols engraved on each stone. He stopped at the third that he came to.

"This one," he said. On the stone was the symbol the Ancient Guardian had directed him to look for.

Tobias and Meara circled the room and came up beside him. Meara took hold of Jake's arm, Tobias rested a hand on his shoulder. Jake looked from one to the other, let out a nervous breath.

"Luck to us, then," he said. If the thread was still there, the side-passage should take them to the landing and the world where they would likely spend the rest of their lives, if he was successful.

He had been in this position once before.

"Let us be off, nephew," said Tobias.

Jake looked at Meara. "Last chance, Meara."

In answer, Meara took hold of Jake's wrist and lifted his hand to the stone. She had made her choice long ago, back when she first insisted that he needed her as a guide into the Outland, back at the start of his first quest.

The journey through this passage was no different than any other. They were quickly enveloped in white, awash in a rush of light. Moments later they stepped out into a large clearing, the ground covered in a dry, mulchy layer of dead leaves and dry twigs. Beyond the clearing was a thinly treed forest of alder and scattered patches of fern and salal. The canopy was open enough to allow the sun's rays to reach the forest floor.

"Are we home?" asked Meara. "This looks like—"

"The Outland?" asked Jake. "I don't think so."

"Not the Outland that you know, my dear," said Tobias.

Jake pointed to the only trailhead leading away from the clearing. "This way."

"What are we looking for?" asked Meara.

"Haven't a clue."

Chapter Fifteen

The trail emptied at the foot of the steps leading up to the front door of a temple. It had been an easy two hour walk through a thinly treed forest that looked very much like the Outland back home.

"This looks promising," said Jake, admiring the temple.

"And familiar," said Meara. This temple had none of the additions that had been incorporated into the temple near Serpent's Keep, but the main structure looked much the same. "On the outside, anyway."

Tobias appeared distracted. "I expect we'll find much the same within as well," he said.

Jake led the way up the steps and to the door. He knocked. After half a minute with no response, he pushed down on the handle and pushed the door open.

The foyer was identical to that of the other temple, likely as all the temples. He called out, and when there was no answer, he tried again. Again there was no response.

"No one home," he said to the others. "Abandoned?"

It may or may not have been abandoned, but the foyer at least was clean and neat, with nothing to indicate the temple was being neglected.

Jake looked from one hallway to another, chose one and started into it. Tobias held out a welcoming hand to Meara for her to follow Jake, and he brought up the rear.

The way grew darker as they worked their way deeper into the temple, with the only light coming from narrow windows in the empty rooms they passed. They worked their way to the temple library. As the rest of the temple, this library was very similar to the one they all were familiar with. There were several tables in the center of the room, and the walls were lined floor to ceiling with shelves weighed heavy with old and very old books. Midway along the left wall was the honeycomb of diamond-shaped cubby holes filled with scroll tubes. A set of tall, narrow windows were evenly spaced along the far wall.

Jake looked about the room, then walked over and stood near one of the tables. He looked disappointed.

"What were you hoping to find, Jake?" asked Tobias.

"I'm not sure," said Jake. "I figured if there was a clue, it would be here."

"A logical assumption." Tobias worked his way to another table. He pulled out a chair and sat down.

"What now, sirs?" asked Meara.

Jake shook his head and sat on the corner of the table. He studied the room. "I still think it's here."

Meara began to wander about. "Eerie. Really eerie. It looks so much like ours."

"That it does," said Jake.

"Could that be the clue you're looking for, sir? The library, the temple, just like ours?"

"It's no coincidence that one of the temples is here." Jake looked over at Tobias. "Here, where the Ancient Guardian sent us."

"Coincidence, no. I wouldn't think so," said Tobias.

"You said there were a number of temples."

"That I did," said Tobias. "Six, actually; all very similar in design. As you see."

"And the Ancient Guardian was behind their creation..."

"That he was." Tobias leaned back and casually folded his arms across his chest. "Once the gates had been realized, and to some extent the secondary threads, Aldwyn sought to establish a society that existed external to humans and Jahai, a brotherhood that would stand outside and bear witness."

Meara gave a smile from across the room. "Master Peter has said as much."

"Yes, well… that was the original purpose of the brotherhood, and of their temples."

"It changed? The purpose?" asked Jake.

"The origin was lost over the centuries. And so the purpose has taken on less meaning."

Jake absently watched as Meara continued to wander the library, looking at the books on the shelves, stopping and looking at the tubes of scrolls resting in the diamond-shaped honeycomb shelves.

He moved to the chair and sat down, looked across the table to Tobias. "Okay… so how does this tie to what we need to do?" he asked.

"It doesn't. At least not directly."

"And indirectly?"

"Well, Aldwyn sent you here to isolate Janice from the rest of the web."

"Yes," Jake urged.

"To this temple; to isolate this temple from the rest of the web."

"Okay…"

"Therefore, both this temple and Janice are in this little corner of the web."

Jake frowned. "That's indirect, all right."

Tobias straightened in his chair, rested his elbows on the table. "And yet…"

"Yes?"

"I do not believe it is as simple as Aldwyn has made it out to be," said Tobias. "The key to isolating this part of the web lay not in the connecting thread itself, but in the temples."

"I don't understand," said Jake. "What do you mean, the temples?"

"The six temples were originally all in one location, in one Outland. Once completed, Aldwyn sent them out across the web as part of the original purpose, so that the brotherhood could '*bear witness*', as he described it."

Meara stepped back to the table. "I get it," she said. "Serpent's Keep, the Outland, the Temple."

"Sent there by Aldwyn centuries ago," said Tobias, wearing a half-smile.

That explains a lot about Serpent's Keep, thought Jake.

"Are you saying that I need to bring the six temples back together?"

"Perhaps so," said Tobias. "Aldwyn sent them out along special threads. Those threads, having no other purpose, no doubt remain; the temples remain connected. They all have a connection to each other, and to this place. There were stories, even back then, that the Outland was alone in the universe, isolated in the web; hence its name."

The Outland...

Tobias continued. "Perhaps if the Outland was brought together again, the temples were returned home, that may sever the thread that brought us here today."

Jake rested his elbows on the table and rubbed his face with the palms of his hands.

"Okay, let's say that's so. Why didn't Aldwyn just tell me that?"

"He didn't tell you how to disconnect the thread, did he?"

"He told me the way would show itself."

Tobias unfolded his arms, straightened and sat forward in his chair. "And I believe it has," he stated calmly.

"Again, why not just tell me?"

"Asking you to disconnect the thread and trap yourself here is one thing, Jake," said Tobias. "But the six temples and their corresponding Outlands are populated."

Jake realized what that meant. "Oh," he said.

"Oh, my," said Meara. "It's not just us. We'll be trapping everyone here."

"I believe so," said Tobias.

"Serpent's Keep?" she asked.

"Serpent's Keep is an integral part of the Outland."

Jake let his arms slide from the table. There was a lot to take in here; six temples, one unified Outland. By bringing them together, this isolated corner of the web would be cut off from the rest of the universe, and the thread they had traveled through to get here would separate from the rest of the web.

Jake looked up from the table. "Janice isn't here," he stated. "Not yet."

"I believe she has made one of the other temples her home base," said Tobias.

By bringing the temples together home to a unified Outland, I will bring Janice here as well.

When Jake came into the mess hall, Meara was already sitting at one of the tables eating from their rations.

"Good morning, Meara." He sat at the table opposite her, sorted through the rations and picked out a cloth-wrapped block of cheese. He unwrapped it and tore a piece from the block and tossed it in his mouth. "We're still on rations, I see."

Meara took a drink from her glass of water. "I could find no food."

"I didn't really think you would." This temple may have been left in good condition, but its occupants had abandoned it long ago. "Have you seen Tobias?"

"He told me he was going to meditate."

Jake nodded absently. He selected a bag of dried fruit, opened it and began picking through the bits of fruit.

Once they did what needed doing, they were going to have to go in search of a food source. Their rations were running low.

Jake chose not to bring that up just now.

Meara indicated the dried fruit, meats and cheese blocks that were set out on the table. There wasn't much there.

"This is all there is, sir."

Okay, so let's bring it up...

If this Outland was anything like their Outland, there was food out there. Meara had been good at finding what they needed during their earlier quest.

Jake looked carefully at a dried apricot and took a bite from it. "It'll do," he said.

"Sir?" Meara asked.

Jake poured a glass of water from one of the canteens, then refilled her glass as well. "What about water?" he asked.

"Pump in the kitchen," she said. "It works."

"Good, good..." Jake drank deep from his glass. They ate quietly from their rations. "Meditating, huh?"

"Yes sir," said Meara. "He does that."

"Yes. I know."

Tobias had been committed to meditating in the mornings while he and Jake were traveling the side-passages, but since coming out of the threads hadn't meditated once that Jake knew of.

Meara closed the ration packet she had been eating from. "I think I'll take a walk outside, sir; I'd like to get a look at the grounds."

"Good idea," said Jake. "We'll meet back here later."

Jake watched her leave the mess hall, then finished up his breakfast of cheese and dried fruit. Leaving Tobias to his meditation and Meara to her walk then, Jake returned to the library.

He didn't really have a plan in mind; rather he didn't have anywhere else to look. If there was a thread to be pulled anywhere in the temple, wouldn't it be in the repository of all knowledge?

He felt himself drawn there.

Entering the dimly lit room, the morning's gray light was barely pushing through the tall, narrow windows on the opposite wall. He started along the near wall of shelves. He stopped after several steps and looked over at the tables in the center of the room.

There was a large, loosely-rolled scroll sitting on one of the tables, bound with thin twine. He was certain that it hadn't been there before. Jake had been the last to leave the library the night before, and he doubted that either Tobias or Meara had returned during the night. And in any case, would either of them have left a scroll on the table, loosely bound in twine?

Jake looked uneasily about the library. There didn't appear to be anyone hiding in the shadows. Could there be someone else, somewhere else in the temple? Absolutely. The temple was a big place, with a lot of empty rooms.

Jake grew more uneasy still. He moved apprehensively over to the table. He looked quickly about the room again, then back to the scroll. The parchment was deeply yellowed. It was old, very old.

A pull of one end of the twine and he was able to unroll the scroll and smooth it out flat across the table.

It was a map. There was a temple displayed there. Another there… and another there. Six temples, set across what must be the unified Outland.

Jake looked up from the scroll, looked warily about the library, then back over his shoulder toward the door leading out into the hall.

He was alone.

He looked down again at the ancient map.

This was it. The key. Somehow, this was it. Whatever *it* was. And someone had left it here for him to find.

Martin and Janice stood before the table, looking down at an ancient scroll. There were several bright lamps in the room, pushing shadows away. The shelves of the library were empty, all the books and scrolls having long since been removed.

Janice didn't much like this old temple, but it did serve well enough as a base of operations.

"It was just sitting here," said Martin. "No one knows where it came from, how it got here. It was just… here."

Janice looked up from the map, glanced around the room at the empty shelves. Further down one wall, the honeycomb of scroll cubbyholes was as empty as the rest of the room.

She looked back at the map. Six temples were displayed in an expansive forest landscape.

She knew what this was meant to represent. They all knew the stories.

Aldwyn's temples.

Janice looked up again, looked about the room again. A hot tingling numbness coursed through her body.

How did this get here?

Aldwyn stood before the portal hovering in the very center of the round chamber. The portal shimmered, the earlier image slowly washing away, a new image forming.

An image now of a temple ruin, piles of stone rubble and half-rotted wooden beams. A dragon sat high on the broken remains of a wall. Its eyes were closed, its wings were folded along its sides.

Aldwyn lifted a hand before him, slowly rolled his fingers. A large scroll materialized in his hand, yellow parchment loosely bound with thin twine.

This would be scroll number six...

He held the scroll out, midway between himself and the portal. It vanished, leaving Aldwyn's hand empty now before him.

The winged dragon felt a tingling in his mind.

Lamal opened his eyes. He tilted his head, looked down from his perch atop the broken wall down to the rubble below amongst the temple ruin. There was something there. There was something there that hadn't been there before.

Lamal stretched out one wing, then the other. Holding both out then for balance, he lifted himself off the wall and dropped down to the rubble. He landed a few yards from the object.

It was a scroll. He had heard of such things. He had seen one once before, though he couldn't remember when or where.

He took a step forward. He reached a claw out to the thing that shouldn't be there.

Janice reached out and brushed a hand across the parchment that was spread out before her.

Jake leaned forward, laid a hand palm down on the ancient scroll.

Tobias was sitting on a wooden chair in the monk cell, his eyes closed, his hands resting in his lap. There was a narrow cot on his left, a small window set high on the wall behind him. The cell door in front of him stood open.

The universe was quiet. Tobias was one with it and yet outside of it, alone and yet a part of everything.

Something had brushed at his mind...

He turned his head slightly.

Something was there... something reached out to him from the quiet.

Tobias opened his eyes.

Mr. Griffin moved to the edge of the second floor deck. The streets of the village were quiet. Few could see what he saw, isolated as they were by the high stone walls that enclosed Serpent's Keep. Most would live their lives without ever seeing the lands of the Outland beyond those walls.

He heard the door behind him open and close. Mrs. Hodges came up beside him. They both stood silent for a few moments.

"Just as you said, Mrs. Hodges," he said evenly.

From the mansion's upper floor deck it was possible to see the Outland beyond the village walls; a mix of fir and oak and alder, the canopy hid the numerous dangers of the strange land. To the west, the spires of the temple rose above the treetops in the distance.

There was something different this day. The canopy had always had a familiar pattern of evergreen and deciduous, of color and texture and shadow. That pattern was different now, the change evident to anyone who spent time on this deck taking in this unique view and the warmth of the afternoon sun.

And there was something more...

The spires of the temple, poking up through this newly unfamiliar canopy, were nearer to the village.

The temple… it was closer. How was that possible?

Looking to the north, Mrs. Hodges indicated something in the distance. "Look," she said.

It was another pair of spires, just visible rising above the canopy.

It was another temple.

"The Outland has been reshaped," said Brother John.

"That and more," said Master Peter.

They were standing on the roof of the east wing of the temple. From here they could see a great distance in every direction.

More than simply reshaped…

The Outland, always vast, stretched out now to the horizon, to all horizons, the treetop canopy a blanket that lay over the landscape as far as the eye could see.

Serpent's Keep was there, visible only as a break in the trees to the east, as always… but there was something wrong about it. Studying it now, the sight of it made Peter uneasy.

And then he realized that the village was considerably closer than it had been only yesterday, much closer than it should be.

Looking off to his left, he saw something else that shouldn't be there. Poking up through the canopy were the spires of yet another temple.

"Are you up for a walk, John?" he asked.

Brother John was looking at the same temple spires. They looked to be a morning's easy walk, assuming there were no difficulties traveling through the woods.

"Certainly, Master Peter."

§

Natan stood alone in the center of the village plaza. A heavily muscled Thrauhm dragon watched from a discrete distance, two others stood watch at the roundhouse, but the village was otherwise quiet.

Natan's attention was on the sky. It was as still and quiet as the village. Sensing movement near the roundhouse, he glanced once at the building, focused again on the sky.

Khol came out of the roundhouse and walked over to stand beside the Jahai leader. He did not look up at the sky, did not look directly at Natan. He studied the village around them.

"The thread is no more," he stated matter-of-factly.

"They were successful, then."

"We can assume so, Natan." Khol's expression was stiff, unyielding. "Natan... it was our last functioning passage stone."

Natan said nothing to that. He already knew the other passage stones had gone silent.

The silhouette of a Lynhaur dragon glided above them, slowly circled over the village before coming down half a dozen paces in front of Natan and Khol. It folded its wings against its side and strode awkwardly to stand before them.

"What news, friend?" asked Natan.

"Changed," said the dragon. "All changed."

Natan nodded gravely, his fears realized. He looked coolly at Khol, turned again to the flying dragon.

"Describe this change, my friend," he said.

"Trees. All trees. Only trees. Nothing. Nothing. Village... we... alone."

Chapter Sixteen

Brother John led the way across the forest floor, Master Peter two paces behind him and three brother monks bringing up the rear. They had left the trail when they were thirty minutes out from the temple, but the Outland here was easy travel, with a sparse forest and only scattered vegetation of giant fern and salal. The ground was covered in a layer of dried leaves. The day was warm but not hot; the sky, visible through the thin canopy, was a pale bluish gray.

Late in the morning, John stepped out onto a wide trail, smooth with a light-colored soil and hardy tufts of dry grass and aromatic weeds. Following this new trail would continue them in the direction of the nearby temple newly appeared.

Half an hour later they came into the clearing in front of the temple. It was much like theirs, and yet not. While the basic building structure of their own Serpent's Keep temple had been added onto a number of times over the years, this temple looked to have been unchanged since it was originally constructed.

To their left, the grounds were clear to the corner of the temple and beyond. To their right, there was a tall, green wall of a hedge that continued around the corner.

The group of monks stood silent for several long moments, taking it all in.

"Well, now that we're here..." Master Peter began. "I suppose we should see whether anyone is home." He started up the steps, Brother John following right beside him. The others waited below.

The doors ahead of them opened as Peter took the top step and reached the landing. Tobias Quigley stepped outside. He put on a welcoming smile.

"Peter, my friend; and Brother John. How good of you to drop by."

§

Brother John pulled the library door gently closed, leaving Master Peter to try to sort out recent events with Master Tobias and young Jacob. Walking the hall, he was again struck by just how similar this temple was to his own, and yet how so very different. This temple left him with the feeling that it wasn't lived in. It lacked the personal effects and touches, the things that one would expect to see in a sanctuary where the brotherhood walked the halls that he now walked, that sat at the tables in the mess, that slept in the rows of monk cells, that studied in the library, conversed with one another in conference rooms. While he had no idea what had happened to these distant brothers, he had the sense that they had been gone for a very long time.

He reached the front foyer, stood in the center of the room. It was quiet. The temple was quiet. His own temple was always quiet, but not like this. There was a hollow silence to the place.

He went to the front door and stepped outside. Meara was standing below at the foot of the steps. She looked back over her shoulder, up to John on the porch.

"Hello, John. Did they throw you out?"

John seldom read Meara very well. He just assumed that she was serious. "I have little to contribute at this time."

"Uh, huh," Meara sighed tiredly. She moved away from the steps, indicated that John should follow. John took a few moments to consider whether or not it was a good idea. He finally descended the steps and walked over to where Meara waited.

They walked to the corner of the temple and then up to the tall hedge. Meara led John along the hedge to an open iron gate. Beyond the gate, on the other side of the hedge, was an overgrown garden of flowering shrubs, raised vegetable beds and short hedges. They walked a narrow path along the outer perimeter of the enclosed garden.

"Nice, huh?" asked Meara.

"It was, once," said John. The garden at least would qualify as a personal touch by the previous occupants of the temple.

"Yeah," Meara sighed. She brushed a hand across a large bush that pushed into the path, threatened to overwhelm the path. The garden hadn't been tended to in years. "I suppose it could use some sprucing up."

"Some."

They walked in silence for a time.

"You should have done something like this in your temple," said Meara.

"We have a vegetable garden," said John.

"Yes, but not, you know… a garden."

"Our garden suits our needs just fine, Meara."

They followed the walkway roundabout and continued into the heart of the garden.

"Master Quigley says there are six temples," said Meara.

"From his deciphering of the scrolls, Master Peter has recently deduced as much," said John. "They were created for the use of the brotherhood."

"And now Jake has brought them together again."

Brother John noted the informal reference to Jacob Quigley.

"So he's *Jake* now?"

"He insisted. He said that he didn't like me referring to him as *Master Jacob.*"

"And what about Master Quigley? *Tobias?*"

They reached a stone bench. Meara brushed dried leaves from the seat and sat down.

"Master Quigley will always be Master Quigley," she said.

John agreed with a knowing half smile.

"So he shall," he said.

Brother John considered the end of the bench, brushed a lone leaf aside and sat down beside Meara. He clasped his hands in his lap. He looked across the narrow walk at the vegetation gone wild after years of neglect.

Yes, young Jacob Quigley had brought the six temples together, after being apart for who knew how long. More than that... the Outland. There had always been something distinct about the Outland. It had always stood apart from the rest of the world.

Now it was home.

And it was one. The Outland was now one; unified.

"You and your father spent a lot of time in the Outland," John observed.

"We did," Meara stated. "My father had a unique relationship with the Outland."

"I would agree. I believe he enjoyed his time out there."

"Yes. He did."

"You did not?"

"I always gave it the respect it deserved."

"I see." Brother John was looking across the walk at overgrown bush. There were several birds moving about within the branches and leaves. Juncos, he believed.

But his thoughts had already moved beyond the garden; his thoughts were beyond the hedge that enclosed the garden.

The Outland is now one...

Jake, Tobias and Master Peter were hovering over the scroll that was spread across the table. Tobias indicated one of the temples represented on the parchment.

"This is where we are," he said.

Master Peter placed a finger on another; he tapped twice. That was his temple, where he had spent much of his life. He then drew the finger across the scroll to the image of a village enclosed by a wall.

Tobias nodded. Meara would be pleased. *Serpent's Keep...*

He looked across at Jake. The boy had been unusually quiet.

"Something on your mind, Jacob?"

Jake stared down at the scroll, at the landscape that it represented. What had happened?

He had placed his hand on the ancient parchment, and six temples had been pulled across an unseen web underlying the universe and brought to this place, to an Outland unified.

Is this what I had been sent here to do?

He had no doubt that this was so.

He nodded calmly at the scroll.

"You figure Janice is in one of those other temples?"

"I figure," said Tobias.

"Janice?" asked Peter.

"Kinda the reason for all this," said Jake. He folded his arms across his chest. They needed to be sure. "I suggest a tour."

"Agreed," said Tobias.

Corwin turned left out of the wider hall and moved into the narrower hallway. He followed it into the castle's inner foyer, crossed the room and opened the heavy double doors. He entered the round chamber room. The observation portal in the center of the room had gone dark, hung now there as a dull gray silhouette.

Aldwyn was standing near the French doors, looking outward, his back to the room. Corwin moved quietly across the room and stopped one step behind Aldwyn. He waited for some sign from the master of the castle. None came.

"Aldwyn?" he urged at last.

"Yes, Corwin?"

"Sir… the outside."

"Yes." Aldwyn stated calmly.

"There is nothing there. It's gone."

"Yes, Corwin. I know."

"Sir? The Dark Path? You knew, sir?"

Aldwyn turned his head and looked back at Corwin for the first time. He gave his companion a confident smile.

"All will be well, my friend."

"Of course, sir." Corwin didn't look all that reassured, despite his belief in Aldwyn. "The Dark Path, sir."

A gentle smile from Aldwyn; perhaps he should have offered Corwin the chance to leave. That was no longer an option. The Dark Path was gone, and there was no other path from the castle.

He placed a hand on Corwin's arm.

"There was no other way, my friend. The greater charge necessitated a number of alterations to the web; that would include the loss of the path."

"I understand, sir," said Corwin. "We are on our own then, sir?"

"For the foreseeable future."

Corwin steeled himself. Very well. So be it.

"Dinner, sir?"

Aldwyn's smile broadened. "That would be fine, my friend."

Chapter Seventeen

Mrs. Hodges walked Serpent's Keep's main thoroughfare toward the marketplace, pulling her empty wire cart behind her. She was as yet unsure of what was happening beyond the walls of the village, but between the strange skies and shifting Outland landscape, the world was obviously changing and she wanted to make sure that the Quigley Estate was prepared. The supply room and pantry were both well-stocked, but they could do with more perishables.

It was early afternoon and the thoroughfare was crowded with villagers. From the bits of conversation that she heard in passing, a few were concerned with what had happened beyond the walls, but most had no idea that anything had changed. Most were simply glad that the atmospheric disturbances had died down and they were taking the opportunity to enjoy the pleasant weather of the past few days.

Turning into the marketplace, she was surprised to see that many of the booths were already closed for the day and there were only a few shoppers milling about.

She noticed then Meara and a robed monk standing near the closed booth of Meara's mother.

When had they returned?

Mrs. Hodges dragged her cart across the plaza. As she drew nearer she recognized the monk that was standing with Meara. It was Brother John.

There was no sign of Master Quigley or young Jacob.

"Meara! You're back."

"Yes, ma'am," said Meara. "Just this hour."

"And you are well, I see. And what of the others? What of Master Quigley and Jacob?"

"Out there still, Mrs. Hodges. But not far. In the Outland."

"Ah, yes. The Outland."

"More than a few changes there, Mrs. Hodges." Meara indicated the closed booth. "I see my mother closed early today."

Mrs. Hodges acknowledged that with a nod, then looked to the monk, who had stood silent until now. She hadn't seen John since he had left the village to join the brotherhood.

"John. It is good to see you."

"Thank you, Mrs. Hodges," said John. "You appear well, as always."

"Tough as leather and just as long-lived," she said. "And what of Master Peter? He and I chanced to have a conversation not so long ago."

"He is with Master Tobias and his young nephew; they are on a bit of an explore."

And with that the discussion turned to the six temples and the reintegration of the Outland.

"Rather mystifying," sighed Brother John.

"Mystifying, perhaps," said Mrs. Hodges. "But to be honest, it does explain a lot."

"That it does," said Meara. "If only my father was here to witness it."

"I believe that Master Gyles knew more than he knew," said Mrs. Hodges. She looked again to John. "Speaking of family, John... have you seen yours?"

"Not yet, ma'am." John looked uncomfortable.

"Do so." Mrs. Hodges gave him a stern look. "I shall be asking them about you later."

"Of course, Mrs. Hodges. I shall."

"Good."

Janice was sitting on the top step of the temple's front porch, her elbows on her knees, her hands clasped, fingers intertwined. She was both physically and mentally drained, having come down now from running nonstop for so long. She would never admit it, not to anyone, but there was a part of her that was relieved it was over. She could stop now. She could rest.

And it was over. She was sure of that. She knew what had happened and what it meant. Aldwyn, safely ensconced in his high castle, had sent his surrogates out to restore his beloved Outland and once again isolate her, imprison her here and prevent her from completing her mission.

Martin came into the clearing from an overgrown trailhead directly opposite the temple steps. He had been out there for more than an hour, wandering the landscape of the Outland. Janice felt sorry for him, and couldn't help but give him a sympathetic smile as he walked up to the bottom step.

Martin had desperately wanted for there to be no difference out there, had wanted to return with news that all was well, that all was as it had been, that the way was yet open to travel the web.

"I am sorry, Janice," he said.

"Poor Martin," said Janice. "We already knew as much."

"But couldn't there be a way... couldn't there be a portal, some path... some way?"

Janice took a long, deep breath, slowly shook her head. "Not this time."

It took Martin another half minute to finally accept what she had said, even already knowing the truth. He climbed the bottom step then, turned about and sat on the steps below Janice. The two sat quietly, each in their own thoughts, until the sound of twigs snapping pushed in on the silence.

They looked up in time to see Tobias and Jake come into the clearing.

"I've been expecting you," said Janice.

"Hello, Janice." Tobias looked at the temple, back to Janice sitting on the step. "You all settled in?"

"I don't see as there's much of a rush," she said. "Do you?"

"I do not."

A shadow passed across the clearing. Tobias lifted his gaze from Janice to the sky overhead. The dark silhouette of a flying dragon glided above them.

"Isn't that the dragon we saw on the Dark Path?" Jake asked quietly.

"Jamal," said Tobias. "To be expected. He returned with his temple."

Evening had come. Lamal drifted casually in the graying sky. The expanded landscape of the Outland passed beneath him, growing darker and more shadowed as day turned to dusk.

Up ahead then, he could see a darker gash that lay across the landscape.

Lamal reached the Great Ravine, circled and looked down into the gorge. Fellow dragons were coming out of their cliff dwellings to welcome the evening; silhouettes gliding above the forest canopy that blanketed the ravine floor.

Lamal circled downward as he slowly descended into the ravine.

Chapter Eighteen

Master Peter closed the leather-bound book and slid his chair back from the table. He looked about the library, stood then and carried the large volume back to the shelves set into the back wall.

The library; his library; his temple. Home.

He had visited three of the other temples over the last few days, having returned home just the evening before. It was good to be home. As similar as the temples may appear on the surface, they were actually very different. It wasn't just the superficial changes that had been made over the centuries. There was something much deeper, something integrated within the very fabric of each temple. The brotherhood of each had made each temple their own in very personal and subjective ways, and this individual quality was felt the moment one stepped through the front doors.

Walking the halls now, that which made this temple home for Peter felt warm and real. He was one with the temple, as were his brethren. Such was the heart and substance of the brotherhood.

He poked his head into the mess, saw that lunch wasn't quite ready. Brother Steven held up a hand, indicating five more minutes.

Peter continued down the hall, turned down the narrow passage to the north tower. He climbed the circular staircase up to the top landing, then the ladder up to the roof access. Once on the roof, he walked across to the roof edge and took in the scene that was spread out before him.

The view was the same view that he had been witnessing from this rooftop for decades, and yet it was now very different. The sky overhead was a cloudless blue, hovering above a canopy of evergreen and oak and alder. The village of Serpent's Keep was there, visible as an open expanse in the Outland to the east.

But the Outland was different. The Outland had always reached to the horizon, but the horizon appeared much further now. And then there was the very configuration of the canopy. The pattern of evergreen and deciduous had changed.

And of course the distance between the temple and Serpent's Keep had changed. It was more than just illusion; those who had walked the trail reported that the village was indeed much nearer.

And then there were the spires poking up through the canopy, visible evidence of the presence of the arrival of the other temples. From here Peter could see the spires of two of those temples, both of them to the north. He had visited both, and one other that wasn't visible from here. Janice had been found in one; another was empty, the third was home to fellow monks, distant members of the brotherhood. Of the two temples that he had not visited, he had been informed that one was a ruin, the last occupied by another group of monks.

Brother John came out onto the roof and stepped up beside Peter.

"Hello, John. How was your visit?"

"Fine, Master Peter. Mrs. Hodges sends her best."

"A lovely woman."

"Yes." John had returned from the village the day before, but this was his first chance to meet with Peter. And it hadn't been chance. He had sought him out. "Master Peter, when you have a moment, can you drop by the meeting chamber?"

"I'm sure the arrangements are fine, brother," said Peter.

"Nonetheless." John waited.

"Very well," Peter sighed. Movement in the nearby trees below caught his attention. Looking closely, he saw a line of figures traveling along the trail toward them. "And here they come," he said.

Looking below, Brother John watched as a group of monks from one of the nearby temples came into the clearing. "They're early," he said.

"Invite them to lunch," said Peter. "A shared meal is a wonderful opportunity to begin forming a bond between our two temples ahead of the meeting."

"Yes, sir." John was nervous. This was to be the first of what would no doubt be a number of meetings between the two temples and it was important that it go well. He wished that he had been given more warning, more time to prepare. "I shall see to it," he said, started back across the rooftop to the access door.

"John," Peter called after him.

"Sir?" John stopped and turned back.

"Your visit to the village. I understand you had a chance to visit your family."

"Yes sir," John said, a bit hesitantly.

"It went well?" Peter asked. "Not to pry, not looking for details."

"It went well enough, Master." John's family hadn't been very supportive with John's decision to join the brotherhood, and he hadn't seen them since he left the village for the brief journey to the temple.

"Good enough, Brother John. I hope I haven't made you uncomfortable."

"Not at all, sir. Thank you, sir."

Peter gave a dismissive nod. "I'll be down presently."

"Thank you, sir." John turned about and left the rooftop.

Master Peter focused his attention again to the Outland beyond the temple grounds.

He was looking forward to this new world.

Tobias Quigley descended the stairs from the second floor. He crossed the front hall to the archway and entered the kitchen in the back of Quigley Mansion.

It was good to be home.

As much as he enjoyed his ventures out there... anywhere out there, coming home always felt good; this time all the more so. His trips were usually weeks in length. Not so this time; beginning with the quest, then his time spent trapped in a landing, then the side-passage travels with Jake, finally the journey on the Dark Path and beyond, had lasted several years.

Yes, it was good to be home. He planned on staying a while.

Mr. Griffin and Meara turned to him when Tobias came into the kitchen. They looked to have been in conversation.

"Mr. Griffin, Miss Gyles." Tobias walked around the island counter and took a glass down from the cupboard. "How goes your morning?"

"Just fine, Master Quigley," Mr. Griffin answered. "Can I help you with anything?"

"Nope." Tobias found a pitcher of iced tea in the refrigerator, filled his glass. He sat at the counter. "Just getting reacquainted with the place."

"Of course, sir."

Tobias took a drink from his glass, looked across at Meara. "How about you, my dear? Good to be home?"

"Yes sir."

There wasn't much fervor behind the answer.

"Uh, huh." Tobias held back a grin. "You can't wait to get back out there, eh?"

"I can do without the daily risks to life and limb, sir."

Tobias slowly nodded, took another drink from his iced tea. He sat the glass down on the counter in front of him. "You've earned a bit of peace, Meara. Enjoy it."

"I shall, Master Quigley." Meara looked to Mr. Griffin, back to Tobias. "I should return to my duties."

Tobias lifted his glass. "Of course. Good morning to you."

Meara nodded to Tobias and left the kitchen.

"Her last day?" Tobias asked Mr. Griffin.

"Tomorrow, I believe."

"I wish her well."

"Of course, sir."

The back door opened and Mrs. Hodges entered the kitchen, pulling her wire cart behind her.

"Ah, Master Quigley," she said. She swung the cart around and parked it. "Lunch in half an hour."

"I can hardly wait, Mrs. Hodges."

"You've little choice in the matter. Half an hour."

"Yes, ma'am. I'll do my best." Tobias gave a side glance and wink to Mr. Griffin, turned again to Mrs. Hodges. "Yep. Good to be home."

I think I'll stay a while.

Jake leaned back in his chair and let Sparta refill his coffee cup. Looking about the café, He gave a nod to Mr. Dante, who was sitting at his regular table. There was a young couple sitting at a table near one of the windows, deep in conversation.

"Wallace will have your soup and sandwich ready in a couple of minutes," said Sparta.

"I'm not in any hurry." Jake took a sip from his coffee.

"Does that mean you're home for a while?"

Jake didn't really want to discuss his plans with Sparta.

"Let's just say I have time for a long lunch," he said.

"I see." She rested one hand on her hip and gave him a playful look. "Do you have something against settling down, Jake?"

"Not at all, Sparta," he said. "It's just that events always seem to get in the way."

"Events do look to have your name on 'em, that's for true." Sparta saw Wallace put Jake's lunch up. She gave Jake a side-glance as she went to fetch it. "Soup and sandwich, coming up."

Sheriff Smith came into the café half a minute later as Sparta returned with Jake's bowl and plate.

"Hello, Sheriff," Jake prompted. "Pull up a chair."

"Thank you, Mister Quigley." The sheriff looked to Sparta as he sat down. "Just coffee, Sparta."

Jake swallowed a spoonful of soup and took a bite of his sandwich, looked across the table.

"All quiet in the village?" he asked, though he knew the answer. There really wasn't much change before and after recent happenings, particularly once the skies settled down.

The village was the village.

"Back to normal, for the most part," said the sheriff.

"That's good."

"So what are your plans now, Jake?"

"I thought I'd try my hand at surveying." Another spoonful of soup. "The Outland needs mapping."

"Ah, so you're off again."

"A few short trips, to start; then, we'll see. We'll go from there." Jake watched Sparta bring a cup for the sheriff. She filled it from the carafe and quietly left. "But then, I'm guessing you already knew that."

"I may have heard something about it." He turned his cup about and picked it up by the handle. He took a sip. "Nothing covert, Jake. Meara's mother told me."

"I hope she's not upset." Jake knew that the woman had lost her husband to the Outland.

"Not at all. She knows her daughter."

"Good to hear," said Jake. "Meara was great out there."

"No doubts there. It's easy to see her father in her."

Jake took a bite of his sandwich. "I get that," he said.

"And she's a good choice to team up with on your surveying," said the sheriff.

"Yeah," said Jake. "I didn't really have much say in the matter."

Sheriff Smith grinned as he finished the last of his coffee. He turned down a refill from Sparta and slid his chair back.

"I should get back at it." He stood, pushed his chair under the table. "So, you're heading out day after tomorrow?"

Meara's mother had been quite the informant.

"That's the plan," said Jake.

"Maybe I'll see you before you leave." The sheriff gave a nod goodbye, stepped away from the table and left the café.

"Pie?" Sparta was standing beside Jake, watching as he put the last of his sandwich in his mouth.

"Excuse me?" Jake mumbled through his food.

"Pie. Apple."

"Um... okay."

"Coming right up." Sparta started away.

Jake leaned back, glanced about the café. Mr. Dante was eating pie. The two sitting at the window were eating pie. A woman at the small table in the corner, *when had she come in?* was eating pie.

Life in Serpent's Keep wasn't going to be bad at all.

~ end Serpent's Keep Two - the Six Temples ~

| 3 |

Serpent's Keep 3 - the Outland

Chapter One

The gently rolling landscape of the northeastern Outland was a blanket of fir and alder, the forest canopy unbroken but for the occasional grassy meadow or small lake, the occasional spire of one or another of the six temples that were poking up through the trees. The setting sun's multi-colored rays streaked through the upper branches of the green canopy with very little managing to reach the forest floor below.

Jake and Meara had found their way to an isolated clearing a hundred feet or so off the main trail. They had cleared away the thick mulch from the center of the clearing and the flickering light of a campfire pushed the shadows of dusk into the surrounding trees and undergrowth.

Jake was sitting near the fire. A bloodied, hastily applied bandage was wrapped around his left forearm. Meara, one of her hands also wrapped in a bandage, her cheek swollen and showing the early signs of bruising, was cleaning an open wound on Jake's temple. She rummaged around in a gray canvas bag and brought out a small plastic vial. She opened it, dabbed some of its contents onto a square cloth and applied it to Jake's head wound. Jake stiffened but managed to hold his silence.

Jacob Quigley was now in his early twenties, but something in the eyes reflected the life experiences of someone much older. Meara, just coming out of her teens herself, carried the wisdom of someone well beyond her years.

Just at the moment though, none of that seemed to matter for either of them.

Meara finished the first aid work on Jake's head wound and turned her attention to his arm. She carefully unbound the temporary bandage, exposing a three inch long gash, half an inch wide, dark and bleeding.

"Gruesome, but clean," she said. She brought a bottle out of the first aid bag, opened it and poured the clear liquid liberally into the wound.

"Oh boy..." said Jake, hissing through clenched teeth.

Meara grumbled out a low *yup* as she worked. She squeezed the gash closed with one hand as she tightly wrapped the arm with a clean bandage. Finished then, she began tossing the dirty bandages into the fire.

"Thanks," said Jake. He looked about their surroundings. "Waddya figure, Meara? Two days from the village?"

"Yes sir. About that. Maybe three." Meara put the first aid supplies back into the bag. She sat back then and looked up at the darkening sky. "Best we stay here tonight, start out at dawn."

Jake gave a nod in answer. He shifted about and faced the small fire. The forest around them was quiet ahead of the night, the encroaching shadows of dusk growing quickly darker.

"That shouldn't be a problem," he said then, almost to himself.

"Yes sir," said Meara. "We weren't followed."

"No, I expect not."

There had been just three bandits, and two of them had suffered injuries much more severe than they had dealt to Jake and Meara. The third had run off with minor wounds. Jake guessed the three were what had constituted one of the lesser bands and were not part of either of the two main bandit groups that roamed the Outland. Neither of these two larger bands was thought to be currently in this part of the Outland.

There was the wolf pack however, a large group of *smart wolves* that roamed a wide range of the Outland, coming and going at will from some unknown location. Worse yet, its leader had a particular grievance against Jake and Meara.

Jake indicated Meara's bandaged hand.

"How's the hand?" he asked.

Meara absently worked the fingers. "Fine, sir."

"Good..." He pointed then to Meara's discolored cheek. "That's gonna bruise."

Meara shrugged and said nothing.

Jake looked about them again.

"I'll fix us something to eat," he said. "You stand watch."

"Yes sir." She considered then. "Sir?"

"Yeah?" Jake was reaching for his backpack.

"One of the temples." Meara indicated west. "It's maybe half a day from here."

Jake brought a bag of rations out of his pack, dug around again for the deep metal dish. He looked then from Meara to the west.

"That might not be a bad idea," he said noncommittally.

"Yes sir." Meara clambered slowly to her feet, using her staff for support. "I'll give the perimeter a check."

The southland temple, unlike the temple near the village of Serpent's Keep, had changed little since its original construction, with just a few additions completed over the many years. There was the main building, the two short wings and a handful of separate outbuildings. A pair of spires rose high above the sanctuary, poking above the canopy of the surrounding forest. A knee-high wall ran the perimeter of the roof of the central structure.

Master Peter stepped out of the temple's primary meeting room, crossed the foyer and started into the main hallway of the east wing. He entered the dining hall.

Only two of the tables were occupied, despite this being midday. He walked across the room to the serving table, picked up a bowl of stew and a spoon, and sat at the nearest empty table.

Peter was in his early sixties, though he could pass for someone much younger. He was dressed in the traditional heavy brown robe of his temple, bound at the waist with a tan cloth belt. His dark brown hair, curling around his ears, was in a constant state of disarray.

His meeting with the head staff of this temple had gone well. Peter had gotten along very well with the abbot and they had felt as brothers from their first meeting, despite their two temples having long been separated. They spoke of the work of their two sanctuaries, the ancient history of the six temples, and what role the temples might play in the recently reintegrated Outland.

Master Peter intended the brothers of the temples to take on a leadership role in the Outland.

The two temples had already worked together to reestablish a presence at another temple in another segment of the Outland, this one long abandoned. No decision had yet been made regarding yet another, distant sanctuary that was now occupied by Janice and the Rhetani.

As for the other two temples, no one had yet reached the distant temple known to exist far to the north; the sixth temple, a ruin now little more than jagged shards of broken walls, had been visited only once and was not thought to be recoverable.

Brother John entered the dining hall with Master Edmund, the temple abbot. Edmund gave a nod to Peter before walking over to one of the occupied tables that he might talk with his monks. John collected a food bowl from the serving table and sat at the table with Peter. He considered the gray contents of his bowl, stirring it with his spoon.

"Believe me when I say that I am most grateful for their hospitality, Master Peter," he said quietly. "That being said, I am all the more appreciative of the bounty of our own sanctuary."

"We are indeed blessed, John," said Peter. He swallowed a spoonful of his stew. "Still, it is not so bad."

John lifted a spoonful from his bowl, let the contents settle in his mouth for a moment. He swallowed, tried a charitable smile. He was only partially successful.

"What next, sir?" he asked.

"Home I believe, where we shall prepare for a journey north."

"To the North Temple then," said John.

The monks had developed or reestablished an extensive network of trails throughout much of the Outland over the past few months, but there were no known trails in the far north. They would be trailblazing much of their journey to the North Temple.

"It should prove to be most interesting," said Peter. "No doubt quite the experience."

"Yes sir," said John.

Master Edmund finished his conversation with the two monks at the other table, stepped across the room and stood before Peter and Brother John. He clasped his hands before him and gave a broad smile.

"And how is the stew today, brothers?" he asked.

"Just fine, Master Edmund," said John. "Thank you."

Peter gave a quick glance and smile to John, again to Edmund. "The generosity of your temple is very much appreciated."

"Yes," John said quickly. "Much appreciated."

"Our pleasure, to be sure." Edmund nodded in welcome. Prior to the reintegration of the Outland, visitors to his sanctuary had been almost unheard of.

"Brother John was just commenting on your hospitality," said Peter.

"You are very kind, Brother John," said Edmund, smiling even more broadly.

A young, small-statured monk stepped into the doorway and looked about the dining hall. Seeing Edmund, he moved quickly across to the table. He stood silent beside Edmund and waited to be acknowledged.

"Yes, Brother Gerald?" prompted Edmund.

"So sorry to bother you, Master Edmund," said Gerald. "We have just received word. Brothers Jasper and Hugh... they are bringing Jacob Quigley and his associate in."

"Pardon?" said Peter, setting his spoon beside his half-empty bowl.

"Yes, Master Peter." Young Gerald wasn't sure whom to address. He decided on his own abbot. "They suffered some injuries, I understand. Attacked by bandits, I understand."

"Thank you, Gerald," said Edmund. He turned to his guests as everyone stood. "Shall we go to meet them?"

Peter and John followed Edmund out of the dining room and down the hall to the front foyer. Stepping through the heavy front doors, Peter moved across the porch to stand at the top of the steps. Only moments later Jake and Meara came into view in the clearing below; several monks were walking beside them, ready to assist if needed. Brother John stepped past Peter and quickly descended the steps to help.

Master Edmund stood beside Peter.

"Walking wounded, it would appear," he said.

"It would take more than a bandit attack to bring down those two," said Peter.

"So it would seem."

Sheriff Smith stood in front of the café, having just finished an early lunch. He looked up and down the wide, cobblestone street that was the main thoroughfare of the village. He was in his late forties, tall with broad shoulders. He was dressed in light brown slacks and a long-sleeved button shirt; a simple badge pinned above his left shirt pocket identified him as sheriff.

He had been sheriff for much of his adult life and it showed in the calm, confident way that he carried himself. He was quite comfortable in his role as the sheriff of Serpent's Keep.

He stepped away from the café and started down the street. The buildings to either side were mostly single storey, with only an occasional two-storey structure. At first glance, the village looked like something out of the distant past, but closer examination showed a curious mix of eras. The street lamps lining the thoroughfare were both gas and electric. The buildings were rustic but clean, made of stone, wood, brick or adobe. The windows had glass panes set into wood frames. Doors rested on heavy hinges and had heavy latches.

Very little had changed in the village since the reintegration of the surrounding Outland several months earlier; this, even with the increased isolation from the outside world.

Sheriff Smith started across the street. He stopped when Mrs. Hodges called out to him.

"Mrs. Hodges," he said, giving a nod hello. "How are you today?"

"Just fine, Sheriff. And you?"

"I am fine indeed, ma'am."

He turned then and the two of them started walking, Mrs. Hodges pulling her two-wheeled wire cart along behind her. She was evidently returning from the market plaza.

Mrs. Hodges was in her sixties, medium height, with strong facial features and sharp eyes. Her medium-brown hair was streaked with gray, was long but kept pulled back. She had run the housekeeping and the kitchen at the Quigley Estate for as long as Sheriff Smith could remember, at least as long as he had been the village sheriff and for years before that. She had changed hardly at all in all those years, was as alive and as spry and healthy as ever.

"How go things at the mansion, Mrs. Hodges?" he asked.

"All is quiet for the moment, Sheriff," she said. "Master Quigley and young Jacob are both away just now."

"So I was given to understand."

"Yes. It is just me and Mr. Griffin, and Mr. Griffin is often mistaken for being absent, the way the man blends into the woodwork."

Sheriff Smith smiled. "I have often had that impression of the man."

They walked in silence for a few paces, then stopped as they reached the door of the sheriff's office. Mrs. Hodges pulled the cart up close and stood it on end.

"I have been meaning to drop in to see you, Sheriff," she said. "A question, if I may."

"Of course, ma'am. What is it?"

"Well, sir," she started. "To now, the Outland was the Outland and the Village was the Village. I have never felt, not in all my years, I have never felt the Outland might be encroaching on Serpent's Keep. All the dangers were on the other side of village wall. Within these walls, we were safe."

"I would consider that a reasonable assumption, Mrs. Hodges." The sheriff thought on that for a moment. "Ma'am, I understand your unease. Indeed, much out there has changed. The Outland is now a very different place. But I can assure you, we recognize that we are in a new world. We have adapted as necessary."

The sheriff had worked with the Captain of the Watch to enhance the security at each of the village gates. Two person teams now walked outside the village wall. Small teams periodically went into the Outland, walked the north road to the Farm and the west trail to the nearby temple. The Farm now had fulltime security.

All of this meant that the village residents rotated duty through the civilian guard much more quickly.

"Is there something specific that concerns you?" he asked.

"Not directly," she admitted. But there were those who visited her back-alley booth seeking special preparations to take with them into the Outland. They came to her with stories, and with fears of what they might next face in the Outland.

There were new dangers out there.

"No," she said then. "I suppose not. Not directly."

Sheriff Smith put on his most supportive, assuring expression; well-practiced, in times like these.

"Do not worry, Mrs. Hodges," he said. "What needs to be done is being done."

"No doubt," she sighed.

"Please, don't hesitate to come to me with your concerns. You no doubt hear from folks who are not likely to come to me."

"I'll do that," said Mrs. Hodges. She shifted her wire cart around, prepared to leave. "I should go."

"It was good to see you," said the sheriff. "And please, Mrs. Hodges. Don't worry. We're ready for whatever might come our way."

"Yes. I'm sure you are right. Thank you, Sheriff."

The sheriff watched Mrs. Hodges continue down the thoroughfare, pulling her cart along behind her. He took out his key then, took the final step up to the door of his office. He unlocked the door and went inside.

It was a small room, furnished with a desk, a filing cabinet and a couple of chairs. Another door led to a short hall with bathroom, storage closet and several cells.

Smith went to the small table in one corner behind his desk. He picked up the coffee pot, flipped the lid and held the pot to his nose: it smelled old but drinkable. He poured the last of the coffee into a ceramic mug, turned back to his desk and sat down, the chair screeching painfully. He was just pulling himself forward when the door opened and Mason came into his office.

Sheriff Smith leaned back, to another squeal from the chair, and brought the cup to his lips. He took a long swallow as he watched Mason close the door and step fully into the room.

Mason placed a hand on the back of the guest chair and looked across the desk to the sheriff.

"Sheriff Smith," he stated.

"Hello, Mason. What can I do for you?" The sheriff took another sip from his coffee. He stared into his cup, gave a grimace.

Okay, not as drinkable as he had first thought...

He indicated the guest chair. Mason considered, finally stepped around the chair and sat down.

"Sheriff Smith," he said again.

"Mason." Smith sat forward, eyes on Mason as he absently set the cup down. "Is there a problem?"

Most of the citizenry considered Mason to be the village eccentric, and his actions and pronouncements did little to dissuade them of that belief. But the man's observations often turned out to be dead on. He took careful handling, and took a disproportionate amount of the sheriff's time, but Smith never dismissed Mason out of hand.

"A problem, sir?" Mason responded sharply. "The outside world that was once known to be out there is lost to us. We are wholly alone."

"That's not really news, Mason," said Smith. This was an earlier observation of Mason's that had proven true. There had been no contact with the outside world for a long time, since well before the bizarre changes to the Outland. The Outland, in which the village of Serpent's Keep existed, was now a world unto itself.

"And yet you sit there as if nothing has changed," said Mason.

There must be something in the air...

Sheriff Smith pushed his cup aside. He would need to make a fresh pot. "Our interactions with the outside were always infrequent, and you yourself have argued more than once that what little contact there was with the outside was never good for us."

"Not the point. Not the point."

"Okay," said Smith. "And the point would be..."

Mason leaned forward, slid forward in the chair. He placed his forearms on the sheriff's desk.

"Our isolation is not our vulnerability, sir."

"It isn't..." Smith said flatly.

"No sir. It is not. It is rather the false sense that all that can be seen can be controlled."

"Excuse me?" Smith prompted. Getting Mason to get to the point was often a chore.

"There are those, those out there in this new, greater Outland, who see what has happened as their opportunity to step in and impose their will, their philosophy, upon us all, upon this world with very real borders."

"All right, Mason," said Smith. *Yes. There is definitely something in the air.* He leaned back in his chair to its accompanying squeal. "What do you suggest we do about that?"

"We need to send out another team," said Mason, sliding his forearms further onto the desk.

"You mean the Road?" A team had been sent out weeks before to verify that the outside world was no longer there. They had followed the road that led from the village front gate to the outside world beyond; the real world.

What they found was that the Outland was indeed alone.

"The Road," said Mason. "Yes."

"Mason, you know better than I that there is no longer a world beyond our own. There is nothing out there."

Wow, thought Sheriff Smith. *To say that out loud...*

Mason gave a sharp nod. "I have just said as much."

"Mason." Sheriff Smith rubbed at his temple. "What do you want?"

"I want to know what has *replaced* the outside world."

"Excuse me? You want what?"

Mason slid back from the desk and let his arms drop into his lap.

"There is *something* out there," he said. "There is something beyond our world, out there, where the outside world used to be. If we are to stand against those who would dominate the Outland, dominate us, we must seek an ally."

"An ally," Sheriff Smith said in a sigh. "Assuming there is actually something out there, something that the last team did not find, I would hasten to add, what makes you think that this *something* would be our ally?"

"Will they?" said Mason. "I do not know. Let's find them. Let's ask them."

Sheriff Smith let that last settle in. He leaned further back in his chair, studied the odd little man sitting on the other side of the desk. Mason, in turn, sat silent, waiting for the sheriff to come to a decision and get things going.

Smith sat forward and turned about in his chair.

"I'm going to make some fresh coffee," he said. "You want some?"

Chapter Two

Jake folded his blanket and set it at the foot of the cot. He sat down then and pulled on his hiking boots and started lacing them up. Filtered sunlight streamed in from the small, narrow window behind him and onto the floor of the sleeping cell, the only light in the room.

Dressed then, he pushed his backpack under the cot and left the cell. The hallway was similar to those that he had found in all the temples. Widely-placed oil lamp sconces were mounted on the walls, their dull light managing to push back the dark just enough that Jake could see where he was going.

He found Meara in the dining room, sitting alone with a bowl of oatmeal. Jake collected a bowl for himself and sat at the table opposite her.

"Good morning," he said.

"Sir." Meara kept eating her breakfast.

Jake glanced about them. Three monks were in the room, each sitting alone at their own tables.

Monks were monks, no matter the temple; usually up well before dawn, an early breakfast, and off then to their duties. Being this late in the morning, these three probably worked some odd shift or had just returned to the temple from some outside errand or other.

Jake looked over his spoon to Meara. The bruise on her cheek had had enough time to begin showing its colors; a mix of dark purple and midnight blue.

"Does it hurt?" he asked.

"Sir?"

He pointed with his spoon. "The bruise. Kinda ugly."

"It's fine, sir. It only hurts when I'm reminded of it."

"Right. Gotcha."

For a few long moments they each focused on their breakfast, spooning oatmeal.

"You?" she asked then. She indicated the wounds at his temple and on his arm, both freshly cleaned and treated by the monks.

"Oh, I expect I'll live," said Jake, shrugging. Unseen were the bruised ribs, which were tightly bound beneath his shirt.

"That's good, sir."

"That it is," Jake said calmly; another spoon of oatmeal.

They ate in silence for several minutes. They were just finishing their breakfast when Master Peter entered the dining hall. He looked quickly about the room before stepping over to Jake and Meara's table.

"And how are you two feeling this morning?" he asked.

"Well enough, Brother Peter." Jake indicated a chair.

Peter pulled out the chair and sat down.

"Well enough to travel?"

"We'll be heading home in a few days," said Jake.

"Good, good," said Peter. "I'm sure you can take whatever time you need."

"They've made us feel very welcome."

"To be sure. Master Edmund has been most gracious to us as well," said Peter. "Listen, should you feel up to it, we will be starting out for home tomorrow. You are certainly welcome to join us. Again, should you feel up to it."

Jake looked across the table to Meara. "Waddya say, Meara? You feel up to it?"

"Safety in numbers, sir," she said in answer.

"My thoughts exactly," said Peter. As precarious and downright unsafe as the Outland had been in the past, it was more so now; dangers familiar and known, dangers new and as yet undiscovered.

This, young Jacob and his companion knew all too well.

"All right, then," said Jake. Turning to Peter, "I guess we feel up to it."

"Very good," said Peter. He slid his chair back and stood up. "There is much yet to do this morning. I will see you two later."

"Yes, Master Peter," said Meara.

"Until then," said Jake.

Peter took several steps toward the door, came to an easy stop and looked back.

"Ah. Jacob. I meant to ask..."

Jake was gathering up their bowls and spoons. He stacked them and looked to Peter. "Yes?"

"Has there been any word of Brother Tobias?"

"We left the village a couple of days after he went out," said Jake. "We've been out of touch since."

"Too bad, too bad," said Peter.

"Sorry."

"No. Not at all." Peter gave a smile, turned again and left the dining hall.

Tobias Quigley finished filling his canteen, screwed on the cap and got back to his feet. He looked up and down the creek as he slipped the canteen into the holster on his hip. He picked up his backpack, slid his arms into the shoulder straps, clipped the belt and started out again.

He had been working his way deeper into the Great Ravine since early morning. If a portal yet remained to reach any of the Jahai communities, which had been closed to the Outland since its reintegration, it would be in the Great Ravine. Tobias had nonetheless taken the long way around to get there, wanting to touch base with the handful of side passage access points that had once existed in each of the long-segregated Outland landscapes.

The gateways existing in the primary Outland had long ago been closed off, this back when Tobias' nephew Jacob had restored Serpent's Gate. Unknown to Tobias until later, though, was that a few side threads had remained.

Now... following the reintegration of the Outland itself and the secondary closure of the web, if any threads remained out there, doubtful really, they would be isolated and nearly impossible to find.

Tobias came to a stop. He dropped slowly to one knee in a smooth, easy motion and went perfectly still.

Up ahead, in the distance...

A shadow had moved across the trail ahead, gliding through the mote-filled stream of sunlight that reached through the canopy and down to the forest floor.

He watched and waited, studying the shadows.

There. Again. Nearer now.

A dark silhouette moved out of and back into the darker shadows in the trees.

Tobias brought his knife out from its boot sheath. He didn't expect bandits in the Great Ravine, but best be ready.

A lone Bentai Jahai stepped into the small clearing ahead, some twenty feet in front of Tobias. He stopped, paused, watching Tobias for reaction.

The Bentai were much more humanoid in physical appearance than other Jahai species, and this one managed an almost human stance, despite its dragon-like features.

Tobias slowly stood, returning his knife into its sheath. He smiled, gave a formal nod.

He recognized this Jahai.

"Khol," he said. "My friend."

Khol nodded formally in return. He was about a head taller than Tobias, with sloping shoulders, a large head and a protruding snout. He had extraordinarily long fingers ending in curved black claws. He was dressed in an open leather vest and a calf-length skirt.

"Dear friend Tobias Quigley," he said.

"Do you travel alone, my friend?" asked Tobias.

"Most sadly, yes."

Khol served at the side of Natan, the leader of the Jahai. He would not be apart from Natan of his own choosing.

"I am sorry to hear that," said Tobias. He moved nearer Khol, who also stepped closer. "You were separated from the Jahai Village then."

The Jahai Village, known to most non-Jahai as the Village of the Dragons, was the administrative capital of the Jahai outside of the Jahai home worlds. It was the site of the Grand Hall and the home of Natan.

"I was." Khol was quite despondent. "I was away from the Village when the event occurred, the dissolution of the web. I was left behind."

"And you now seek a thread."

"I have found none to now, neither to return home nor anywhere else."

"I too search for a way to reach your brethren," said Tobias. "We can seek a thread together, if you wish."

Khol tilted his head. He pushed his snout forward.

"I would like that, Tobias Quigley," he said.

"Very well, friend Khol." Tobias started forward, allowing Khol to follow beside him. "Let us talk of our separate travels to now as we walk."

Tobias and Khol continued further into the Great Ravine together.

Janice reached the trailhead and stepped into the wide clearing that was spread before the temple the Rhetani had taken possession of. Martin followed, stepping up beside her. Both carried light packs on their backs, wore utility belts with canteens and sheathed knives strapped to their hips.

They had been gone three days. It felt good to be home.

Janice was a well-kept middle-aged woman, with a smooth complexion but for the slightest onset of wrinkles at the corners of her sharp blue eyes. Her brown hair, unchanged for years, was full, falling to her shoulders.

Martin, in his late thirties, was a short, squat man with disheveled hair and ill-fitting clothes. He had been Janice's assistant for several years, though it seemed much longer to him.

"That is surely a sight for sore eyes," he said, admiring the rundown temple.

"So they say." Janice shifted her backpack and started across the clearing toward the front steps.

The temple was very much as the others, with but a few additions since its original construction. It had been abandoned at some point after the division of the Outland, and had been empty at the time Janice and Martin had found it. They had settled in well before the Outland's recent reintegration, and it was now the official headquarters of the Rhetani, at least so far as Janice was concerned. They had no way of knowing if there were any of the Rhetani high council remaining; if there were, there was no way of contacting them, no way to reach them.

A few Rhetani stragglers, finding themselves isolated from the outside world and alone in this reintegrated Outland, had managed to find their way to the temple over these past months. And so Janice was slowly rebuilding the Rhetani.

She reached the top step as the heavy double doors of the temple opened and Thomas stepped out.

"Janice," he said. "It is good to see you safely home."

Thomas was a few years older than Janice. He was tall, thin, his short hair beginning to gray. His clothes, while old and thread-bare, were clean and neat, as was the man himself.

"Thank you, Thomas." She slipped out of her backpack and handed it to Martin. "Thank you, Martin."

Martin took the backpack, gave a nod to Janice; a nod then to Thomas as he stepped past him and went into the sanctuary.

Janice turned around and looked out across the clearing and to the surrounding forest beyond.

"Have the security issues been taken care of?" she asked. Janice had grown increasingly concerned with the temple defenses. There had as yet been no indication that any of the bandit bands had reached this part of the Outland, but she was certain that it was only a matter of time.

"Yes, ma'am," said Thomas. "Most of the required measures have been implemented, the remaining soon will be."

Janice gave a curt nod in response. There were as yet only a handful of Rhetani living at the temple, so they had had to get creative with the security measures. She had noted on her way in the clearing away of the surrounding brush, though she had not seen the alert trip wires and other perimeter measures.

Barely visible had been the guard on watch up on the roof. Even with all members included in the guard rotation, with so few Rhetani most would be pulling a three hour shift every two to three days.

She would review the security measures being implemented within the temple itself later.

Thomas realized that Janice would not be responding further. He cleared his throat.

"Ma'am," he prompted. "Your trip. Was it successful?"

With each journey out, Janice and Martin pushed the boundaries of their territory, searching for resources the temple might be able to use, looking for anyone living nearby, whether they be potential allies or possible threats.

And they sought other Rhetani, stragglers left behind in one or another of the long-separated Outland segments at the time they had been brought back together.

"Martin has the list," she said. Martin mapped their travels as they went, marking the locations where they had identified resources to be brought back to the temple.

"I'll detail a team," said Thomas.

Janice gave another curt nod, acknowledging Thomas' statement. She turned to him then, contemplated for a moment, again looked outward.

"Thomas," she began.

"Ma'am?"

"I believe we should consider an alliance, of a sort, with one of the bandit bands."

"Janice, I—"

"I understand your concern," she said quickly, cutting him off. "Believe me, I do. Any such association would be limited in scope and the parties would maintain both distance and autonomy."

"To what end, if I might ask?"

"Of course, Thomas." Janice grew thoughtful. "Such would serve two purposes, I should think. First, we are as yet too few in number to push ahead on our plans regarding the Outland populace."

"True enough," Thomas said, reluctantly.

"And with an alliance, the bandits are less likely to mount an assault on our little sanctuary."

The bandits may not be an immediate threat, thought Janice, *but it is only a matter of time...*

"With all due respect, of that I am not so sure."

"You think not?"

"I believe they are just the sort to bite the hand that feeds them." Thomas gave a gentle nod. "Ma'am."

"Oh, I don't intend to feed them, dear Thomas," she answered, a hint of a smile. "I intend to play them."

Thomas didn't appear sufficiently convinced, but he would let it go for now. They would meet on this further, of that he was sure. Janice was not one to jump into something like this without collaborating with her staff and coming to some consensus.

"Yes, ma'am," he stated.

They stood in silence then, looking out across the clearing and into the surrounding forest.

The Outland was a strange world, filled with strange things and myriad possibilities.

Chapter Three

The trail was wide enough that Jake and Meara were able to walk side by side. They were traveling one of the main trails of the network of trails that connected several of the temples of the Outland. Two monks followed at some distance behind them, another two walked ahead. Ahead of these walked Master Peter.

It was near midday and they had been hiking since before dawn. The day was gray, the air cool; a thin mist drifted through the sparsely treed forest on either side of the trail. Jake felt each step in his ribs, bruised and still bound in bandages.

Upon further consideration, it might have been better had they waited another day or two and let Peter and his group leave without them, and so giving Jake more time to heal.

The pain must have shown on his face and in his gait.

"Would you like me to ask them to stop for a bit, sir?" asked Meara. "We could all do with a rest."

"I'm good," said Jake. "We'll be stopping for lunch soon enough."

"Yes, sir."

They continued on in relative silence. They had spoken very little since leaving the temple, and their traveling companions were not much for casual conversation in any case.

The procession slowed then, without coming to a full stop, when the young monk that had gone ahead of the group reappeared. He stepped into line beside Peter as they continued walking. He spoke to Peter in a hushed voice.

Peter did stop then and looked back to the line of travelers spread out along the trail behind him. He waved Jake and Meara forward and waited.

"I'm afraid we will need to travel off the main trail for a time," he said calmly. "One of the bandit bands has established what Brother Oliver described as a semi-permanent encampment some short distance ahead of us."

Jake remembered having passed the trailhead of a side path about ten minutes back. He nodded over his shoulder and asked if that trail would take them around.

"Not directly, no. I suggest we go off trail here," said Peter. He indicated the forest to their left. He knew of a much narrower, less-defined animal trail that paralleled the main trail some half mile away, roughly following a small, meandering creek. They could follow that until they were well past the bandit camp.

Jake nodded silent agreement.

"Very good, then," said Peter. He indicated that Brother Oliver should lead the way. The young monk stepped off the trail and started into the forest.

Peter looked to Meara, then to Jake. He gave him a sympathetic smile.

"We'll break for lunch once we reach the creek," he said and then followed after Oliver.

"After you," Jake said to Meara.

It was late in the evening, nearing midnight. The Quigley Estate was quiet. A single, vintage ceiling fixture offered the only light in the kitchen.

Mrs. Hodges was puttering around the high-ceilinged kitchen, dressed in a thick, fluffy robe, well-worn slippers and a scarf to tie back her hair. She half-filled a tea pot and put it on the stove, turned on the burner. She set a box of tea bags on the center island counter and went to the cupboard to bring down a tea cup.

Mr. Griffin appeared in the doorway, dressed in an ankle-length housecoat.

"Mrs. Hodges," he said softly. "Are you having trouble sleeping?"

Mrs. Hodges turned quickly about, hand to her chest.

"Oh dear," she said, a heavy sigh. "You startled me."

"I do apologize." Mr. Griffin stepped over to the island counter and settled onto one of the tall stools.

Mrs. Hodges brought two tea cups down from the cupboard and set them onto the narrow counter next to the stove. She sat then opposite Mr. Griffin.

"I find a full night's sleep more difficult to come by these days, Mr. Griffin."

"Yes," said Mr. Griffin. "As do I."

"We be a couple of old fools, wandering about this old mansion at all hours, worrying about Master Quigley and young Jacob."

Mr. Griffin leaned forward and rested his arms on the counter.

"The boy has acquitted himself well enough," he said.

"And yet... here you are."

"Yes, Mrs. Hodges," sighed Griffin. "Here I am."

They sat silent for several moments. The teapot began its slow, growing whistle and Mrs. Hodges stepped over to the stove. She waited until the whistle reached a high pitch, then took the teapot off the heat. She placed a tea bag into each cup and poured.

"Chamomile," she said over her shoulder. "It should help with sleep."

"Thank you, ma'am."

Mr. Griffin watched Mrs. Hodges step back to the counter and set the cups down between them. Mrs. Hodges settled back onto her seat, absently dipped the tea bag in her cup.

"They've been gone a long while, Mr. Griffin," she said.

"They've been gone longer in the past, Mrs. Hodges; now and again."

"Six weeks is a long time with no word, all the same."

"I'll not start worrying just yet." Mr. Griffin carefully squeezed his tea bag, set it on the saucer and lifted the cup to his lips.

"And yet... here we are," said Mrs. Hodges.

"Yes." Mr. Griffin took a second sip of the tea, set the cup back onto the saucer. "Here we are."

§

Jake stood looking down at the small campfire, the flickering light of the flames reaching past him and out to the wall of trees and undergrowth that enclosed the clearing. Several of the monks that were traveling with him were sleeping nearby; several others stood watch, were little more than shadows within shadows in the surrounding forest.

It was late, well after midnight; the sky overhead was black and starless, the overcast from the day continuing deep into the night. Jake had just come off watch and wasn't yet ready to crawl under a blanket and return to sleep. Meara came into the clearing then, her own turn at watch also over. She stood beside Jake and looked down at the fire, held her hands out to try to catch what little heat rose from the flames.

"Hardly worth it," she mumbled softly, careful not to wake the sleeping monks.

"What's that?"

She gave a nod to the campfire, so small that it did little to provide warmth while putting out just enough light to attract the attention of anyone or anything within a hundred yards.

They were miles past the bandit encampment. Still, there were others out there, and other dangers.

"It's a psychological thing," said Jake. "You can't have a camp without a campfire."

"Yes sir," said Meara. She was sure that she had said that to him a long, long time ago.

She knelt down nearer the fire, seeking out what little heat emanated from the glowing coals beneath the flames. It felt good on her face.

Jake squatted onto his haunches, onto his heels, rested his elbows onto his knees, as he continued to stare into the fire.

"It will be good to be home, eh Meara?" he asked. "All the conveniences of home?"

"It will," noncommittally.

Jake looked up, looked over the fire and across to the world around them. They had spent weeks mapping this sector of the now much larger Outland, all with an eye as to how the village of Serpent's Keep might fit into this new world, what this new landscape might offer the village and what the village might have to offer this isolated new world.

"You've always appreciated the Outland more than I, sir," said Meara.

"And yet, here you are."

"Of course." She gave only the quickest glance over to Jake before looking again to the fire. "I couldn't very well let you stumble around out here on your own, sir. Who knows what might happen?"

Jake pushed down a grin, returned his focus to the glowing, shimmering coals.

"Thanks," he mumbled. He silently appreciated Meara's rare attempt at humor.

At least, he hoped it was humor...

"You're welcome," she answered.

As he had expected, Tobias had found the Lynhaur caves in the cliff wall deserted, the village of flying dragons set deep in the Great Ravine having been abandoned well ahead of the dissolution of the web. What he had hoped against hope, however, was that he might find a side passage, even a fraying thread, that might have survived and might still be connected to one of the Jahai villages. The Great Ravine had always been a focal point of the web and there had been the possibility, however small, that somehow some thread might have survived.

But Tobias had found nothing.

He reached down now, picked up several pieces of wood and tossed them into the fire, creating a cloud of sparks above the flames. He looked beyond the fire to the caves cliff wall. Khol had settled at the base of the wall for the night, dragons not being particularly fond of campfires.

Sitting around the campfire appeared to be a primarily human thing.

It would be morning soon. Even now, the cliff wall rising up behind Khol was beginning to lighten, shadows slowly being pushed aside, revealing the black mouths of the dozens of shallow caves that were set into the rough rock.

Khol shifted his weight, leaned forward and slowly rose up. He looked about the clearing, beginning to shade to gray but for the campfire, with Tobias sitting beside the fire.

He walked over and stood opposite the fire from the human.

"Have you slept at all, Tobias Quigley?" he asked.

"Enough, my friend," said Tobias. He looked up. The sky was just a shade lighter than just a few minutes earlier. "It will be morning soon."

"Yes," Khol stated flatly. He breathed noisily through his snout, looked carefully at Tobias. "What will you do now, Tobias Quigley?"

"I shall continue my search," said Tobias. "Beginning right after breakfast."

"I see. And where will your search take you?"

To some of my old stomping grounds, thought Tobias.

"I'm not sure just now," he said. "And what about you, friend Khol? What will you do?"

"I will seek out others as myself," said Khol. "There are certainly those who were left behind in the Outland at the close of the web."

"No doubt, no doubt." Tobias considered then. "Lamal has been seen."

Lamal, the Guardian at the ruined temple that had last been located along the Dark Path, had been a silhouette in the sky above the Outland in recent weeks, seen a number of times over the past several months. Quite to be expected, as the temple ruin was a part of the reintegrated Outland.

"I have seen Lamal with my own eyes," said Khol. "I was unfortunately not able to draw his attention."

"Unfortunate indeed," said Tobias. "I do have a suggestion, friend Khol."

Khol tilted his head slightly, a Jahai sign of curiosity. "Yes?"

"The temple ruin has likely remained Lamal's home base."

"Almost certainly."

"It is quite some distance from here," Tobias said, still considering. "What say you and I travel there together? I can continue my search along the way, and who knows what we might find once we get there?"

"I see," Khol said, thinking the idea through. "Perhaps others in my situation may have already sought out or will yet seek out Lamal's temple."

"Quite possible, indeed." Tobias turned his focus to the campfire before him. The flames flickered; there was a crackling sound as embers settled into the coals.

Khol took a step to one side, took several steps back. He shifted and slowly settled down, watched the human, studied the human. He tilted his head slightly.

Tobias caught the gesture while continuing to watch the fire. He reached out to the side, gathered up several sticks and tossed them into the fire.

"But first, breakfast," he said.

Chapter Four

TahLyn led the small group of Jahai across the gray, desolate landscape. She was of the Bentai species, a small figure alongside the two much larger reptilian-like Thrauhm Jahai that walked with her. Above them, a winged Lynhaur glided in slow circles.

The world around them was a featureless, near colorless plain spread out beneath a gray, featureless sky. They had travelled three hours from the landing and had found nothing, were now on their way back home.

Up ahead then appeared the dark silhouette of a short, squat feature.

One of the Thrauhm pushed out his overlarge head and gave a deep snort-like noise.

"I see it," said TahLyn. Glancing above, she watched the Lynhaur widen its circling, pushing nearer their target.

It took another minute's travel nearer for the silhouette up ahead to begin to take on its true shape. The obelisk stone was chest high to TahLyn, square with a smooth top. Their Lynhaur traveling companion had landed and had settled in beside the object, was placidly waiting for the others.

"Go home now?" it asked. It tilted its head.

"Yes," said TahLyn. "We go home now."

If the thread is still there, she thought, studying the obelisk. *We will find out soon enough...*

She looked calmly to her companions in a silent impetus. In response, each of the Thrauhm reached out to her and rested their clawed hands on her shoulders. The Lynhaur ambled up beside them, placed a hand on them.

Ready...

TahLyn reached out and held a hand above the obelisk. She hesitated a moment, then lowered her hand onto the surface. The smooth stone felt cool against the thick skin of her palm.

There came the familiar rush of white empty. It washed over them, through them, past them...

A moment later...

They were standing beside a stone obelisk very similar to the one they had just left behind. This one stood a dozen yards off a wide trail that cut through a field of low, yellow brush.

They were back on the Dark Path.

This was the furthest they had managed to travel the Dark Path, and getting this far had been difficult, with each journey's success uncertain. The Path was disjointed, broken, in disarray. Travel would appear normal, untroubled, only to suddenly fragment, fall apart, and they would find themselves isolated, the world around them unrecognizable.

They had found a handful of side passages, each thread unreliable, leading to dead landscapes, uninhabited landscapes, with unfamiliar landings. To now, they had been unable to reach Aldwyn and his castle, this being one of their goals.

They started along the Dark Path towards home. After most of a day's travel they reached the tall, wooden double gate. One of the Thrauhm stepped forward and reached out, pounded on the gate.

They waited.

After several long moments they heard the wooden crossbar slide aside and the double gate opened. A young Bentai stood beyond the gate. He stepped to one side and gave a welcoming bow to the travelers.

"Thank you," said TahLyn, passing through. Her two Thrauhm companions followed closely behind her. The Lynhaur came last, passing overhead, flying above the gate, its wings spread wide, gliding in the general direction of the Jahai Village.

With the gate again locked, the Bentai on watch hurried forward to take the lead, escorting the returning team back into the village. They were met by Natan in the center of the plaza. The Jahai leader dismissed the escort to return to his duties. He then thanked the two Thrauhm companions and dismissed them as well.

"Attend me, TahLyn," he said then. He turned about and TahLyn stepped in beside him. They started back across the plaza. Natan listened as TahLyn detailed their latest journey into and along the Dark Path. The report was similar to those of the half-dozen previous reports she had presented.

As best as could be determined, the Dark Path and any threads were isolated, connected to nothing. The Path and the village were alone, torn from the rest of the world, from the rest of the universe; they had been separated from the other Jahai as well, and from the Jahai home worlds.

And beyond this, the Dark Path and the Jahai village had been torn from the Outland.

Natan could only hope that his assistant Khol, his friend, was well.

That the Jahai Village and Dark Path had remained together had initially been considered most fortunate. The phenomenon that was the Dark Path had always been something special, something uniquely Jahai, uniquely of the Jahai Village.

It should now be their way home.

As yet, it was not. As yet, the Jahai Village and the Dark Path were alone.

"We will go out again, Natan," said TahLyn, having completed her report. "A day, and we will go out again."

They reached the doors of the Grand Hall. Natan stopped, turned about and looked out across the plaza. TahLyn, standing beside him, waited.

"Your opinion regarding the threads, TahLyn."

"Natan?"

"What few threads you have found have been broken and, if viable at all, they took you nowhere."

"That is so," said TahLyn. "Perhaps the next."

"Perhaps," sighed Natan.

TahLyn again waited. Natan grew distant, thoughtful.

"I would ask something of you, TahLyn," he said.

"Of course," said TahLyn. "I serve the Jahai."

"Thank you." Natan turned to look directly at her. "Gather what supplies you feel warranted for an extended journey; as much as you can carry."

"Yes, Natan."

"I wish for you take the Dark Path as far as it will take you."

"Yes, Natan." TahLyn hesitated. "Natan, we have traveled twice the distance previously known, without reaching its end."

"I know," said Natan flatly.

Natan asks for something more...

"I see," she said.

Natan turned his focus again to the plaza. Several Jahai were milling about; it was otherwise quiet.

"Take it to its end," he stated. *Find the castle, my young friend. Find Aldwyn...*

"Yes, Natan." TahLyn gave a brief, abbreviated bow of the head. "We will journey to its end."

Natan gave an acknowledging nod without turning to look at her. "Thank you, TahLyn."

It was good to be home.

Master Peter finished his meeting with the temple staff, in which he was assured that there had been no major disasters in his absence, and stepped out of the conference room and into the hall. He followed the passageway into the west side wing, nodding acknowledgments to brother monks that he passed along the way. He took the narrower hall down to the medical room. He found Jacob Quigley sitting on the examination table, where he was being attended to by Brother Drake, the temple's elderly medical administrator.

Jacob lifted his arms to allow Drake to wrap his bruised ribcage with fresh bandaging.

"How does he look, Brother Drake?" asked Peter. "Will the young man survive?"

"The recent journey will delay his healing, Master Peter," said Drake, a bit grumpily.

"I'm fine," said Jake.

"He is well enough." Drake finished the wrap. He stepped aside and handed Jake his shirt.

"Good, good." Peter stood before Jake. "You are welcome to stay with us for as long as you have need, Jacob."

"I appreciate that, but I'm anxious to get home," said Jake.

"I understand, of course."

"Nonetheless," Drake interjected. "A few days rest would be best."

"Thank you, Brother Drake," said Jake. He began putting on his shirt. "Meara and I will be heading to the village in the morning."

Drake shook his head as he began gathering the old bandages and his medical gear. *To be expected...*

Peter gave a sympathetic nod. "Of course, of course."

"I'm half a day from Mrs. H's kitchen," Jake slid off the examination table. "*It be calling to me.* I have no choice but to answer."

"Then answer the call you must," said Peter. He took a step back to the door, stopped and looked back. "But I would rather you didn't go alone. The well-traveled path from here to Serpent's Keep might not be safe, what with all that has been happening these last few months. I will ask two or three brothers to tag along."

"That is not necessary, Brother Peter."

"Nonetheless."

Jake finished buttoning his shirt. "Sure. Much appreciated. Have you seen Meara?"

Peter continued to the door. "I believe she is in the dining hall."

There was no movement. Short, thick tufts of grass and weeds grew in the seldom-traveled trail. A wall of trees and brush pushed up against one side of the trail; a field of tall, yellow grass spread wide along the opposite side. The afternoon sun shimmered orange-yellow against the pale blue sky.

The faint hint of a breeze began then, evident only by the slight wave of the dry grass, as yet the only sign of movement.

A sound then, distant, indistinct, drifted across the silence.

More moments then... it was a man's voice; casual, conversational. No words could yet be discerned.

Two figures appeared far down the trail, walking side by side. As they drew slowly nearer, one could be seen as human, the other a Bentai Jahai.

Long seconds later, the two ever nearer... the human was Tobias Quigley, the Jahai was Khol. Tobias traveled now with a tall, wooden staff, made from a six foot long tree limb, slightly gnarled, slightly crooked, freshly cut and trimmed.

Tobias was doing most of the talking. He was accustomed to traveling alone and was perfectly happy on his own; he actually enjoyed the solitude. He found himself a bit uncomfortable when traveling with a companion, whether it be his nephew Jake or in this case with friend Khol. And for some reason he felt it his duty to fill the quiet that he otherwise preferred.

Khol, for his part, was content to walk in silence and didn't really understand Tobias' need to fill the void.

Khol didn't notice that Tobias had stopped talking. He did sense that the human had slowed his pace. Tobias slowly came to a stop, then; he held a staying arm out to Khol.

Khol reached out with all his senses. He saw nothing in the forest of trees to their left, saw no movement in the field to their right but for the slight wave of grass being generated by the breeze.

He listened. His keen hearing caught the occasional stirring and chirping of small animals, the brush of wind across the grass.

Khol caught a smell then in the breeze; a musty animal scent that shouldn't have been there.

He looked side-glance to Tobias. Tobias gave an acknowledging nod without looking to his companion. He was focused on shadows in the trees a dozen paces or more ahead on the left. Khol could sense that Tobias was readying himself to respond to an impending threat.

With hardly a sound then, two *smart wolves* leapt out of the trees and onto the trail some twenty feet ahead. Tobias stood ready, unmoving, watching.

These wolves were bigger, bulkier than the normal wolf, with broader shoulders. Their heads were large, their faces almost flat but for the snout.

And their eyes betrayed that something was going on in there.

The lead wolf, a hand taller than the other, took a cautious step forward, stood his ground and studied Tobias and Khol.

"Hello, young friend," Tobias stated calmly.

The lead wolf showed no response; he stood silent, watching, waiting.

Tobias heard the slightest of sounds behind them; paw pads dropping onto the trail as one or more wolves leapt out of the forest.

Khol half turned his head just enough to see that there were indeed two wolves watching from a dozen paces back along the trail.

"Two more," said Khol quietly, looking forward again.

"Thank you," said Tobias, continuing his focus on the lead wolf.

"Uh, huh..."

Tobias gave a thin smile.

"You are far from home, friend," said Tobias to the lead wolf. "And you are on your own."

The lead wolf tilted its head a few degrees, gave a slight twitch.

"That is it then, is it?" asked Tobias. "Striking out on your own?"

The lead wolf took another cautious step forward, straightening its head. The wolf behind it made no move.

There was no sound from the two smart wolves standing in wait behind Tobias and Khol.

"Tobias?" Khol prompted, hardly a whisper.

Tobias gave a nod to the lead wolf.

"Our young friend there," he said. "A young Alpha. And he is no longer comfortable taking orders from the Leader of the Pack."

"Yes?" asked Khol.

"He is looking at starting a pack of his own." Tobias turned half about, glancing back at the two smart wolves behind them. He looked forward again, gave the hint of a smile to the young lead wolf. "And I suspect there are more than just the four of you."

The lead wolf lifted his head, kept his focus on Tobias.

"Yes," said Tobias. His eyes drifted briefly to the shadows in the trees on their left. "I believe you will do well, my friend."

Khol shifted, leaned near Tobias.

"Does he know who you are, Tobias Quigley?" he asked. "Are we... all right?"

As they watched, the lead wolf took another cautious step forward. It tilted its head, straightened, gave another twitch.

"He knows who I am," said Tobias. "As for our health and welfare... that has yet to be determined."

Khol gave a low grumble, gave a studied gaze to one and the other of the wolves in front of them.

Tobias held his staff forward, planted it firmly on the hard surface of the trail.

"As I respect the Pack of your youth, my young friend, I respect the Pack that you now lead," he said.

The lead wolf gave a brief jerk of the head. It took another soft step forward, now near striking distance. The wolf behind him also took a step forward.

Tobias held his ground.

"I suggest that you and I come to the same accord as I at present hold with your brethren."

The wolf made no movement at first, gave no indication that he had even heard Tobias. Several moments more, and he took one step back, stopped.

He warily eyed the human and the Jahai.

"Tobias Quigley?" Khol asked.

"The young leader considers," said Tobias.

Another several long moments...

The lead wolf gave a slight snort. His head twitched. A moment more, he turned suddenly and leapt off the trail, back into the shadows of the bordering forest. His companion quickly followed, as did the two behind Tobias and Khol.

Tobias heard the faint rustling of perhaps a half a dozen more smart wolves moving deeper into the forest.

Khol let out a long grumbling sigh.

"I believe his agreement with you was made half-heartedly, Tobias Quigley," he said.

"I believe you are right," said Tobias. He brought his staff back and started forward. "I suggest we put some significant distance between us and this new Pack."

"A good idea," said Khol.

"And I believe we will have to go off trail soon," Tobias continued. "Assuming we are where I think we are."

"I'm good with that."

Tobias gave a grin.

"Yes. It wouldn't hurt."

Chapter Five

Master Peter enjoyed watching the sunrise from his temple's roof deck.

No. Not the sunrise. Rather, Peter liked to view the Outland through the sunrise. He came up onto the roof deck before dawn most mornings whenever he was home, whenever his early morning duties allowed.

The world was in predawn gray. Mist drifted slowly through the trees and about the temple grounds, rolling across the clearing that was spread out before the front steps of the sanctuary. A slight, damp breeze brushed Peter's face. It was cool but refreshing. His heavy monk's robes kept him warm.

He turned to look to the east. The village of Serpent's Keep lay in that direction, just half a day's easy hike. As he watched, rays of color formed on the horizon and then streaked across the forest canopy and to the temple. The clouds of mist that were rolling through the trees filled with orange and red.

He heard the door behind him open and gently close. Moments later Brother John stood beside him.

"Good morning, Master Peter," said John.

"Yes it is, John."

John looked admiringly out across the surrounding forest.

"It is good to be home," he said.

"It is." Peter glanced briefly at John, again then to the view. "Still, it was a successful journey, wouldn't you say?"

"I suppose it was."

"Come now, John," said Peter. "Our visits to our brethren's temples. It was quite an education."

"Yes sir," said John. "It was."

Peter let his gaze drift to the north. He nodded slowly then, half lost in thought.

"The North Temple," he said finally.

"Master?"

"It's waiting for us."

"It will happen, Master Peter."

"Of that I have no doubt, John," said Peter. "It will be a journey unto itself."

"Have you found anything further?" John knew that Master Peter had already spent time in the library since their return, likely researching the six temples, the temple in the far north isolated from the others.

"A bit," said Peter. He shrugged then. "In fact, not so much."

"You will, sir."

More likely we will just strike out and hope for the best, thought Peter.

Hearing the temple's front door down below them open and close, followed then by the sound of the shuffling of feet in the otherwise quiet morning, both Peter and John leaned forward and looked down into the clearing in front of the sanctuary. A group had started down the steps from the porch. Stepping away then, they started into the open, a robed monk leading the way. Jake and Meara were following closely behind, with two more brothers bringing up the rear.

"There they go," said Peter.

They were on their way to Serpent's Keep. John looked up, looked east across the treetops. They should be there by midday.

Peter watched as the group reached the far side of the clearing and entered the trailhead, disappearing into the trees.

"You can still catch up to them, John," he said. "Join them."

John had family in Serpent's Keep. They hadn't been all that keen on John becoming a monk, and John had only recently begun reaching out to them after years apart. He had visited with them twice in recent months.

"Not necessary, sir," said John.

"All right," said Peter. "The offer stands."

"Thank you."

"Though..." Peter stared at the empty trailhead, raised a brow. "You'll have to hurry."

The trail between the temple and the village of Serpent's Keep was well traveled, the most traveled path of all the Outland. Until recently it had also been considered relatively safe, at least safer than many of the other, more obscure trails of the Outland.

Now though, the reintegration of the far-flung components of the greater Outland had brought with it a whole new bunch of dangers.

It was so sad...

"Thank you no, sir," said John. "I believe I'll skip this trip."

Peter nodded in answer. He returned his gaze to the eastern horizon. The sunrise was complete, the golden orb now sitting atop the trees. The dawn colors were fading to pale blue and gray.

Peter turned away from the roof's edge.

"I'll be in the library," he said and started to the door.

Janice was kneeling in the shadows of the trees, huddled behind brush. She looked out across the narrow dirt road to the Farm. The morning mist that had been hovering above the fields had burned off, and the day looked as though it was going to be clear if a bit cool.

Martin was kneeling beside her, studying the scene in silence. Beside Martin was Kailee, Thomas' young assistant. She was there in Thomas' stead, he having insisted that he should remain at the Rhetani-occupied temple and continue with the security enhancements. Kailee was in her mid-twenties, though looked even younger. She had been part of Thomas' small group since well before the recent events surrounding the shutting down of the gateways and then the rejoining of the Outland.

Janice and her two companions had been considering the situation at the Farm for several hours. From what they had been able to observe, security was light, though greater than it had been in the past. A pair of well-armed security walked the perimeter of the village farm. Several others, nowhere to be seen at the moment, walked routes in and about the cluster of buildings in the heart of the farm.

There was very little movement, not so much as a breeze to stir the grass in the nearer fields. The only activity was near one of the larger farm buildings, where several farm workers were gathered beside a row of wagons. Two of them looked to be finishing up loading one of the wagons as two others stood nearby.

"I don't know, Janice," said Martin. "Taking it wouldn't be a problem. Security isn't that strong, and there aren't all that many hands. But keeping it, that's something different." He leaned forward and looked down the dirt road. "We'd likely have company before long."

Janice's expression remained unchanged.

Kailee gave a confirming nod.

"I'm afraid he's right, ma'am," she said. "We are so few, and the layout of the farm being what it is... we would never hold it."

Janice's expression continued to remain unchanged. Her focus was solely on the goings-on hundreds of yards distant, near the cluster of buildings.

"Ma'am?" Kailee prompted. "Why take the farm at all? Why not just take the wagon train while it's en-route to the village? No fuss."

"We're not looking for supplies, Kailee," said Janice coolly. "We're looking to establish the Rhetani presence."

"Yes, ma'am," said Kailee. "Of course."

Janice slid back a bit further into the shadows. So did Martin and Kailee. Janice looked to her companions, then again to the farm.

"We need to have a meet with the bandits," she said.

"A meet?" asked Martin.

"The bandits?" asked Kailee. "Ma'am?"

"The bandits," said Janice, giving a slow nod. "Perhaps hire them first to assist with the takeover, then keep 'em on as security."

Martin looked very skeptical.

"Oh, Janice..."

"Yes," she sighed. "I know."

§

Charles Victor, the manager of the village farm, stood with arms folded, watching the hands tie the canvas cover over the lead wagon. Charles was in his sixties, his hair beginning to gray, his skin weathered from half a century working in the fields, most of that time managing the farm.

His assistant, half Charles' age, stepped up beside him, beside the wagon. He pulled at the edge of the canvas as if to ensure that it was secure.

"Do you see them?" he asked Charles, pointedly ignoring the three people that were huddled in the shadows of the trees on the other side of the dirt road, several hundred yards distant.

"Yes," said Charles. He casually looked over at one of the hands, tying the line to keep the canvas in place. "I see them."

Jake was sitting in a wooden folding chair, a small wooden side table beside him on which sat a tall glass of iced tea. He was wearing a jacket, as the evening was rather cool.

He was home, the Quigley Estate. He was relaxing on the mansion's second floor deck, which was enclosed on three sides and looked out across the village and the village wall to the west. The temple was out there in the Outland. On very rare occasions one could see the gleam of the sun against the spire; not so today.

Several of the street lamps along the village's main thoroughfare were already lit against the dusk. Several windows were aglow, with warm light filtering through closed curtains.

The door behind Jake opened and quietly closed.

Mr. Griffin stood beside Jake then, looking out at the village.

"Are you sure you should be up and about, young sir?"

Jake picked up his glass of iced tea, took a drink, set it back on the table.

"I'm fine, Mr. Griffin," he said.

"Mrs. Hodges instructed you to rest." Mrs. Hodges had given him the medical once-over and redressed his wounds.

"I am resting."

"Yes," Mr. Griffin said stiffly. "So I see."

Jake glanced up at the tall figure standing beside him, again looked outward.

"How's Meara?" he asked.

"Doing well, I understand. She is visiting her mother."

"That's good." Jake took another drink from his tea, leaned back in the chair, keeping the glass in hand.

"Anything from my uncle?"

"Nothing from Master Quigley," said Mr. Griffin. "That is not unexpected."

"No. I suppose not." Jake frowned. "Still..."

"Yes, sir," agreed Mr. Griffin.

Jake took another long drink from his iced tea.

A gentle slope fell away from the ridge down to a thinly wooded forest of oak and alder and evergreen. Broken building spires rose up from a shallow basin just beyond the trees; nestled in the basin was the temple ruin, a cluster of interconnected buildings, now little more than the jagged outlines of broken walls. It looked much as it had during Tobias' previous visit. But there were a few differences visible, even from this distance. He could see movement, several Jahai moving about in the ruin. He could see broken stone blocks now stacked, forming the structures of cave-like shelters.

Lamal was circling overhead, a winged silhouette set against an evening sky of fading blue with wide swathes of darker blue and violet and burgundy splaying out from the west.

"There is not much left," said Khol. He knew of this temple ruin, when it had been known to be reachable along the Dark Path, but he had never actually been there, had never seen it.

It felt somehow strange to Khol that he should visit it now that it was no longer a milestone on the Dark Path.

They took the switchback trail down the hillside, followed it then through the woods and straight on to the site of the ruin, finally then to a set of stone steps that led up to what had at one time been the front double doors of the temple. It was now nothing more than the splintered remains of a door jamb; they stepped through it to a foyer with no ceiling or walls, with the shards of tall, broken spires rising up on either side.

Spread out before Tobias and Khol were rotted wooden beams among broken stone and chunks of concrete, wall foundation footings outlining the vestiges of hallways and rooms and sleep cells. Set in amongst these were the simple structures that had recently been put together to serve as shelters.

A few yards to Tobias' left stood a large Thrauhm Jahai; reptilian, heavily muscled, its large head leaning cautiously forward. Its nostrils expanded and contracted, sniffing.

"Blood of Tobias," it stated brusquely. It tilted its great head, shifted its gaze to Tobias' companion. "Khol."

"It is good to see you, Mauch," said Khol.

"Welcome," Mauch said, then straightened. "You pass."

"Thank you, Mauch," said Khol, nodding. He and Tobias continued into the ruin.

A shadow passed over them and danced across the broken stone of the ruin. There came the thrumming sound of beating wings. Lamal hovered a moment ahead of them, drew his legs out and forward and grasped the top of a broken wall. He shifted around and settled atop the wall, facing the new arrivals.

He silently watched the human and the Bentai Jahai maneuver through the ruin and approach. He recognized the human.

"Tobias," he said.

"Hello, friend Lamal." Tobias indicated his companion. "This is Khol."

"Khol," said Lamal.

Khol gave an acknowledging nod. "Lamal."

Lamal looked again to Tobias.

"Something happened, Tobias Quigley," he stated matter-of-factly.

"Yes."

"We are no longer on Pelonar." Lamal lifted his gaze, looked outward, beyond the temple ruin that had been his home for so many years. "Outland."

"That is correct," said Tobias. "The Outland is again one. The temples have been brought together."

"Home," said Lamal.

"That it is, friend."

Lamal lowered his gaze, looked briefly to Tobias, then to Khol. He looked about the temple.

"Friends come. Some come. Some come."

"I am glad," said Tobias. He turned to Khol. Khol was looking about the ruin, noting his brethren moving about the remains of the sanctuary. He quickly identified three species of the Jahai, maybe ten or twelve individuals all total. Perhaps there were more beyond his view.

Khol sensed his friend Tobias watching him. He turned to him.

"This is good," he said.

"Yes, friend Khol," said Tobias. "It's a start."

Chapter Six

Janice stood at the top of the steps, hands clasped behind her back, waiting. The late afternoon was drifting into evening and the clearing before her was filling with shadow.

The doors of the Rhetani Temple opened behind her. Martin came out onto the porch and stepped up beside her. Janice ignored his presence.

They waited.

The air felt heavy, thick. After several cool days, this day had been warm, moist, with little to no breeze. It took a little more effort to breathe.

Janice heard movement in the trees beyond the clearing. From the sound, there were several people approaching, following the trail, avoiding the security trip wires.

Thomas appeared at the trailhead. He saw Janice and Martin standing atop the steps as he entered the clearing, his two fellow team members coming into the clearing behind him. He approached the stone steps and stopped. He placed one foot on the bottom step and looked up at Janice.

"Janice," he said.

"Hello, Thomas," she said then. "It is good to see you back safely. It went well?"

"They have agreed to meet with you," said Thomas.

He waved a hand for his team to step forward, indicated then that they should go inside. They climbed the steps, gave silent nods to Janice as they moved around her and Martin and went into the temple.

Janice kept her attention on Thomas. She indicated for him to continue.

"They are intrigued at the suggestion of an association," he said then. "They would like to hear more."

"They have agreed to the meeting arrangements?" she asked.

"Of course," said Thomas, climbing the steps. "They appeared to be amused by the neutral location proposal."

"Well, that's unsettling," said Martin.

Janice actually managed the hint of a smile, quickly let it fade.

"Thank you, Thomas," she stated. "You should go get cleaned up. Dinner is in an hour."

"Yes, ma'am." Thomas crossed the porch and went inside.

Janice looked side-glance to Martin. Another smile formed and then faded.

Something to say?

"Martin?" she prompted.

"I've said it before, Janice," said Martin. "You can't trust them."

Janice gave a tired sigh, frowned and looked out across the clearing. The shadows moving through the surrounding trees were growing darker, the sky overhead grayer.

"Thank you, Martin," she droned. "I shall keep that in mind."

Brother John opened the door to the library and quietly entered the room. The walls were lined floor to ceiling with shelves filled with old volumes. Midway down the room an entire section of the wall was covered with a honeycomb of diamond-shaped compartments filled with scroll tubes.

Master Peter was sitting at one of the several tables in the middle of the room. A lone pole lamp illuminated an unrolled scroll that was spread out across the table before him.

John moved quietly across the room and stood before the table facing Peter.

Peter leaned back in his chair.

"Good evening, John," he said, carefully rolling the scroll.

"Master Peter."

Peter slipped the scroll into its tube, stood as he fitted the cap.

"Is there a problem?" he asked.

"No sir."

Peter nodded absently as he walked over the scroll compartments. He slid the tube into its shelf and began looking through the shelves for another, very specific scroll.

"So?" he asked, somewhat distractedly.

"Well," John said hesitantly. "Not a problem so much as an increasing concern."

"Uh huh." Peter read the label on the side of tube. "Ah. This is it."

John followed Peter back to the table. "It is the Rhetani, sir."

"Uh huh." Peter sat at the table. He pulled the cap off the tube, reached in with two fingers and carefully pulled out the scroll. "I'm listening," he said, unrolling and spreading out the scroll. It appeared to be a skillfully detailed map.

"We have been observing an increasing amount of activity in and around the temple that they have occupied," said John. "Quite a lot of comings and goings."

"I see." Peter did look up from the scroll. "Any ideas on what they're up to?"

"It can't be good."

"Really? Why not?"

This caught John off guard. "Well... *um*... they are Rhetani, after all."

"Right." Peter returned to studying the scroll. "I'm surprised at you, Brother John."

"Yes, Master Peter." John appeared genuinely chagrined. "I'm a bit surprised myself. I apologize."

"Yes," Peter said, sighing. "Still; history would suggest that it would be best that we know what they are up to."

"Yes, sir."

"Surveillance continues, of course?"

"Of course," John stated firmly. "Discretely."

"Good, good," said Peter, the matter seemingly settled for now. Studying the scroll, he ran a finger across the parchment near the top left corner. "As best I have been able to determine, the North Temple is here..." He let his finger drift in a wide arc. "Somewhere."

Brother John hovered over the table and studied the diagram where Master Peter was indicating.

"Yes, sir."

"Mmm." Peter then slid his finger south several inches. "Our network of trails only gets us to here."

"That leaves a lot of uncharted country, Master Peter."

"That it does, my friend," said Peter. His brow furrowed as he continued to study the diagram. He glanced up then to John, gave him a slight grin. "Are you up for it?"

"Absolutely, sir."

"Good, good." Peter returned his focus to the map. He ran his finger in a circle over the top-left quadrant. "Please ask one of our brothers to prepare a map of this area; something that we can take with us."

The midday sun shone through the one window of the café, the outside light shimmering dully across a wide swathe of the reddish-brown wooden floor, its surface incredibly smooth from decades of cleaning, sweeping, scrubbing, polishing, and tens of thousands of footsteps.

Nine small square tables lined three of the walls, with one of those tables set directly beneath the window. Six larger tables were evenly spaced about the floor. Salt & pepper shaker sets and wooden napkin holders were set at each table.

Cosmo Dante, the owner of the only bank in the village, was sitting at his regular table set against the back wall. A thin, middle-aged man was sitting at the table beneath the window. Both men were focused on their lunches.

Jake was at one of the tables in the center of room. At the moment he was working on a bowl of soup; a half sandwich was on a small plate beside the soup bowl.

Sparta came from behind the counter and walked over to Jake's table, refilled his glass of iced tea.

"How is everything, Jake?" she asked.

"Excellent, Sparta," said Jake. "My compliments to Wallace."

"I'll be sure to pass that along," she said and took the half-dozen steps over to Mr. Dante's table.

Sheriff Smith came into the café. Standing just inside the door, he looked briefly about the room before walking over and sitting at the table next to Jake's.

"Young Mister Quigley," he said. "How's the soup today?"

"Quite good, Sheriff." Jake set his spoon into the empty bowl and pushed the bowl aside. He picked up his sandwich, took a bite. "The ham and cheese isn't bad either."

"I'll hold you to that, sir," Sheriff Smith said lightly. He looked in Sparta's direction. Her attention was on Mr. Dante, but she did manage a quick glance to the sheriff. They exchanged nods and Smith looked again to Jake.

"I heard that you picked up a few scrapes and bruises your last trip out," he stated. "I trust you are well on the path to recovery."

"I'm fine, Sheriff. The extent of my injuries was exaggerated just a bit."

"That's good to hear; and it's good to see you out and about."

Both looked up then as Sparta approached.

"Sheriff Smith," she prompted. "How goes the day?"

"Most satisfactorily, Miss Vesper." The sheriff shifted in his chair and smiled. "I have it on good authority that today's soup and sandwich special is quite good."

"Far be it from me to argue with that, Sheriff," said Sparta. "An iced tea with that?"

"Why not?"

"Great." Sparta left to give the order to Wallace. He was visible through the food-up window, moving about in the kitchen.

Sheriff Smith shifted about again to look across to Jake.

"Say... Jake," he started. "I don't suppose you've run into Mason since you've been back?"

"I can't say I've had the pleasure." Jake took a swallow of his iced tea. "This is my first chance to get out of the house. Why do you ask?"

The sheriff considered a moment, then pointed to an empty chair at Jake's table. Jake waved him over and Sheriff Smith changed tables. He scooted his chair forward.

"Mason says that we need to find out what is beyond the Outland."

"Wasn't it Mason who first suggested that we were alone? That there is nothing out there?"

"Actually," the sheriff sighed. "What he told me, in no uncertain terms, which is suggestive on its own, is that we need to find out what has replaced the outside."

"Replaced?"

"Exactly."

"I see." Jake took a moment to consider. He stared at his tea glass, then again looked up at Sheriff Smith. "Are we talking about the Road here?"

"He insists that we send a team out."

"I thought you already did that."

"I did. And they went far enough out confirm that the Outland is alone."

"Then I'm not sure—"

"Mason insists there is something out there. And he insists that we must find out what it is."

"I see," Jake repeated. "I guess."

Jake had traveled that road a number of times when growing up, spending summers at the Quigley Estate from the time he was twelve through his mid-teens. His journeys by bus from the outside world to the front gates of Serpent's Keep had seemed normal enough to a young boy; or at least as normal as his uncle's unique and distinctive village.

"And you're thinking that I'm the one to check it out?" he asked.

"I don't want to push you into doing anything that you don't want to do, Jake."

"Really, sheriff; I don't know that that's possible."

A slight smile from the sheriff. "I suppose you're right about that. You are your uncle's nephew, Mister Quigley."

"I'll take that as a compliment."

"As it was intended." Sheriff Smith saw Sparta come around the counter with his lunch. He leaned back in his chair to make way for her.

"Here you are, Sheriff," said Sparta. She lifted the bowl of soup from the tray and set it on the table. She set the sandwich plate and iced tea beside the bowl.

"Thank you much, Sparta." He waited while Sparta set out his silverware.

"Enjoy." Sparta gave a smile and returned to behind the counter.

"I wish I could go myself Jake, but circumstances being what they are..."

"Not a problem," said Jake. "Really. I'm glad to do it."

The sheriff scooted forward and picked up his spoon.

"I do so enjoy the food here," he said. "I can't imagine it's as good as Mrs. Hodges' cooking."

"I come here for the change in scenery," said Jake.

"I hadn't thought of that. And that would no doubt be in between your jaunts into the scenic Outland." Sheriff Smith took a spoon of soup, groaned appreciatively.

"Well that would be a different matter entirely."

"Of course." Sheriff Smith set down his spoon, picked up his glass of iced tea. "To the Road, then?"

Jake raised his glass. "And to wherever it may lead."

TahLyn, the young Bentai Jahai, waited with the other three of her team at the edge of the Jahai Village plaza as Natan crossed the square and approached them. It was early morning, quite early for dragons, and so there were very few others about.

The winged Lynhaur standing beside TahLyn shifted anxiously, eager to be off. The two large Thrauhm, carrying the team's packs of supplies, waited patiently a few yards away, near the head of the path that would take them to the gate and on to the Dark Path beyond.

Natan reached the team.

"TahLyn. You are ready." It was a statement, not a question.

"We are, Natan."

"Very good." Natan looked briefly at the others of the team. "You are well supplied?"

"We have all we need and more," said TahLyn. She couldn't be sure of that, of course. This time out, they did not know how long they would be traveling the Dark Path.

As long as was necessary.

Natan spoke then to the entire team.

"The good will of all goes with you," he said. "To the journey's end."

"The Dark Path must have an end and we will find it, Natan," said TahLyn. "We will reach it; we will stand before Aldwyn."

Natan took a step back, and then another, and gave the team a slight bow of the head.

"Off then," he said.

TahLyn turned about without another word. Ahead of her, the Thrauhm started into the trail. TahLyn and the Lynhaur followed. It took several minutes to reach the tall, wooden gate; before the gate waited another young Bentai. Seeing the team approach, he lifted the crossbar and set it aside, opened the gate. The two Thrauhm stepped to one side and let TahLyn and the Lynhaur pass through the gate first.

Standing beyond the gate, TahLyn noted a change in the Dark Path since their last visit. The world before them was grayer, murkier than before. The air felt heavier, the sky lay more heavily upon them.

The Dark Path most certainly didn't have a mind of its own, but it was almost as if it knew they were coming, knew what was to be attempted and wasn't at all happy about it.

"Not right," said the Lynhaur. It opened and closed its wings; a clear indication of its disquiet.

"A gloomy start, to be sure," said TahLyn. "But the path lay ahead; it is there for us to follow."

The gate closed behind them. TahLyn noted the sound of the crossbar being put back into place. She tilted her head then and gave an unspoken signal to the Lynhaur. The winged Jahai stepped forward, took another step and slowly spread its wings; several more steps then as it lifted from the trail and ascended into the sky.

For the eighth time in recent months, TahLyn started away from gate and onto the Dark Path.

This time there was but one purpose.

They would travel the Dark Path to its end. They would find and stand before the Ancient Guardian.

Chapter Seven

Master Peter had never traveled this part of the Outland. But then, up until a few months ago this part of the Outland had existed in some other landscape, on some other plane.

There was a trail here, having been created by monks who had worked nonstop these past months to connect the temples that had been brought back together with a network of well-defined trails. Peter walked the wide trail now, with Brother John walking beside him. They were quiet for the most part; what few conversations they had spoken had been in low voice. Two young monks walked ahead of them, one behind the other. The two others of their small group followed a few yards behind Peter and John.

The world was eerily quiet, even for the Outland. The trees here were the same trees as the rest of the Outland, the brush the same as the brush in the forest undergrowth around Peter's home temple.

And yet, this Outland felt different. It even sounded different.

It wasn't different. Peter knew that it wasn't. And yet...

The two monks walking ahead of him stopped. One spoke briefly to the other, then both looked back to Peter and waited for him to reach them.

"This is it, Master Peter," said one of the monks. He looked off trail, to the north.

So this was where they would have to leave the trail, to walk the forest floor, and hope to find the North Temple, still miles distant. They could easily miss it. They could easily pass by it to the left or to the right and never see it.

Peter looked to where the brother monk had indicated, into the forest. According to the map that had been copied from the scroll that Peter had found, this was their route to the long lost temple. It looked no different than any other part of the Outland; same trees, same undergrowth, same shadows; same mote-filled rays of sun streaking through the canopy down to the forest floor.

It gave him the heebie-jeebies.

"Lead the way, brother," he said.

The monk gave Peter a nod and stepped off the trail, the second monk following. Peter held a hand out for John to go next, and Peter followed after, with the others of the group bringing up the rear.

They were quickly enveloped in the shadows and the shifting sunrays beneath the forest canopy. The sound of their footfalls on the mulchy forest floor was surprisingly loud in the otherwise silent world, wafting out and away through the surrounding trees and brush.

They traveled single file in a generally northerly direction for several hours, occasionally having to veer left or right to work their way around natural obstacles. No one spoke. Now and again they heard the sounds of small animals moving about in the brush or the mulch, the wisp of a breeze drifting through the forest.

In the late afternoon Peter noticed a large dark shadow far up ahead, the silhouette coming into and out of view through the trees. As they drew nearer, he saw that it was a hillock of a sort, a cluster of granite stones rising up from the forest floor. Standing before it, the mound was eighty feet wide, thirty feet high. The crown was still well below the top of the canopy. It had the look of a massive pile of large granite rocks dumped in the forest and then left behind.

Peter looked at the others of the team. They were already beginning to walk along the base of the mound, starting to work their way around it.

"Hold up," he said. He considered for a few moments, looking carefully at the mound of granite. He began scrambling up the rock face then, finding handholds and footholds.

"Master Peter?" John asked, questioning.

"A moment, John."

Peter worked his way to the top of the hillock. The summit, such as it was, was fairly wide, with numerous pockets and bulges. The hilltop was wide enough to accommodate the six of them with plenty of room to spare. One of the pockets would serve well as a fire pit, with the surrounding stones offering seating. There was a broad, flat area that would work for sleeping.

Most importantly, it offered a view of the surrounding area and was defensible.

Just in case...

Peter looked up into the sky. It was beginning to gray. He moved to a high spot, stepped up and looked outward again. He wasn't able to see much above the canopy without stretching on tiptoes.

He stepped down and worked his way back to the edge of the hillock.

"Come on up," he said. "We'll spend the night here."

Khol walked slowly, carefully along the top of the broken wall. To his right was the temple ruin, bustling now with activity as debris was being cleared away and crude, almost cave-like dwellings continued to be put together. The Thrauhm Jahai were doing most of the heavy lifting, while the smaller Bentai such as Khol did most of the supervising and the directing.

He stopped midway along the wall; he watched the activity for a few moments more before turning about and settling down to look outward, away from the ruin.

It was midafternoon. The sky was dark gray, the air wet. It had rained off and on through much of the day, and looked to Khol that it would rain again before dusk.

A rough trail wound away from the wall below him and through the surrounding short brush ahead before disappearing into the stand of trees some hundred yards distant. The bare soil of the trail shimmered with the damp; the brush to either side of the trail was slumped heavy with moisture.

A figure appeared then, coming out of the trees. It was a human.

It was Tobias Quigley. He carried a light backpack on his back; a utility belt with canteen and knife sheath was strapped to his waist. He followed the trail toward the broken, jagged wall of the ruin, gave a wave to Khol as he approached.

Khol gave a half nod of his large head in response. He watched then as Tobias climbed the set of rough stairs that had been formed using a stack of broken, concrete chunks of wall, then took the several steps to the Bentai.

"Friend Khol," said Tobias. He was looking into the ruin, noting the activity. There was a large group of Thrauhm and Bentai at work deep within the ruin. A smaller group worked nearer, below and just to Tobias' left, where two Thrauhm were clumsily attempting to remove chunks of debris. It wasn't easy. Thrauhm were large and strong, but they weren't built for carrying heavy blocks.

"Was your day successful, friend Tobias Quigley?" asked Khol.

"Oh, I don't reckon I would call it that," Tobias said with a sigh.

"That is too bad. I am sorry."

Both stood silent then, looking into the ruin. The activity was a welcome distraction.

"Not that I expected to find anything," said Tobias at last.

"And yet you go out each day."

Tobias gave the suggestion of a smile. "That I do," he said.

"I suppose it is a human thing," said Khol.

"No doubt," Tobias said, chuckling lightly. "Hope, when all reason says no."

"I understand."

"I appreciate that, friend Khol."

This temple ruin, as all the temples, had been sent to an alternative plane when the Outland had been pulled apart. The difference here was that the temple ruin had also been a part of the Dark Path, a unique and rather ambiguous entity. With the return of this temple ruin as part of the Outland, might some connection to the Dark Path have come with it? If so, might Tobias be able to travel the Dark Path? If so, the Jahai Village waited for Tobias at one end, Aldwyn and his castle at the other.

It was increasingly obvious that Tobias was unlikely to see either. He had found no sign that any connection to the Dark Path had followed the temple ruin.

"What will you do now, friend Tobias Quigley?" asked Khol.

"Oh, I'll hang around a few days," said Tobias, considering. He indicated the work going on below them. "Maybe I can help."

"I am sure your help would be appreciated," said Khol. "And what will you do then?"

"I expect I'll be moving on. I should probably check in at home. I have been told now and then that folks worry about me."

When it came to human humor, Khol was never quite sure; friend Tobias Quigley's humor in particular. As such, he found it best to take whatever the human said at face value.

"Then check in you should, friend Tobias Quigley."

They fell into a comfortable silence then. The air smelled of the approaching late afternoon rain.

Khol didn't like rain.

Jake stood with his back to the wrought-iron front gate of the Quigley Estate, his small backpack at his feet. It was early morning and the sun had yet to show itself. The air was clear and clean from the rain of the day before.

The estate took up most of the north side of the narrow lane, the grounds enclosed by a high fence. Across the road was the village plaza, a park surrounded by its own tall wall. Jake could see the sprawling lawns and winding walkways of the park through the opening of the park's wide north entrance that was set into the wall directly opposite the estate.

Jake turned at the sound of the Quigley Mansion's door opening and closing. Looking through the estate's gate, he saw Meara standing on the porch. She was slipping into her backpack. The pack belt clipped into place, she took the steps down to the front walk. Jake opened the gate and she stepped through.

"Sorry I'm late," she said.

"You're not late. I'm early." Jake made sure the gate was locked, then picked up his own backpack and slipped into the straps. "Are you ready?"

"I sure am," said Meara. She looked back through the gate to the mansion. "Mrs. Hodges was not happy at missing you. She wanted to prepare a breakfast for you."

"Mrs. H always wants to prepare a breakfast for me," said Jake. "I do love that woman."

"Yes sir."

They started away from gate and walked down the center of the narrow lane toward the center of Serpent's Keep. Reaching the main thoroughfare, they turned left and walked to the village's main gate. They met no one along the way. The village was for the most part still asleep.

Civilian guards stood to either side of the open double gate. They gave Jake and Meara simple nods of acknowledgement as they passed through. Mason stood alone half a dozen steps ahead. He looked ready to go. He was dressed in old jeans and long-sleeved shirt, carried a faded and frayed backpack. His hiking boots, however, were quality and looked to be broken in, ready for the journey that lay ahead.

"Good morning, Mason," said Jake, stepping up beside him. He looked up the Road ahead of them.

"Hello." Mason did not look to Jake. His focus remained outward, beyond the village, almost as if he was able to see what waited out there for them.

Meara kept her distance from the two men, some two paces behind them. Mason had always been vocally over-protective of Meara, of *Mr. Gyles' little girl,* and that had always rubbed her the wrong way.

She chose instead to keep her distance. She watched and listened as Jake tried to strike up a conversation with Mason. She thought that odd, really. Jake was well-liked by most who met him, and he was friendly enough, but he wasn't all that talkative.

She heard Jake ask one question and then another. Mason gave one word responses each time. Jake eventually gave up, gave a final nod and joined Mason in simply looking silently out at the world beyond the village.

It was another couple of minutes before the sheriff came through the gates, escorting the last two of the team that were going on this journey. Meara knew them both, of course; the village was a small community after all. Betty was a full-time member of the civilian guard, young and smart. She knew her business. Carlo was a bit older, somewhere in his late forties. He owned the handmade furniture shop, and sometimes worked guard duty for the wagon convoys coming from the Farm.

Sheriff Smith stood beside Meara as the others continued past, giving Meara good-morning nods on their way to Jake and Mason.

"Good morning, Meara," he said.

"Sheriff," she acknowledged.

"I wish I was going with you." He looked passed the others to the Road, then up into the sky. "The rain stopped. It should be a nice day."

"Uh, huh." Meara looked from the others to the sheriff. "What do we expect to find out there?"

"I haven't a clue."

"Then what are we doing?"

"This is Mason's little get-together."

"Sheriff... that's crazy."

Sheriff Smith grew thoughtful.

"Mason thinks there's something out there," he said then, giving a nod in Mason's direction. "He's probably right. He often is."

Meara had known Mason her entire life. As eccentric as he was, as peculiar as he was, she had to admit that his... *observations...* were weirdly accurate.

Still...

"And?" she asked.

"And..." The sheriff reconsidered. "Listen, whatever Mason's motivation, I would like to know what's out there, whatever it is. It might help us, it might not. Whatever, I think it best that we know. Don't you?"

Meara stared ahead, watched as Betty and Carlo continued to get acquainted with Jake.

"Hmm," she said noncommittally. She saw then Jake turn and look in her direction. He was ready to go. "That's it, then," she said to the sheriff. She shifted her backpack, adjusted the belt.

"Good luck to you, Miss Gyles."

"Thanks," she said. "See ya."

Meara joined the others. Sheriff Smith watched them from a distance as they prepared to depart. Jake looked back at him, gave him a wave. The sheriff gave a pensive wave in response.

Jake led the way, starting down the Road; the same road that he had traveled each summer by bus when he came to Serpent's Keep to visit his mysterious Uncle Tobias.

A young man came through the gate and walked up to the sheriff. Geoff occasionally helped the sheriff, though he most often worked as an apprentice to Numidia, the village blacksmith.

"They're off, then?" he asked, watching the team continue away, down the Road.

"That they are." Sheriff Smith turned and started back toward the gate. "What is it, Geoff?"

"The Farm is under observation, Sheriff." Geoff followed quickly beside the sheriff. "They're being watched. Mister Victor has seen 'em. They're spying on 'em from across the road."

"I see." Sheriff Smith stopped, quietly considered. "That can't be good."

"No, Sheriff. That's what I thought."

"All right." The sheriff started again, passing through the gate and into the village. "Let's put together a team. Get 'em to the Farm."

"Yes sir."

"And find Wanda," said the sheriff. "Ask her to drop by my office at her earliest convenience."

"Yes sir."

Wanda was the head of the Civilian Watch. She was in her late sixties, gray hair turning silver; she ran the Watch with an iron fist well-fitted inside a foam glove.

Well into the village now, Sheriff Smith stopped again. He put his hands into the pockets of his light jacket. He looked up into the heart of Serpent's Keep. The sun was coming up, the early rays of dawn shimmering along the bricks and flagstones of the main thoroughfare. There were a few people out and about now, the day just getting started.

It won't stop with the Farm, he thought to himself. *They'll bring it here...*

"On your way, Geoff," he said.

The narrow dirt road wound its way through a landscape of grassy fields, with only an occasional twisted, ancient oak tree or thicket of yellow and brown brush to disturb the scene. The air was still, the morning sun already warm. Now and then Jake heard the buzz of insects, but mostly there was only the sound of their own footfalls, the sound of his own breathing.

Jake had never traveled this road on foot. He had only seen this passing landscape through the scratchy windows of the bus, through his eyes as the young boy visiting his uncle over the handful of summers that now seemed so long ago.

The old bus had come from another time, an old, creaky vehicle out of the 1940s. It was easy now to be drawn back to those trips from the real world to the village; the smell of aging plastic and worn leather, of hot motor oil. The windows, warm to the touch; the sound of sheet metal popping in the summer heat; the dull drone sound of the engine; the grumble of the tires on the dirt road.

Jake had almost always been alone on the bus but for the elderly driver; it has always been the same driver: an old man in faded blue slacks and shirt, his silver hair pushing out from under a faded blue cap; pallid skin, dull gray eyes. He always had a smile and a nod for Jake when the boy climbed on board, was always quiet en route, never speaking to his lone passenger.

And then one summer, Jake didn't travel to Serpent's Keep. Reaching his middle teens, Jake's life in the real world grew too busy to spend his summer months at the Quigley Estate.

Several years later, Jake grown then to a young man, came the letter: Tobias Quigley had passed away, or so it was thought, and he had left his entire estate, and his quest, to his nephew Jacob Quigley.

And so Jake's final journey down the Road, an ethereal journey from the real world to the almost otherworldly village of Serpent's Keep; a last journey taken in the antique bus, driven by an ancient driver with gray eyes and a faded blue cap.

The bus had left him at the front gate of the village before disappearing back down that dusty road. Jake had stepped through the gate and into another world, a world that he had somehow never truly seen during those summers' past, that he could never have imagined; that could never have existed in the real world.

He had entered his uncle's world.

Now Jake's world...

So much had happened between then and now.

Jake listened to his soft footfalls on the dusty road, to the gentle breeze brushing across the tall, yellow grass of the sprawling fields to either side, took in the warm smell wafting up from the grass and out across the road.

Jake slowed, stopped. He took a moment to let all his senses reach out to all the elements of the morning. It was all so different when on foot; not at all as it had been to that young boy looking through the dull, faded glass of the windows of the old bus.

"Is something wrong?" asked Meara.

It took a moment for Jake to come back from wherever his distant thoughts had taken him, to realize that someone had spoken to him, had asked him a question.

He looked at Meara, standing beside him, then to Mason and the others of the team, standing several steps behind him.

"No." He turned from them, looked again up the dirt road; there was another slow curve up ahead, and then a long straight stretch. "Sorry."

He started forward again. Meara fell in beside him.

Mason looked to Betty and Carlo, gave a grumpy frown and followed.

Chapter Eight

Master Peter was only half listening. Brother John was talking in a hushed tone, as the heavy quiet of the surrounding forest demanded. The younger monk was speculating, not for the first time, on what they might expect when they finally found the lost North Temple.

Peter thought it unusual, really. Voicing such speculation was not in Brother John's nature. The near-ethereal atmosphere of this northern Outland that they now traveled must have been playing with his unspoken thoughts.

Peter stopped. He listened now, fully, to something that had brushed at his senses, to something coming from somewhere far past Brother John.

John turned and looked back to Peter.

"Master Peter?"

Peter let his hearing reach out across the forest floor. The others of the team stopped, did their best to hold their silence. John tried to hear what Master Peter had heard.

He heard nothing.

He looked curiously at Peter, shook his head.

Peter was sure that he had heard something that was not of the forest; not the breeze drifting across the floor, not the small animals that scurried about.

Something. There had been something out there...

Again, the breeze across the floor, through the brush, through the leaves of the canopy. A little animal was scurrying nearby through the mulch of the forest floor.

And that was it. Whatever it was, whatever he had heard... it wasn't there anymore.

"Never mind," Peter said at last.

He started forward again. John stepped up beside him, the others followed behind.

Three young men were huddled in the shadows, kneeling behind thick brush. They wore dark green robes, their hoods pulled up over their heads; monk robes, though different in style and color than those of the group of monks they were secretly observing.

The sounds of soft voices carried across the forest floor from the strangers being watched. The two walking at the head of the group were in quiet conversation; the others following their leader and his assistant walked in silence.

These monks traveling from another land had been seen descending Granite Mound after spending the night there, and had been under observation ever since.

They were in all likelihood brethren from one of the temples that had been separated from their own so long ago. By all indications they were traveling to the Temple. They didn't look to be a threat, were likely seeking out lost brothers following the recent upheaval.

They would nonetheless continue to be closely watched.

The three observers slid slowly back, moving deeper into the shadows. They slipped away then, traveled quickly and silently, and hurried to move out ahead of the strangers.

Janice slowly circled the clearing, walking around the tall stone that stood in its center. She was looking outward, studying the perimeter, looking for possible threats. Could someone hide there? Could someone attack from over there?

She slowed as she pointed to a thicket, waved her hand. A young woman stepped up to the brush and began clearing it away. A young man was already clearing brush away from another location.

Janice turned finally to the stone itself. Martin and Thomas stood to either side of her. Thomas studied the stone as Martin watched Janice.

The clearing was half a day's march from their Rhetani temple. The stone looked very similar to those of the gateways that had been tied directly to Serpent's Gate, those that had gone silent when Jacob Quigley had brought together the Serpent's Gate artifacts.

This stone, however, stood in a clearing in a segment of the Outland that had until recently existed in a whole other world, in another plane. Janice had heard nothing of such portals existing in the other segments of the Outland. Had this been an actual gateway? Had the act of bringing the Serpent's Gate artifacts together reached out as far as the lost lands?

Janice stepped forward and rested a hand against the rough rock. It was cool to the touch. She brushed her hand across it, brought her hand back and looked at her fingertips, rubbed them together. She turned about and looked again about the clearing. The targeted vegetation had been cleared away. All looked ready.

Thomas glanced up into the sky, then to the trailhead opening in the perimeter. The opening was shrouded in shadow.

"Any minute now, ma'am," he said.

Janice acknowledged the observation with a nod.

Someone appeared in the trailhead then. The woman was another of Janice's team. She stepped into the clearing and moved to one side, stood out of the way.

They're coming...

Janice heard them then, following the trail, coming nearer. A few more moments and shadows appeared. A figure then; a large man entered the clearing, looked quickly about. Satisfied, he moved aside. Another figure, then another, stepped into the clearing.

Five then, finally; four men and a woman. Their clothes were ragged, could definitely use a wash, as could the bandits themselves.

One man stepped forward, ahead of the others.

Thomas leaned nearer to Janice. "Ma'am," he mumbled under his breath.

That was the leader, then.

Janice gave only a slight welcoming nod to the man.

Thomas cleared his throat. "Welcome, Captain," he stated formally.

Captain looked to be in late forties. He had rugged features, bristling whiskers, and sharp eyes that looked always to be amused by what they were seeing.

"Thomas," Captain stated coolly, those sharp eyes remaining on Janice.

"I present Janice," Thomas offered. "Principal of the Rhetani."

"So I hear," said Captain. He looked about the clearing, then at the stone behind Janice. "Interestin' choice for a meeting."

"We like it," said Janice, her tone firm, strong.

Only then did Captain again move forward. He stopped two paces from Janice, his focus now on the stone.

"I 'been here coupla' times," he said. "Weird rock."

"Yes," said Janice, not deigning to look behind her. She had already seen the stone, time now to focus on the subject at hand.

Captain spread his feet, taking a solid stance. He folded his arms across his chest.

"So. Whatcha got? What's the deal?" he asked. Behind him, his team formed a line against the perimeter of the clearing, spacing well apart.

"I propose a temporary alliance, you and I," said Janice.

"Yeah..."

"You are of course familiar with the Village Farm?"

Captain took a moment to consider where this might lead. His eyes sparkled. There was a twitch at the corner of his mouth. There was almost but not quite a smile.

"And you are suggesting..." the sentence drifted.

"I am." Janice moved her gaze across the faces of those standing in line behind Captain. She focused again on Captain. "It could be of benefit to us both."

"No doubt." Captain lifted a hand from this folded arms, raised a finger. "Point of order, oh Principal of the Rhetani. Why do we need you?"

"I would argue that the greatest benefit to you would be to actually take possession of the Farm, not just grab a bag of potatoes and run. Such would be better accomplished by us working together, you and I; such details would need to be worked out, of course."

"Of course." Captain frowned. "Sounds like a lotta work to me."

Janice had expected as much.

"Right," she sighed. "And then of course there is the Village."

This got Captain's attention. For a moment this showed on his face, but was as quickly masked. "Yeah?" he urged.

"A percentage of the spoils," she said, smoothly.

"Again." Captain raised a brow. "Why do we need you?"

"You and I both know that taking Serpent's Keep would be a far from simple matter."

"Then why bother? Why not just hit the Farm, take what we want and quietly depart?"

"I want the Village," Janice stated calmly. "You quite obviously need what the Farm has to offer. We both do."

"Uh, huh." Captain mulled that over. "And ya' got a plan."

"I do."

"Uh, huh." Another few moments to consider. "That percentage of which you dangle. It's gonna have ta' be pretty big."

Behind him, the big man grinned broadly. The others maintained their stone expressions.

Janice let a gentle smile show.

"I feel certain that we can work out an arrangement that will be satisfactory to us both," she said.

Camp had been set up alongside the Road; the road and the camp shimmered in the glow of thousands of bright stars. Jake walked around the small campfire and stood looking down into the flames. Betty and Carlo were sitting cross-legged opposite the fire from Jake, Carlo holding a metal cup in his lap. Betty said something, voice low, but Jake couldn't hear what she said.

Looking up from the fire, Jake could see the slight, short figure of Mason standing at the edge of the camp. Mason's back was to the camp; he was looking out across the field. He had been unusually quiet since they had started this journey.

"There she is," said Betty, this time loud enough that Jake could hear.

He turned about and looked up the Road, the dirt surface aglow beneath the starlight. Meara was strolling down the center of the road, her figure similarly luminous. Reaching camp, she stepped up beside Jake. He raised a brow, giving her a questioning look. She shook her head in response.

Once camp had been established, she had insisted on walking a ways further up the Road, wanting to ensure no dangers lay immediately ahead in the dark. This had become a daily ritual of Meara's that Jake had grown accustomed to in their past travels, and that Jake had come to appreciate.

It was nice to know their surroundings when settling in for the evening.

The journey so far had been uneventful, very quiet. They had made good time, walking a constant, steady pace, stopping every few hours for short breaks, a half hour for lunch, stopping each evening at sunset. The countryside remained mostly unchanged; fields of tall grass, occasional lone trees and clusters of brush.

It was the same landscape that Jake had traveled through by bus those summers past, yet it seemed curiously different. On foot, walking the road, it was somehow different than when viewed through the windows of the bus. It had seemed normal back then...

Was it really different now?

Maybe it was Jake that had changed.

He backed away from the fire, took the few steps up onto the road. He stuffed his hands into the pockets of his jacket. He let his eyes adjust, then looked up and down the road.

In those summers past, traveling to the village from the outside world, the old bus would turn off the two lane county highway of the real world and start down this dirt and gravel road. Jake remembered that it took about three hours back then to get to the gates of Serpent's Keep; about a hundred miles.

So... had the outside world still been out there, it would as yet be another several days' journey.

But then, the outside world, *the real world,* wasn't out there. Not any more. This much they knew.

So what would they find? How long before they found it? Where were the boundaries of their world and what lay beyond, if anything?

Meara left the fire and joined Jake. She looked past him and up the road, then the other direction. The shell of stars above set it all near incandescent.

"Is everything all right, sir?" she asked.

"Everything is fine, Meara."

Meara looked up and down the road yet again. "Good," she said softly.

Jake looked side-glance to Meara, half turned and looked out across the field beyond the camp.

"I was just thinking," he said, almost to himself.

Meara leaned a bit nearer.

"Sir?"

"I was thinking of the ledge above the Great Ravine, the ledge that looked down into the ravine."

Jake and Meara had camped that night on the ledge. They had looked down into the ravine as dusk was falling, had seen silhouettes and shadows gliding above the forest blanketing the ravine floor.

That had been the first time that either of them had seen dragons...

"That was a long time ago, sir," said Meara.

And so much has happened since, thought Jake. *Such a long journey.*

"Yes. A very, very long time ago," he said, as if to himself.

This road was that ledge. Up ahead were the silhouettes of dragons.

The main thoroughfare of Serpent's Keep lay in a murky, silvery gray fog; the row of street lamp globes hung in a drifting night mist some twelve feet above the brick surface of the pedestrian street, each lamp a dull, yellowy gold, the hazy glow just reaching the ground.

Sheriff Smith passed beneath one of the street lamps, passed through its cone of light. It was late evening, the village was quiet, its citizens having settled into their homes for the night; lit curtained windows shone through the fog, aglow with both electric light and oil lamps.

The sheriff continued his rounds, passing beneath the next lamp; the intersection beyond lay half in shadow, half in light. Reaching the corner, he turned and walked into the dark of the narrow side street. Diffusely lit light fixtures hung on the south walls every few dozen paces.

He reached the west gate guard station at the end of the street. The woman standing civilian watch stepped out of the guard shack, stood before the heavy wooden gate and gave a nod to Sheriff Smith.

"Good evening, Sheriff," she said.

"Rebecca." Sheriff Smith acknowledged the young woman, then looked past her to the gate. "How are we doing this evening?"

"All's quiet. Team two checked in a couple of minutes ago."

Several two person teams walked the perimeter on the other side of the wall, a relatively new security measure. The teams stopped at each gate and checked in with the watch on duty.

Sheriff Smith looked from the gate again to Rebecca. "Do you need anything?"

"I'm good."

"Great." The sheriff hesitated, then turned to leave and continue his rounds. "You have a good evening, then."

"Sheriff?" Rebecca called after him.

He turned back, waited.

"Sorry, Sheriff; but..." Rebecca wavered, wore a guilty expression. "Have you heard anything from the Farm?"

Rebecca's kid brother was a member of the team that had been sent to help defend the Farm, should it be necessary. Sheriff Smith understood, and tried to appear supportive, but there really was very little that he could say to reassure her.

"No, ma'am. It's really too soon."

"Right, right," mumbled Rebecca. "You're right."

"You hang in there, Rebecca."

"Yes. I'll do my best."

Sheriff Smith took a step back toward her.

"Rebecca, I believe absolutely that Ethan will be back here giving me headaches in no time."

Rebecca managed a smile. "I'm sure you're right."

"I wouldn't say it if I didn't believe it."

"Thank you, Sheriff," she said after a long pause.

Sheriff Smith gave a comfortable smile in response, stepped back and turned to walk the narrow dark side street back to the main thoroughfare.

He had the other gates to visit this evening.

TahLyn sat in the heart of the large clearing, staring up into the night. The splay of stars were unfamiliar to her. Such had been the case each night of this journey.

The clearing they had settled into for the night was well off the Dark Path, enclosed on three sides by tall brush. The Lynhaur dragon sat a few yards from TahLyn, a dark shadow in the shadows, wrapped within its wings against the cool of the night. The two large Thrauhm of the team were squatting at opposite sides of the clearing, facing outward; they were asleep and yet not asleep, ready to respond to any threat that might come near.

TahLyn let her eyes close. She listened to the dull whisper of white noise around her. She let out a long, slow breath, the wide nostrils of her snout expanding. She let her thoughts drift back along their journey so far, for the most part uneventful, to where they now found themselves.

They were still several days from the farthest point they had previously reached along the Dark Path, and yet TahLyn had already noted differences from their previous journeys. There were the changing shell of stars each night, yes, but also milestones that she had noted previously were no longer there, new landmarks taking their place. On any other trip out they would be investigating each of these changes, but not on this journey. This journey had but one purpose, and TahLyn refused to be distracted by the admittedly curious alterations to the Dark Path.

A rustling, hollow swishing sound reached into TahLyn's thoughts, drifted into her thoughts. Her eyes opened; she gazed about.

All was still. She listened. There was only silence, in the clearing and beyond.

Movement then...

The Lynhaur opened its wings to the rustling of wing against body, stretched them out, then drew them in, folded them back against the sides of its body.

Silence again...

TahLyn half-turned her head and looked over at the two Thrauhm. One sat with eyes closed, the other was calmly watching TahLyn.

TahLyn gave a very brief, short nod.

The heavyset Thrauhm, mollified, heaved a long, slow breath and closed its eyes, ready to respond as needed.

TahLyn shifted about, looked about, looked beyond the clearing. The night was so very still, so very quiet. There was not even so much as a breeze to brush across the grass, to push through the surrounding brush. Glancing above, the thousands of unfamiliar stars splashed across the jet-black night sky, painted a silvery glow over the landscape.

TahLyn returned her attention to her companions in the clearing. Their presence comforted her. She shifted again and settled again into her sleep position.

And yet... she was not ready to sleep.

She would rest, then; that, at least.

She let her eyes slowly close, let her thoughts wander where they would.

The night passed.

Chapter Nine

Master Peter and his traveling companions had been walking through the forest since just after dawn. The midmorning air was cool, the overcast gray sky visible now and then through the leaves and branches of the forest canopy above them. There was no sign of the sun.

Up ahead, the young monk leading the way stopped, looked back to the others. He waited then for Peter and John to catch up to him.

"What do you have?" asked Peter.

The young monk indicated ahead of them.

Just visible through the trees, several hundred feet ahead, was the front of a building, its stone steps leading up to a set of heavy doors.

"The North Temple," said John.

"It would appear so," said Peter. He gave the young monk a pat on the shoulder and moved out ahead, leading the way.

They stepped out of the trees as a group. As they did, two figures came through the temple doors and stood at the top of steps. They were dressed in monk robes, but robes different than those of Peter and his temple; different in style and color. Theirs were dark green, with narrow collars and tailored hems.

"The Lost Monks," Peter said quietly, calmly. When one of the younger companions gave him a curious look, he indicated those standing at the top of the steps. "The robes," he said. *The robes of the Ancient Monks.*

Peter moved forward and stood at the foot of the steps.

"We have traveled a long way," he said.

"So you have," said one of the two standing at the top of the steps. "The Serpent's Keep Temple."

"We are occasionally referred to as such. My name is Peter."

The monk let his gaze drift from one to another of the arrivals, returning then to Peter.

"I am August, abbot of this sanctuary." He indicated the monk standing beside him. "My associate, Brother Tarrant."

"The North Temple," said John.

August looked to John, initially curious, then in understanding.

"We have been alone for a very long time," he said then.

"The Lost Monks."

"The Ancient Monks," said the young monk standing beside John.

Master August again appeared curious, wrinkling a brow, questioning, but said nothing.

"If I might," said Peter. "The scrolls describe the disappearance of the distant North Temple long before the division of the Outland and the scattering of the temples, which itself was a very long time ago."

"I see." August considered, then turned and indicated the sanctuary's front doors behind him. "Please. I would like to hear more."

Meara stopped. Jake and Mason were far ahead along the Road, walking at an easy pace. Betty and Carlo, trudging several steps behind Meara, moved up beside her, said nothing, waited.

Meara pulled her canteen out of its holster, twisted off the cap and took a swallow. She looked about at their surroundings.

The landscape had changed over the last few days. The fields to either side were dusty, barren; there were occasional clumps of vegetation scattered about, brown with brown leaves and bare branches.

The air was dry, warm. The sun was sitting low on the horizon.

Meara noticed then that Jake and Mason had stopped and were looking back at them. She closed her canteen and returned it to the holster on her hip, looked side-glance to Betty and Carlo.

Carlo lifted a brow. *Lead the way...*

As they drew near Jake and Mason, Meara saw a large, boxy silhouette a few hundred yards beyond. Something was sitting alongside the road; pre-dusk shadows were swathed over the object and the desolate landscape stretching away to either side of the road.

"What is that?" she asked.

"Let's find out," said Jake. He led the way then, and they continued down the center of the road. After a few dozen yards the boxy silhouette took on the shape of an old bus. It looked very much like the bus that Meara had occasionally seen pulling up outside the village's main gate.

They reached the vehicle. Meara looked from the bus to Jake.

Jake had a strange, puzzled look on his face.

Mason lifted a hand and rested it on the side of the bus, as if to make sure that it was really there.

Jake moved to the door, hesitated and then pushed it open. He gave one tentative look to Meara before climbing inside.

"Mason?" asked Meara, looking over at the little man.

Mason lowered his hand, took a step back and slowly shook his head. Meara took several steps back then and took it all in; at the bus parked alongside the Road, at their desolate surroundings.

The bus appeared to be abandoned. More than abandoned; it looked to be long abandoned. It was covered in years of dust and dirt, the windows now opaque with gray grime. The tires, the rubber faded gray, were near flat, several sitting on their rims.

Jake reappeared in the open door. He looked all the more bewildered.

"Nothing," he said. "Empty."

"Is it...?" asked Meara.

Jake stepped down, stepped away from the bus.

"Oh, yes," he said. "It's the bus."

"Of course it is," grumbled Mason.

It was the same bus that Jake had taken each and every time he had traveled from the outside world to Serpent's Keep.

"How can that be?" she asked. "This bus has been here a long time."

"I know."

"A very long time, Jacob Quigley," said Mason.

"I know." Jake turned about, gave the old bus a long, careful study. "I was on this very bus a couple of years ago."

"What are you saying?" asked Betty, asked Carlo, at almost the same time.

"It's been sittin' here a lot longer than a couple of years, sir," said Meara.

"I know."

Mason frowned, pursed his lips, gave another even darker frown; he looked at the bus through bushy brows. "Time's different out here," he grumbled.

Jake thought about that for a long moment, looked back then down the Road, back the way they had come: to the Outland, to the village of Serpent's Keep.

"Or it's different back there," he said, tentatively. *It's us existing out of time...*

Meara glanced up at the sky, looked to the west. The sun was sitting low on the horizon.

"It'll be dark soon," she said. "Maybe we should stop for the day."

"I'd rather not," said Jake firmly. He started down the Road, leaving the others to follow.

"All right," Meara mumbled.

Charles Victor was kneeling behind the stack of empty wooden crates, leaning around and peering around the crates enough to be able to see what was unfolding in the open compound area in the center of the farm. The farm manager's shotgun was leaning against the boxes beside him.

Eighteen year old Ethan was kneeling beside him. He had a slight frame, wore loose-fitting shirt and pants. He was looking at Charles Victor's bloody shirt.

"Are you all right?" he asked.

"Don't you worry about me, Ethan," said Charles. The wound in his side had been bound, the bleeding stopped. He shifted his weight from his left knee to his right, taking the pressure off his injured side.

He watched as a group of ten to twelve raiders worked their way into the farm's compound. Several of the raiders confronted a handful of farm defenders head-on as other bandits pushed still other defenders back into the main barn. The direct hand-to-hand lasted only a few moments before the fights broke up and the defenders retreated into one of the smaller barns.

Charles slid back behind the crates, squatted fully onto his haunches. He wore a dark, fretful frown.

"Mr. Victor?" asked Ethan.

Charles shook his head. It was all but done. No one had been killed as yet, so far as he could tell, but the farm was all but lost, and Charles didn't know what would be coming next.

What do they want beyond produce? Is this all for a few potatoes and onions?

He was startled at the sound of three gunshots. He pushed off his haunches and onto a knee, peered again around the stack of crates.

There was no movement in the farm compound, but he could hear struggling going on inside the barns. Briefly then, he saw figures moving behind and between the barns; thin wisps of smoke hovered in the air.

Another group of bandits were meeting with some resistance...

Charles slid back, turned and looked carefully at Ethan.

He's just a kid. What's he doing here?

"Are you up for a jog?" he asked.

"I guess so," said Ethan, no idea where this was going.

"Good. I need you to do something for me."

"Sure, Mr. Victor. Anything."

"Hurry back to the village. As fast as you can."

"Sir?"

"We're all but done here. Get to the sheriff. Let him know what's happening. Give him the numbers. We appreciate the folks that he sent our way, but it isn't near enough. We need help."

"All right." Ethan looked anxiously about. "I can do that."

"I know you can," said Charles. He shifted again, placed a hand on the boy's shoulder. He gave a nod to the south. "Cut across the southwest forty, come out onto the road as far south as you can. Don't stop till you reach the village."

Charles struggled then to his feet, turned and looked around the crates. There was no movement, no sign of the bandits.

"It's all clear, boy," he said over his shoulder. "Go now. Good luck."

"I'll bring back help, sir."

Ethan scrambled to his feet and started across the field. Charles continued to watch for signs of trouble until he was sure the boy had made it safely away. Only then did he reach down and pick up his shotgun, step around the crates and start across the open space between the crates and the nearest farm building.

He would try to reach the defenders that were currently taking on the band of raiders on the other side of the farm, beyond the barns.

TahLyn came upon what looked to be a long-abandoned human campsite. Brush enclosed the clearing, in the center of which was a small circle of stones, the cold ash remains of a campfire.

She lifted her gaze from the tiny fire pit to look beyond the perimeter of brush. Beyond the camp, the vast plain spread out across the landscape in all directions. The purple silhouette of a distant mountain range lay across the horizon; still several days' travel distant.

It was believed the Ancient Guardian lived in a castle in the mountains. TahLyn hoped what lay on the horizon was in fact the home of Aldwyn. She had sent the Lynhaur ahead to see what was to be seen.

She turned to the pair of Thrauhm Jahai. The large dragons waited patiently just beyond the clearing. One, seeing the Bentai Jahai turning to look to them, tilted its head slightly, expectantly, its mouth opening, closing.

"Yes," TahLyn stated. "We have hours remaining to us before night. Let us continue."

Both Thrauhm rose up, readied. They waited.

TahLyn left the clearing and started walking again, continuing in the direction of the mountain range, currently little more than a smudge of silhouette on the horizon. Her Thrauhm traveling companions followed quietly behind.

Tobias was sitting on a fallen tree lying alongside the trail. He was eating a late lunch, munching on dried fruit and jerky. The forest was very thick here. The trail before him looked to be seldom used, was little more than an animal trail, and was used by very few animals at that.

Tobias had left the site of the temple ruin several days before, starting out in the morning after bidding farewell to Khol. He had grown rather close to the Bentai during their travels and their time together at the temple ruin. He hoped to see him again before too long, and looked forward to checking in on the work being done to create a permanent presence at the ruin site. Several different species of dragon continued to trickle in a few at time.

He estimated that he had another five or six days of rations, including nuts and cheese, dried fruit and jerky. Making a side trip on his way home may not have been the best idea, as it put him at least another week from Serpent's Keep, but his curiosity had gotten the best of him. He had never been to that region of the Outland, as it was a newly reunited section, and he wanted to give it a quick visit. On his way back now, he had yet to reach familiar territory.

He picked up his canteen, took a long swallow of water. He checked to see how much he had left. He would need to find a water source soon.

He closed the canteen and set it on the log beside him, then leaned his head back and let what sunlight that managed to reach through the canopy warm his face. It was early afternoon. He should be starting out again soon, as he had another four or five hours of daylight.

Just another five minutes...

There was a sound then, some yards distant, reaching through the trees.

Someone or something was traveling along the narrow trail; a number of footfalls, the occasional pushing aside of branches of brush bordering the trail, occasional deep grumblings and grunts.

There was more than one of them, then; quite a few more. And they were coming in his direction.

Tobias waited. Whoever they were, whatever was coming, they would be here soon enough and threat or no, there was little that he could do about it now.

He reached down and picked up his canteen as he watched the trail, barely visible amidst the thick, encroaching brush. He unscrewed the cap, took another swallow. He held the canteen in his lap.

He would do his best to appear unconcerned, even indifferent, to what might be coming.

A dragon appeared then, working his way along the trail; it was a young Bentai, easily maneuvering his way through the overhanging and encroaching brush. Following behind him walked a large Thrauhm Jahai. The Thrauhm had to push aside branches and thick brush to follow.

Tobias could just see other Jahai following behind the Thrauhm; at least one more Bentai and perhaps several other species.

The lead Jahai stopped a few paces from Tobias, warily eyeing the human. The Thrauhm hovered behind the Bentai, towering above the smaller Jahai, watching the human.

Tobias calmly took a swallow of water from his canteen.

"Hello friend," he said then. He set the canteen on the log beside him. He stood, gave a bow of welcome.

The Bentai appeared uncertain at this, a human making a Jahai gesture. Behind him, the Thrauhm lifted its head high, looked down from on high.

Tobias noted that the dragons further back along the trail were doing their best to peer around the larger dragon, struggling to see what was happening.

"Human," the lead Jahai stated.

"That I am," said Tobias. "I am Tobias Quigley."

The Bentai tilted his head, taking in the unfamiliar words of the human, saying nothing.

Hmm, thought Tobias. *Not so impressed.*

"You have traveled far?" he asked.

"Far," said the Bentai. It looked left, looked right, looked again to the human. "We were in web. We were in thread. Bad then. Something bad. We were in gray land, long time. Empty land. Long time. Very long time."

Since the time of the closing, thought Tobias. *A very long time, indeed.*

"I am pleased that you survived such a difficult ordeal, friend," said Tobias.

"We were there," said the Bentai, flatly. "Now we are here."

"You are strong Jahai," said Tobias.

The Jahai looked again from side to side. He tilted his head to look intently at the human.

"Where is *here,* Tobias Quigley?" asked the Bentai.

"Ah," said Tobias. He stepped back, leaned back against the fallen log. "That may take a bit of telling, friend."

Chapter Ten

Jake was standing the last watch. He was out on the Road, the overnight campsite just a few yards off the road. It was early morning, pre-dawn. There had been very little cooling overnight and it looked to be another warm day on the way. Such had been the case the day before, and the day before that. The increasingly barren terrain they were traveling through seemed to reflect the warm, dry weather.

This was not the landscape that Jake remembered from his bus trips to the village, and yet the Road continued before them. They had now traveled far beyond the reach of the last team that Sheriff Smith had sent out.

What was out there? What lay ahead?

There was stirring in the camp. Glancing back, Jake saw that Meara was moving about under her light blanket, just pushing it off. She sat up.

It was quite warm...

Jake again focused his attention outward, then up the Road. The stars had disappeared and the sky was black; the eastern horizon had yet to show any hint of sunrise, leaving the dirt road in darkness. Across the road, the field lay empty and black.

Meara walked over and stood beside Jake.

"Morning," she said quietly, careful not to wake the others.

"Meara," said Jake. "What are you doing up so early?"

"It's too hot to sleep."

Jake agreed. He had in fact started his watch period early, unable to sleep.

He looked back to the others in the camp. They were little more than bundles of shadow encircling the remains of the dinner fire, now only ash.

"That it is," he managed to say, before turning again to look up and down the road.

"You've been awfully quiet the last few days, sir," said Meara. "Is anything wrong?"

Jake had to think about that. Perhaps she was right. He supposed he had been distant of late.

"Most everything, I expect."

"I see. So, nothing specific then..." said Meara, managing a smile.

"Nah," Jake said, shrugging. "Just... it's a lot to take in."

"A lot of questions, and not many answers," agreed Meara.

"You see that too, then."

"Kinda obvious."

Jake said nothing. He noticed the hint of color beginning to form along the distant eastern horizon. Looking about, the black was just beginning to gray; not much, but a little.

"Sir?" Meara prompted.

Jake looked side-glance to Meara, then away.

"Sir?" Meara asked again. "Sir, are you thinking that Mason is right? You know, that we are out of time? In some kind of time bubble?"

"Some kind," Jake mumbled.

"Yeah," Meara sighed. "I think so too."

Some kind, thought Jake. *Outside of the rest of the universe... doesn't that put us out of time? Doesn't that put us in a bubble?*

But what did that mean? If out of time, *when* were they? What did that mean? Did *when* even mean anything anymore? Was the outside world moving forward without them? Was time in the Outland moving at all? Was it static?

Geez...

The discovery of the bus had changed everything, and yet had changed nothing. They knew that the world outside had disappeared, that the Outland was alone. The question of time may have complicated things, but so far as day-to-day life in the Outland it meant little.

Jake let out a loud sigh.

Dawn colors began to paint across the eastern horizon.

Dawn. Another day. Time...

Jake spoke while looking up the road, a winding band of black turning a shimmering brownish gray.

"You're not regretting coming along, are you Meara?"

"I expect you know me better than that, sir."

"Expect I do," said Jake. He watched the horizon. He liked to stand the last watch, liked the sunrise.

The world around them quickly lightened then, black to gray to splashes of orange and red and yellow.

"It's a nice change from the Outland," said Meara.

Interesting choice of words, thought Jake. *She gets it. We are no longer in the Outland.*

So, where are we? Not in the Outland, yet not in the outside world.

We are somewhere in between.

He sensed movement behind them, a stirring in the camp.

The others were beginning to wake.

"I should get the coffee going," he said.

Peter followed Brother Tarrant down the narrow hall of the west wing of the North Temple, each of them passing through the dull yellow orbs of light that were formed by the widely spaced lamps. The air was musty and there was the faint taste of lamp oil on the tongue. Back home, in Peter's own temple, they had long ago added ventilation to this hallway and to the east wing hall to help freshen and clean the air.

He might mention the option to Master August if the subject ever presented itself and Peter could do so without seeming to offend. In their time here Peter had found that while August was hospitable and cordial, he was quick to become defensive, and for what Peter thought to be the most minor of reasons.

Despite this, and despite their very different personalities, Peter liked the abbot and they got along well enough. Master August was a pleasant host and Peter was enjoying his time at the North Temple. Their exchange of information was ongoing, with unexpected discoveries coming daily, many having to do with their divergent histories since the disappearance of the North Temple. So, while Peter looked forward to returning home, he had not yet set a date to depart.

Brother Tarrant opened the door near the end of the hall. Peter followed him through and into the North Temple's library. He stood in the middle of the room, lit by half a dozen lamps placed strategically about the library. It was very similar to the library back home, with the walls lined floor to ceiling with shelves filled with old books, and a section of diamond-shaped honeycomb shelves filled with scroll tubes. In some way that Peter couldn't point to, this library had an even stronger air of antiquity than their own. It smelled of old paper and oiled papyrus, of book glue and centuries-old wood.

But then so did the library back home. So what was it? There was something different about this library, something that spoke to Peter of the distant past.

He hoped that before he left here that he would be able hear what it was trying to tell him.

Master August approached from the far end of the room with several scroll tubes tucked under his arm.

"Ah, there you are Peter," he said. He gave a smile to Tarrant. "Thank you, Tarrant. That will be all."

Tarrant nodded and backed away, turned about and left the room, closing the door behind him. August walked to a table that was cluttered with papers, folders and a large ceramic mug. A pole lamp stood directly beside the table. He set the scroll tubes onto the table and dropped himself into one of two chairs. He scooted the chair forward and picked up the mug, took a long swallow from the contents and watched Peter sit in the chair opposite.

"Your morning goes well?" asked August.

"I've been meditating in the garden," said Peter. "It was quite pleasant."

"Yes. One of my favorite places to go when I'm seeking to quiet my thoughts and feed my soul."

"I can certainly understand why it would be so." Peter leaned forward, placed his forearms on the table and clasped his hands. "You asked to speak with me."

"That I did, Peter. That I did." August pulled himself nearer the table, moved a few items aside and held the mug between his hands and leaned forward. "I've been assimilating the information that you have provided regarding the network of temples into the information that we have here; the data detailing the temples before our isolation, what information there is following the dispersal of the temples that you have described. I have attempted to mesh that data, if you will, with that of our own history, both before and after our isolation from the other temples, and the facts as we have always understood them."

"Quite the project, I would imagine," said Peter.

"To be sure," August stated evenly. Key to his investigation was the ability to reinterpret what he thought he knew, and importantly the ability to interpret the data that was contained in their scrolls from his newly modified perspective. August found that he had needed to reevaluate all that he thought he knew, to step back and explore the world around him with a different set of eyes.

Brother John stepped out of the garden, followed the walk along the wall of the North Temple's main building. Coming around the corner, he found Master Peter standing at the top of the front steps. Peter appeared to be lost in thought, though he did silently acknowledge John when he climbed the steps and stood beside him.

"Master Peter," said John. "I was told that you were meeting with Master August. I trust it went well."

Peter let his gaze drift across the clearing and above the forest of the Outland beyond. He took a moment to gather his thoughts.

"We have always been rather pretentious when it comes to our temple," he said at last. "In relation to the other sanctuaries. Have we not?"

"I haven't given it much thought, really," said John, unsettled by the question. "Until quite recently, we were alone."

"On our own, perhaps, but not alone. We knew that our brethren were out there, somewhere."

"I suppose that is so," John said, his thoughts jumbled. "That happened long before my time."

"Hmm," Peter mumbled. "Mine, as well."

"Sir?"

"Nonetheless..." said Peter, his own thoughts drifting.

"Yes sir..."

They stood silent for several very long moments then. It was late afternoon, the air was warm and still. John thought he saw movement in the trees, small animals moving about in the shadows; creatures were just beginning to move about after a long day of slumber.

"We were apart from one another for far too long," sighed Peter.

"We were, sir."

Peter looked briefly at John, forward again.

"Ours was not the original temple," he said.

"Sir?" John had always thought the temples had been built at about the same time, when he thought about it at all. Looking at them now, they were certainly designed and constructed similarly.

"If there was what one would call a primary sanctuary, it was this one," said Peter. "The North Temple."

"It does seem to stand apart from the others," said John.

"Hmm," sighed Peter. "Knocks us down a peg, doesn't it?"

"I don't understand."

Peter managed something between a grin and a smirk. He had always felt his own temple to be special. After all, there was Serpent's Gate, primary to the outworld gates, literally at their front steps.

Nothing but happenstance, as it turned out. The purpose of the temples had been to bear witness to the good and the bad of humankind, with but a tenuous relationship to the gates.

"August believes there is a strong connection between the North Temple and the Ancient Guardian," said Peter.

Of course he does... thought John.

"And is there?" he asked.

"Maybe," shrugged Peter. "Maybe it has something to do with the North Temple disappearing all those years ago; long before the division of the Outland."

"I see," said John.

"Really?" Peter looked to John, again to the sky hovering above the Outland. "I wish I did."

Sheriff Smith's footfalls sounded down the narrow side road deep into the north end of the village. He stopped at an unmarked door located midway along the long brick wall that spanned the length of the road and the row of buildings behind it.

He hesitated a moment, as if gathering up the courage to face what waited for him inside. He reached out then, opened the door and entered the Adventurer's Guild.

The front foyer was a small room; off-white colored walls, gray carpet, soft lighting. A tall, elderly man in conservative slacks and jacket stood behind a high counter of dark wood. A set of double doors in the wall beside and behind the counter stood slightly ajar. The low rumbling of a dozen quiet conversations could be heard coming from beyond the doors.

"Good evening, Sheriff Smith," the man behind the counter said softly, his tone formal.

"Good evening, Broderick." The sheriff stood facing the doors, a hand resting on the countertop beside him.

Broderick looked to the doors, then to the sheriff.

"They appear to be friendly enough this evening, sheriff," he said reassuringly.

"Good to hear." Sheriff Smith knew everyone in the room. He knew everyone in the village.

He just didn't like speaking to a crowd.

To it, then...

He stepped through the doors and entered the guild's main hall. It was a spacious room, though not overly large. There were half a dozen round tables scattered about the floor, with a handful of smaller tables set along the walls and interspersed with high-backed chairs. This evening, all the tables and chairs were occupied.

Most of the conversations stopped as Sheriff Smith crossed the room, moving between the tables. He placed a hand on one shoulder and another, mumbling an occasional 'hello' or a 'good evening'.

Reaching the far wall, he turned about and faced the room. Ethan, the young man that had brought Sheriff Smith the news from the Farm, was sitting at a nearby wall table with his sister Rebecca.

The sheriff looked from Ethan to the room at large.

"Thank you for coming, everyone," he said. "I won't take too much of your time."

He paused briefly as another person came into the room. It was Wanda, the captain of the Civilian Watch. She gave an apologetic smile and then stood with her back against the wall beside the double doors, folded her arms across her chest.

Sheriff Smith gave her a nod of welcome, looked again about the room, let the room fall quiet. All eyes fell on him; all in the room grew expectant.

"You all know what's happened at the Farm," he said then. He looked over to Ethan, gave him an affable smile, turned again to the room, his expression again growing dark. "I won't go into details, beyond to say that the severity of the attack is beyond appalling."

"Has anyone been killed?" asked a middle-aged woman. Sheriff Smith knew that her son had been one of those sent to help defend the Farm.

"I do not believe so," he answered. He glanced to Ethan, who gave only the slightest shake of the head. He turned back to the woman. "Injuries, to be sure, but we do not believe anyone has been killed."

"What now?" asked a man sitting at another table.

"That is why I have asked you all here." Sheriff Smith stepped near Ethan and his sister. He placed a hand on Ethan's shoulder, took a few moments to look at each person in the room. "We have been asked to provide further assistance. We will provide that assistance."

"Sending more out to the Farm?" asked the man.

"That's right."

A number of people began talking at once. The sheriff heard a few rumblings of concern about leaving the village undefended.

"Hold on, folks." Sheriff Smith stepped away from Ethan, held up his hand. "A moment, please."

He waited for the loud din to fall to low grumblings. He indicated Wanda then, who was still standing at the back of the room.

"Wanda will be meeting with her team leaders in the morning to organize additional enhancements to the village defenses. I can assure you we will be well prepared for any eventuality."

"We thought that with the Farm," came from one in the crowd.

"That's true enough," admitted the Sheriff. "I take responsibility for that."

"Not yours alone, Sheriff," said another. "It's on all of us."

"I appreciate that, but it was my call." The sheriff's expression brokered no argument. "Now. The situation at the farm will be resolved. And the village is another matter entirely."

"That it is," came from one in the crowd.

"We are prepared for any eventually," the sheriff stated again, firmly.

A return of the grumblings then, some of doubt, others of hesitant acceptance; most agreed.

"In the meantime," Sheriff Smith continued, urging quiet. "Wanda has designated a team leader from the guard who is at this moment organizing the team that will be heading to the Farm at first light."

He took another few moments to look directly at the men, women and young people in the room. He expected that most everyone in the room, most everyone in the village, would be asked to volunteer to defend the village. He also fully expected that most, if not all, would step forward and accept.

"We will get through this," he said. He paused then, gave a general nod to all. "Together."

And with that the meeting began to break up. Wanda caught the attention of several in the room, led them out of the guild hall. Most everyone else remained, however, and the hall filled with the growing rumble of a dozen conversations.

The sheriff caught Ethan's attention and the young man came over, his sister Rebecca right beside him.

"How are you feeling, Ethan?" asked the sheriff.

"I'm fine, Sheriff. Just fine."

"Good to hear. Listen, I know you're anxious to get back to the Farm, but I have something else in mind for you."

"Sure, Sheriff," said Ethan. "Whatever you need."

Rebecca looked on with concern. She was glad that Ethan wouldn't be going back to the Farm, but she was apprehensive about what the sheriff was going to ask of her brother.

"I appreciate that, Ethan," said the sheriff. "So, here it is. I would really like for you to make a trip out to the Temple. I need you to tell Master Peter what's happened."

"Sheriff?" asked Ethan.

"Trust me," said the sheriff. "It's important that he knows what's going on. Can you do that for me?"

"Are you worried they might attack the Temple?" asked Rebecca.

"That is certainly a possibility," said Smith. "They should be prepared for that, but actually... Master Peter might be able to offer some assistance."

"Really?" asked Rebecca. *What can a bunch of monks do?* she wondered to herself.

"Really," said the sheriff. "You would be surprised."

"Okay, Sheriff," said Ethan. "Should I leave now?"

"Best not just yet. It'll be dark before long." Sheriff Smith placed a hand on the young man's shoulder. "The morning will be soon enough."

"Sure, Sheriff. You got it," said Ethan after a long pause. "I'll leave at first light."

Rebecca took a step in the direction of the door, looked from Sheriff Smith to her brother.

"Let's go, Ethan," she said. "If you're gonna be headin' to the Temple tomorrow, there's prep to do."

Ethan gave an uncomfortable grin to the sheriff as he took a shuffling step toward his sister.

"Guess I gotta go, Sheriff."

Sheriff Smith nodded farewell to the young man and watched Ethan and his sister work their way through the still mingling crowd and to the door. Several others followed, though most of those who had attended the meeting remained.

Friends and neighbors, ordinary folks, being asked to do stand up and do extraordinary things.

Sheriff Smith wished he felt as confident about their future as he let on.

Chapter Eleven

The animal trail that had paralleled the road running from the Farm to the village turned sharply and emptied onto the road itself. Janice stopped, took a step back from the road. From here she could see the Serpent's Keep wall and the north gate just a few hundred yards further south.

Thomas, the man that Janice most relied on to handle the security of their Rhetani temple, stepped up behind her and looked past her. He moved then beside her, studied the empty road north and then south. He watched as a pair of guards followed the village wall, passed the gate. They continued on along the wall until they disappeared from his view.

"All's quiet," he said, looking again north up the road. They had witnessed a group of villagers from Serpent's Keep traveling the road an hour or so after dawn, heading for the Farm. Other than that, they had seen no one since they left the assault team encampment several hours northwest.

Janice gave a casual glance up at the sky and sun, back behind them into the woods.

They should probably move back further off the road.

She looked up at the sky again, checked the sun's location again: it was about an hour till midday. The rest of her team would be breaking camp soon and starting their way.

"Let's find a spot to bivouac," she said. "Lunch in an hour."

Thomas placed a hand on Janice's arm, gently pulled them both back further into the trees, further from the road. Alert now, Janice silently complied.

They held silent and motionless.

A long minute later Tobias passed by, walking the road at an easy pace, staff in hand, heading to the village's North Gate.

The North Gate was unique among the village gates in that it had a smaller door set into the larger double gate that was used only when the produce wagons needed wider passage on their way to or from the Farm. Tobias approached and pulled on a rope hanging from a hook and running through a hole in the wall.

He waited.

Several moments passed before the guard standing watch on the other side of the gate called out to him.

"Who calls?"

"Tobias Quigley."

Another moment, then Tobias heard the sound of the heavy crossbar sliding aside. The smaller gate opened; a young man took two steps back and waited. Tobias stepped through the gate.

"Welcome home, Master Quigley," said the guard.

"Thank you, young man. It is good to be home." Tobias stepped past the guard and continued into the village.

The main thoroughfare that he walked and the side streets that he passed were strangely quiet, all but empty. Looking into the market plaza, he noted that most of the booths were closed; the three or four patrons that he saw wandering the marketplace for the most part passed the handful of open booths without stopping.

He passed no one while walking the thoroughfare down the center of the village. Indoor lighting shone through the window of the café, but there was no sign of movement within. On the other side of the way, the window shutter of the sheriff's office was open.

Tobias continued on to the side road of his estate, followed the estate's fence to the wrought-iron gate. Overhanging trees put the street and the estate into shadow. He unzipped the inside pocket of his jacket and brought out his key, unlocked the gate.

Entering the Quigley Mansion, he stood in the middle of the foyer and slipped out of his knapsack. He took a moment to let the soothing atmosphere of home envelope him.

How many times over the years had he come home, stood in that very spot and let this room warm and heal his soul?

Hundreds of times at least...

"Master Quigley. Welcome home, sir." Mr. Griffin was standing at the top of the stairs. He tried his best to maintain a calm decorum as he descended. "It is so good to see you, sir; so very good to see you."

"Thank you, Mr. Griffin. It is good to be home," said Tobias. He raised a brow. "It is, is it not? Good to be home?"

"Sir?"

"I've just had a rather disquieting walk through the village," he said. "What have I missed?"

"That would depend, Master Quigley," said Griffin. "What do you know of recent events?"

"Dear Mr. Griffin. I do miss our little chats."

"As do I, sir," said Mr. Griffin. He went on then to describe the attack on the Farm and the teams that had been sent out to defend it. He noted the sheriff's concern that the village might be next.

The Farm, thought Tobias. If he had taken his normal route home he would have walked right passed the farm. He had instead gone cross country through the woods, coming out onto the road well south of the farm.

He took a moment then to consider. Would bandits have made such an assault on their own? Uncertain, but if so they would have grabbed what was immediately at hand and then ran. Tobias doubted they would occupy the farm. They weren't farmers, and in any event he didn't believe they would want to take on the wrath of the village what was certain to follow.

Were the Rhetani behind this? Was Janice behind this?

If so, then the village could very well be a target.

"I've no doubt the sheriff has things well in hand," Tobias said. He would need to drop by the sheriff's office.

"I believe you are correct, sir," said Mr. Griffin. "And he has been working closely with the captain of the Watch."

"Good, good." He looked to the archway leading to the kitchen and dining room. "And how is Mrs. Hodges?"

"Quite well, sir. I am expecting her return before lunch."

"Ah, *lunch*. What a lovely word." Tobias picked up his knapsack. "I'll stow my gear and get cleaned up." He took a step toward the staircase, stopped and looked back to Mr. Griffin. "What of my nephew? Causing trouble, I trust?"

"He has come and gone, Master Quigley. Sheriff Smith sent him on a mission of sorts up the Road."

"Really?"

"Following up on some concern of Mason's, I understand."

"Is that so?" Tobias asked thoughtfully, considering. He liked Mason. The man occasionally wandered into the rather unconventional, but he was never to be dismissed outright.

"He left several days ago," said Mr. Griffin. "Young Meara went with him; as did Mason."

"Sounds like fun," he said, continuing on then to the staircase. "Too bad I wasn't here in time to join them."

"Yes sir." Mr. Griffin started then toward the kitchen. "I will let Mrs. Hodges know that you are home the moment she returns."

Charles Victor and four others sat with their backs against the back wall of the main barn. His shirt was caked with dried blood. The others showed similar signs of injuries. All looked exhausted, several appeared defeated.

Not so Charles Victor. His expression remained defiant.

An armed bandit stood silent watch from a safe distance. He and his fellows had successfully taken the Farm, though few of them knew what they were supposed to do with it now that they had it.

The young man standing guard certainly had no idea.

Would they force these prisoners into farm labor? To what end?

And would they be able to hold onto the farm? Wouldn't the village try to take it back?

Why don't we just load up a wagon with some food and get out of here?

Another of the bandits came around the corner and stood beside the guard. He leaned in and asked the guard a question. In answer, the guard nodded in Charles' direction.

The bandit stepped forward and stood before Charles.

"You run this place?" he asked harshly.

"I'm the manager," said Charles.

"Come on." The bandit took a step back and waited, his weapon at the ready.

Charles clambered slowly to his feet, walked where the bandit indicated, the bandit following two steps behind. He was led around to the front of the barn, the large doors standing open, to where the man Charles thought to be the leader of the bandits waited.

"Here he is, Captain," said the bandit escort.

Captain gave little acknowledgement. He was quietly taking in the view that was spread out before him. The Farm was a well maintained, well managed facility; a handful of beautiful barns, assorted smaller buildings, a small home, and sprawling fields reaching out in all directions from the heart of the farm.

"A nice place you have here," said Captain, not deigning to look at his prisoner.

"Thanks," Charles grumbled. "What do you want?"

Captain did smile then, glancing briefly at Charles before returning his gaze to their surroundings.

"It looks like I have what I want, my man. Don't you think?"

"You don't strike me as a farmer."

"No," Captain smirked. "No, I suppose not."

"So then, you've gone to a lot of trouble to steal a few potatoes."

"Oh, I've never been a big fan of potatoes," said Captain. He smiled. There was something menacing in that expression; but then Captain was well practiced. He knew how to work it. He was good at it.

He hesitated just the right amount of time, then took a step away from the barn. He took another step. Folding his arms, he spoke calmly over his shoulder to Charles.

"How long you figure?" he wondered aloud. "Before we see something more coming up that road?"

"I couldn't say," said Charles. "What do you want from me?"

Another smirk from Captain.

"You mean... now?"

"Why did you ask for me? Certainly not just to revel in your victory."

"Certainly not, sir." Captain turned about and faced Charles Victor. He considered, gave a half turn of the head and a slight nod. "One might consider the events here to be mere distraction. The lady certainly does."

"The lady," Charles stated matter-of-factly.

"Yes. Bit of a know-it-all, really. I don't much care for her." Captain looked briefly about, then directly at Charles. "This is her bit, you know. We thought it might be fun."

"You're having a good time, then."

"No, not really," said Captain with a shrug. "The spoils should be good. Then there's the other. The rewards."

"The other," Charles stated. "Of course."

Captain grinned. "Yeah."

A young woman in faded pants and shirt, blood on one of the sleeves, came around the corner of the barn. She stopped briefly beside the man that had escorted Charles to their leader; she whispered something and then stepped up beside Captain. Captain leaned in, listened a few moments.

He pulled back, a sign of dismissal. The young woman departed.

"Ah, so..." Captain said to Charles, then indicated Charles' escort. "The gentleman here will return you to your friends. We will have to pick this up again later."

"Problem?" asked Charles, raising a single brow.

Captain only grinned at Charles snide insinuation.

"It is what I live for," he said, almost cheerily.

The escort moved into position, frowned and silently ordered Charles to move out ahead of him.

The world around TahLyn and her companions was flat and dry, mostly desolate with occasional islands of gray vegetation. The sky overhead was a cloudless, dull, dusky gray. It never changed, never growing darker, nor brighter. There was no sound, no wind, no movement but for TahLyn and her two Thrauhm dragon companions walking across the barren landscape. The Lynhaur had again been sent out ahead, had been gone most of the morning.

They came upon a small cluster of scraggily shrubs and TahLyn stopped for a short break. The two overlarge Thrauhm settled onto their haunches a few yards away, looked indifferently about them and patiently waited.

The days and nights to now had passed relatively uneventfully. They had travelled terrains of forest, of rolling hills of yellow grass, of barren landscape, journeying ever onward, ever hopeful, now far beyond the farthest reaches of their previous journeys on the Dark Path.

One of the Thrauhm rose up then, took two awkward steps and pushed his great head forward, half-turned his head, eyed the sky in the distance.

TahLyn turned about, looked up into the sky to where her companion was indicating.

A silhouette was set against the pale blue; distant, very distant, but slowly coming ever closer.

Though there was never any real doubt, it was another minute before the silhouette could be recognized as their Lynhaur companion; another minute still before it was circling above them, slowly descending. It finally landed half a dozen long strides from TahLyn.

"I am pleased at your safe return," said TahLyn. "What have you for us?"

"I bring news," said the Lynhaur. It took three short steps, pulling its wings back firmly against its body.

"How so, friend?"

"Mountains," said the flying dragon. "High mountains. Much high. Fill horizon."

"Yes?" urged TahLyn. The Ancient Guardian dwelled in just such a mountain range.

"Saw castle in mountains. Castle. Castle," the Lynhaur stated.

TahLyn stepped forward, stepped around the Lynhaur. She looked to the horizon. Whatever lay ahead was as yet just a smudge of purple silhouette on the horizon, but now she knew, knew for certain, that it was there.

The Dark Path would take them to the Ancient Guardian.

TahLyn spoke then without turning to her companions.

"We have hours yet before night descends." She started forward. "Let us continue."

Chapter Twelve

After the evening meal, Master Peter returned to his sleeping cell to pack up his few belongings in preparation of their early morning departure from the North Temple. Peter and his companions would be leaving before dawn.

They had talked just that morning about possibly starting for home in another two or three days. They had actually begun making plans, then just hours later Brother Tarrant returned from another of his excursions into the Outland with news of bandit activity in the south. Tarrant and his team had been out a number of times since the reintegration of the Outland and such observations were growing more frequent. Tarrant also reported having met with a group of travelers on this latest jaunt. They described to him what sounded to be organized attacks on large groups and several permanent establishments, which was something new for the bandits. And their attacks were growing more brazen and more violent.

While there had been no mention of an immediate threat to their home temple, Master Peter and Brother John were both anxious to get back, just in case. Their sanctuary was always ready for possible assaults, had been since the temples were first established, but with this latest news they weren't comfortable with not being there.

They needed to get home.

Brother John appeared at the open door of Peter's cell.

"Master Peter."

"John." Peter closed his pack. "Anything wrong?"

"I'm just about to go out for my evening walk. Would you like to join me?"

"Thank you, no," said Peter. "There will be plenty of that come tomorrow."

John chose not to remind Master Peter that an evening walk really had nothing to do with walking.

"Yes sir," he said. "Very well, I'm off then."

"I'll see you in the morning," said Peter. He lifted his pack and set it against the wall.

"Yes sir. In the morning then." John left Peter and continued down the hall to the foyer. Once outside, he stood at the top of the steps for a moment and took in the evening air. He descended the steps and walked around to the side of the sanctuary and entered the garden. He followed the wide, winding walkways and paths, bordered by flowering shrubs, passing the occasional wood bench set back off the walks. He came up then to one bench that was occupied.

The abbot of the North Temple looked up at the approaching monk.

"Ah, good evening Brother John," said August.

"Master August," said John with a slight nod. He glanced about them. "It is a pleasant evening. Is it not?"

"That it is." August looked about, again to John. "You will be leaving us, then."

"Come the dawn," said John. "We have much appreciated your hospitality."

"It was our pleasure, I assure you." Master August grew thoughtful, then gave a slight smile. "I admit that we were a bit out of practice, what with our isolation; a most acute isolation, to be sure."

John considered that, finally turned about and sat down beside the abbot. He glanced over at the monk, then ahead, at their surroundings.

"Well, you know, the *Lost Monks* and all," said John. "You've done quite well, really."

"Thank you." Master August had only just begun getting his head around the whole Lost Monks, Ancient Monks story. Seeing their disappearance from the perspective of the other temples, and the inferred connection to the Ancient Guardian, he supposed that it was understandable.

"Odd, you know," said John, almost casually. "The Temples, all together again; the Outland, so much more than I could have imagined."

"No doubt," said August. "Your Temple having stood alone; your temple and the village."

"You know of Serpent's Keep?"

"But of course," said August, quite matter-of-factly. "The home of Tobias Quigley."

Janice walked through the main gates and entered Serpent's Keep for the first time in many years. She and her teams had silently worked their way along the village walls, avoiding the side gates and instead assailed the village through the front gates. They easily overwhelmed the sentries that had been posted there, the guards quickly retreating back into the village.

Out ahead of Janice, the two assault teams were rushing up the main thoroughfare, each with its own specific target. She had left the attack on the Farm to Captain and his bandits, while the teams now before her were a mix of both Rhetani and bandits. She would as soon not have involved bandits at all, but as yet there were only a few dozen Rhetani. They couldn't do this on their own.

She turned off the thoroughfare, leaving the teams to their tasks, and entered the park. There was no one there. She followed the walkway across the park and to the gate opposite the Quigley Estate.

Sheriff Smith hovered over the heavy table. He folded his arms and studied the map of the village that was spread across the tabletop. Standing opposite him, Wanda moved a wooden piece an inch across the map, considered, moved it again; she considered again, finally satisfied.

There were seven brown pawns and two red pawns set about on the map.

"Hmm," mumbled the sheriff.

"All is going as anticipated," said the captain of the Civilian Watch.

"Hmm," said the sheriff again. He unfolded his arms, leaned forward and rested his hands on the table. The seven brown pawns, representing groups of villagers, were in position, ready to confront the two smaller attack teams. The village groups were made up of men, women and even older children, virtually the entire population of the village, each led by a member of the Civilian Watch. Wanda was certain they could successfully stand against Janice's assault.

Sheriff Smith was less confident, but he and Wanda had done all they could to prepare. They had even correctly anticipated the assault coming through the main gate.

A young girl, no more than twelve, came into the room. She stood at attention and handed Wanda a folded piece of paper.

"Thank you, Connie," said Wanda. She read the message, gave a smile and a nod to the young girl. "Dismissed."

"Yes ma'am." Connie turned about on her heels and marched out of the room.

Connie took her duties very seriously.

Wanda looked down at the map. She moved one of the red pawns forward, moved two brown pawns directly in front of it.

Sheriff Smith gave long sigh.

"All right, then."

Janice stood across the road from the Quigley Estate.

She recalled the last time she had walked through the wrought-iron gate and up to the heavy door, the garish dragon doorknocker set at eye level. The visit had not gone particularly well. Her argument with Tobias Quigley had been rather heated. Their conflicting views regarding Rhetani philosophy had ended a long relationship.

That had been so very long ago. Back then, the village had been little more than half a dozen buildings scattered about, surrounding Tobias' fenced estate grounds.

She crossed the road now, reached out and checked the gate: locked, as expected. She considered attempting to climbing over but decided against it. She started along the wall surrounding the estate grounds looking for an easier place to hop over than a gate with spikes.

Mr. Griffin stood at the top of the stairs, watched Janice come through the front door and move into the middle of the foyer.

"This way, ma'am," he stated formally. "Master Quigley is expecting you."

"Of course he is," said Janice. She crossed the foyer and climbed the stairs, quietly followed Mr. Griffin down the upstairs hallway.

The deck was much as Janice remembered, though she had only been there a few times. It was enclosed on three sides and open to the west. Tobias Quigley stood near the edge, looking out across the village.

Janice stepped up beside him. Tobias clasped his hands behind his back, continued looking outward. He slowly lifted his gaze from the village to the Outland beyond the west wall.

"Hello, Janice," he said.

Looking down into the streets, Janice saw that they were empty but for a handful of people running from the main thoroughfare into the market plaza at the north end of the village.

"I wasn't sure that I'd find you here, Tobias," she said.

"Oh, I wouldn't miss it."

"Is that so?"

"Absolutely." Tobias turned then to look at Janice for the first time. "Are you here to measure for new curtains?"

"Just checking out my new digs."

"I see." Tobias returned his gaze outward. The streets remained surprisingly quiet. "Honestly, I don't believe things are going as well for you as you think, Janice."

"It's a bit early to come to that conclusion, Tobias."

"Oh, I don't believe so."

Both were quiet for a few moments. Tobias glanced back at the silent Mr. Griffin, who stood waiting near the door. He turned again to look briefly at Janice, then outward, to the village streets and beyond.

"Working with bandits and hooligans, I see," he stated. "I'm disappointed in you, Janice."

"They are but a tool," said Janice. "Nothing more."

"I was always led to believe the Rhetani were more idealistic than that; goals attained through unsavory means are tainted and therefore unworthy."

"Evolving circumstances call for measures that we wouldn't have considered in times past."

Tobias looked directly at Janice. "Has the passage of time changed you so very much?"

"Not really." Janice grew thoughtful, introspective. "Though... I suppose we were quite the wide-eyed romantics back then, we little band of crusaders."

"Perhaps," agreed Tobias, turning to look beyond the village walls. "But it would so appear, each with our own unique perspective on just what it was that we were crusading."

"Hmm," sighed Janice. "And the direction that each would take that crusade. What we would do with it."

"It was not I who fell in with a cult, Janice."

"Cult? Mudslinging now, Tobias?"

"Hurt feelings, Janice? It doesn't become you."

They fell silent yet again. There was some movement in the streets below, an occasional crying out in anger or in strife.

Janice thought it much quieter and calmer than she would have expected, but she managed to hide a growing concern.

"Do you see them much?" she asked. "Our comrades from back then?"

"Now and then," he sighed. "Though not for some time. Jacob, more than I; in his travels."

"Jake. Yes," Janice grumbled. "A bit of an irritant, if you ask me. Where did you find the boy?"

Tobias managed a smile.

"Another life, a different world," he said softly. He lifted a curious brow. "My nephew, don't you know."

"Yeah, so I heard. That would take some explaining."

"Quite."

Another few moments, and then Tobias glanced back to Mr. Griffin, standing near the doorway. He gave the slightest of nods before again looking out across the village.

At that, Mr. Griffin took a step forward, raised a brow to Janice.

"Ma'am," he stated firmly.

Janice looked curiously at Tobias, her expression slowly shifting to confusion.

"It was good to see you, Janice," Tobias said dismissively, his focus remaining outward.

Janice half-turned, looked from Mr. Griffin to Tobias.

"Yes, well," she said. "I will see you again; real soon."

Tobias gave a slight grin, took a long, quiet breath.

"But of course."

Tobias entered the estate's upstairs library. The room was high-ceilinged, with shelved walls, a cherry-wood desk and a leather chair; two high-back chairs sat in one corner beneath a single pole lamp. It wasn't a very large room, and all available space was filled with books.

Stepping up to a section of shelves along the left wall, Tobias reached up and casually pulled at a large book with the title "Creatures in Myth" stenciled on the spine. He heard the catch release, the sound coming from behind the shelves.

He pulled at the shelf section, exposing the access. Stepping through the opening, he felt along the wall on his left and flipped the switch. Three recessed ceiling lights lit up the room; a hallway, twelve feet wide and twenty feet long.

This was Tobias' Hall of Statues.

The six statues stood on short pedestals, three along each side wall, set about five feet apart. They reached nearly as high as the very high ceiling. Each was a unique species of dragon.

The six races of the Jahai.

Tobias walked down the middle of the hall between the statues. He turned left and entered his command center. There was a large, heavy desk near the far end of the room, facing the left wall. The only chair in the room was a large, leather chair behind the desk.

Stepping up to the paneled wall opposite the desk, Tobias pushed a horizontal wood strip to the accompanying sound of another click. He pushed open the hidden door and walked into the supply room.

When he came out a few minutes later, Mr. Griffin was standing beside the desk, waiting.

"Ah. Mr. Griffin." Tobias walked around the desk and dropped into the chair. "How goes the scuffle?"

"The scuffle, sir?"

"The fracas, the confrontation; the battle?"

"Yes, sir. It goes well enough, sir. So I understand. Minimal bloodshed, so I understand."

"Good, good," said Tobias. "I don't mean to make light. Anxiety showing through, I suppose."

"Yes sir."

"And Janice?" asked Tobias, looking up at Mr. Griffin.

"She has departed the estate and grounds."

Tobias could have sworn he saw the hint of a smirk on the face of the stoic Mr. Griffin.

"Good, good," he said again. "I imagine she'll be leaving our fair village soon enough, once reality has had a chance to settle in."

"I would imagine so," agreed Mr. Griffin.

"Which reminds me," said Tobias. "I'll need two week's rations put together."

Mr. Griffin glanced over at the supply room, again to Tobias.

"You are preparing to leave, Master Quigley?"

"That I am, Mr. Griffin; once the dust has settled here."

"Very good," said Mr. Griffin. "I shall advise Mrs. Hodges."

"Thank you." Tobias hesitated then, grew thoughtful. He leaned back in his chair. "The changes out there aren't done just yet, Mr. Griffin. There are the changes that I know are coming, and more yet that I don't. I don't like the not knowing part."

"Yes sir. Of course not, sir." Mr. Griffin took a step back. "I'll see to the rations."

"Thank you, Mr. Griffin."

Tobias watched Mr. Griffin leave the command center, then slowly turned about in his chair. Lost in thought for a minute, he absently glanced up at the old map that was hanging on the wall behind the desk. He gave the map a frown…

Well, that's' going to take some updating...

Jake didn't recognize this stretch of road, hadn't for a number of days now. He was walking well ahead of the others, quietly taking in the solitude of the landscape. The tall grass of the surrounding fields waved gently in the slight breeze.

Far up ahead, what Jake believed to be a wall of trees stretched across the distant horizon. At the moment it was little more than a smear of dark lying across their path.

They walked on. Another hour passed. The silhouette took on the form of a wall of forest. Another half hour and Jake could make out the individual trees.

He slowed his already easy pace. Meara stepped up beside him as he stopped.

"That's the Outland," he stated flatly.

"That's impossible," said Meara. She looked back behind them, along the road they had been traveling for days. "We left the Outland when we left the village."

"Sorry, Meara, but that's the Outland. The North Outland, I'd say."

"But—"

"There. Look." Jake was indicating a spire poking up above the treetops.

"A temple?" Meara asked haltingly.

"North Temple, my guess."

"The Lost Temple? But, how do you figure?"

"The temples are all in the Outland. That includes the North Temple. And I don't see those spires belonging to any of the other temples that we've been to."

"Well, yes sir, but… we've been traveling south," Meara insisted. "Always south. Now we're in the North Outland?"

"Soon will be."

"What, we've gone around the planet?" Meara asked, attempting humor. It fell flat.

"However it's happened, Meara, we're here." Jake gave a nod to the trees. "Serpent's Keep and everything you know is that way."

Meara considered, finally indicated the temple spires, ahead and some way to the right.

"If that's the Lost Temple…"

"Then that's where we need to go."

TahLyn continued to work her way up the switchback trail, her two Thrauhm companions trudging very awkwardly along behind her. Rays of sunlight streamed through the trees. The castle was still far above them, intermittently coming into and disappearing from view. The Lynhaur was gliding overhead, circling, watching and waiting.

The afternoon passed quietly; the only sounds were those of the Thrauhms dragging their feet along the trail and their heavy breathing.

Finally then, coming around another switchback, TahLyn suddenly found herself standing directly before the castle. A human stood at the top step, looking down at her, his hands clasped behind his back.

TahLyn moved across to stand at the base of the steps, eyes always on the human. The man was tall, had a thin face, startlingly bright eyes and smile, and long, salt-and-pepper hair. He was wearing loose pants and a long-sleeved shirt, soft shoes.

Aldwyn... the Ancient Guardian...

The Lynhaur dragon glided down from above, dropped down onto the porch a few yards from the Ancient Guardian. It spread its wings, closed them and tucked them along its sides. It shifted sideward then and settled in beside Aldwyn.

The Ancient Guardian acknowledged the Lynhaur, looked again to TahLyn, who continued to stand patiently at the foot of the steps.

"I am Aldwyn", stated the Guardian. "I bid welcome to you all."

"Thank you, Guardian. I am TahLyn." TahLyn indicated the others. "My traveling companions."

"My friends," Aldwyn nodded and smiled.

"We have traveled the Dark Path from the Jahai Village seeking the Ancient Guardian and his guidance."

"My my," said Aldwyn. "I am humbled, to be sure."

The large door behind Aldwyn opened and another human stepped out onto the porch. Corwin, the Ancient Guardian's assistant, was of average height, with pale skin, dark eyes and heavy brows. He was dressed in a heavy brown robe, similar to the garb of other monks that TahLyn had met.

He acknowledged the new arrivals by offering a slight bow, then spoke softly to Aldwyn.

"All is prepared," he said.

"Very good, Corwin," said Aldwyn. He spoke again to TahLyn. "Appropriate accommodations have been prepared for your associates, TahLyn." Aldwyn bowed first to the pair of Thrauhm, then half turned to the Lynhaur and gave a short nod. "Corwin will direct you."

"My pleasure," said Corwin.

"TahLyn," Aldwyn stated then, took a half step back and turned aside. He held out a welcoming hand. "This way, if you would."

Chapter Thirteen

Late afternoon was giving way to another warm dusk; a hint of orange lay across the west horizon at the edge of a near endless world of evergreen and alder and oak, a seemingly endless forest spreading out in all directions from the cluster of granite stones rising up from the forest floor.

Peter was sitting alone atop the Granite Mound, quietly eating his meal, spooning the thick stew from a large bowl. Three of his five traveling companions were sitting nearer the small campfire, finishing up their own early dinners. Another of the monks was standing on a small knob of rock at the far side of the hillock, looking outward.

John walked over to Peter. He sat beside him and set his empty bowl aside. He looked out at the approaching sunset.

"We made good time," he said, filling the silence.

"We did," said Peter. He spooned the last of his stew, sat the bowl beside him.

They could hear their companions behind them, shifting about near the fire pit as they ate their meals, talking quietly among themselves. The atmosphere atop the cluster of rocks was pleasant enough, almost comfortable.

"The weather has changed," John said then. He continued to look to the trees. They were for the most part just below or just at the level of the top of the surrounding canopy. "So still; the air is heavy."

"Hmm," Peter muffled absently. "Humid."

"It's almost like a whole different Outland."

Peter sensed that as well. Still, true as it was, he said nothing.

John brought his knees up, rested his elbows on them and clasped his hands, intertwining his fingers. He glanced back over his shoulder, turned forward again.

"It'll be good to get home."

"It will."

John shifted, adjusted his elbows resting on his knees.

"Master August knows of our temple," he said.

"So I understand."

"And of the village," said John. "And of Tobias Quigley."

"Uh, huh."

"How can that be? The Lost Monks..."

"That I do not know."

John shifted again, leaned further forward, kept his eyes forward."

"Could it be true?" he asked. "A relationship between the Lost Monks and the Ancient Guardian?"

Peter considered.

"Certainly possible," he said at last.

They fell into silence then, the quiet stretching out for half a minute. The sky overhead grew increasingly gray. John mumbled something about there being things to do, then reached for his bowl and stood up. He offered to take Peter's bowl.

Starting away, he suddenly hesitated as he looked outward. He took a halting step nearer the edge.

"Master Peter," he said softly, speaking over his shoulder.

Peter got to his feet and stepped over to stand beside John. He looked in the direction that John had indicated.

A rolling fog was drifting through the forest. It was a thick mist, roiling, rolling, plodding through the trees and encroaching upon the cluster of rocks on which they stood.

"I see," said Peter.

John stepped then to the very edge, looking down into the narrow clearing between trees and rock.

Something there... something in the fog; a darker shadow in the drifting shadows; it appeared to be the silhouette of a man.

"Master Peter?" John urged, not taking his eyes off the shadow.

Peter moved nearer the edge of rock, standing again beside John.

A young man stepped out of the fog. He took the few steps and stood then at the base of the rock wall. He was dressed in canvas pants, a heavy shirt and jacket; a small daypack was strapped to his back.

"That is most interesting," said Peter. He didn't recognize the boy, wondered silently whether he was from Serpent's Keep.

Ethan glanced up, saw the two monks looking down at him. He raised a hand uncertainly, gave a hesitant half wave in greeting.

The pedestrian thoroughfare of Serpent's Keep was eerily still, eerily quiet. The dull, gray evening lay heavily over the village, dampening all sound. A young man wearing a long tan leather coat moved cautiously three paces ahead of Janice, ever watchful for potential threats. None came.

The man turned into an alley. Janice reached the alley moments later and followed him in. The third of the small group, a young woman with long, matted hair and a flannel shirt followed Janice.

Janice had met up with the two only minutes earlier as she was working her way through side streets and back alleys toward the village's east gate and had continued on together.

They turned into a narrow passage and then stepped toward the gate at the end of the way. They approached a pair of guards, members of the civilian watch, who stood at the ready.

"Let us pass," Janice stated coolly.

"I think not, ma'am," said one of the guards.

"It's all done," said Janice. "Do you really want things to get ugly now, when all we want is to leave?"

"It's not our call, ma'am."

Janice looked from one to the other. Both were armed, though they kept their weapons holstered, hands resting casually on the handles. She wasn't armed herself, but her companions were. Both looked ready to act if called upon.

Janice hadn't expected to just walk out, but this looked as though it wasn't going to end well.

So be it. She had no intention of being held prisoner by the likes of simple villagers.

"All right, then." She prepared to signal her companions.

A sound came from behind her... shuffling, movement. Janice hesitated, as did those standing beside her.

"Let them go," came a woman's voice. It was calm but steady.

"Ma'am?" asked one of the guards.

"Open the gate."

"Yes, ma'am." The one guard signaled the other, who moved to open the gate.

Janice glanced back behind her. A woman stood in the center of the alleyway, two others stood behind her; all looked ready to respond as needed.

Janice gave a brief nod to the woman.

Wanda, the head of the civilian watch, did not respond. Her gaze was sharp, her expression firm, almost severe.

Whatever... thought Janice. She turned forward again. The gate was opening, the guards moving to either side. They gave her a cold look as they waited.

Janice stepped forward, walked between them; she ignored them as she stepped through the gate and out of the village, her companions following.

Wanda watched them leave. She gave a sharp nod to the guards. One closed the gate, the other lifted to wood crossbar into place.

A dark frown then, Wanda turned about and walked between the two watch members standing with her and left the alley.

Jake stood in the center of the Road, his hands stuffed into his jacket pockets. He was looking ahead at the wall of trees, the stand another thousand yards further on. The road ended at the forest wall. The sun had set just minutes earlier and the west horizon was painted in quickly fading orange. The landscape to either side of the dirt road lay in low, scrubby grass and weeds.

Meara and Mason stepped up beside Jake, the others of the team stopping a few yards behind him.

"I believe the answers we're looking for are in there," said Mason.

"Uh, huh," droned Meara. "And you have the questions all ready?"

"I have a general idea."

"Really?" Meara frowned.

"I do," Mason stated flatly. Then, "Our journey has certainly raised additional concerns, but my overall apprehensions remain the same, and so my questions."

He seemed quite satisfied with his response.

"Uh, huh," Meara droned again.

Jake had heard it all before and chose to stay out of the back and forth bantering. He looked up at the gray sky, then nodded to a wide spot in the road just ahead.

"We'll camp there tonight," he stated, then looked again to the wall of trees. "It'll be dark soon."

"Right," said Meara. "As good a place as any."

"We'll head in come morning."

Mason only grumbled assent, took a few steps out ahead of them and stood looking to the trees. Betty and Carlo moved off the road to begin setting up camp.

"Waddya think, sir?" asked Meara.

"About?"

"Mason," said Meara, looking curiously at Mason, standing silent, unmoving, studying the forest they would be going into in the morning.

"I've learned not to dismiss his observations out of hand," said Jake. He sensed Meara's raised brow and grinned. "I know. I sound like Sheriff Smith."

"Yes sir," Meara said softly. "Still, whether or not he knows the questions to ask, we could do with some answers."

Up ahead, Mason took another slow step forward, continued to study the increasing shadows moving about in the trees.

Meara set her plate aside, stood and walked up onto the road. She walked over to Jake, who was standing with his plate in hand, finishing his meal. He said nothing, and for a long minute neither did Meara.

"It sure is quiet," she said at last.

"I'd be surprised if it wasn't."

"Guess that's so."

They fell quiet again, another long minute passed.

Meara looked about them, curious, thinking...

"The outside," she said, quietly so as not to disturb the evening. "What's it like?"

"Outside?"

Meara indicated the distant horizon, as if there was something beyond. "The world out there, where you grew up."

"Ah." Jake considered, held out his empty plate and shook off what crumbs might remain. "Crowded big cities, towns small and big, sprawling corporate farms; lakes and mountains; oceans. Lots of oceans."

"Did you like it there?"

Jake shrugged. "Some, I guess. A lot of it was too crowded, a lot of it too noisy."

"That sounds... not so good."

"Some of it wasn't. But a lot of it was nice; really nice."

"Oh," said Meara, not totally convinced. "What about your family?"

"There was just my mom."

"Were you close?" Meara was close to her own mother.

"I guess so." Jake gave a shrug. "Being just her and me, you know. It was just kind of how it was."

"Yeah, I can see that." Meara appeared a bit uncomfortable, then. "So now, you know, not being able to home again."

"Serpent's Keep is home now," said Jake. He took a moment, considered. "Mom passed away a couple of years ago."

"I'm sorry."

"Yeah, well," Jake gave another shrug. "Like I said. Serpent's Keep is home now."

"And you have family here. Your uncle." She wondered then, "Master Quigley... your mom's brother?"

"No," said Jake. "I don't think so."

Meara waited for more, but Jake didn't offer any more.

"So..." Meara pointed, indicated the road ahead of them. "I think I'll take a walk."

Captain walked across the Farm's main compound to the larger of the barns. He worked his way around to the side of the barn and down to a side door set near the middle of the building. He glanced about before entering. All was calm and quiet; it was late evening, the sky was clear, gray and quickly growing darker.

The farm manager's office was sparsely furnished with a desk and chair, several guest chairs; one short file cabinet and a small table were against the back wall. A window near the door let in the fading evening light.

Captain stepped around the desk to the counter and poured himself a cup of coffee. He settled then into the desk chair, leaned back and took a deep swallow of the hot coffee.

He looked about the room, scowled.

This just wasn't him; an interesting diversion perhaps, but nothing more than that. He looked forward to handing this off to Janice and moving on. He would honor his obligations to the strange, crazy lady and provide support as agreed to, but Captain was ready to return home. Supplies had already been loaded onto several wagons in anticipation of his departure.

The door to the office opened and one of Captain's lieutenants came into the room. He stood at the desk and waited to be acknowledged.

Captain took another sip from his coffee, looked over the cup at the young man.

"What is it?" he asked.

"We have word from Serpent's Keep, Captain," he stated. "The assault did not go well."

Captain stared down at his coffee, leaned forward and set the cup onto the desk. He smirked, leaned back in his chair and rested his hands on his belly, intertwined his fingers.

"I expected nothing else," he said. His expression grew dark. "Did we lose many of our own?"

"Uncertain, Captain, but I do not believe so. A number are being held captive, many have withdrawn. We should have more information soon."

"Very well. Any news of our partner in crime?"

"The Rhetani woman? Not as yet, sir."

There was a knock at the door. It opened and a middle-aged woman took one short step into the room.

"You should come outside, Cap'n," she said. "Something ya' need to see."

She waited until she saw Captain lean forward and stand, then turned about and left the office. Captain and his lieutenant followed her outside.

Standing then in the center of the compound, the woman to his left and his lieutenant on his right, Captain took a long swallow of his coffee and looked out, across to the road that bordered the farm. It was lined with dozens of villagers and robed monks. They were simply standing there, shoulder to shoulder, as if waiting for some sign to move in.

"We are way outnumbered here," said the lieutenant.

"Uh, huh," Captain stated calmly. He took a final swallow of coffee. "The supply wagons?"

"Left some time ago. They are well away, Captain."

"All right." Captain looked about the compound, to the buildings, to the surrounding fields. He absently handed his empty cup to the lieutenant. "I think we're about done here."

"Yes sir," said the lieutenant.

Captain looked to his left, raised a brow to the woman.

"Yes, Cap'n," she agreed.

Chapter Fourteen

Darkness had closed in on the rock outcropping. The robed monks were gathered around several small campfires that were set in shallow depressions on the knoll's flat crown, the firelight reflecting against the silhouettes of the huddled figures. Peter and John were sitting at one of the fires with young Ethan, the boy from Serpent's Keep.

Ethan had been sent to the temple by the sheriff of the village, the sheriff seeking the help of the monks. Finding that Master Peter was not at the sanctuary, and hearing that the temple abbot had gone north, Ethan had decided on his own to follow after him.

Peter hadn't been surprised to hear of the assaults on the Farm and the village, but he did find it curious, and a bit disconcerting, to hear that the Rhetani had sought the assistance of bandits.

What must the Rhetani have been thinking to choose to dance with the devil?

Perhaps the number of Rhetani was much less than previously suspected. Perhaps very few had been caught up in the Outland reintegration and were now forever beyond the Outland. This was possible, as little was really known of the goings-on within the walls of the temple that had been occupied by the Rhetani, and it could very well be that there was only a handful of the cult here in the Outland.

If their numbers were in fact few, and in spite of this they had decided nonetheless to conduct a simultaneous assault on both the Farm and the village, they might indeed have felt they needed the assistance of the bandits.

Peter thought it to be a desperate move. Should they succeed, what did they believe would happen next? Peter foresaw nothing good for the Rhetani, the bandits being bandits and the Rhetani being Rhetani.

Not that it would ever come to that, with or without the assistance of the monks that the village sheriff was seeking. Serpent's Keep may have appeared vulnerable from the outside, but Peter knew that to be illusion. Given the devotion of the citizenry to their home and the actual configuration of the village itself, any attempt to take and then keep Serpent's Keep would be met with tremendous obstacles.

Peter looked across the fire to Ethan. The boy was quietly munching on dried fruit and nut mix as he stared into the flames. Peter had promised him that help was on the way and he seemed reassured by that.

William, the monk that Peter had left in charge of the temple, had certainly understood the situation just as Peter knew it to be, and he would have responded just as Peter would have. Help was no doubt on its way to the village farm, may even already be there.

Which brought to mind a question, one that John had been first to voice aloud.

Time. Distance. Something wasn't right.

How had Ethan reached Peter and his companions so quickly? He hadn't traveled nearly the distance from the temple that he should have. And he hadn't been on the trail nearly long enough.

Did the strange fog have something to do with that? How could that be possible?

"If I were to hazard a guess, I would say that the Outland has not fully settled," Peter had suggested.

"The landscape is reshaping, still forming? Reforming?" asked John.

"Perhaps," said Peter. "And perhaps time itself, as well."

"If that be so," John sighed thoughtfully. "Then I suppose I should be more mindful of my evening walks from now on. Who knows where I might end up?"

Perhaps we should all be mindful of the possibility of becoming separated, thought Peter.

"For the time being, let us stay within sight of one another," he agreed. "At least until we get home."

"As to that," considered John. "The rest of our journey may prove interesting."

"Indeed."

"I don't understand," said Ethan. "I had no problem."

"And neither shall we," said Peter. "We will be home before you know it."

"And then?" asked John.

"We shall review the situation and respond accordingly." Peter turned to Ethan. "All will be well, my young friend."

Ethan appeared comforted by that. A great weight had been lifted from his shoulders. The sheriff had given him an important task. That task, his mission, had been accomplished. He was content now to follow Master Peter's direction.

He looked forward to returning home.

An hour before dawn in Serpent's Keep, the world dark and still and quiet. The Quigley mansion was a shadowy black form along the heavily shadowed side street. Within its walls, the rooms and halls of the mansion silently waited for morning.

The kitchen was lit by one of the light fixtures that were set in the high ceiling. Tobias stood at the island counter, just finishing putting supplies into his backpack.

Mrs. Hodges, dressed in a thick, fluffy robe, handed him a brown paper bag.

"Your breakfast," she stated matter-of-factly.

"Thank you, Mrs. Hodges." He took the bag, rolled it and stuffed it into one of the side pockets of the backpack.

"Will you be meeting up with young Jacob, Master Quigley?" asked Mrs. Hodges. She was worried about Jake and Meara, though she tried not to show it.

"I don't think so. I'm afraid he's gone in one direction, while I will be heading in another altogether." Tobias closed the backpack and fastened the clasps. He lifted the backpack from the counter.

"I see," said Mrs. Hodges.

Tobias sensed her concern, then. For Mrs. Hodges, Jake would always be the little boy forever getting underfoot all those summers ago.

"He'll be fine, Mrs. Hodges," he said. "I have no doubt of that."

"I'm sure he will," she answered, perhaps too firmly. She managed a slight smile then. "Meara is watching over him."

"There. You see?" Tobias slipped a backpack strap over one shoulder. "I'm off then."

"So you are." Mrs. Hodges folded her arms across her chest.

Tobias reached out with his free hand, rested it comforting on her arm. He gave her a sympathetic smile.

"And as for me, madam; just another stroll in the wilderness." He stepped away and started toward the archway leading out of the kitchen.

Mrs. Hodges spoke softly after him, "The world isn't what it once was, Master Tobias."

"All the more reason to do a little exploring, my dear," he called back over his shoulder. He stepped through the archway, walked quietly from the back of the house and into the front foyer. The room was dimly lit.

Mr. Griffin came out of his room, tying the belt of his housecoat.

"On your way I see, sir," he said.

"I am." Tobias turned to look back at Griffin as he slipped fully into his small backpack. "You take care of things."

"It is what I do."

"That it is." Tobias turned and started again to the front door. "A sharper eye, my friend. As was recently pointed out to me, the world is not what it once was."

"Yes sir." Mr. Griffin stood unmoving, two steps from the door to his rooms. "Enjoy yourself, sir."

"Thank you, Mr. Griffin. I'm sure I will."

§

Jake and his traveling companions stood at the Road's end. The forest wall was up ahead, beyond a meadow of grass and wildflowers. It was just past dawn, the sun rising above the horizon on their left, spreading dawn colors across the meadow.

As inviting as this looked, it only reminded Jake once again that they were definitely no longer traveling the route from the outside world to the village, those summer bus trips he had taken as a child.

He readied to start across the meadow.

Meara placed a hand on Jake's arm. "Uh… what's that?"

Thin streams of fog began creeping out from the trees. The fog grew thicker as it gently rolled across the meadow toward Jake and the others.

"You don't see that every day," said Jake.

"It's about what I would expect, all things considered," said Meara.

"It's a sign," said Mason.

"A sign of what?" asked Meara, with more than a hint of irritation.

"We are being called," said Mason. "What we seek lay within."

"Right." Meara was growing annoyed with Mason's cryptic comments that took them nowhere they wouldn't be going in any case.

"Good to know," mumbled Jake. He took a long, deep breath. "Shall we?"

"Sure," grumbled Meara. "Why not?"

The others stepped up beside Jake and Meara, each giving a strong nod to Jake.

"All right, then," said Jake. He stepped forward, led his companions across the meadow, into the fog and into the forest.

TahLyn followed Aldwyn's assistant down one hallway and then another. Corwin was patient and yet insistent, pausing to wait for her at one turn and then another. For her part, TahLyn had never felt so uncomfortable. Passageways such as this were very oppressive to her.

Why do humans create such things?

She stepped from yet another passage and into a large foyer. There were a number of closed doors along the walls. Corwin stood before a set of large, heavy double doors, again waiting patiently for TahLyn. He turned then and pushed down on the wooden handles and pushed open the doors. He stepped through and stood to one side, allowing TahLyn to enter the room beyond.

It was a round chamber, forty feet across, with russet-brown stone walls and a domed ceiling. Several chairs and side tables were set against the wall to TahLyn's left, beside a set of French doors leading outside. Light spilled onto the chamber floor from the doors' inset windows.

Aldwyn was standing before the main feature in the room, what at first suggested to TahLyn a thin curtain of water, four feet across and seven feet tall. It hung midair in the middle of the chamber, two feet above the floor. It was half an inch thick. It shimmered and sparkled.

Aldwyn looked back at TahLyn, gave her a soft smile. He turned again, facing the portal, moved around the portal and looked back through it to TahLyn.

"A window on the universe," he said. He lifted a hand and gave a gentle wave, the portal shimmered and cleared. An image appeared... the open plain that TahLyn and her companions had traveled. The cloudless sky was a bright blue. He waved again, the image faded and a moment later a new one appeared; a forest canopy, the green spreading out as far as could be seen.

"You can travel where you wish?" asked TahLyn.

"Sadly, no. It is a viewing portal only." Aldwyn moved around the portal and approached TahLyn. Behind him, the portal again took on the appearance of a thin curtain of water.

"Friend TahLyn," he said then. "You are rested from your journey?"

"I am quite well, Guardian," said TahLyn. "Thank you for your hospitality."

"You are quite welcome," said Aldwyn. "And I do apologize for not being more attentive to my guests. Busy, busy, you know. I trust Corwin has stood well in my stead?"

TahLyn gave an acknowledging nod to Corwin, who was standing silent near the door. "He has been most courteous."

"Very good," said Aldwyn, walking to the chairs and side tables that were set against the wall near the French doors. He poured water from a decanter into a tall glass.

"Water?" he asked.

"No thank you."

"Nature's tonic." Aldwyn took a long drink and set the glass back onto the table. "So. Your quarters. Satisfactory? Please, if you need anything, do not hesitate to ask."

Individual quarters had been prepared specific to the needs of each of the three Jahai species. TahLyn's room was surprisingly similar to her dwelling back home, a high-ceilinged, dome-like room with no furniture to get in the way. Once settled in, she had visited the two Thrauhm and the Lynhaur. Their quarters likewise met their needs, the Lynhaur's quarters being similar to a shallow, cave-like room that opened to a plaza; the Thrauhm quarters were almost cavern-like, also opening to the same plaza.

"There is nothing more we could ask for, Guardian," she said. She bowed her head first to Aldwyn, then to Corwin. "We are humbled by such thoughtfulness."

"We could do nothing less, friend." Aldwyn stepped to the French doors, opened them. "Walk with me, please."

TahLyn followed the Ancient Guardian outside. It was good to be in the open once again. They followed a gravel walkway out to the middle of the garden, where Aldwyn stopped; he looked up at the clear sky, seemed momentarily lost in thought.

TahLyn was content to wait, content to stand silent under the open sky.

Aldwyn turned finally then to his guest. He asked of the Jahai village, suggesting that he knew of the purpose of TahLyn's journey, her reason for seeking the Ancient Guardian.

TahLyn took a moment to try to organize her thoughts, began then awkwardly stumbling through trying to explain that while those within the village were doing well enough, the village itself was... all alone. She quickly tried to describe what was happening to the Outland.

Aldwyn calmly held up a quieting hand.

He let TahLyn know that he knew of the situation regarding the Outland. He asked then for more information regarding the Jahai village, of its relationship with the Dark Path. He asked about Natan, leader of the Jahai.

TahLyn was warmed by the curiosity of the Ancient Guardian. It was clear to her that the Ancient Guardian was quite familiar with the Jahai, and more than that, that he cared for their wellbeing. She did her best to satisfactorily respond to all of his questions.

"Can you help us, Guardian?" she asked then. "We are alone. Threads along the Dark Path are broken. We have been unable to find a thread from the village to our fellows. Can you help us?"

Such threads no longer existed, and any threads that did remain were torn and frayed and unreliable. It was not in Aldwyn's power to repair such passageways. And while there might be someone out there who may hold the secret to redirecting or repurposing threads to connect to new gateways, such was not within Aldwyn's abilities, even if one could be repaired.

Not that all was lost to the Jahai village. While they would in all likelihood not soon see their home worlds, they need not remain alone.

It was not certain, but it may be possible for the village to come home to the Outland.

"Can you do this?" asked TahLyn.

There had been a number of issues with the reintegration of the Outland. This, Aldwyn had observed from the first. He had attempted to make minor corrections of his own, but his abilities, trained as he had been by those who had come before him, were in fact quite limited.

And then had come the isolation of the reintegrated Outland, suddenly separated from all that was *out there,* all that lay beyond. Upon witnessing this, Aldwyn found it easier to implement minor additional corrections, smoothing the rough edges of the Outland.

As yet, the Dark Path and Aldwyn's castle remained separate from the Outland, though the Outland was within reach of his viewing portal. The Jahai village, with its own tenuous connection to the Dark Path, was also beyond the Outland.

Not a part of the Outland and yet apart from the outside world, they appeared to exist in a realm all their own.

"We are in this together, friend TahLyn," said Aldwyn. "Together we will join with our fellows in the Outland, or together we will build our world here. In either case, the Jahai village is not alone."

Chapter Fifteen

Janice stepped out onto the smooth surface, a narrow ribbon of ancient roadway covered in a coarse yellow-green grass; sixty feet wide, smooth and straight, it ran east to west as far as the eye could see.

Her two companions moved up beside her.

"Isn't this the North Highway?" asked Devon, the younger of two.

That it is, Janice thought, though she said nothing.

It wasn't the same stretch of the highway that they were all familiar with, but it was definitely the North Highway.

"But... we crossed the North Highway two days ago," said Peg. She was considerably older than Devon, and a few years older than Janice. Her hair had gone salt and pepper over the last few months.

"That we did," said Janice.

"Then where is our sanctuary?" Peg looked back into the woods, from where they had come, as if she could somehow find the answer there.

They should certainly have reached their temple by now. They had noted changes to the landscape some ways back, and had continued to travel the direction that should have taken them home. Janice didn't believe they were lost, but had quickly come to realize that they were not where they thought they were, that the temple was not where it used to be, where it was supposed to be.

There were some major modifications going on, shifting in both landscape and time.

Nonetheless, Janice was still surprised to come upon the North Highway a second time.

"Interesting," she mumbled, mostly to herself.

Her traveling companions, both having escaped the village with her, appeared particularly shaken by recent events. Janice didn't know either of them very well. While they were both lifelong Rhetani, they had only recently arrived at Janice's temple.

"What do we do now?" asked Devon.

Janice looked across the roadway. The thick forest beyond was set back from the highway some thirty or forty feet. She looked then to their right and studied the ribbon of highway running to the vanishing point far in the distance. She looked to the left then. It was much the same; empty, somehow drawing her in.

She started left, began walking down the center of the North Highway.

"Janice?" Devon asked, prompting. "Where are we going?"

Janice didn't answer. She kept an easy, steady pace. Devon and Peg followed. They walked in silence for some time. It was some minutes later that Janice noticed a faint shimmering far, far ahead. She continued walking, though her pace began to slow.

Another two minutes and the horizon grayed, a misty flowing swirl; a fog was slowly creeping out from the horizon and crawling along the highway toward them.

Janice stopped, Peg stepped up beside her. Devon took an extra step ahead of them, frowning.

"What is that?" he asked.

Peg only gave a soft *hmmph* in answer.

"Yes," said Janice, looking to Peg. She moved up then and placed a hand on Devon's shoulder. "I think that's something I'd like to check out," she said.

A fog, faintly aglow with the midday sun, drifted across the landscape. It slowly thinned to a heavy mist, revealing a forest, a clearing, and the thin band of grass-covered highway, smooth and straight, reaching to either horizon.

Meara stepped out of the trees and started across the clearing. Mason was half a dozen steps behind Meara, Jake and the others not far behind. Reaching the highway, they stood together on the grassy-covered band of roadway.

"Curiouser and curiouser," mumbled Jake, looking west then east.

The others looked questioning at Jake.

"Yes," said Mason, agreeing with the observation while not knowing the source of the phrase. He could see, as they all could see, that this was the North Highway, though no one recognized this particular stretch of the road.

"No. No, this isn't right," said Carlo. "I don't care how twisted the Outland got, or how we ended up north when we traveled nothin' but south, we shouldn't be anywhere near the North Highway."

"Our world continues to reshape itself," said Mason. This may not have been what he had been expecting when he insisted they journey the Road in search of he knew not what, but it was certainly a good to know...

"Yes," said Jake. He looked curiously at Mason. "Are you thinking...?"

"Just a thought."

"What is it?" asked Meara. She considered a moment, and then, "Oh. I see."

"Well I don't," said Carlo.

"Neither do I," said Betty.

Meara waited for Jake or Mason to speak up. Neither did. Meara turned to Carlo and Betty.

"The question is... are these continuing changes the result of the original reintegration of the Outland, or are they guided by the unseen hand of someone else?"

She looked to Jake for confirmation. He gave a curt nod. She stepped then away from the group, again looked one direction and then the other. She half turned back to the others.

"Pick a direction," she stated.

Jake stepped forward, moving past Meara. He looked back to Meara, then Mason. Mason stepped up beside him. A silent moment passed, then both simultaneously indicated east.

She walked around them and led the way east, grumbling, "Well, that's just weird."

Corwin stepped out onto the castle's front porch and moved up beside Aldwyn. He stood silent, waiting for a sign of acknowledgement. Aldwyn was lost in thought, his gaze taking him out to the world before them. The open plain stretched out from the base of the mountain range; the Dark Path was out there somewhere.

"Our guests?" asked Alwyn at last, continuing to look outward.

"All are well," said Corwin. The Thrauhm were in fact quite comfortable, content to remain in their quarters until they were needed. The Lynhaur spent as much time on the wing as in the castle.

TahLyn, the young Bentai, did seem anxious to return home with the news that she had found Aldwyn, that they were not alone, that Aldwyn knew of their plight, that he cared and that he intended to help.

Movement caught Corwin's attention and he glanced up. The Lynhaur was circling above, hundreds of feet overhead. It glided outward, away from the mountains and out over the plain.

"Will you be able to do something for them?" asked Corwin.

"I'm working on it," said Aldwyn. In point of fact, his struggles to make even the most minor of corrections to the issues resulting from the reintegration of the Outland were limited to pushing forward those changes that had previously been initiated but were not yet fully realized.

It was not within his abilities to recreate a passage to the Jahai home worlds. The young Bentai had accepted that. But Aldwyn believed that it might be possible, that it was within his capabilities, to find a frayed passageway on the Dark Path that connects to a landing in the Outland and, while not repair it, at a minimum smooth the frays and restore some reliability.

"And by assisting the Jahai, what of our own isolation?" asked Corwin.

Aldwyn and Corwin had lived in near isolation for years, and Aldwyn was forever tied to the castle that lay at the end of the Dark Path. But there had previously existed numerous threads stretching out from the Dark Path to all quadrants and corners of the web. This had been lost of late, and so had nearly blinded Aldwyn, leaving him with only fragmented and unreliable images of what lay out there.

A single stable thread from the Dark Path to any landing in the Outland would restore at least some sense of normalcy and go a long way to restoring Aldwyn's windows.

"I'm working on it," Aldwyn said again, now almost a whisper.

Tobias was standing on the front porch of the temple, his backpack resting at his feet. He looked up into the clear sky, then out to the trailhead of the path leading back to Serpent's Keep.

He was unsure now of the direction to take.

There were only a few monks remaining in the temple behind him. According to William, the monk that had been left in temporary charge of the sanctuary, Master Peter had gone in search of the North Temple with a small group of fellow monks, while others of the brothers had gone to the Farm to help defend against the bandits.

The temple monks had been called upon more than once over the centuries to stand against those who would do wrong, whether in defense of their own or to protect those in need. Tobias Quigley had stood with them more than once.

It would be a mistake to underestimate their abilities.

The door behind Tobias opened and William came out onto the porch. He handed Tobias a rolled scroll, a copy of the map that had been prepared for Master Peter.

"Thank you, William," said Tobias. He knelt and slipped the scroll into a side pocket of his backpack.

"Master Peter should be returning before long," said William. He had already explained that word had been sent to Peter with news of what had been happening. "You are welcome to wait."

"I thank you, but I best be off." Tobias lifted his backpack and moved to the top step.

"As you wish, sir."

"I appreciate all your help." Tobias slipped his arms through the backpack straps.

"Our pleasure," said William. "Be well, Tobias Quigley."

Tobias gave a nod in answer, started down the steps. Working his way across the clearing, he decided that he would need to stop by the Farm and ensure that all was well before continuing on to the North Temple.

He looked back once to the temple before entering the surrounding woods, gave another nod to the monk standing at the top of the steps.

Sheriff Smith stood in front of the Farm's main barn. He looked out beyond the compound and the cultivated fields to the dirt road running alongside the farm. A large group of monks were walking along the road, on their way back to their temple.

He looked then about the compound. The world was strangely quiet, the old normal for the farm.

The farm manager came out of the barn.

"Sheriff," said Charles. "I thought you had already started back."

"Just about." He sensed movement and looked to his right. He saw a small group of villagers and monks just disappearing between two of the buildings.

They were part of a contingent of villagers and monks that were remaining at the Farm, both to help restore things and to be there and ready should the bandits decide to return. They had been driven off, but they may have gotten a taste for fresh fruit and vegetables and decide that it was worth the cost to make another visit.

Charles looked back at what had drawn the sheriff's attention. He gave an approving nod to the work going on.

"It won't be long," he said. "We'll have things back on track."

"Of that I'm sure. Did we lose much?"

"We'll be supplementing from stores for a few months, but we'll be all right." Charles gave another nod then in the direction of the sound of hammering just coming from behind the barn. "And we're putting together a couple of new wagons.

"Let me know if you need any more help." Sheriff Smith held out his hand. Charles took it and they shook. "I'll let the folks back home know how the farm is faring."

"Tell them not to worry," said Charles.

"I'll do that." Sheriff Smith started away, toward the road.

Charles called after him. "We got off easy this time, Sheriff. Injuries and all," he said. "It could be worse next time; could be a lot worse."

The sheriff gave only a slow nod of acknowledgement, turned away and started again for the road and home.

Chapter Sixteen

Master Peter called for a brief halt, the group having been hiking steadily since their midday lunch break. He sent one of his brother monks ahead a hundred paces to stand watch, another to backtrack along their path the same distance.

The Outland forest floor they traveled was little changed since leaving the North Temple some two days earlier. The canopy overhead would let sunlight stream through and then would not. The forest was quiet but for the occasional sounds of birds in the trees, small animals scurrying about the mulchy floor. The strange fog would appear, would drift through the trees and then slowly fade.

The young man Ethan had been quiet for most of the journey. He had commented to Master Peter as an aside several times that the way they traveled appeared not to be the same as his travel out, but acknowledged that he might be mistaken.

Peter looked over now at the boy. Ethan was sitting off by himself, his back to a tree. The other brother monks were sitting together some few yards away.

John returned from a short foray through their surroundings.

"All's quiet," he said, stepping up beside Peter.

"Thank you, John."

One of the two monks sent to stand watch up ahead returned, stopping when within comfortable speaking distance.

"You might want to come have a look at this, Master Peter."

"What have you found, brother?"

"It looks like some changes in the forest going forward... I don't want to get too far ahead on my own."

That being the case, Peter called the brothers standing rear watch back and the group moved out together, the afternoon break ending a minute or two earlier than planned.

Peter began noting a change after only a few dozen yards, a thinning of the forest further ahead, a brightening of the canopy. They met the second of the monks sent ahead and continued then, Peter walking in front.

The trees stood farther apart here, the trunks were more slender and lighter in color. The canopy was ever thinner, with fewer leaves clinging to spindly branches.

Fog began to form again up ahead, drifting in and about amongst the trees. It rolled slowly across the forest floor toward the group of travelers.

And then Peter came out of the trees and stepped onto a wide band of yellow-green grass that cut across the Outland as a ribbon of roadway sixty feet wide, smooth and straight, as far as Peter could see.

The others of the group followed him out onto the roadway. The sky was clear and bright blue, the slight breeze was warm.

"I suppose we should have expected something like this," said Peter. "But I didn't."

Brother John stood in the middle of grassy road, casting his eyes to the east. "This can't be."

"Oh, but it can," said Peter.

"We shouldn't be anywhere near the North Highway," said another of the monks.

"And yet, it is so."

Ethan was standing a few yards ahead of John. He lifted a hand and pointed.

"Look," he mumbled.

There was a shifting of shadows up ahead, where the highway met the horizon. Moments later then, the shadows took on the form of the silhouettes of people walking the North Highway.

§

Corwin stood atop the front steps, watched as TahLyn led the two Thrauhm downslope, away from the castle, to the trailhead below and into the trail that would take them down the mountainside and eventually onto the plain beyond. For the Thrauhm Jahai, it would be a lumbering, awkward hike down the steep, winding switchback down the mountain.

The three Jahai entered the trailhead and disappeared into the trees. Corwin lifted his gaze then to the sky, looking for the Lynhaur. The winged Jahai was nowhere to be seen, was probably in the low clouds that were hovering above the plain, drifting in an unseen breeze. The shadows of the clouds were scurrying across the landscape below.

Corwin turned about and started through the doors... there was work to do. The castle wouldn't clean itself.

First though, he was to report the departure of the Jahai to Aldwyn.

He entered the dome-ceilinged viewing room. Bright daylight was splashing across the floors and walls. Aldwyn was moving in slow circles around the portal window. His movements were smooth, instinctive. He was physically present, but his mind was somewhere else, somewhere distant.

Corwin always sensed something sorcerer-like about the Ancient Guardian when he was lost in such episodes. Aldwyn tended to play down his abilities, but Corwin had witnessed near mystical accomplishments many times over the years. Understanding that science underlay Aldwyn's powers did not make them any less incredible to Corwin.

Corwin moved off to one side to wait. He watched in silence as Aldwyn continued to slowly circle the portal, the Ancient Guardian's senses, powers and energies focused completely on the portal, merging with the powers of the portal, slowly becoming one with whatever mysteries lay deep in the heart of the portal.

The Ancient Guardian was far from this room, far from this castle.

Within the window portal, swirling images faded in and out, appearing and disappearing, shadowy tableaus drifting from one setting to the next. Barren landscapes, windswept plains, rolling hills blanketed in green forest.

A group of humans gathered along a ribbon of grass-covered roadway.

The last image faded...

Corwin saw then the haunting, shadowy image of Aldwyn's silhouette through the watery curtain of the portal window.

Chapter Seventeen

There wasn't a cloud in the sky.

Meara couldn't remember the last time the sky had been so clear, so blue; weeks at least, maybe months. And warm. The day was warm. Not the slightest breeze, making the afternoon all the warmer.

The group ahead continued to approach, walking toward them along the North Highway. There were at least half a dozen of them, still too far away for Meara to note any of their features.

"Warm day," she said, giving a brief side-glance to Jake, standing beside her. The others of their party were standing behind them, shuffling apprehensively.

Jake glanced up at the sky, returned his attention to the approaching group. Their silhouettes shimmered in the heat. "I expect it'll get warmer before the day is done," he said.

"I can't remember the last time it was so warm," said Meara. "The air is so still."

Behind them, Mason took half a step nearer. "It's the whole world," he said. "The whole world is still. And quiet."

"Uh, huh," said Jake.

The approaching group drew nearer, walking at a cautious, steady pace. Meara could see now that most of them were dressed in monks' robes.

She recognized the two walking in front.

"It's Master Peter," she stated. "And John."

"So I see," said Jake. He saw then that one in the group was dressed in simple shirt and pants, a light jacket. He thought he recognized him... a kid from Serpent's Keep.

Meara recognized him too. "Ethan is with them," she said.

Right... Ethan, thought Jake. *Kid brother of one of the women of the watch.*

"I wonder how he ended up way out here with a bunch of monks," he said.

Mason stepped up beside Jake and Meara.

"I gotta wonder what the monks are doing out here at all," he said.

"They're monks," Jake said frankly. "Monks do whatever it is that monks do."

Mason frowned at that, but then gave a nod. "Expect that's true."

"Still," Jake sighed. "Be interesting to find out if they're out here for the same reason we're out here."

"Where they're coming from," said Mason.

"And if they've been seeing what we've been seeing," agreed Meara.

"Yes," said Jake. "That to."

The evening brought no relief from the heat. The air weighed heavy, the world was as still and as silent as ever. Master Peter and Jake stood apart from the simple camp that had been established. Behind them, Meara was in quiet conversation with Brother John, with Ethan close by, having attached himself to Meara.

The other monks were gathered in two groups to one side of the campsite, while the others of Jake's team had settled in near the small campfire, Carlo heating a pot of stew over the glowing coals.

"Most interesting indeed," said Peter. "Most."

"Just plain peculiar, you ask me," said Jake.

"I no longer consider any of recent events to be peculiar." Peter grinned, shook his head. "That your journey south should deliver you here is almost to be expected these days."

"And interesting..." Jake mumbled, quiet sarcasm.

"Exactly."

Jake considered, looked then back the way they had come, forward then up the North Highway from where Peter and his group had come. He gave Peter a questioning look.

"And if we went back that way, the way we came? Or if you returned where you came from? What do you suppose we'd find?"

"Ah," Peter said thoughtfully. "Now there is an interesting mental exercise."

"Uh, huh. Interesting."

Peter and Jake turned then at Meara's approach.

"Carlo says the stew's ready," she stated.

"Excellent," said Peter. He looked over to the center of the camp. Ethan was standing near the fire, looking in their direction. "You seem to have made a friend, Meara."

"I'm a familiar face," she said matter-of-factly. "Someone from home."

"Of course," said Peter.

"An island in the storm," said Jake.

Meara clearly didn't recognize the phrase, gave a half-hearted *uh, huh*, gave a nod back toward the campfire.

"Whenever you're ready," she said, turned away and started back.

Jake looked about them, looked back along the North Highway.

"You're heading home, then?" he asked Peter. Both were concerned about the attacks that Ethan had described to Peter.

"That's the plan."

"Assuming it's still there."

"Oh, it's still there, Jacob," said Peter confidently. "You have said as much in describing your experiences. Our combined observations only confirm it."

"The reintegrated Outland is doing a bit of ongoing reshaping..."

"As best we can comprehend what we are witnessing. It is quite beyond human experience, after all."

"Right," Jake sighed. He again considered. "And since Serpent's Keep, and your temple, are both in the heart of the Outland..."

"And as we are most assuredly in the Outland..."

"Then they should be here and we should be able to get to them."

"Exactly," said Peter. He pointed south. "That way."

Jake turned his gaze in the direction that Peter indicated.

"Right," he said again, not at all confident.

"Would you care to join us on our little hike?" asked Peter, grinning.

Aldwyn wore a pallid look, his skin pale, his eyes opaque, his expression distant. His right hand was raised, his fingertips just touching the thin veil of the window portal. The watery curtain reflected against his silhouette, the silk of his long robe iridescent.

The image within the portal shimmered and wavered, waned and then coalesced. TahLyn was walking the Dark Path; her Thrauhm companions followed behind her, one behind the other. The Lynhaur was nowhere to be seen, was likely on the wing above.

They approached the gateway, a passage entrance, distinct from any milestone they may have seen en route to now. It manifested no solid form. It was rather a wavering of the atmosphere along the path. The path beyond the threshold was visible and yet indistinct.

TahLyn slowed her pace, stepped cautiously nearer and then stopped. She was drawn to the entrance, sensing that this gateway was something different.

This could be it. This could be the way.

The flying dragon appeared in the image, settling down near TahLyn. It folded its wings and stepped closer.

TahLyn looked to the Lynhaur, then back to the two Thrauhm. She gave an almost human-like half-bow of her large, heavy head and looked forward again to the threshold.

In the castle of the Ancient Guardian, in the round viewing room, Aldwyn stood before the window portal.

He slowly lowered his hand to his side.

§

TahLyn stood atop the ridge with her companions. The gentle slope fell away down to a thinly wooded forest of oak and alder and evergreen. Broken building spires rose up from a shallow basin just beyond the trees. Nestled in the basin was the temple ruin.

Even at this distance, TahLyn could see a number of Jahai moving about among the jagged outlines of broken walls.

The temple... thought TahLyn. *Lamal's temple...*

She turned slowly about. The wooded landscape stretched out in all directions as far as she could see.

The Outland... she thought, not yet ready to voice the words aloud. *This is the Outland.*

She turned forward again, looked across to the temple ruin.

The Lynhaur stepped awkwardly forward, stood beside her.

"Many Jahai," it said.

Both of the Thrauhm grumbled and growled agreement. "Jahai."

TahLyn saw then a winged silhouette in the distant sky, approaching from the left. It glided in and began circling about high above the temple.

"Lamal," said TahLyn, speaking aloud for the first time since their arrival.

"Lamal," agreed the Lynhaur. It worked its wings against its sides.

TahLyn looked briefly to the Lynhaur, quietly noting its eagerness.

"Go, friend," she stated. "Speak with Lamal."

"I go."

The Lynhaur stepped to one side, stepped forward and readied its wings. Leaning forward, it took several hurried steps as it spread its wings and lifted from the ground, into the air.

TahLyn watched a moment, then again looked about.

The gateway was there, several yards behind the pair of Thrauhm, little more than a disturbance in the air, the threshold a gentle shimmer of the atmosphere.

A doorway between the Dark Path and the Outland.

We are no longer alone, thought TahLyn. *The village is not alone.*

She looked over at the Thrauhm. They were obediently standing by, though barely able to contain their enthusiasm, looking to the ruin and their fellow Thrauhm.

"Soon," she said to them. "We first have a task to complete."

They shifted their weight from one foot to another.

They awaited instructions.

"Find stones, this size," she said, holding her clawed hands before her, a foot apart. She pointed then. "We must build a marker there, by the gateway."

The Thrauhm went quickly about their task. While she waited, TahLyn considered their next actions. She would need to return to the Dark Path and then on to the village as soon as possible. Natan must be told. The Jahai leader would be pleased. TahLyn had reached the end of the Dark Path. TahLyn had found the Ancient Guardian.

The Ancient Guardian was a friend to the Jahai.

Perhaps this was not a path between their village and their Jahai home worlds, but it was good news nonetheless.

The Ancient Guardian had given them a passageway between the Dark Path and the Outland, a path from the Jahai Village to Lamal's temple.

They were no longer alone.

Tobias followed the small group of monks into the clearing and started across toward the front steps of the North Temple. They stopped as another monk, coming through the front doors, descended the steps and indicated the path leading around the sanctuary's main building.

Tobias gave a silent thank you nod to his escort and followed the monk. The path led to a narrow gate opening into the garden. Stepping aside, the monk held a hand out for Tobias to enter.

Tobias found Master August kneeling before a raised garden bed, weeding. Seeing Tobias, the abbot stood and brushed the dirt from his hands.

"Ah! Hello! My dear friend Tobias!" he said. He rubbed his right hand on his robes and held it out.

"And hello to you, August," said Tobias, shaking the monk's hand. "You are looking well."

"As are you," said August. "Perhaps a bit gray about the edges."

"You are too kind."

"I am seldom accused of that, friend." August indicated the bench nearby and they sat down. "Tobias, how was your journey?"

"Uneventful," said Tobias. He glanced about. "The garden is little changed; as pleasant as ever."

"But a few seasons have passed since your last visit, Tobias." August gave a slight, knowing grin. "Though I understand that quite a bit more time has passed *out there.*"

"And now we come back to my showing gray about the edges," said Tobias.

"Oh, not so gray as to reflect the passage of years that I've been advised of," said August. "And therefore such evidence would suggest to me that you've done some moving about, perhaps taken advantage of the web."

Tobias looked down at his hands, rubbed his palms and clasped his hands together.

"Quite so, friend August," he sighed. He sat back. "Quite so."

August slid back then and rested an arm on the back of the bench.

"So... we are returned to the Outland," he said matter-of-factly. "The Outland... coming together again after all these years."

"That is so. And then some."

"From what I understand, there is as yet some significant settling going on."

"That is true as well," said Tobias. "Which is causing some confusion and some frayed nerves among the populace."

Master August gave a few thoughtful nods. He brought his arm down. "Would this settling of the landscape be an ongoing part of the reintegration process? Or might there be some external influence at play here?"

"Ah... you perhaps refer to our friend Aldwyn."

"He has crossed my mind," said August. "Have you seen him recently?"

"Some time back; not since all of this." Tobias turned to look at his friend. It was as if they hadn't been apart at all, and at the same time at been apart for decades. "I take it you haven't talked with him?"

"I have not. Not since... *this,*" said August, indicating the garden and the North Temple. He gave the hint of a smirk. "A bit more than a few seasons," he said.

Tobias gave a light chuckle. He leaned forward then and stood. He stepped away from the bench.

"You appear to have done well," he said.

"Well enough." August again rested an arm on the back of the bench. "You?"

Tobias thought of his answer for a long time, spoke then without looking back at his long-lost friend.

"Duties performed, responsibilities met," he said quietly. "A life well lived, with few regrets."

"And what of Janice?" asked August.

"Well... there may have been a disappointment or two along the way." Tobias looked back over his shoulder, forward again. "As I said, a few regrets."

Chapter Eighteen

Mrs. Hodges filled a small thermos with milk from the fridge; she wrapped her sandwich in wax paper. Leaving the estate, she walked across the street and through the park's wide side gate. Seeing Mr. Griffin, she walked across the park and stood across the picnic table.

"Mind if I join you?" she asked. She sat then, not waiting for him to answer.

He gave a brief welcoming nod as he continued selecting pieces from his cup of trail mix, steadily eating one after the other.

Mrs. Hodges looked about them. It was a pleasant afternoon; there were a number of people in the park.

"A lovely day," she said.

"Yes," said Mr. Griffin. He ate his trail mix as he watched Mrs. Hodges pour milk from her thermos, then methodically unwrap her sandwich. She meticulously smoothed out the wax paper.

They ate in silence for several minutes. Mr. Griffin picked at his trail mix. Mrs. Hodges ate her sandwich and drank her milk. The sounds of children playing drifted across the sprawling lawns of the park.

Mrs. Hodges pulled a napkin from her pocket and wiped at the corner of her mouth. She carefully folded the wax paper that had been used to wrap her sandwich, slipped it into her pocket. She took the napkin then and wiped the inside of the cup, returned the cup to the thermos.

She set the thermos aside. She looked to Mr. Griffin for a moment, then looked about the park again; she glanced up at the blue sky. The breeze was slight, the sun felt warm on her skin.

She looked again across the table at Mr. Griffin. He had finished his cup of nuts and raisins. He looked silently back at Mrs. Hodges, said nothing.

It was just another day for the staff of the Quigley Estate.

Mrs. Hodges sat up straight and placed her hands in her lap. She was growing increasingly concerned for Master Quigley and Jacob. The days and then weeks continued to pass with no word. They had been gone for than two months now, Jacob starting down the Road, Tobias heading into the Outland and who knew where.

Mr. Griffin was beginning to annoy her. She knew that he was as concerned as she was, but he persisted in feigning indifference.

They had known each other for decades, had worked together for decades. Each knew the other better than anyone knew either of them.

They were more family than family.

And then there are days...

Mrs. Hodges gave an audible sigh, frowned and then let the thought pass. Mr. Griffin was Mr. Griffin and would always be so.

Sheriff Smith entered the park through the main gate. Wanda, the Captain of the Civilian Watch, walked with him. From what Mrs. Hodges could tell, they appeared unconcerned. Theirs was a casual lunch hour walk, enjoying the pleasant day as all the others in the park. They were in quiet conversation. Mrs. Hodges noted an occasional smile and even a light laugh.

Yes, some sense of normal was returning to Serpent's Keep; this, despite what was happening in the Outland, and despite recent events; and despite the significant and quite visible increase in their defenses, both here in the village and at the Farm.

Serpent's Keep had always had the wall, the gates and the civilian watch, these since the earliest days of the village. These had always seemed enough. They had never had to deal with a serious threat. Dangers had always existed beyond the walls of course, in the Outland, but no serious threat had ever breached the walls and entered the village.

They had been shaken out of their complacency; they had survived the attacks on the village and the farm and so had taken lessons from the experiences and had applied what they learned to enhance their security.

And now, within its walls, the village of Serpent's Keep was slowly returning to normal.

For Mrs. Hodges this meant worrying about Master Quigley and young Jacob whenever they were away.

They should be home by now.

She looked again across the table to Mr. Griffin. He was looking out across the park at the children playing, at families gathered around picnic tables and at villagers strolling along the winding walkways.

He seemed to sense Mrs. Hodges' eyes upon him and turned to her. A few moments passed as he sensed her thoughts, her concerns.

"Soon, Mrs. Hodges," he stated. "I am confident they will return soon."

And then there are days... she thought again.

Jake walked with Master Peter through an unfamiliar woodland. Meara was ahead of them, walking with the monks of Peter's group, young Ethan amongst them.

The others of Jake's group followed a dozen paces behind him; Jake occasionally heard the whisperings of Mason as he struggled to explain to Carlo and Betty how what they were experiencing with the shifting of time and landscape somehow fit into his original observations and their reasons for starting down the Road.

Jake caught very little of what was being said, but what he did hear made little sense to him.

He caught then a hint of humor brush across Peter's face.

"He's not as crazy as he comes across," said Jake. He wondered why he felt the need to defend Mason to Peter.

"Of course not, Jacob," said Master Peter. "I would never presume."

"Eccentric, yes. I mean, sure..."

They fell silent again. There was only the sound of the footfalls of the three groups of travelers as they tread across the mulchy forest floor.

"He really does sense things," Jake said then. "It's uncanny, really."

"I have no doubt of that," said Peter. "I have known a few such as he in my time. Spirits with a deep, living connection to our world that exists on some level quite apart from our own, that they do not understand and could never explain. I doubt they even see it, as they have never known anything else."

"Sounds about right," said Jake, glancing back behind them as they walked. Mason and the others were some dozen paces back. Mason gave a placid nod to Jake. Uncomfortable now, Jake turned forward. "He is peculiar, though. No getting around that."

"Rather colorful, to be sure," said Peter.

They both noticed then something going on up ahead. Several of the monks had stopped, grouped together, Ethan with them. They were talking amongst themselves. Meara and one of the others were continuing ahead.

Jake and Peter continued forward, wary now. As they approached the group, they saw that Meara and the other monk, twenty feet or so further on, were talking with a tall, thin, middle-aged man, dressed in simple pants and shirt.

Peter and Jake left the group of monks and approached Meara, the monk and the stranger.

"The gentleman is concerned for our welfare," said the monk. "It would seem."

"I see," said Peter.

The stranger said nothing, took half a step back. Too many people were within reach of his safe zone.

Meara looked from Master Peter to Jacob.

"The Rhetani's temple is up ahead," she stated.

"Is that so?" Peter prompted, raising a brow to the stranger.

"So he says," said Meara.

"You're Rhetani?" Jake asked the man.

In answer, the stranger looked back over his shoulder, spoke in that direction.

"There are a number of defensive measures set out, up ahead," he said. "If you wish to visit our sanctuary, I will need to guide you through."

"Booby traps?" asked Meara.

The stranger looked back at Meara, then Jake and Peter. The others of the group were clustered together further back.

He said nothing.

"That is very thoughtful of you," said Peter. "We accept your kind offer."

"We do?" asked Meara.

Peter gave a pleasant smile, held out a hand for Meara to take the lead.

"Okay, sure," Meara grumbled. She moved up beside the stranger. The two then started away. Jake and Peter followed several steps behind them, the others some distance further back.

"Might I ask," the stranger said hesitantly to Meara, breaking the silence. "Have you seen Janice?"

"Janice?"

"Janice. The principal of our order."

"No," said Meara. No, sorry. I haven't."

"Perhaps your friends."

"No. I am sure not."

"I see," he said. A few more yards, then he nodded to their left, Meara followed his steps around some unseen trap. She looked back over her shoulder to ensure the others were following in their footsteps.

"We grow concerned for her," said the stranger. "The last word we have is of Janice departing Serpent's Keep. We have heard nothing since."

"I'm sorry," said Meara. "We've been away for some time."

"I see," the stranger said again. He led Meara around another obstacle, silently indicating that she should stay close.

They continued the rest of the way in silence.

Master Peter came out of the Rhetani temple, descended the front steps and walked to the middle of the clearing. He looked about, taking in the early evening.

While the Rhetani hadn't exactly welcomed them with open arms, they hadn't been discourteous either. It was as if the visitors had no connection to the village or the farm. They offered their guests a light meal and a number of sleeping cells for the night.

Peter had gone out of his way to show appreciation. His fellows followed his direction and similarly demonstrated their appreciation, albeit with minimal enthusiasm.

They would continue their journey the following morning.

Peter saw a figure standing motionless just beyond the treeline. The man's back was to Peter, but he recognized him as Martin, Janice's long-suffering assistant.

Peter walked the rest of the way across the clearing and into the trees. Stepping up beside Martin, the man mumbled under his breath to watch the booby trap, indicating a barely visible trip wire that Peter had somehow managed to avoid.

Martin's melancholy hung heavy in the air. Then, he had been gloomy since Peter and his companions' arrival.

"We live in strange times," said Peter.

"That we do," said Martin after a long moment. "I wonder where it will lead, Master Peter. I wonder where it will take us."

"I am confident the path ahead will lead us to a future that we will all be eager to embrace," said Peter. "Though there may be an obstacle or two set before us along the way."

"Some of us may face more and greater obstacles than others."

True enough, thought Peter. *But then, that is always the way.*

"Some will no doubt create their own obstacles," he said.

"Of that I am absolutely certain," said Martin. He fell silent. He took a step forward, looked absently into the shadows that were moving about in the trees as early evening drifted into dusk. There was a soft, cool breeze.

He stuffed his hands into his jacket pockets.

Something has happened to her...

He took another short step forward.

The shadows were only shadows.

Peter moved up to again stand beside Martin. He recognized the source of Martin's disquiet; the man wore it on his sleeve for all to see.

"There could be any number of reasons that she has not yet returned, Martin," he said.

"I know," said Martin.

"Of course you do," said Peter. "You are a true and loyal friend, Martin. Janice is fortunate to have such a friend."

"We have been together a long time."

"I sense more than two walking the same path, my friend."

Martin gave a barely perceptible shrug. "Maybe so."

They were quiet then for a long time. The air grew ever cooler. Peter considered excusing himself to allow Martin his thoughts when Martin looked side-glance to Peter, again forward.

"Loyalty," he said then, quietly. "I suppose so. To now, what loyalty I may have felt in the past toward Janice has always been tied to the Rhetani cause."

"The Rhetani," Peter said coolly, giving a noncommittal nod.

"As it may," said Martin, holding up a silencing hand. He considered letting the whole matter drop, after some seconds finally spoke then so that only Peter could hear. "Over the years, you might say that my personal views have diverged somewhat from those of the Rhetani."

From what little Peter knew of the Rhetani, once enraptured by their dogma, to find one's way out of their miasma would seem to be just about impossible.

Perhaps Martin's unique circumstances had allowed him the opportunity to bear objective witness to the personal cost of fealty to the

Rhetani. Peter himself had on more than one occasion been witness to the withering away of the inner being of those lost in the blind pursuit of similar dogma.

And Rhetani was all-demanding, all-consuming. Individualism was given over to absolute fealty to the name that was Rhetani. Civilization and Rhetani were one. There were no thoughts that were one's own that had not been first provided by the Rhetani. Belief was what Rhetani said it was.

Religion was the belief of the Rhetani. Civilization was the belief of the Rhetani. There was no political structure other than the Rhetani.

There was no war. There was no conflict. There was only Rhetani. And that was good. With Rhetani would come universal peace.

The Rhetani and their doctrine would spread to all worlds, across all times.

Martin shifted about and looked to Peter.

"I had not considered it loyalty as such. It simply was." Martin turned around and looked back to the sanctuary now given over to the Rhetani. "Perhaps that is the power, the mesmerism, of the Rhetani."

"And now?"

"And now..." Martin considered, tried to put his thoughts into words. "I would say that my fidelity to their cause is much diminished, Master Peter." He turned to look Peter in the eye. "To be clear, my loyalty to Janice has not."

So Martin had indeed witnessed the cost of fealty to the Rhetani; the cost to his friend Janice.

"And what of Janice's beliefs, my friend?" asked Peter. "Is not her loyalty to the cause as strong as ever?"

"Very likely," Martin said despondently.

"And so, Martin," Peter stated. "You have a dilemma."

Martin stared ahead, his focus on the spreading shadows in the forest before him. Dusk was fully upon them. Night was not far behind.

"I do not," he said.

So... thought Peter. *Martin will follow Janice wherever her path may take them, setting aside his own beliefs. How sad.*

"Dilemma avoided," he said. It was clear that Martin's fealty to Janice was as strong as hers to the Rhetani.

The withering away of the inner being.

Peter wished there was some way to reach out to this soul and bring him back; he had tried to save others in the past. He had failed.

Martin was too far down the path. He would have to find his own way.

Peter placed a comforting hand on Martin's shoulder.

"I am confident that your friend will be home soon," he said. He turned about then and walked back to the clearing, across to the front steps of the sanctuary. He took them slowly and went inside.

Tobias and August stood on the grassy band that was the North Highway; the ancient road stretched away toward the horizon. Several of August's fellow monks were walking slowly along the highway a few hundred yards further on, studying the woods along either side of the road.

It was late evening, the sun having set half an hour earlier. It would be dark soon and they needed to start thinking about getting back.

"We discovered it yesterday," said August, indicating the highway. "Newly arrived, so far as we can determine."

Tobias gave a curious side-glance to August as he watched the monks working their way along the wide, grass-covered ribbon.

"Yes," said August, responding to Tobias' raised brow. "This area has been well explored; has been visited quite recently. I can assure you that it wasn't here just a few days ago."

"Interesting," said Tobias. The evening air was cool. He stuffed his hands into the pockets of his jacket. He looked back behind them, around them. They were about an hour's easy walk from the North Temple.

"It was to be expected," said August. "Should your assumption be correct that the Outland has been seeking a complete return to its original state."

"Quite right," said Tobias. Evidence suggested that the reintegration of the Outland sectors had triggered a reset, the greater Outland attempting a return to all as it was so very long ago.

But there were also clear indications, at least to Tobias, that there was additionally an external hand at work. There were adjustments and minor tweaks being made that were beyond the scope of the ongoing Outland reintegration.

Tobias knew of only a handful of people capable of attempting these modifications.

The North Highway, however, was surely a part of the Outland's reset.

Tobias took a step forward, spoke back over his shoulder.

"It takes one back, doesn't it?" asked Tobias, looking down the ancient road.

"If this goes as I expect, the highway should go full around the Outland." said August. "And soon."

"Well, if nothing else, it should make my journey home a lot easier." He turned about walked to August and continued past. "It will be dark soon. We had better start back."

Chapter Nineteen

The vast expanse of cultivated, well-tended fields spread out and away from the dirt road that ran along the western edge of the cleared land, cut from the forests of the Outland long ago. A cluster of buildings formed a compound of sorts in the heart of the village Farm.

A wagon sat in the middle of one of the fields, a group of men and women working nearby. Other than the deliberate, unhurried activity near the wagon, the farm was eerily still. A whispering hint of voices drifted across the landscape as they worked.

A small band of travelers walked along the road, silent, with even the sound of their footfalls muffled. Jake and Meara looked weary, their steps plodding and methodical. Betty and Carlo traveled ahead of them some twenty feet further up the road. Mason followed far behind Jake and Meara, seeming to be lost in his own world, having appeared so for days.

Movement near the wagon caught Jake's attention. He looked out across the field as he continued walking.

The man he recognized as the farm manager had stepped around the wagon, stood beside it now. He waved to the travelers walking along the road, now just passing parallel to the wagon and those who were gathering and loading vegetables.

Jake lifted a hand and gave a half-hearted wave in response. They continued on. A quarter of an hour later they passed the southern-most fields of the farm, commonly referred to as the south forty.

Master Peter and the other monks were no longer traveling with them. Jake and his group had parted ways with the monks and young Ethan several days earlier. Coming upon a fork in the well-traveled trail they had been following, Peter had felt the right fork would take them back into the heart of the expanded Outland, while Jake felt the left fork would likely lead them nearer Serpent's Keep.

It was possible they were both right, so the decision had been made to split up. If nothing else, should one group reach home and not the other, folks might have an idea where to look for them.

And then there had been Mason. Mason wanted to follow the left fork.

So be it.

There had been a near visible sense of relief amongst Jake's group when they came upon the Farm. Reaching the farm meant that home was only about half a day's hike down the road.

At least... they hoped the village was there.

Those they had seen working in the fields had seem unconcerned. That had been a good sign.

In any event, they would know soon enough. The road between farm and village was very familiar to all of them.

Jake and Meara found themselves silently indicating one and then another landmark they recognized as they passed; a particularly unique stand of trees, a large stone, a fallen log.

"What's the plan, sir?" asked Meara. "Once we're home."

"I expect that depends on what we find," said Jake. "I'd really like some down time."

"How do we explain what we found?"

"There is that," Jake sighed. "I suppose we just set out the facts, don't try to explain it."

Meara glanced briefly back to Mason.

"Mason's been quiet," she said, looking forward again. "I wonder what he'll have to say."

"Maybe we'll leave the interpretation to him," said Jake.

Meara grinned at that. "Yes sir."

They walked in silence another few minutes. At one point, Jake pointed to a large, towering cluster of berry bushes that he recognized.

She nodded acknowledgement, pulled a handful of berries as they passed by.

"Sir," she said then, almost tentative. "Are you serious about taking some time off?"

"Absolutely."

They traveled another dozen steps.

"Good," she said then.

"Absolutely," Jake said again. "We could all use a break."

"Yes, sir."

"Yes..." Jake said after a long moment. "Lay about the mansion, get in Mr. Griffin's way, drive Mrs. H. crazy. You know... just like old times."

"Yes, sir."

"What about you, Meara? Any plans?"

"I thought I'd help out at the market booth," she said. "I haven't spent much time with my mother lately."

"Sounds nice. Your mother will like that."

"She just has me," said Meara. "I mean, she has her friends at the market, but family, just me."

"I'm sorry I've taken so much of your time."

"Not at all, sir. I wouldn't have missed any of it."

"I appreciate that," said Jake. "I couldn't have done it without you."

They continued on for another few minutes.

"Sir?" Meara prompted.

"Yeah?"

"Do you really think we're going to have some time off?

"We can always hope," said Jake.

He saw then Betty and Carlo come to a stop up ahead. They were standing near a wide spot in the road, often used by travelers between the Farm and Serpent's Keep to take a break.

"Good idea," he said to Meara, then gave a raise of the hand. "Let's take five," he called out.

§

Peter stepped out onto the roof of the temple. He walked casually across to the edge, stood then with his hands clasped behind his back. He looked east, beyond the Outland to the sun climbing above the horizon.

Dawn had already come. He had missed the sunrise.

The temple had survived well enough without him, of course. He had expected nothing less. But these last mornings since his return had seemed busier, fuller than in times past, and he had yet to meet the sunrise.

Much had happened these past few months; past several years, actually. Gone was the calm tranquility of the Outland, the unchanging landscape of the world in which the temple, Peter's temple, had existed all these years. Their universe was in flux, unsettled, shifting beneath their feet. Even the passage of time itself, it would seem, was uncertain.

And so what of the future?

The temples were coming together in a loose association, forming a guild of sorts, though their role in the final design of the Outland was not yet known.

Of course not. The nature of the Outland itself had yet to be realized; nor its place in the universe beyond.

What new purpose might lay ahead for the monks in this new world, for a new purpose there must be. And what might be Master Peter's role in the new Outland?

His path, and the paths of his fellow monks, would unfold ahead of them as the landscape of the Outland was realized.

Peter could wait. He would watch, witness and be ready to serve as needed. He would help shape this world as needed, would stand ready to lead his monks into their new role as needed.

Peter gave a final appreciative look about the Outland; the forest canopy was shimmering in the early morning light.

Ah well, the day wasn't getting any younger...

He turned about then and left the rooftop.

The temple hallways were in shadow, with just half the sconces lit this early in the day. He passed a number of monks along the way; some were on their way to morning studies, others preparing to work outside in the vegetable gardens. Some had maintenance duties or kitchen detail.

He found Brother John standing at the door to the mess. John gave an acknowledging nod and indicated the dining room.

"She's having breakfast, sir."

"Thank you, John." Peter stepped through the doorway.

Janice was sitting alone at one of the tables, spooning oatmeal from a bowl. She gave no sign of having noticed Peter. No one else was in the hall.

Peter went to the buffet table and gathered a bowl of oatmeal and a spoon. He joined Janice, sat at the table opposite.

"Good morning," he said quietly.

Janice glanced across the table at Peter. She said nothing and returned to her breakfast.

A group of monks returning from one of the other temples had come across Janice the day before. She had been tired, hungry, disheveled, and though unwilling to admit it had clearly been lost. It took very little persuasion for her to accept their invitation to join them.

Master Peter had been able to get very little from her as to where she had been, what she had been doing all alone in the Outland wilderness. He gathered that she had become separated from her companions while on her way to the Rhetani temple; and though she didn't actually say so, Janice's omissions made it clear to Peter that the shifting of landscape and time had mystified and confused her.

What she wanted now was to return to the Rhetani temple; much had happened and there was much to contemplate. Peter had promised that he would take her there himself.

What place might the Rhetani have in this new world? It was obvious to Peter that it would not look anything like what Janice and her cohorts might have envisioned. This was not the universe that they had at one time sought to dominate. This Outland would not willingly accept their hand.

Peter suspected their dominion would likely never spread far beyond the confines of the temple in which they now resided.

And Janice?

Peter considered the woman sitting across the table from him, just finishing her breakfast.

Her sense of identity had been shaken; her purpose made uncertain. He saw as much in her eyes, in her manner. She had done bad things in the name of her cause, a cause that she had believed in to her very core, and it now seemed to have all been for naught.

What was left now to her?

Peter would take her home. He would watch her climb the steps and walk through the large, heavy doors. What she did once within the walls of their sanctuary was not up to him.

Whatever her history, he would bid her well.

The sun shone through the few tall, narrow windows of the dining hall.

The day was not getting any younger…

Peter focused on his bowl of oatmeal.

The Dark Path was a visible thing; a thin, winding, shadowy trail running snake-like across the barren plain that was spread aglow beneath the starry sky. A waning half moon hung in the eastern night sky, climbing slowly above the nearby range of mountains that stood silhouetted against the horizon.

Aldwyn sat before a small fire, the campsite several yards off the trail, at the base of the mountain range where mountain met plain. The thin, bare, twisting branches of the short shrubs enclosing the campsite shimmered in the firelight.

Aldwyn lifted his gaze from the fire. A lone figure was approaching, coming up the Dark Path. Distant at first, the man's pace was steady but unrushed. As he drew near, his features shifted from shadow to form, showing in the light of the fire.

He stepped off the trail and stood opposite the fire from Aldwyn. He looked up at the mountainside, the castle unseen in the dark. His gaze lowered then to where the trail of the Dark Path reached the hillside and disappeared into the trees.

He looked finally to Aldwyn.

"Aldwyn," said Tobias. "I was just on my way to see you."

"I know," said Aldwyn. He indicated that Tobias should sit.

Tobias took a moment to study the ground, then shifted his weight and eased down to his knees. He dropped back then and sat down, crossed his legs.

"All too quiet," he said. "I can hear my bones creaking."

"I'll be sure to bring chairs next time," said Aldwyn.

"I'd appreciate that." Tobias adjusted his position, got more comfortable. "August sends best wishes."

"How kind. I trust all are well."

"Quite well." Tobias again looked up at the black shadows of the mountainside. "I'm surprised to see you here, Aldwyn... this far beyond your castle walls."

"Pleasant walls they be," said Aldwyn. "But I sometimes find them confining."

Tobias understood that. He felt much the same after too many days in the mansion of the Quigley Estate.

"We share that, my friend," he said. "I have the freedom to take these occasional walks. To now, you sir have not."

"Yes, well..." Aldwyn gave a sigh, took in a long breath as he looked about them. "I'm afraid this is it for me. This is as far as my *walks,* as you say, can take me."

"Too bad. Nonetheless, you have managed to broaden your boundaries considerably."

"An unexpected benefit of my recent endeavors," said Aldwyn. "Endeavors that have made your journey here possible."

While visiting the temple ruin of the Jahai, Tobias had been surprised when a group arrived from the Jahai Village. They had in turn described the new portal forming between the Outland and the Dark Path.

And so then Tobias' journey here...

He uncrossed his legs and shifted, leaning heavily on one hand.

"Quite a lot going on," he said, looking carefully at Aldwyn. "A lot of changes."

"Very little of it is my doing, Tobias." Aldwyn clasped his hands, placed them in his lap. "I do wish I could have done more."

"I'm not sure what more need be done, friend." Tobias continued to study Aldwyn's expression. "We're about done then?"

"You mean is the Outland and our environs now what they will be?"

"And don't forget time. All settled?"

"I am not all knowing, Tobias. You know that more than anyone. But should I be called upon to say yay or nay, I would say yay. We're about done."

"I hope you're right." Tobias lifted a brow and gave something between a smile and a frown. "We have a lot of nervous folks back there, not sure what's coming, not sure what's already come."

"It'll no doubt take time for the dust to settle."

They fell silent; there was the crackle of burning branches in the campfire, the shimmering glow of coals at the base of the flames. Aldwyn lifted his head, half-turned to face the slight breeze; it felt cool on his face.

"We are apart from the outside world, Tobias."

"I've been told," said Tobias. The team sent out from Serpent's Keep had returned with news that the Outland was alone, that there was no avenue to what they called the real world.

Hearing later that Aldwyn had created a portal from the Dark Path to the Outland had been good news to Tobias. It meant that the Jahai Village was in essence now a part of the Outland.

And of course at the opposite end of the Dark Path was Aldwyn's castle.

"It is good to have you with us, friend Aldwyn," he said.
"It is good to be here, friend Tobias."

Chapter Twenty

What had been referred to simply as the temple ruin, and that for so long had been home to Lamal, the lonely Jahai Guardian, was much changed. Much of the debris had been cleared away and dozens of rustic stone structures now lined wide walkways. The craggy shard remnants of the old outer temple walls now formed a stone palisade that encircled the Jahai settlement, of late given the informal name of Sanctuary.

This was Natan's first visit to Sanctuary, his first time away from the Jahai Village since the discovery of the Dark Path portal to the Outland. And while the village would remain the administrative capitol for the Jahai outside the Jahai home worlds, Sanctuary was destined to become the primary colony for the Jahai. Dozens of Jahai representing a number of the dragon species already called Sanctuary home.

Natan walked the main path through the settlement, his friend and assistant Khol by his side. Many of the Jahai lined the path to watch their leader pass by. Natan gave respectful nods to them as Khol pointed out the work that had been done, the work yet to do.

They reached the center of the settlement, where more Jahai stood quietly by.

There was very little work going on during his visit.

Natan held his arms at his sides, the clawed fingers of his hands pressed firmly against his thick thighs. He turned slowly about, tried to make eye contact with each of those standing in silent respect about the compound. He lowered his large head in acknowledgment to several.

He looked then at the structures that encircled the compound. These were community buildings, serving the needs of the settlement. Beyond these were the private dwellings, built to the specific needs of the different species of Jahai. All were built using the recovered stone and beam materials of the temple ruin.

"I am quite impressed," said Natan to Khol.

Several of the Jahai standing nearby gave sharp nods of appreciation.

"They have worked very hard, Natan," said Khol.

"It shows." Natan looked then to the crowd. "You should be very proud of what you have accomplished here, my friends."

There were more sharp nods of appreciation, as well as mumblings and grumblings and grunts and growls of thank you.

Khol allowed this for another few seconds, then indicated to Natan that they should continue. He led Natan to a narrow walkway, which they followed to another path that ran along the base of one of the outer walls. They climbed a staircase of stone blocks to the top of the wall.

From here they were able to see out across the surrounding forests of the Outland. They stood quiet for some time, taking it in. The wooded landscape stretched out in all directions as far as the eye could see.

It was a landscape the Jahai would have to share. Hidden in those forests were other temples, these inhabited by humans. And out there somewhere was Serpent's Keep, home to friend Tobias Quigley and his nephew Jacob Quigley.

The Jahai had never lived in such close proximity to humans. There were relationships, to be sure, but this was different. And there had been the Great Ravine, but it had been isolated and secreted. As for the Jahai Village, it had not existed in the Outland and required several portals to reach.

Sanctuary was to be a new experience, and where it would take them was not yet known.

Natan tilted his head to look side-glance to Khol.

It was good to have his friend again by his side. With this, at least, there had come some slight return to normal. With Khol's return had come a sense of relief; a great weight had been lifted that Natan had not realized he had been carrying.

Khol's support would help much with whatever was to come.

Looking outward again, Natan saw a shadow flickering across the treetops. Glancing up, he saw the silhouette of a Lynhaur, the flying dragon gliding high above the canopy.

"Lamal," said Khol. "He spends much of his time up there, out there. I believe he much enjoys the change in circumstance."

"Lamal has gained a new freedom, has he not? No longer bound to ancient obligations."

"That is true," said Khol. His Bentai face managed what might be considered a smirk. "I think he just likes to fly."

Sheriff Smith opened the door and came into the newspaper editor's front office. The room was small; the desk was cluttered with paper and folders, the shelves that lined the walls were filled with haphazardly stacked books, binders and files. The large front window, with *Village Gazette* stenciled on the glass, let in the only light.

There was no one in the room. Smith took a step to one side and looked through the open door set in the center of the back wall. An old printing press dominated the center of the back room. The machine looked to be well maintained, while the rest of the room was as cluttered as the front office.

Jeb Rainey was standing behind the press, wiping his hands with a cloth. The owner and editor gave a wave as he finished up whatever he was doing.

The Village Gazette was published weekly. Each issue of the sixteen page newspaper was filled with news articles, feature pieces, and just enough advertisements to keep Jeb Rainey from having to get a real job.

Sheriff Smith sat on the corner of the desk and waited. Half a minute later Jeb came into the room.

"Sorry to keep you waiting, Sheriff," he said. Jeb had a pleasant face and manner, bright inquisitive eyes. Anyone who knew Jeb, which was just about everyone in the village, knew also that there was a quick, sharp mind behind those eyes.

Smith pushed himself away from the desk as Jeb dropped himself into the chair behind the desk.

"The world keeping you busy, is it?" asked the sheriff.

"Not so as I can't get my six hours sleep a night." Jeb offered the sheriff the guest chair. "How about you? What brings you to my door?"

Smith slid the chair over to just in front of the desk and sat down.

"Things have quieted down considerable, for the most part," he said.

"So I've noticed," said Jeb. He gave a wink. "Slow news week, you know."

"Yes, of course." Sheriff Smith leaned back in the chair, placed his hands on the chair arms. "Which leads me to what brings here."

"Ah. Is that so?"

"That story in the last issue," said the sheriff. "The Mason piece."

"I hope I didn't get anything wrong, Sheriff. It was, after all, from Mason's perspective."

"Not at all. As you say, the story was written from Mason's viewpoint. And that was made clear."

"Good." Jeb slid forward, straightened and placed his forearms on the desk. "Then what can I do for you, Sheriff?"

Sheriff Smith leaned forward now, elbows on his knees.

"It was something that you reported, something he said."

"Sure..."

When Mason had gone with Jacob Quigley in search of what lay beyond the village, down the Road, he had told Sheriff Smith that there was indeed something beyond, that there was a world outside, but an outside that had replaced the outside they had known. It was important that they bear witness to what lay beyond, that the survival of those in the Outland, those in the village, might very well depend on what lay beyond.

Returning from their quest, Mason and the of the team spoke instead of a world beyond that lay forever out of their reach. The Outland was alone, a land of its own place and of its own time.

It was also an Outland brought together and again whole, of a history none in the village had known lay in their past.

Now, perhaps, if what Sheriff Smith had read in Jeb's newspaper was true, there was something more...

Mason now suggested that a reconstituted Outland had been torn from the fabric of one existence and was now in another, albeit empty void. Additionally, this had been the result of the actions that had initiated the reconstitution.

"In the article," said Smith, "Mason is saying that whatever outside universe might exist, it doesn't exist where we are."

"Yes." Jeb gave a slight, knowing smile. "Which goes just a tad beyond what he and the others said upon their return."

"Just a tad."

"And you are wondering if I had any more information, information that ended up on the cutting room floor."

"Something like that," said Smith.

"I'm afraid it's all there in the piece, Sheriff. I did try to dig deeper, but that's all he had." Jeb slid his arms off the desk, leaned back in his chair. "You know Mason. He's not one to hold anything back, so I felt confident at the time that that was all there was."

"I thought that might be the case."

"Perhaps if you talked with him yourself; you being the sheriff and all."

"I already did. As you say, he's not one to keep his thoughts to himself, and he told me no more than he told you."

"Then I'd say that's all there is."

"I suppose so. At least for now," said the sheriff. He fell silent then, frowning. Jeb Rainey studied the man's face, his expression.

"It doesn't really change anything, does it?" asked Jeb. "I mean, whatever is or isn't out there in the beyond, we are here, we're on our own, and the dust in the Outland has settled."

"Has it?" asked the sheriff.

"Settled, you mean? The monks think so. The Quigleys think so. Even those dragons, the Jahai, think so."

Ah, yes... the Jahai. They were going to take getting used to. They were something completely new to most of those in Serpent's Keep.

"Our world may be on its own," said Sheriff Smith. "But it's not the world we knew."

Jeb Rainey leaned further back in his chair.

"A more interesting world, I would argue," he said. "We have been much too complacent to now."

Jake was sitting on the top step of the Quigley Estate mansion's front steps, his elbows resting on his knees. It was late morning, and the weather was pleasant. He could hear children playing in the park across the street.

Life in Serpent's Keep was slowly returning to normal, however isolated the village might be.

Mr. Griffin came around from the side yard, a pruning saw in hand. He was dressed in work clothes, sweat on his brow and his hair damp. He looked very much out of place.

Jake couldn't help but grin, though he quickly pushed it down.

"Mr. Griffin," he said. "How go the toils?"

A young plum tree had been damaged in a storm a week earlier. Mr. Griffin had just gotten around to pruning away the broken branches.

"It is all taken care of, Master Jacob."

"It'll live then?"

"I would think so." Mr. Griffin wasn't quite sure whether the question had been sarcasm.

"Good to hear." Jake gave a nod in the general direction of the pruning saw that Mr. Griffin was holding. "You should have let me take care of that, Griff. No problem, you know."

"The care of the grounds is part of my duties, Master Jacob."

"Sure, but—"

"If you wish a set of daily chores, young sir, I would suggest that you take the matter up with your uncle."

"Sure," said Jake, not able to push down a second grin. "Maybe I'll do that."

Mr. Griffin gave a terse nod in response, took the bottom step.

"I understand that you have taken on several community responsibilities," he said then. "I would not want you to become distracted from your new duties."

Jake had reluctantly accepted a seat on a newly formed committee, its role being to advise the village council regarding foreign relations... meaning the village's relationships with any and all Outland communities.

The seat had been offered to Jake after Tobias turned it down. Pleading time constraints, he suggested that he would not in all likelihood be available for most meetings. He subsequently agreed to serve as a consultant.

"I don't expect my committee duties to take up all that much of my time, Mr. Griffin," said Jake. He stood then. "They promised as much."

Now Mr. Griffin managed a hint of a smile. He gave only a half nod in answer.

Jake started down the steps then.

"I'm off," he said. "Having lunch at the café today."

"Is Mrs. Hodges aware that you will not be home for lunch?"

"I have so informed our dear Mrs. H." Jake started toward the gate. He stopped and looked back. "Would you care to join me, Mr. Griffin? I believe today's special is hearty vegetable stew and freshly baked bread."

Mr. Griffin had already started up the steps.

"I think not, Master Jacob. If you will excuse me, I must get cleaned up."

"I'm happy to wait," said Jake. "No rush, really."

"No," Mr. Griffin stated firmly; quite firmly in fact. "Thank you."

"Sure." Jake reached the gate and opened it. "Your loss."

"I understand." Mr. Griffin was at the front door. He looked briefly back.

There was no one at the gate. Jake was already gone.

Mr. Griffin turned away from the door and moved back to the top step. He could hear the children playing across the street, heard parents calling after them. A breeze was wafting through the trees lining the street, the aging leaves rustling.

Autumn was fast approaching.

Mr. Griffin turned back to the front door of the Quigley Mansion. He opened it and stepped inside.

He had to get cleaned up and dress.

There were duties yet to perform this day.

~ *End Serpent's Keep 3 – the Outland*

| 4 |

Jahai Encyclopedia

The Jahai are the twelve dragon species of the four habitable planets of the Jahai system.

The Jahai had joined with Tobias Quigley and stood watch for a thousand years as Guardians of the Artifacts, the components of the gate that had been distributed to the Other Worlds by Tobias.

The Jahai Species

Bentai

The Bentai are much more humanoid in physical appearance than other Jahai species. They tend to be a head taller than the average human, with sloping shoulders, a large head and protruding snout. They have extraordinarily long fingers ending in curved claws. Unlike other Jahai species, Bentai wear clothing, albeit simple, usually open leather vests and calf-length skirts. The Bentai are the primary administrative class of the Jahai. The leader of the Jahai is Bentai.

Lynhaur

One of several of the flying species of dragon. Colored in multiple shades of green and brown, the Lynhaur are sleek, but with powerful hind legs, slightly smaller front legs that can be used as arms and hands. Their leathery wings are folded and bundled on their back when not in use.

Thrauhm

Thrauhm are heavy, well-muscled, with thick legs and neck, are broad chested and have an overlarge head. They are intelligent but have limited language and simple speech.

Zelhaur

The Zelhaur are a lizard-like species well-suited to the desert, their home environment the arid southern continent of the innermost world of the Jahai planetary system. The Zelhaur body is slung between short, powerful legs, its belly and tail held up off the sand.

Slyruhm

The amphibian species of the Jahai dragon; sleek, silky water serpent at home in the water. The Slyruhm has a small head in relation to its long, undulating serpentine neck, a sharp protruding chin and large dark eyes. They are articulate, well-spoken.

Jehnlaur

Gentle and slight, the Jehnlaur are thin and agile, bipedal with delicate hands and fingers. They mother their young for several years. They frequently care for and are protective of the Chenling species.

Venerahn

Long, very slender body, spindly legs; overlarge wings are nearly transparent. They are highly cerebral, live most of their lives alone.

Chenling

Sometimes referred to as "Little Ones" by humans, Chenling have all the dragon features of the larger Jahai species, but are no larger than midsize dogs. They commonly live in groups in underground tunnels and labyrinths, but will also individually attach to other dragons or humans.

The Four Friends

The four distinct species of the fourth planet in the Jahai system are referred to as "The Four Friends". They seldom leave their home world, are seldom seen by other Jahai species, and very little is known about them.

www.ingramcontent.com/pod-product-compliance
Lightning Source LLC
Chambersburg PA
CBHW030348310726
48979CB00001B/223

9781947231511